AMERI
THEY KEEP TH
ASTON

BUT NOW TH

AT THE HEART OF . . .

DREAMLAND

DEPARTMENT OF THE AIR FORCE

Project 1633B-154 Update

AIM-154 ANACONDA

Engagement	Air-to-Air / Air-to-Ground Tactical
Power Plant	Ramjet Assist / Hydrazine
Length	172 inches
Launch Weight	378 pounds
Diameter	13 inches
Wingspan	24 inches
Range	130+ miles
Speed	Mach 5.5
Guidance System	Inertial, Command, Infrared, and Active-Radar Guidance
Warhead	Radar-Fuzed 45-pound Directed Frag or Thermium Nitrate
Deployment	Classified
Aircraft Platforms	Air Force: EB-52, EB-1

• Warhead

• Guidance Electronics

• Anti-Jam GPS Receiver

• Satellite Data Link Terminal for In-Flight Communications

• Main Fuel Tank

• Wing and Wing Door Deploy System Folding Wings, Wing Slot Doors Open During Wing Deployment and Close After Wing Deployment to Provide a Clean Aerodynamic Fuselage

• Main Solid Rocket Motor Components

• Ramjet System: Ramjet Compression / Combustion Chamber

DALE BROWN'S

Dreamland
RETRIBUTION

DALE BROWN and JIM DeFELICE

HARPER

An Imprint of HarperCollins*Publishers*

This is a work of fiction. Names, characters, places, and incidents are products of the author's imagination or are used fictitiously and are not to be construed as real. Any resemblance to actual events, locales, organizations, or persons, living or dead, is entirely coincidental.

HARPER

An Imprint of HarperCollins*Publishers*
10 East 53rd Street
New York, New York 10022-5299

Copyright © 2007 by Air Battle Force, Inc.
ISBN: 978-0-06-088946-3
ISBN-10: 0-06-088946-2

First Harper paperback printing: September 2007

HarperCollins® and Harper® are registered trademarks of Harper-Collins Publishers.

Printed in the United States of America

Visit Harper paperbacks on the World Wide Web at
www.harpercollins.com

10 9 8 7 6 5 4 3 2 1

Dreamland: Duty Roster

Lieutenant Colonel Tecumseh "Dog" Bastian

Dreamland's commander has been mellowed by the demands of his new command—but he's still got the meanest bark in the West, and his bite is even worse.

Major Jeffrey "Zen" Stockard

A top fighter pilot until a crash at Dreamland left him a paraplegic, Zen has volunteered for a medical program that may let him use his legs again. Can Dreamland survive with a key member away?

Captain Breanna "Rap" Stockard

Zen's wife has seen him through his injury and rehabilitation. But can she balance her love for her husband with the demands of her career . . . and ambitions?

Major Mack "The Knife" Smith

Mack Smith is the best pilot in the world—and he'll tell you so himself. But filling in for Zen on the Flighthawk program may be more than even he can handle.

Captain Danny Freah

Danny commands Whiplash—the ground attack team that works with the cutting-edge Dreamland aircraft and high-tech gear.

Jed Barclay

The young deputy to the National Security Advisor is Dreamland's link to the President. Barely old enough to shave, the former science whiz kid now struggles to master the intricacies of world politics.

Lieutenant Kirk "Starship" Andrews

A top Flighthawk pilot, Starship is tasked to help on the Werewolf project, flying robot helicopters that are on the cutting edge of air combat. Adjusting to the aircraft is easy, but can he live with the Navy people who are in charge of it?

Captain Harold "Storm" Gale, USN

As a young midshipman at Annapolis, "Storm" Gale got Army's goat—literally. He and some compatriots stole the West Point mascot just before the annual Army-Navy Game, earning instant acclaim in the Navy. Now he's applying the same brashness to his role as commander of the *Abner Read*. An accomplished sailor, the only thing he hates worse than the enemy is the Air Force.

From the Authors:
The Story so Far . . .

Two weeks ago tensions began building between Pakistan and India after a series of guerrilla attacks against Indian oil terminals and other assets. The Indians blamed the strikes on Pakistan and threatened to retaliate; the Pakistan government believed that India had staged the attacks as a pretext for making its own raids on Pakistani facilities. With both countries edging toward war, the Chinese sent their new aircraft carrier, the *Khan*, into the Arabian Sea to protect its ally Pakistan and shipping. Within days the three countries stood at the brink of a nuclear exchange.

The United States, with friendly relations toward both Pakistan and India, was caught in the middle. Convinced that the acts of sabotage stoking the tensions were being launched by a third party, the President sent the Dreamland team to monitor the situation. And when war seemed inevitable, he came up with a novel idea to stop it—radiation-emitting weapons called "EEMWBs," whose E wave radiation would paralyze electronic devices for miles and miles, effectively neutering any nuclear bombs or warheads.

With help from the cutting-edge littoral attack destroyer *Abner Read*, the Dreamland team discovered that the war was being provoked by a private Iranian force headed by Val Muhammad Ben Sattari. The son of a powerful Iranian general who had clashed with Dreamland some years earlier, Sattari believed that Iran would benefit from a conflict that destroyed its main competitors in the region. But before the Dreamland team could apprehend the Iranians, disaster struck—the Indians launched their nuclear missiles, and the Pakistanis retaliated. Colonel Tecumseh "Dog" Bastian immediately ordered his aircraft to intercept the missiles over India. They were successful, knocking out not only the weapons but all electronic devices over a wide swath of the subcontinent. Bastian then led his own suicidal attack on the Chinese aircraft carrier *Khan*. Out of missiles, he threatened to crash his Megafortress into the *Khan*'s V-shaped flight deck if it didn't put its nuclear bomber back in its hangar deck. After ordering his crew to eject, Dog aimed the nose of his plane at the carrier. Bare seconds before he would have crashed, the *Khan* stood down. Nuclear war had been prevented.

But things were hardly finished for the Dreamland team. Indian antiaircraft missiles had seriously damaged the plane containing Bastian's daughter, Captain Breanna "Rap" Stockard, and her husband, Major Jeffrey "Zen" Stockard. Breanna managed to get the plane over the ocean, where most of the crew parachuted into the sea below. Then she and her paraplegic husband prepared to bail out together as the plane augured in.

War may have been prevented, but with the sun coming up, more than two dozen nuclear weapons were scattered around the Indian subcontinent, and a host of Dreamlanders were in the ocean, hoping to be rescued . . .

Prelude:

Annihilation Averted

———

THE V-SHAPED DECK OF THE CHINESE AIRCRAFT CARRIER *Khan* grew in the screen as the plane approached, its color fading from dark black to gunmetal as the focus sharpened. There was an aircraft at the catapult launcher on the right side of the screen; on the left, an antiair missile foamed and flew out of the frame. The deck continued to get closer and closer, until the shadow of the approaching aircraft, an American EB-52 Megafortress bomber, appeared directly below. The early morning sun rode almost on the plane's back, and the shadow engulfed the aircraft carrier's deck, as if the plane were swallowing the ship, not the other way around.

Red, computer-generated letters flashed at the bottom of the image.

COLLISION IMMINENT.
COLLISION IMM

The image went black.

"Is that real time?" shouted Jeffrey Hartman, who'd just entered the room.

"No, Mr. Secretary," said Jed Barclay, the National Security Council deputy responsible for liaisoning with Dreamland during Whiplash missions. "It's three minutes old."

"Jesus. Did the plane crash or what?"

"Um, it made it, sir. The video cut out as a latent effect from the, uh, T-Rays. S-S-Scientists say it's kinda like a sunspot effect. This is the airplane over here."

Barclay pointed to the smaller screen at the front of the situation room. Centered on the Arabian Sea, the screen mapped the waters off the coast of India and southwestern Pakistan. A bright red blip headed southward; this was the Megafortress that had just narrowly avoided diving into the Chinese aircraft carrier. The time flashed at the bottom, indicating Washington, D.C., and the time in Karachi, Pakistan—an arbitrary point selected as a reference for the operation, which was taking place across several time zones.

"The Chinese stood down?" said the Secretary of State. "They didn't launch their nuke?"

"Yes, sir. The President managed to convince the government, and Dog must've gotten through to the captain of the carrier. They sent the nuke plane back into the hangar."

"Dog?"

"Um, that would be Lieutenant Colonel Bastian, Mr. Secretary."

"Oh, yeah, the Dreamland flyboy."

President Kevin Martindale, who'd stripped off his jacket and tie, looked up from the secure communications console at the far end of the room. He'd just finished a conversation with the Russian prime minister, explaining that the U.S. had intervened in a three-way conflict between Pakistan, India, and China, arresting a nuclear exchange with the help of newly developed terahertz radiation weapons called EEMWBs— Enhanced ElectroMagnetic Warfare Bombs, generally pronounced as "em-web." The missiles—the word bomb in the title was a misnomer—the "T-Rays" fried most electronic devices within a five hundred mile radius of the explosion.

"About time you got back, State," said Martindale.

"The Pakistanis were quite difficult and—"

"Never mind. Get over here. I need you to talk to the Indian prime minister."

"On my way."

Hartman turned to Jed. In a whisper he asked if they'd gotten them all.

"All of the nukes both the Indians and the Pakistanis fired were neutralized," said Jed.

"Good work."

Hartman patted Jed's shoulder, as if Jed had personally knocked all of the missiles down.

Jed pulled over a chair and dropped down into it. The Dreamland force had averted a nuclear war. But at what cost? Power failures were cascading across the subcontinent; it was likely that power would be disrupted throughout Pakistan and in India at least as far south as Hyderabad. It would take weeks, perhaps even months, to restore it all.

Meanwhile, all but one American spy satellite in the area had been disabled. And contact had been lost with two of the Dreamland aircraft, one of which was almost certainly shot down.

That aircraft happened to contain Jed's cousin, Jeffrey "Zen" Stockard, the head of Dreamland's Flighthawk program.

"Young Jed," said the President, "get over here and help me again with these projections."

"Yes, sir," said Jed, getting up from his console. Then, glancing again at the frozen main screen, he whispered a prayer. "I hope you're OK, Jeff. Jesus, I just hope you're OK."

I

Downed Airmen

———

WIND WHIPPED THROUGH THE MEGAFORTRESS COCKPIT AS Colonel Tecumseh "Dog" Bastian leaned the plane as gently as he could onto her left wing, aiming to take a slow circle north of the Chinese aircraft carrier *Khan* and its escorts. He'd ordered his five crew members to eject when it looked as if he'd have to crash the Megafortress into the *Khan* to prevent it from launching its nuke-laden bomber against the Indians' capital. Now that the Chinese had stood down, he turned his attention to his people in the water.

Ordinarily, the Megafortress's flight computer would have recorded the plane's position when the crew bailed, and then computed their likely landing area. Slapped into Search and Rescue mode, the computer would have projected a likely search area on the windscreen, along with convenient markers showing Dog where to look. He could have switched the Megafortress's sensor inputs over to infrared and in a few moments picked out the bobbing bodies of his crew.

That wasn't going to work now. Pressed into service to prevent a world war, *Wisconsin* had not been shielded against the T-Rays. Its brains had been fried over northern India; the only electronic device still working was a satellite radio that had been kept in a shielded box until after the explosions. Dog knew he would have to find them the old-fashioned way, with a pair of Mark 1 human eyeballs, now seriously derated due to fatigue.

Flying the EB-52 without a copilot was generally not

difficult, but flying it without its computer was an entirely different story. Add the fact that his joystick, pedals and throttle were now connected to hydraulic backups, and the plane demanded every bit of his considerable piloting skills. The fuselage, ordinarily a slick, carefully stream-lined airfoil, had five holes in it where the ejection seats had gone out. Dog had to alternately wrestle and baby the aircraft to get it to do what he wanted.

He found a patch of air around 2,500 feet that the Mega-fortress seemed to like, and rode it around in an elongated circle, looking for the orange life rafts that should have in-flated as his crew descended.

"Dreamland EB-52 *Wisconsin* to crew—Mack, Dish, Can-tor, where are you guys?" he asked over the shielded radio.

There was no answer. The survival radios the crew mem-bers carried had been in cases shielded against the T-Rays, but the otherwise stock devices had relatively limited ranges, and it was likely they were having trouble picking up *Wis-consin*'s transmission.

At least Dog hoped that was the case. He didn't like the alternatives.

He pushed the plane lower and slower, trying for a better view. Displeased, the *Wisconsin* responded by literally flap-ping its wings—the flexible carbon-composite extensions at the very ends of the slicked-back wings began to oscillate.

The effect felt like a stutter in the stick. After a few hairy seconds, Dog realized that the shudder wasn't a prelude to a nose dive; the *Wisconsin* chugged away at a hair under 200 knots, level as a laser beam and precisely 753 feet over the waves, according to the old-style analog altimeter.

A test pilot undoubtedly would have made a note of the phenomenon so he could discuss it with the engineers when he got home. Dog, a fighter pilot by training and inclination, did what most fast-jet jocks would do—he pushed the plane another notch, taking her down to five hundred feet and slowing her to 160 knots.

He trimmed the control surfaces like a yachtsman tacking

into the final leg of the America's Cup. The plane bucked, but then smoothed out as he reached five hundred feet. He found he had to keep a good deal of pressure on the stick to keep the nose up, but the plane felt stable. The ocean spread out before him like a smooth blue carpet, with the faint pattern of dark blue seashells arrayed shoulder-to-shoulder, uninterrupted as far as the eye could sight.

Not what he wanted to see.

He broadcast again on the emergency channel.

Still nothing.

He reached across the console, inadvertently changing his pressure on the stick. Immediately the Megafortress dipped to its left. He quickly added power and began to climb.

Something glinted to his left as he went to back the throttle off.

"Dreamland *Wisconsin* to crew—Mack? Anybody?"

"We're all here, Colonel," answered Major Mack Smith.

"What's your situation?"

"Treading water."

"Where are your life rafts?"

Mack explained that the men had purposely sunk their chutes and rafts to make it harder for the Chinese to find them. They had two backup, uninflated rafts in reserve.

"The Chinese stood down," said Dog. "They're not going to use their nuke."

"We'd still rather not be eating dinner with chopsticks tonight, Colonel," said Mack.

"Go ahead and inflate the rafts," Dog told him. "I'll get the *Abner Read* to come north to pick you up."

The *Abner Read*, an American littoral destroyer, had been shadowing the Chinese fleet during the conflict. They were roughly fifty miles away when Dog last checked; it might take them two hours or more to get there.

"You sure the Chinese aren't going to interfere?" Mack asked.

"They took several hits during the conflict. It looks like they're spending all their energy just keeping the ship afloat," said Dog. "If the *Abner Read* can't come, I'll ask the Pakistanis to send one of their ships. They have some patrol vessels to the northeast."

"No way—they'll just hand us over to the Chinese."

"They're our allies," said Dog, though he wasn't sure how far to trust them—the Pakistanis were allied with the Chinese as well, and during the conflict the two forces had worked together against the Indians.

"I still think I'd rather swim," said Mack.

"Careful what you wish for, Major."

Northern Arabian Sea
0730

"COLONEL SAYS THE PAKISTANIS MAY RESCUE US," MACK told the others.

"The Paks?" said Sergeant Peter "Dish" Mallack. "Fuck that. They were just trying to blow us out of the air."

"They'll turn us over to the Chinese," said Technical Sergeant Thomas "T-Bone" Boone. "I ain't wearing no Asian pajamas for the rest of my life."

"Yeah, I'm with you there," said Mack.

Dish and T-Bone were radar systems operators; aboard the *Wisconsin* they'd kept track of hundreds of contacts—Indian, Pakistani, Chinese, and American—as war threatened. Now they were just swimmers, and not particularly good ones.

Two other men had gone out with Mack—Lieutenant Sergio "Jazz" Jackson, the Megafortress's copilot, and Lieutenant Evan Cantor, who along with Mack had been piloting the Flighthawk remote control aircraft from the Megafortress's lower deck. Cantor had hit something on the way out of the aircraft and broken his arm; his face was deeply bruised and he seemed to have a concussion. Dish, the best swimmer of the bunch, had lashed himself to the lieutenant, helping to keep the younger man awake. Fortunately, all of their horseshoe-style life preservers had inflated; Mack couldn't imagine staying afloat without them.

Mack turned to look to the south. He could see the mast of one of the *Khan*'s escort vessels, a destroyer, he thought, though he was far from an expert on ships. Behind it two thick curlicues of black smoke jutted from the water. The smoke came from ships damaged by the Indians; the *Khan* was farther east, marked on the horizon by a plume of white smoke—mostly water vapor rising from the hoses the crew was spraying on the parts of the ship damaged by missiles.

American missiles, for the record.

"If they pick us up, Major," said Dish, "they'll have a hell of a lot of questions about our plane. There's no way they're going to just let us go."

"We're not going to be picked up by the Pakistanis, or the Chinese," Mack told them. "We're going to get over to the *Abner Read.*"

"Hey, guys, I'm starting to get a little cold," said Cantor.

Mack looked over at Cantor. His teeth were chattering.

"All right. We open one life raft," said Mack. "We use that to get the hell out of here. Jazz, do the raft. Hang in there, Cantor. Dish'll start a fire for you as soon as we get it open."

Aboard the *Abner Read*, northern Arabian Sea 0736

CAPTAIN HAROLD "STORM" GALE PUT HIS HANDS AGAINST the sides of his head, trying to stop the ringing in his ears. He'd been slapped against the deck and bulkhead several times by salvos from attacking aircraft and missiles. His head hurt, but he decided arbitrarily that it wasn't a concussion, and that even if it was, it wasn't worth going to sickbay for.

The jagged cut in his leg from exploding shrapnel might deserve attention, but since the bleeding seemed to have slowed to an ooze, he'd deal with that later.

The ship herself was in good shape. The holographic damage control display on the deck of the *Abner Read* showed that she had sustained only minor damage despite the onslaught of missiles fired at her over the past hour.

What bothered Storm—what truly pissed him off—was the fact that his nemesis also remained afloat despite his own attack. The Chinese aircraft carrier *Khan* had taken three missiles from the *Abner Read*, and possibly a fourth from one of the destroyer's smaller escorts, known as a Sharkboat, and the S.O.B. was still sailing.

Unlike the Indian carrier he had sunk some hours before.

"Captain, communication coming in from Fleet."

"Give it to me."

"Storm, Storm, Storm!" exclaimed Admiral Jonathon "Tex" Woods. "What the hell are you up to now?"

"Admiral."

"You sunk the *Shiva*?"

"I believe that's correct, sir. The Indian carrier is gone."

"Great going, Storm." The admiral's voice swelled with pride, as if he were Storm's greatest fan and biggest admirer. In fact just the opposite was true. "And you disabled the *Khan*?"

"I'm not sure of the damage to the Chinese, Admiral. The Dreamland people helped—they were invaluable."

"You're being uncharacteristically modest, Storm—a welcome development! Even if you are complimenting Lieutenant Colonel Bastian and his crew."

Storm scowled. He didn't like Bastian very much, but the colonel and his people had done an excellent job—and helped save his ship.

"The *Abe* is steaming north to take up a patrol off the Indian coast," said the admiral, referring to the USS *Abraham Lincoln*, one of the Seventh Fleet's attack aircraft carriers and Woods's temporary flagship. "Once the *Abe* is on station, you'll receive new orders. In the meantime, get no closer than five miles to another warship—Chinese, Indian, Pakistani, or Croatian, for that matter."

Storm had no intention of getting involved in another

firefight; he was out of Harpoon antiship missiles, and Standard antiair missiles as well. But the order angered him.

"Why am I being ordered to withdraw?"

"You're not being ordered to withdraw. All combatants have agreed to stay five miles apart. You have a problem with that, Captain?"

Woods's belligerent tone was somehow more welcome than the phony proud-father routine he'd started with.

"I don't have a problem, Admiral."

"Good," snapped Woods. "There'll be a bottle of scotch with my compliments when you reach port."

Woods signed off. Storm called up the navigational charts on the holographic display at the center of the bridge and had his navigator plot a course south. As he was about to relay their new orders to his exec and the rest of the ship, the communications specialist buzzed in with a new call.

"Cap, we have Dreamland *Wisconsin* on the Dreamland channel. It's Colonel Bastian. The signal's not the greatest; he's using a backup radio."

Storm fumbled with the control unit on his belt. Squelch blared into his headset before he clicked into the right frequency.

The funny thing was, it seemed to clear the ringing in his ears.

"Dreamland *Wisconsin* to *Abner Read*. Can you hear me?"

"This is Storm. Dog, are you there?"

"I thought I'd lost you," said the Dreamland commander.

"I'm here," Storm told him. "We've sustained light damage. We're rendezvousing with one of our Sharkboats and then sailing south."

"Five of my people parachuted into the water near the *Khan*," said Dog. "I need to arrange a search."

"Give me the coordinates," said Storm.

"I'm afraid I can't. My locator gear was wiped out by the T-Rays. They're roughly twenty miles due north of the *Khan*."

Storm bent over the holographic chart, where the computer marked the ships' positions with three-dimensional images.

He was about sixty nautical miles away; cutting a straight line at top speed would get him there in two hours.

Except he couldn't cut a straight line and stay five miles from the Chinese ships.

"See if you can get me a better location, Bastian," said Storm. "I'll get there as soon as I can."

Aboard the *Wisconsin,*
over the northern Arabian Sea
0738

DOG BLEW A FRUSTRATED WAD OF AIR INTO HIS MASK AND turned his attention back to the sea.

"Dreamland *Wisconsin* to Mack Smith. Mack, the *Abner Read* is on its way. We need to find your precise coordinates for them."

"Not sure how I can help, Colonel," snapped Mack. "Looks like they forgot to put lines on this part of the ocean."

"Can you break out a signal mirror and flash my cockpit?"

There was no answer.

"Mack?"

A beam of light flashed on the port side of his aircraft.

"Keep flashing me," said Dog. He gently nudged the aircraft in the direction of the light, then turned the radio to the Dreamland frequency. "Dreamland Command, this is Colonel Bastian. You reading me?"

"Spotty but we have you," responded Major Natalie Catsman. Second in command at the base, Catsman was manning Dreamland's situation and control room.

"Can you get my precise location from the sat radio?"

"Affirmative, Colonel," she said after checking with one of the techs in the background. "The scientists tell me we can triangulate using your transmission."

Dog heard Ray Rubeo objecting in the background that her explanation wasn't precisely correct and the procedure would yield an error margin of plus-or-minus three meters.

"I'm going to overfly a spot and give you a mark," Dog told her. "I'll try it a couple of times and we can average out the location. I need it for the *Abner Read*."

"Roger that."

Dog lined up the Megafortress for a run over the splotches of light. He got his nose directly on one of the beams and ran it down.

"Now," he told Catsman.

He took the computed position and passed it on to Storm. The navy captain grunted and told Dog it would take "a while" to get up there.

"How long's a while?"

"A while is a while," said Storm. "It may depend on the Chinese. They don't appear to be in a particularly good mood."

True enough, thought Dog. He switched back to the emergency frequency.

"Mack, can you hear me?"

"Just barely," said Mack.

"*Abner Read* is on its way. It may take a couple of hours."

"Tell those fuckers to get the lead out," Mack replied. "The water's starting to get cold. And that ship on the horizon looks like it's getting closer."

"Roger that," said Dog. The ship was a Chinese frigate, and it had in fact turned in the direction of the downed airmen.

Dog banked too aggressively and the Megafortress sent a rumble through her frame.

"Sorry about that," he told the plane. "I don't mean to take you for granted."

Aboard the *Abner Read*,
northern Arabian Sea
0743

LIEUTENANT KIRK "STARSHIP" ANDREWS FINISHED THE survey of the water around the Sharkboat and turned the Werewolf back toward the *Abner Read*.

"Sharkboat, Werewolf survey confirms no mines in the area," he told the crew aboard the small vessel. Roughly the size of a PT boat, the Sharkboat looked like a miniature version of the *Abner Read* and was designed to work with the littoral destroyer. Lacking the bigger ship's comprehensive sensors, the small vessels had proven susceptible to mines earlier in the deployment.

"Thanks much, Werewolf. We are proceeding toward rendezvous."

Starship plotted the course back and let the computer take over the robot helicopter. Developed by Dreamland and originally intended to fight tanks and protected land positions, the Werewolf had been pressed into service as a naval helicopter gunship aboard the *Abner Read*. It proved remarkably adept at the job, so much so that Starship was now practically a regular member of the crew. The Navy people called him "Airforce" because of his service affiliation; the nickname at first had a ring of derision to it, but had come to be a compliment.

Starship rose halfway in the seat and turned around, trying to twist some of the knots out of his neck and back. His station was at one end of the destroyer's high-tech Tactical Warfare Center.

Lieutenant Commander Jack "Eyes" Eisenberg gave Starship a thumbs-up. Eyes was the *Abner Read*'s executive officer, second in command of the ship and the majordomo of Tac, as the Tactical Warfare Center was generally known. Starship gave him a grin and turned back to his computer display.

"Object in water," blurped the Werewolf computer.

"Identify," Starship told the computer. He pointed at the touchscreen, obtaining a precise GPS reading as well as the Werewolf's approximation of its size.

"Unknown. Believed to be human," said the computer.

"Tac—I have an object in the water. Could be a man overboard," said Starship. He took control from the computer and pushed the Werewolf lower, slowing so he could focus the forward video camera better on the object.

The Werewolf looked like a baby Russian Hokum helicopter. Propelled by a pair of counterrotating blades above, the unmanned aerial vehicle had a stubby set of wings and jet engines whose thrust could be tapped to help push its top speed out to nearly 400 knots—roughly twice what a "normal" helicopter could do. It was quite happy to hover as well, though the transition from top speed to a dead stop could be bumpy. In this case, Starship rode the chopper into a wide arc, descending gradually around his target.

"Could be a pilot," he said, studying the screen. "I think it might be one of the Chinese fliers."

"Location," said Eyes calmly.

Starship read the coordinates off. "Smile for your close-up, dude," he told the stricken man, pushing the freeze-frame on the videocam.

"Airforce, what's your status?" barked Storm.

"Downed flier, approximately, uh, let's say ten miles southwest of us, Captain." Starship was used to Storm's gruff way of communicating, and his habit of interrupting after Eyes had already given an order. The captain could be a genuine, class one jackass, but he was a good leader when the shit hit the fan.

Not as good as Colonel Bastian, but few men were.

"How far is that Sharkboat from him?"

"Take them almost an hour to get to him, Captain," Starship told him. "We're a lot closer, just about ten miles, and—"

"Here's what we're going to do, Airforce," Storm told him. "The Sharkboat is going to take flyboy. You're going to hover over him and make sure they find him."

Storm snapped off the circuit. Starship, confused about why a vessel farther away was being tasked to make the pickup, turned around and saw Eyes looking over his shoulder at the Werewolf's video feed. Because of the ad hoc nature of the arrangement, the Werewolf's video and other sensor data was not available at the executive officer's own station.

"Looks scared," said Eyes, bending down.

"Probably in shock," said Starship. Punching out of an aircraft at a few hundred knots took a lot out of the body. And while the Arabian Sea was relatively warm—the surface temperature was no lower than 68 degrees—it was still cooler than a human body. "Sir, you mind if I ask you a question?"

"Fire away."

"How come the Sharkboat is taking him?"

"We're heading north," said Eyes. "Some of your Dreamland guys bailed and we're going to pick them up, assuming we can get around the Chinese."

**Indian Ocean,
off the Indian coast
Time unknown**

TIME PAST MIXED WITH TIME FUTURE, THE PRESENT A TANGLE unrecognizable, bizarrely shaped and shot through with pain.

Time lost meaning, and there was no meaning, there was no present or past, nothing solid, nothing reliable except confusion.

Major Jeffrey "Zen" Stockard lay on his back in the ocean, floating not on water but rocks, black rocks tinged with orange. Flames lapped at his face and his legs were packed solid in ice. When he breathed, his lungs filled with the perfumed air of lilacs.

What happened to me?

The voice came from the sky.

Am I out of the plane?

Zen tried to shake his head and regain consciousness. Instead of his head, his chest shook.

Where is Breanna? Where's my wife?

A black blanket covered his head. He clawed at it, pulled and poked and prodded, but it would not yield. He gave up.

When he did, the blackness lifted to reveal a golden red sun no more than a foot from his head.

The voice spoke again.

I'm out of the plane, but where is Breanna?

Zen blinked his eyes, trying to shield them from the sun. His brain began to sort things out, reconstituting his memory like a computer rebuilding its hard drive. It moved sequentially, from the very beginning, everything rushing together: He was in high school, he was in the Air Force, he had just qualified as a fighter pilot, in the Gulf War.

Good shot, Captain, that MiG never had a chance.

Selected as test pilot, assigned to Dreamland, in love.

Well, you're too pretty to be a bomber pilot, why'd you slap me?

I do, I do, I do the happiest day of my life and no, the damn Flighthawk is going to hit my tail pain just pain just dark blank nothing who cares no one cares never and I will walk damn you all damn everyone because I will walk and I won't walk I won't won't won't will not give up will come back and who I am who I am?

Where is Breanna? Where is my wife?

Bree?

The voice called louder, pleading. Finally, he recognized that it was his voice, that he was calling for his wife, that he wanted her more than he wanted anything, more than he cared for his own life, certainly.

And then time asserted itself, and he was aware of the present. Zen fell into it, consumed by the swirling ocean of gray.

**White House Situation Room,
Washington, D.C.
2145, 14 January 1998
(0745, 15 January, Karachi)**

"THERE'S AN OPPORTUNITY HERE THAT WE HADN'T ANTICIpated." National Security Advisor Philip Freeman's face was beet red as he pleaded his cause. "It's been thrown in our lap."

Freeman glanced at Secretary of State Jeffrey Hartman,

then at President Kevin Martindale. Jed Barclay couldn't remember his boss arguing this passionately before.

"Of course there's risk, but it's not as great as it seems," continued Freeman. "The T-Rays have been much more effective than we hoped. It will be days before power is restored. The *Lincoln* is within a day's sail, and we still have the Dreamland assets in the region. If we recover those warheads ourselves, neither country will be in a position to challenge the other for years—years."

"We need to know definitively where the warheads are before we give the go ahead for an operation," insisted Secretary of Defense Arthur Chastain, speaking over the closed circuit communications system from the Pentagon War Room. "Without that, Mr. President, I can't guarantee success. I'm not even sure I can with it."

"Jed?" said Martindale.

"Space Command is working on the p-p-projections," said Jed, referring to the Air Force agency responsible for monitoring satellite intelligence. "They say they'll have something in twenty-four hours."

"Twenty-four hours!" Martindale never shouted, but his voice was as loud as Jed had ever heard it.

"Mr. President," said Chastain, "it's going to take time to get the area under full surveillance. The satellites we couldn't reposition were lost. Remember, we had to rush the operation before all the assets we wanted were in place, and even if they had been—"

"I don't want excuses," said Martindale. "Jed, tell Dreamland to find the warheads."

"Begging your pardon, Mr. President, but besides Space Command, the National Reconnaissance Office is working on it, and so is Navy Intelligence," said Admiral Balboa, Chairman of the Joint Chiefs. "I'm sure we can cut the time down considerably. We'll have something in twelve hours, maybe less. And the Dreamland people have done enough."

"See what Dreamland can do," Martindale told Jed. He

was calmer now, his voice softer, though it still had an edge to it. "Those scientists can figure it out. They always have some sort of high-tech trick up their sleeves."

"Yes, sir."

"I don't think it's worth the risk," said Chastain. "The *Lincoln* doesn't have ground forces that could make the pickups."

"We have a Marine Expeditionary Force near Somalia," said Freeman. "We can put them into action. And the Dreamland people."

"The Marines are two days away," said Chastain. "At least."

"Not if they stage out to the *Lincoln* and then go ashore," countered Freeman. "What do you think, Admiral Balboa?"

Admiral George Balboa, also speaking from the Pentagon, cleared his throat. While he and Freeman had often found themselves at odds, Jed noted that the two men had been meeting together a lot recently. If Balboa's tone was any indication, they had come to some sort of understanding.

"It might be possible," said the admiral. "The Marine Ospreys can fly to the *Lincoln,* then operate from there or even somewhere onshore until their assault ship arrives. Of course, we need to know where the warheads are. That's the key."

"What about the Dreamland people?" asked Martindale. "Can they recover the weapons?"

"There are too many warheads for them to do it," said Chastain. "And three of their planes have been shot down."

"Jed?"

"Um, their ground unit is intact, but, um, it's not big enough to do it on its own."

"I meant, what's the status of the airplanes?"

"There were three planes on the mission. Two were shot down," said Jed. "The third was the plane flown by Colonel Bastian. He was preparing to crash it into the Chinese aircraft carrier when the Chinese sent their nuclear-loaded bomber back to the hangar deck. So six crews are in the water."

"Have our people been picked up?"

"We're still working on it. This has only happened within the last hour, sir. Thirty minutes."

Martindale took a step toward the video conference screens. "Admiral, I want those people recovered."

"I'm sure they're working on it, sir," said Balboa.

"Work harder." Martindale turned around. "I'll decide what we're doing when I see the data on where the warheads are. But I agree with Philip. This is an historic opportunity. It's worth considerable risk. Now you'll have to excuse me. I have to tell the world what we've done."

**Aboard the *Wisconsin*,
over the northern Arabian Sea
0745**

DOG TACKED TO THE EAST, WIDENING HIS ORBIT. IT WAS VERY possible the destroyer had noticed him circling the area and was coming over to investigate. In that case, he thought he might be able to throw them off by circling around an empty patch of water.

On the other hand, they might be pulling themselves close enough to fire short-range antiair weapons at him. He had no radar warning device, so he couldn't even tell if he was being tracked.

"Dreamland *Wisconsin,* this is the *Abner Read*."

"*Wisconsin.*"

"Dog, we're under way toward your men," reported Eyes, the *Abner Read*'s executive officer. "It's going to take us a little more than two hours to get up there. There are some Chinese ships between us and the fliers. It's possible they may try to interfere, despite the cease-fire. I'll keep you advised."

"Understood," said Dog.

The *Wisconsin* had a little more than two hours' worth of

fuel left in her tanks. He'd need to go south and refuel before the *Abner Read* arrived. The question was, when.

Something flashed from the deck of the Chinese frigate— a missile.

The Chinese had just cast their vote in favor of sooner rather than later.

**Aboard the *Abner Read*,
northern Arabian Sea
0747**

AS STARSHIP SPUN THE WEREWOLF TO THE SOUTH, THE Chinese pilot's head disappeared beneath a swell of water.

"Tac, this guy's not going to make it much longer," said Starship. He watched as the man bobbed back to the surface. The Chinese pilot shook his head and rubbed his eyes. Starship winced—the saltwater probably stung like hell—but at least the man was alive.

"Sharkboat is doing the best it can," replied Eyes.

If the Werewolf were a "real" helicopter, it could have dropped a line from its belly and picked the poor sucker up. But the Werewolf didn't have a line. Its winch pack, used for transporting objects in combat, was aboard the *Abner Read*, but would take at least ninety minutes to install and test.

Then again, they didn't need a winch, just a line.

Starship suggested that he return to the *Abner Read*, where a sailor could tie a rope to one of the Werewolf's skids. He could then lift the pilot back to the ship.

"Why do you think he'll grab onto the line?" Eyes asked.

"We'll tie one of those rescue collars on it," said Starship. "I think he'll grab it if it's in front of his face."

"Let's give it a shot," said the lieutenant commander. "Head back here. I'll have a sailor standing by."

Aboard the *Wisconsin*,
over the northern Arabian Sea
0748

THE MEGAFORTRESS DIDN'T SEEM ANY HAPPIER TO GO FAST than it had slowing down. Dog slicked the aircraft's control surfaces back, rigging her for speed as he prodded the engines. Ordinarily, the aircraft would have responded instantaneously, jumping forward with a burst of speed. But the holes at the top and bottom of her fuselage where the crew had punched out created strong currents of air that fought against her wings' ability to provide lift. She was unbalanced, and moved sluggishly, drifting sideways rather than straight ahead.

"Come on now," said Dog. He tried to correct by adjusting his engines, but was only partly successful; even as he picked up speed, he felt as if he was fighting a stiff crosswind.

The missiles the Chinese ship had launched were HQ-7s, a Chinese version of the French Crotale. Guided by radar from the launch ship, the missiles used an infrared sensor to detonate once they were near their target. Ordinarily the Megafortress would have no trouble confusing the missiles, jamming both the destroyer's radar and the guidance frequency. The aircraft's stealthy radar profile would have helped, reducing the target the enemy had to home in on. But Dog didn't have electronic countermeasures, and the holes in the Megafortress's hull negated the stealthy effects of the plane's skin.

The one thing he knew he did have going for him was the missile's range. Though it was capable of hitting a Mach 2 target at 13,000 meters—roughly eight miles—its practical range was much closer to 8,000 meters. The *Wisconsin* was about 10,000 away.

Dog locked his eyes on the blue sky in front of the windscreen, fighting to hold the *Wisconsin* steady.

"Go," he told the plane. *"Go!"*

Northern Arabian Sea
0750

FROM MACK SMITH'S VANTAGE POINT IN THE WATER, THE missile looked like a white finger jetting across the sky, spewing a trail of cotton after it. The Megafortress seemed to hang in the air, completely unaware that it was in the crosshairs.

"Hit the gas, Colonel," yelled Mack. "Get the fuzz buster going. Jink. Do something, for chrissakes."

"He doesn't have countermeasures," said Jazz, next to him in the water.

"Yeah. Shit."

The missile stopped spewing cotton from its rear. It continued forward another mile or so, then disappeared. The Megafortress continued northward.

Mack turned back to the others. All of them, including the injured Cantor, were staring in the direction of the ship that had fired the missile. Its bow was turning in their direction.

"All right, guys, here's what we're going to do," Mack said. "Number one, we get the other raft inflated and lash it to this one. Number two, we find the *Abner Read*. She's to the southwest."

"Major, that ship has to be fifty or sixty miles from us," said Dish, glancing at Cantor. "I don't know."

"I *do* know," said Mack forcefully. "Let's get this fucking done. And no more bullshit defeat talk."

"I'm not—"

"No more bullshit, period," said Mack, fishing for the uninflated raft kit.

Aboard the *Wisconsin*,
over the northern Arabian Sea
0752

DOG COUNTED OFF SIXTY MORE SECONDS BEFORE ALLOWing himself to believe the missile had missed. He turned the

Megafortress to the west, now well north of the Chinese and his men.

"Dreamland Command, this is *Wisconsin*. I've just been fired on by the Chinese frigate. I'm all right," he added, almost as an afterthought. "What happened to the cease-fire?"

"We copy, Colonel," said Major Catsman. "We're alerting U.S. forces in the area. We're on the line with the White House," she told him, pausing. "They're assuring us a cease-fire has been worked out."

"Well assure them a missile just flew by my windshield."

"Yes, sir." Catsman paused once more, apparently relaying the information. "There's a possibility not all Chinese units got the message," she told Dog. "It's being reissued."

A handy excuse, thought Dog—and one typically employed by the Chinese.

"I'm going to go east and circle. Hopefully he'll think I'm over our guys and he'll change direction," said Dog. "I'm not sure what else I can do."

"Colonel, be advised that our data on Chinese frigates indicate that it's carrying HQ-7 antiair missiles similar to Crotales. You will be within lethal range of the missiles at seven miles."

"I already found that out, Major. But thanks."

**Aboard the *Abner Read*,
northern Arabian Sea
0800**

THE PETTY OFFICER SHOT HIS ARMS INTO THE AIR, SIGNAL-ing to Starship that the Werewolf was clear to launch.

"Werewolf powering up!" said the pilot, louder than necessary. His adrenaline was getting the better of him.

"Werewolf is away," he reported to Tac as the robot leapt into the air. Starship spun his tail, got his nose down and whipped over the waves, racing for the Chinese pilot. The computer marked off his progress in a legend to the right of the red crosshair designating the man's location. He throttled back as he reached the flier. The wash from the blades made the collar at the bottom of the rope dance back and forth. It wasn't going to be as easy to grab as Starship thought.

The man in the water bobbed helplessly as Starship approached. He fired off a round of flares, trying to make sure he had the man's attention, then nudged the Werewolf down until the collar skimmed in the waves. The wash from the rotors beat a circle before him as he worked slowly toward the pilot.

The pilot disappeared in a swell. Starship pushed forward in a rush, then realized that was the wrong thing to do—he was only roiling the water further. He slid the aircraft into a turn and throttled back as much as possible before trying again after the man's head reappeared.

He stopped about four or five feet from the downed pilot.

"Grab it, damn it," he said, sliding the collar right in front of his face, but the man still didn't react.

He's dead, he thought.

Not ready to give up, Starship nudged the stick back gently in the direction of the man. The collar hit the pilot in the chest as a small burst of wind nudged the aircraft downward.

"Grab it!" urged Starship. He flipped on the Werewolf's PA system and told him to take the line. The Chinese pilot still didn't move.

Reluctantly, Starship started to nudge away.

"Tac, I'm afraid—"

He stopped mid-sentence as the screen from the chin cam caught his eye. The pilot had reached out his arm toward the collar.

"Finally," said Starship, easing back.

UP ON THE *ABNER READ*'S BRIDGE, STORM FOLDED HIS arms as he studied the holographic projection of the ocean around his destroyer. There was no way to get to the downed *Wisconsin* fliers without sailing closer than five miles to one of the Chinese ships.

Obey orders and let them die?

The hell with that.

But armed with only his torpedoes, he'd be at a severe disadvantage if any of the Chinese ships became hostile. And the fact that one had just fired a missile at Bastian didn't bode well.

He could turn off all of his active sensors and try to sneak into the area. But he couldn't go blind, and Bastian had told him he'd have to leave the area to refuel. Putting out the *Abner Read*'s passive sensor array would slow him down.

"Eyes, how close to the Chinese pilot is the Sharkboat?" Storm asked, pressing his intercom connection. "How long before it can come north and scout the area for us?"

"Captain, the Werewolf has the Chinese pilot in tow and is inbound."

"How?"

"We had a rope rigged to the aircraft's skid. Airforce thought of it."

Those Dreamlanders—always thinking.

"Let me know when he's aboard."

"Aye aye, sir."

STARSHIP WASN'T SURE HOW FAST HE COULD GO BEFORE the injured pilot lost his grip. He started out slowly, at under ten knots, but the *Abner Read* had her turbines churning, and just to keep up he had to bring the aircraft to thirty knots. With one eye on the videocam showing the pilot at the end the rope below, he nudged up his speed—forty knots, fifty, then sixty. The wind rippled the man's flight suit. Starship imagined it might feel like a motorcycle ride. Then again, it could be the most horrific experience the pilot ever had.

He reached 100 knots before the destroyer came into view.

"Tac, I have our package ready to drop under the Christmas tree," said Starship. "If you can clear me in to land."

"Stand by. Security team to the helipad."

Starship adjusted his altitude as well as his speed, bringing the pilot down about five feet from the waves. Four armed crewmen waited near the bull's-eye on the fanged fantail. Starship tried to get the pilot right between them but moved a bit too abruptly and bowled over one of the sailors. The others scrambled to help, wrestling the Chinese pilot from the collar as they fought the wind from the helicopter above.

"Tac, tell those guys to take it easy," said Starship. Not only was he worried that they were going to hurt the pilot, but their tugs pulled at the Werewolf, wreaking havoc with the controls. The computer kept trying to compensate, fighting Starship as he struggled to hold her steady above the moving ship.

"He's secure," said Eyes finally.

Starship pulled up.

"Airforce, you have your ears on?" barked Storm.

"Yes, sir, Captain."

"I want you to run ahead and get a look at the ships between us and those Dreamland people. We're turning off our radar so the Chinese don't realize we're coming. I want to see what I'm up against."

"On my way."

Aboard the *Wisconsin*,
over the northern Arabian Sea
0805

DOG'S PLAN WORKED—SORT OF. THE CHINESE FRIGATE once more changed direction, sailing toward the spot in the ocean he was circling. But he'd also attracted the attention of a smaller vessel, which was now approached from the northeast. This was a small patrol boat, little more than an overgrown speedboat, but just as deadly to the men in the water. It was also more maneuverable, and more likely to search the area and conclude that the downed airmen were somewhere else.

Dog decided he would try and shoo it away; if nothing else, the frigate would be convinced that he was trying to protect someone there.

The aircraft growled as he pushed her wing down, moving farther sideways than forward and losing altitude more quickly than he'd intended. Dog wrestled it back under control in time to pass by the bow of the patrol boat at two hundred feet—not particularly low, though close enough to see the 40mm double-barreled gun on the foredeck as it swung in his direction.

Dog babied the stick, putting the Megafortress into another turn, this one as gentle as he could manage. He slid down to one hundred feet and came over the patrol boat. The 40mm gun turned again in his direction, but if it fired, Dog never saw the shots. He pulled off as he passed, and by the time he glanced down, saw that the vessel had turned back in the direction of land.

Northern Arabian Sea
0810

MACK WATCHED THE MEGAFORTRESS DISAPPEAR TO THE northwest, once again chased away by the Chinese destroyer. At least it had taken the ship with it this time.

They'd lashed the two inflatable rafts together and put Cantor in one. Mack told them that they'd take turns in the other once they got tired. For now, they were all going to kick in the direction of the *Abner Read*.

Forty or fifty miles on the open ocean was a very, very long distance. But Mack figured that moving was better than floating, and every hundred yards was a hundred yards away from the Chinese.

"Aw, shit," yelped Jazz. "Ah, man."

"What's up?"

"My leg. Feels like I got an iron chain in it."

"It's just a cramp," said Mack. "Work through it."

Jazz continued to curse.

"Take a break, Jazz," Mack told him finally.

"I'm OK, Major."

"Your lips are turning blue. Get in the damn raft. That's an order."

"Yes, sir."

It was only after Jazz pulled himself into the raft, leg twitching, that Mack realized everyone's lips were blue.

"Kick," he told the others. "Let's go. Kick!"

**Aboard the *Abner Read*,
northern Arabian Sea
0810**

THERE WAS ONLY SO MUCH THAT COULD BE DONE TO MAKE a helicopter stealthy, but the Werewolf was small and its ability to fly extremely low would make it hard for the Chinese ships to spot it until it was very close. Starship figured that if he moved fast enough, he could get by any of the ships before they could react and try to shoot him down.

A Chinese guided-missile cruiser presented a particular problem, since it sat almost directly in his path. But the cruiser had been heavily damaged in the battle, and smoke poured from three different places on the ship. The radar warning receiver aboard the Werewolf indicated that the vessel was not using its weapons or even early warning radar; most likely the radar systems had been destroyed. Still, Starship kept an eye on the infrared warning panel as he shot past no more than a mile away, worried that the ship might try firing a heat-seeking missile without locking him up on radar.

With the cruiser in the rearview mirror, Starship put the pedal to the metal and sped over the waves. About three miles from the GPS point he'd been given as the fliers' location, he began rising to get a better view for his radar and other sensors.

The first thing he saw on the synthesized radar screen was

a Chinese destroyer, six miles to the east. Dreamland *Wisconsin* was eight or nine miles north of the destroyer.

So he had the neighborhood, at least.

Starship slowed his speed to eighty knots and did a quick scan of the area around him; he couldn't see anything in the water. He instructed the computer to set up a search pattern; when the grid came up on the screen, he chose the segment closest to the Chinese destroyer as a starting point and told the computer to go.

The Werewolf hadn't actually reached the point when he spotted a pair of rafts and several swimmers three miles to the west. He took back control and turned toward them.

"Werewolf to Tac," he said. "I have our subjects in view. Counting—four—no, five men—two in the raft, others in the water. Stand by for GPS coordinates."

Northern Arabian Sea
0825

THE NOISE REMINDED MACK SMITH OF HIS BROTHER'S whiny two-stroke weed whacker—assuming it had a blanket thrown on it.

The water to the east seemed to bubble up into a moving volcano.

"Chopper," said Tommy. "Ours or theirs?"

They were too far away to see it clearly, but the sound gave it away.

"That's a Werewolf," said Dish.

"Yeah," said Mack. "Has to be from the *Abner Read*."

The robot aircraft banked southward, moving away.

"Yo, Werewolf—where are you going?" grunted Mack. The mouthpiece for his survival radio was integrated with the collar of his Dreamland-designed flight suit, but the radio was in a sleep mode to conserve battery power and had to be manually turned on. Mack reached down to the vest and did so, then repeated the hail, this time with more formality.

Dog, not the Werewolf, answered.

"Mack, that's the *Abner Read*'s aircraft," said Dog. "He's scouting your position."

"*Wisconsin,* can you connect me with the pilot? He's flying to the south."

A transmission from the Werewolf overrode the reply. Neither were intelligible.

"Mack Smith to Werewolf. Yo, you just flew south of us."

"Just getting the lay of the land, Mack," responded Starship.

"Hey, Junior, I don't know how to tell you this, but you're flying over the sea."

"Oh, that's what that blue stuff is. I thought I was upside down."

"You're a joke a minute, kid. How long before you get that tin can you're in up here?"

"*Abner Read* will pick you up in about an hour and a half."

Mack glanced over at Cantor. He was out of it.

"Give me a vector and we'll meet it halfway," said Mack.

"Major—"

"Give me a vector, kid. We're not hanging here all day."

Aboard the *Wisconsin*,
over the northern Arabian Sea
0835

DOG PULLED BACK ON THE STICK, COAXING THE MEGAFOR-tress into a gentle climb. With the *Abner Read* on its way and the Werewolf close enough to talk directly with the downed airmen, there was nothing more for him to do here.

He got Catsman on the Dreamland Command frequency and through her spoke to the KC-10 tanker that had been tasked to Dreamland for the operation. They arranged a rendezvous about an hour's flying time south of his present position.

When Dog finished making the arrangements, he turned back to look for the Chinese frigate. Not spotting it right away, a shiver of panic flew through him. He'd blundered too close, he thought, and was now in range of another missile.

Then he saw the frigate in the distance. It had given up chasing him and was once more sailing back in the direction of Mack and the others.

Northern Arabian Sea
0850

THE WEREWOLF PICKED UP EVERYONE'S MORALE, BUT MACK soon realized that could be too much of a good thing. For while they kicked ferociously for a few minutes, pushing the raft in the direction of the approaching American ship, they quickly ran out of energy. And with the *Abner Read* still far in the distance, they had to conserve their strength.

"All right, new plan," Mack told the others, and felt his teeth chatter as he spoke. "One guy kicks at a time. Two guys, one on each side, rest. Other two stay in the raft. Jazz, how's your leg?"

"Much better."

"Great," said Mack, though he knew the lieutenant was lying. "All right. I'll kick and steer. Idea here is that we're saving our strength. All right? We're all about endurance right now."

"I'll swap with Dish," said Jazz.

"Nah, it's OK," said Mack.

"Dish looks cold."

"I'm OK," said Dish.

Jazz slipped into the water next to him. Mack watched his shock as the water hit him. Then Dish pulled himself into the raft, Mack could see he was both reluctant and grateful.

Mack leaned over toward Jazz. "You hanging in there, kid?"

"I'm with ya, Major."

"Kick slow if you have to, to stay warm."

"Staying warm."

Mack kicked slowly himself, pushing the raft almost imperceptibly. He told himself he was in a survival tank bank at Nellis Air Base, just having a grand ol' time with the instructors, one of whom had been *Sports Illustrated* model material.

Luscious, that.

Mmmm, mmmm, mmmm.

In the raft, Dish shifted around to get closer to him.

"Hey, Major," he said in a barely audible voice. "That Chinese ship. I can see it on the horizon, getting bigger."

Damn, thought Mack, doing his best not to turn around.

**Aboard the *Abner Read,*
northern Arabian Sea
0855**

THE RADAR DETECTOR ABOARD THE WEREWOLF BLEEPED TO let Starship know that the Chinese frigate was looking for it. The ship had changed course and was now making a beeline for the life raft.

"Tac, I need you to take a look at this," Starship said. In an instant, Eyes appeared at his side.

"The frigate is heading in their direction. You think it knows they're there?"

Eyes squatted and looked at the Werewolf control screen, which displayed a situational representation of the area. The sitrep provided a bird's-eye view, augmented with information about the contacts, their speed and bearings. The control computer could gather and synthesize the information from a variety of sources, but in this case it was working primarily with the Werewolf's regular and infrared radar. The destroyer was about four miles from the men.

"They're too far to know exactly where they are," decided Eyes. "But I'd say they definitely know they're in the vicinity."

"How long before they actually see the raft?"

"Hard to tell. It's too small and low on the water to be detected by any radar the Chinese have." Eyes straightened. "That leaves human lookouts. Good glasses, good lookouts . . ."

Eyes didn't finish the sentence. Starship knew that his own Mark 1 eyeballs were capable of picking out a silver speck in a bright sky at four or five miles, no sweat. Here, the lookouts would have a nice orange target on a field of deep blue.

"We have to figure out a way to get them out of there," said Starship.

"That, or get the frigate out of there."

**Aboard the *Wisconsin*,
over the northern Arabian Sea
0900**

THE SUN POURED THROUGH THE HATCHWAY ABOVE THE copilot's seat as Dog turned toward the Chinese ship. Wind surged through the cockpit, grabbing at the folds of his flight suit. He could barely hear his breath in the face mask, which was just as well—he'd started to hyperventilate, too revved on adrenaline.

"*Wisconsin* to Werewolf. Starship, can you go over to the Dreamland Command channel?" he asked over the emergency frequency.

"Werewolf. Affirmative, Colonel."

"Do it." Dog guessed that the Chinese were monitoring the emergency frequency and didn't want them listening in.

"I'm on, Colonel."

"The Chinese frigate is heading toward Mack and the others. How close is the *Abner Read*?"

"Roughly an hour and a half," said Starship.

"Are you armed?"

"Only with .50 caliber bullets."

The bullets were fired from machine guns in the Werewolf's skids. The weapon wouldn't do much against the frigate, and to use it Starship would have to fly well within range of the Chinese ship's missiles.

"*Wisconsin,* he's activated targeting radars," warned Starship.

"Yeah, roger that," said Dog. He took a hard turn, hoping to "beam" the radar, flying in the direction of the waves, where it was more difficult to be detected.

"Still targeting you."

"Just tell me if he fires."

"Werewolf," said Starship, acknowledging.

Dog began a bank, aiming to circle in front of the destroyer and make himself a more inviting target.

It was hopeless, wasn't it? Sooner or later the captain of the frigate was going to figure out what he was up to, if he hadn't already. And by now he'd have realized that the Megafortress was unarmed and impotent.

Well, he was weaponless, but was he impotent?

An hour and a half before, he'd been willing to give his life to keep the Chinese from launching a nuclear weapon and involving the world in a nuclear war.

He could do that now, he thought. If he hit the frigate right, he'd sink it.

He'd have to stay at the stick to do it.

Dog hesitated, then pushed the stick back toward the frigate. He reached for the throttle glide, ready to put the engines to the wall.

"Missile launch!" screamed Starship. And as he did, Dog saw two thick bursts of white foam erupt from the forward section of the Chinese ship.

Northern Arabian Sea
0908

MACK SAW THE MISSILES STREAK FROM THE CHINESE destroyer but couldn't tell what they were firing at. The

Wisconsin, he guessed, though he couldn't see it in the sky.

The Werewolf was skittering around two miles to the east.

Cantor groaned.

"Maybe the chopper can take him back to the ship," said Dish.

"Maybe," said Mack, though he knew that the small helicopter wasn't normally equipped with rescue equipment. "Hey, kid, you still up there? Werewolf?"

"Werewolf."

"We got an injured airman here. It's Jazz—you think we can rig a stretcher up or something?"

"Uh, negative, Major. I have a line running down from the bird and there's a collar attached, but I don't know about hooking up a stretcher. It's a long way back, and he'd have to hold on. I don't think he could make it."

"That's it, kid. You just gave me a great idea. Get overhead right now," he added, as two more missiles flew from the destroyer.

**Aboard the *Wisconsin*,
over the northern Arabian Sea
0908**

ONE HAND ON THE POWER CONTROLS AND THE OTHER ON the stick, Lieutenant Colonel Tecumseh "Dog" Bastian goaded the *Wisconsin* to the southeast, urging her away from the missiles. The weapons were smaller and faster than the Megafortress, and didn't have to worry about dealing with holes in their fuselage. On the other hand, the Megafortress had a five-mile head start and a human pilot guiding her.

Dog pushed the Megafortress toward the waves, trying to get as low as possible without turning his plane into a submarine. The radar in the Chinese destroyer, originally intended for tracking targets tens of thousands of feet higher, lost the aircraft at about a hundred feet, leaving both missiles to use their onboard infrared detectors to find the target.

The first missile, either incorrectly believing it was near the Megafortress or simply deciding it had had enough of the chase, imploded a good mile from the *Wisconsin,* harmlessly showering the sea with shrapnel.

The second missile continued in the right direction. The launch trajectory had sent it climbing over the Megafortress by a few thousand feet. As it corrected, Dog pushed hard to the south, taking his juicy heat signature away from the missile's sensor. The radar on the frigate picked up the plane as it turned, then lost it again, though not before its fitful guidance beam sent the missile into a half loop back toward the target.

Dog didn't know what was going on behind him; he only knew that the farther he flew, the better the odds of survival. He'd been chased by countless missiles, some radar guided, some infrared, a few like this one—a combination of the two. Even with countermeasures, it was always a question of outrunning the thing—"getting where the missile ain't," as an instructor had taught him a million years ago. Jink, thrash the pedals, lean on the throttle—just go.

Drenched in sweat, Dog felt the water rolling down his arms, saturating the palms of his hands. He slid his left hand farther down the stick, worried that his fingers would slip right off.

As he did, there was a low clunk behind him and the plane jerked forward, its tail threatening to rise. He used both his hands to keep control, but even as he did, he felt a surge of relief—the shock had undoubtedly come from the warhead's explosion, and while it must have been close enough to shake the plane, he could tell it hadn't done serious damage.

Leveling out, Dog took a moment to wipe the sweat from the palms of his hands, then pulled back to climb. He glanced over his left shoulder, looking for the frigate in the distance.

He didn't see the ship. But he did see a silvery baseball bat, headed straight for him.

It was another HQ-7 antiair missile, and it was gaining fast.

Northern Arabian Sea
0912

THOUGH IT WAS SMALL, THE WEREWOLF KICKED UP A PRETTY good amount of wind from its props and engines. Mack had trouble keeping his eyes clear as the robo-helo edged in, its rope and sling swinging below.

What Starship had called a collar looked like a limp rubber band—a wet, slimy one that packed the wallop of a wrecking ball. As Mack reached for it, a swell pushed him forward faster than he expected and he was whacked in the neck. He grabbed for the rope but couldn't quite reach it.

"Get that mother!" he yelled.

He put his left hand on the raft and lurched forward, jumping across the tiny boat for the collar. He managed to spear his arm through it and immediately began to spin to the right. T-Bone jumped at the same time and also grabbed part of the collar. Dish reached but missed, grabbing T-Bone instead. The three men crashed together, none of them daring to let go. The tied-together rafts twirled beneath them, one of them nearly swamping.

"I got it, I got it!" yelled Mack. He hung on as the rope bucked back and forth. "Just grab me. Grab onto me and hold onto the rafts. Stabilize them!"

Starship was trying to tell him something, but Mack couldn't hear. He felt the helicopter pulling him upward and tried locking his grip by grabbing his flight suit, so that the sling was tucked under his arm. His right leg tangled in the line they'd used to lash the two rafts together, and he felt as if he was being pulled apart at the groin.

"Hold me and the raft! Hold me and the raft!" he shouted, though by now his voice was hoarse.

They were moving, though he had no idea in what direction. It wasn't exactly what he'd in mind, but it was something.

**Aboard the *Abner Read*,
northern Arabian Sea
0916**

STARSHIP DIDN'T KNOW FOR SURE WHETHER THE MEN IN the raft had snagged the line until he had to struggle to correct for a shift in the wind. He nudged the Werewolf forward and the rafts came with her, pulling through the water at about four knots.

The frigate was still coming toward them.

"Major, I'm going to try increasing the speed," said Starship. "Are you guys all right?"

Mack's response, if there was one, was drowned out by the roar of the Werewolf's blades directly overhead. The engineers who had advertised the chopper as "whisper quiet" obviously had a unique notion of how loud a whisper was.

Starship notched the speed up gently, moving to six knots and then eight. He knew it had to feel fast to the men on the rafts, but it was less than half the frigate's speed, and the ship continued to close. While the helo was too low to the water for an antiair missile, it was only a matter of time before the frigate's conventional weapons could be brought to bear.

"Come to ten knots," he told the computer, deciding to use the more precise voice command instead of the throttle.

As the computer acknowledged, a warning panel opened on the main screen—the frigate's gun-control radar had just locked onto the helicopter.

**Aboard the *Wisconsin*,
over the northern Arabian Sea
0916**

DOG DROVE THE MEGAFORTRESS DOWN TOWARD THE waves, hoping he could get low enough to avoid the radar guiding the missile toward him. He hung on as the *Wisconsin* shook violently, the aerodynamic stresses so severe that he thought for a moment the missile had already caught up. He kept his eyes on the ocean as he slammed downward; when he thought it was time to pull up, he waited five long seconds more before doing so.

By then it was almost too late. The controls felt as if they were stuck in cement. He put his feet against the bulkhead below the control panel and levered his entire weight backward. The plane reluctantly raised her nose, and was able to level off at just over fifty feet, so close he worried that he was scooping the waves into the engines.

Dog's maneuver had cost him so much airspeed that the missile shot past, still flying on the last vector supplied by the guidance radar. He saw it wobbling a few hundred feet overhead; instinctively he ducked as the warhead blew up two or three hundred meters in front of him.

Fourteen kilograms of high explosive was more than enough to perforate an aluminum can, even if that can was covered over with an exotic carbon resin material. But the truly deadly part of the HQ-7's warhead was the shroud of metal surrounding the explosive nut; the metal splinters the explosion produced were engineered to shred high performance fighters and attack aircraft. Fortunately, the designers envisioned that the warhead would be doing its thing behind the plane it was targeted at, not in front of it, and the majority of the shrapnel rained down well beyond the *Wisconsin*.

Not all of it, however. The left wing took a dozen hits, the fuselage another six. A fist-sized slab of former missile punched through the top of the cockpit behind Dog. It crashed into the bulkhead at the rear of the flight deck, spraying more metal around the cockpit. Dog felt a hot poke on his right side, and winced as a splinter rebounded off one of the consoles and hit his ribs. It barely broke the skin, but still hurt like hell.

Clearly, the shrapnel had damaged the plane. He decided a poke in the side was a small price to pay for the near miss, and started to climb again, angling southward, well out of the frigate's range.

**Aboard the *Abner Read*,
northern Arabian Sea
0920**

HANDS ON HIPS, STORM WATCHED THE VIDEO FEED FROM the Werewolf in astonishment. The downed airmen seemed to have formed a human chain connecting their rafts with the robot helo. Any second now, he thought, one of them would suggest the helicopter turn around so they could try boarding the destroyer chasing them.

More guts than brains, that bunch.

He turned back to the holographic table, rechecking the positions of the Chinese ships. Then he reached to the com switch on his belt.

"Sickbay, how's our guest?"

"Conscious, Captain. In shock, though. Looks like a concussion, but no other serious injuries."

"Can he be transported?"

"I wouldn't advise it, sir."

"That wasn't the question."

"If it were absolutely necessary."

Storm flicked the controller. "Communications—send a message to the captain of the *Khan*. Tell him I have one of his pilots and I'm on my way to return him. Tell him I need to talk to him right away."

THE WEREWOLF'S SMALL SIZE AND SHIFTING LOCATION made it difficult for the gun radar to lock, but the Chinese were definitely out to earn an A for effort. The radar warning receiver kept flashing and then clearing, only to flash again.

Finally, a shell arced toward the helo. It missed by nearly a half mile, short and wide to the right. The 56mm gun at the bow was effective at about 10,000 meters; the computer calculated it would be within range of the rafts in another sixty seconds.

Starship notched the speed up to twelve knots.

"Mack, can you get the raft tied in better?" he asked.

When the major didn't respond, Starship tried again, this time yelling into the microphone.

Still no answer. The frigate was now forty-five seconds from range.

"Fourteen knots," Starship told the computer.

Northern Arabian Sea
0923

MACK'S LEGS FELT AS IF THEY'D BEEN PULLED FROM HIS hips. The waves cracked across the bottoms of the two rafts, punching them up and down. This wouldn't have been so bad, he thought, if they bounced together. Instead, they rumbled unevenly, thumping and jerking in a madly syncopated dance. It was as if he were standing on the backs of two rodeo bulls, each of whom were riding in the back of a poorly sprung pickup truck.

T-Bone had his right leg and Dish his left. The others, except for Cantor, were holding onto them.

"Hey, this is fun, isn't it?" yelled Mack, trying to cheer them up.

As if in reply, the Werewolf gave him a fresh tug. He suddenly jerked forward, the ride smoother—too smooth, he realized as he began to spin. He'd been pulled completely from the raft.

"Starship, get me back! Starship!"

Mack spun to his right. He caught glimpses of the destroyer as he spun. The Chinese warship seemed to gain a mile every time he blinked.

Dizzy, he closed his eyes, then quickly opened them as the ocean bashed against his leg. Something flew at him—a bullet from the frigate's gun, he thought. But it was only Dish, leaping out to grab him as the Werewolf swung back with him.

The rafts twirled as the Werewolf once again changed direction.

"Hang on, hang on!" Mack shouted to the others.

"Look!" yelled Dish, pointing behind him in the direction of the frigate.

Mack wanted to scream at him; there was no sense pointing out how close the frigate was. Dish turned around, then looked back up at Mack, a grin on his face.

What the hell are you smiling about? he wondered, then glanced over Dish's shoulder and saw that the frigate had turned off.

**Aboard the *Wisconsin*,
over the northern Arabian Sea
0925**

"THE *KHAN* HAS TOLD THE FRIGATE TO KNOCK IT OFF," Storm told Dog. "They've turned away."

"Why were they firing in the first place?"

"Why do the Chinese do anything?" said Storm. "They gave me some cock and bull story about the frigate captain believing he was rescuing Chinese pilots, but I don't trust them to tell the truth. I don't trust them at all."

Dog wasn't sure what to believe. It was possible that the captain of the frigate believed he was rescuing his own men; the *Khan* had lost most of its aircraft, and the frigate probably wasn't aware that the crew of the Megafortress had jumped out—after all, the plane was still flying.

On the other hand, the transmissions on the emergency or guard band should have made it clear that the downed airmen were American.

Unless, of course, the captain suspected a trick.

"Now don't you go screwing things up, Bastian," added Storm. "Don't use your weapons on the Chinese, as tempting as it may be. Don't even power them up."

"What do you think, I'm going to crank open a window and take potshots at them with my Beretta?"

"I wouldn't put it past you."

Dog snorted. All this time fighting together, and Storm was still a jerk.

"I'm going to have to go south real soon if I'm going to make that tanker," Dog said. "Can you handle the pickup?"

"Go. We have the situation under control."

Under other circumstances, Dog would have flown over the raft, dipping his wings to wish his men luck and let them know he was still thinking about them. But he didn't want to press his luck with the plane.

As he found his course southward, he reached into a pocket on the leg of his speed jeans, fishing for a small pillbox he kept there.

He rarely resorted to "go" pills—amphetamines—to keep himself alert. He didn't like the way they seemed to scratch his skin and eyes from the inside. More than that, he didn't like the idea of them. But there was just no getting around them now. The long mission and the physical demands of flying the Megafortress without the computer or human assistance had left him drained. He worked up some saliva, then slipped a pill into his mouth and swallowed.

It tasted like acid going down.

"Dreamland Command, I'm heading south," he told Major Catsman. "See if you can get the tanker to fly a little farther north, would you?"

II

Lost and Not Found

———

**Indian Ocean,
off the Indian coast
Time unknown**

IT HAPPENED SO GRADUALLY THAT ZEN DIDN'T NOTICE THE
line he crossed. One unending moment he was drifting in a
kaleidoscope of shapes, thoughts, and emotions; the next, he
was fully conscious, floating neck high in the Indian Ocean.
And very, very cold.

He glanced around, looking for his wife Breanna. They'd
gone out of the plane together, hugging each other as they
jumped through the hole left by one of the ejection seats in
the Flighthawk bay of the stricken Megafortress. Eight people had been aboard the plane; there were only six ejection
seats. As the senior members of the crew, they had the others
bail first, then followed the old-fashioned way.

Ejection seats had been invented to get crew members away
from the jet as quickly and safely as possible, before they
could be smacked by the fuselage or sucked into a jet engine.
While certain aircraft were designed to be good jumping plat-
forms, with the parachutists shielded from deadly wind sheers
and vortices, the Megafortress was not among them. Though
Zen and Breanna had been holding each other as they jumped,
the wind had quickly torn them apart.

Zen had smacked his head and back against the fuselage,
then rebounded down past Breanna. He'd tried to arc his upper body as a skydiver would. But instead of flying smoothly
through the air, he began twisting around, spinning on both
axes as if he were a jack tossed up at the start of a child's

game. He'd forced his arms apart to slow his spin, then pulled the ripcord for his parachute and felt an incredibly hard tug against his crotch. But the chute had opened and then he fell at a much slower speed.

Sometime later—it could have been seconds or hours—he'd seen Breanna's parachute unfold about two miles away. His mind, tossed by the wind and jarred by the collision with the plane, suddenly cleared. He began shifting his weight and steering the chute toward his wife, flying the parachute in her direction.

A skilled parachutist would have had little trouble getting to her. But he had not done a lot of practice jumps before the aircraft accident that left him paralyzed, and in the time since, done only four, all qualifying jumps under much easier conditions.

Still, he had managed to get within a few hundred yards of Breanna before they hit the water.

The water felt like concrete. Zen hit at an angle, not quite sideways but not erect either. There wasn't much of a wind, and he had no trouble getting out of the harness. As a paraplegic, his everyday existence had come to depend on a great deal of upper body strength, and he was an excellent swimmer, so he had no trouble squaring himself away. The small raft that was part of his survival gear bobbed up nearby, but rather than getting in, he'd let it trail as he swam in the direction of Breanna.

She wasn't where he'd thought she would be. Her chute had been released but he couldn't see her. He felt as if he'd been hit in the stomach with an iron bar.

As calmly as he could manage, he had turned around and around, looking, then began swimming against the slight current and wind, figuring the chute would have been pulled toward him quicker than Breanna had.

Finally, he'd seen something bobbing up and down about twenty yards to his right. It was Breanna's raft. But she wasn't in it.

She was floating nearby, held upright by her horseshoe

lifesaver, upright, breathing, but out of it. He'd gotten her into her raft, but then was so exhausted that he pulled himself up on the narrow rubber gunwale and rested. He heard a thunderous roar that gave way to music—an old song by Spinal Tap, he thought—and then he slipped into a place where time had no meaning. The next thing he knew, he found himself here, alone in the water.

How long ago had that been?

His watch had been crushed during the fall from the plane. He stared at the digits, stuck on the time he'd hit the airplane: 7:15 A.M.

The sun was now almost directly overhead, which meant it was either a little before or a little after noon—he wasn't sure which, since he didn't know which way was east or west.

Five hours in the water. Pretty long, even in the relatively warm Indian Ocean.

He reached to his vest for his emergency radio. It wasn't there. Had he taken it out earlier? He had the vaguest memory of doing so—but was it a genuine memory or a dream?

A nightmare.

Was this real?

Breanna would have one. Bree—

Where was she? He didn't see her.

Where *was* she?

"Bree!"

His voice sounded shallow and hoarse in his ears.

"Yo, Bree! Where are ya, hon?"

He waited, expecting to hear her snap back with something like, *Right behind you, wise guy.*

But she didn't.

He thought he heard her behind him and spun around.

Nothing.

Not only was his radio gone—so was his life raft. He didn't remember detaching it. His head was pounding. He felt dizzy.

Zen turned slowly in the water, positive he'd seen something out of the corner of his eye. He finally spotted something in the distance: land or a ship, or even a bank of clouds; he was too far off to tell. He began paddling toward it.

After about fifteen minutes he realized it was land. He also realized the current would help him get to it.

"Bree!" he shouted, looking around. "Bree!"

He paddled harder. After an hour or so his arms began to seize. He no longer had the strength to swim, and simply floated with the tide. His voice had become too weak to do more than whisper. He barely had enough strength, in fact, to resist the creeping sense of despair lapping at his shoulders.

Diego Garcia
1600, 15 January 1998

DOG WATCHED THE TANKER SET DOWN ON DIEGO GARCIA'S long runway, turning slowly in the air above the island as he waited for his turn to land. It had taken his damaged plane just under eight hours to reach Diego Garcia, more than twice what it had taken to fly north.

His body felt as if it were a statue or maybe a rusted robot that he haunted rather than lived in. His mind could control all of his body's movements, but didn't feel quite comfortable doing so. He was a foreigner in his own skin.

Eyes burned dry, throat filled with sand, Dog acknowledged the tower's clearance and eased the *Wisconsin* into her final leg toward the runway.

Owned by the British, Diego Garcia was a desert island in the middle of nowhere, a sliver of paradise turned into a long runway, fueling station, and listening post. It was an odd mix of three distinct time periods—modern, British colonial, and primordial—all existing uneasily together.

The rush of air around him seemed to subside as he dropped toward the concrete. The wheels screeched loudly when he touched down, and the sound of the wind and the engines seemed to double. Dog had practiced manual-controlled landings many times in the simulator, and had had a few real ones besides. Even so, his hands shook as the Megafortress continued across the runway, seemingly moving much faster on the ground than she had been in the air. He had his brakes set, power down, and reverse thrusters deployed—he knew he should be stopping, but he wasn't. He deployed the drag chute at the rear of the aircraft and held on.

The world roared around him, a loud train running in his head. And then finally the aircraft stopped—not gradually, it seemed, but all of a sudden.

The *Wisconsin* halted dead a good hundred yards from the turnoff from the taxiway. Dog let go of the stick and slumped back, too exhausted to move up properly. An SUV with a flashing blue light approached; there were other emergency vehicles, fire trucks, an ambulance, coming behind it.

After he caught his breath, he undid his restraints and pulled himself upright. Embarrassed, he flipped on the mike for his radio.

"Dreamland *Wisconsin* to Tower. Tower, you hearing me?"

"Affirmative, *Wisconsin*. Are you all right?"

"Get these guys out of my way and I'll tootle over to the hangar," he said, trying to make his voice sound light.

"Negative, *Wisconsin*. You're fine where you are. We have a tractor on the way."

"Welcome back, Colonel," said a familiar gravelly voice over the circuit.

"Chief Parsons?"

"I hope you didn't break my plane too bad, Colonel," said Chief Master Sergeant Clyde Alan "Greasy Hands" Parsons. Parsons was the head enlisted man in the Dreamland detachment, and the de facto air plane czar. He knew more about the Megafortress than its designer did. "I have only a skeleton crew to work with here."

"I'll take your skeleton over Angelina Jolie's body any day," Dog told him.

"Jeez, I don't know, Colonel," answered Parsons. "If that's the lady I'm thinking of, I'm afraid I'd have to go with her."

* * *

LIEUTENANT MICHAEL ENGLEHARDT HOPPED FROM THE
GMC Jimmy and trotted toward the big black aircraft sitting
on the runway in front of him. The right wing and a good
part of the fuselage were scarred; bits and pieces of carbon
fiber and metal protruded from the jagged holes and scrapes.
The engine cowling on the far right engine looked as if
someone had written over it with white graffiti.

The ramp ladder was lowered from the forward section. Colonel Bastian's legs appeared, followed by the colonel himself.
His face was drawn back; he looked a hundred years old.

"Colonel!" yelled Englehardt.

"Mikey. How are our people?"

"Mack and the others were picked up by the *Abner Read*
several hours ago. They're going to rendezvous with the *Lincoln* and get home from there."

"Good. What about everybody else?" asked Dog.

Englehardt lowered his gaze, avoiding his commander's
stare.

"Dreamland *Fisher* was lost with all crew members," he
said. "Wreckage has been sighted. The *Levitow* is also missing," he added. "It went down near the Indian coast. We're not
exactly sure of the location. A U-2 is overflying the route. The
aircraft carrier *Lincoln* will launch some long-range reconnaissance aircraft to help as well, once they're close enough.
They should be within range inside of twelve hours."

Losing any aircraft and her crew was difficult, Englehardt
knew, but losing the *Levitow* would be especially painful for
Dog—his daughter Breanna was the *Levitow*'s pilot. Her husband Zen had been aboard, leading the Flighthawk mission.

"What about Danny Freah and Boston?" Dog asked.

"They were picked up by a Sharkboat after they disabled
the Iranian minisub. The Sharkboat is due to rendezvous with
the *Abner Read* and another Sharkboat in ninety minutes."

"What's the status of the *Bennett*?" Dog asked.

"Our engine has been replaced and we should be ready to

launch within the hour," said Englehardt. Mechanical problems had scratched the airplane from consideration for the original mission, and while they weren't his fault, the pilot couldn't help but feel a pang of guilt. "I've prepped a Search and Rescue mission and would like to help join the search for our guys."

"Are there still cots in the upper Flighthawk compartment?"

"Yes, sir, but we don't have a backup crew."

"I'm your backup crew," said Dog. "Let's get in the air."

Ring E, Pentagon
0825, 15 January 1998
(1825, 15 January, Karachi)

AIR FORCE MAJOR GENERAL TERRILL "EARTHMOVER" Samson checked his watch. Admiral George Balboa, Chairman of the Joint Chiefs of Staff, was nearly ten minutes late.

Admirals always thought they could be late for everything, Samson thought. But he forced a smile to his face and kept his grousing to himself.

As a younger man, the African-American general would have assumed it was because he was black. But now Samson realized the problem was more generic: no one had any manners these days.

Then again, that was one of the benefits of command: you didn't need manners when you outranked someone.

"General, would you like some more coffee?" asked one of Balboa's aides.

"Thank you, Major, but no, I'm fine."

"There you are, Samson," barked Balboa as he entered the office. "Come in."

Balboa's tone suggested that Samson was the one who was late. Samson hadn't risen in the ranks by insulting his superiors. Especially when, as he hoped, they were about to deliver good news. So he stifled his annoyance and rose, thanked the admiral's staff for their attention, and followed Balboa into his office.

"You've heard the news about India and Pakistan, I assume," said Balboa, sliding behind his desk. An antique, it was said to have belonged to one of the USS *Constitution*'s skippers—a fact Samson wouldn't have known except for the brass plate screwed into the front, obviously to impress visitors.

"I read the summary on my way over," said Samson.

"What do you think of the developments?"

Samson considered what sort of response to give. Though classified, the report hadn't given many details, merely hinting that the U.S. had used some sort of new weapons to down the missiles fired by both sides. It wasn't clear what was truly going on, however, and the way Balboa posed the question made Samson suspect a trap.

"I guess I don't have enough details to form an opinion," he said finally.

"We've shot down twenty-eight warheads," said Balboa. "The Navy sank an Indian aircraft carrier and several Chinese ships that tried to interfere. The President is continuing the operation. He wants the warheads recovered."

"I see," said Samson.

"The Dreamland people were in the middle of things. They fired the radiation weapons. Power is out throughout the subcontinent."

"Uh-huh." Samson tried to hide his impatience. A few months before, he had been mentioned as a possible commander for a new base that would have supplanted Dreamland, but the plans had never come to fruition—thankfully so, because he had much bigger and better things in mind.

Like the job he'd hoped Balboa had called him here to discuss, heading Southern Command.

"Some of the people in the administration didn't understand the potential of the Whiplash concept," said Balboa.

He was interrupted by a knock on the door.

"Come."

One of his aides, a Marine Corps major, entered with a

cup of coffee. The major set it down, then whispered something in Balboa's ear.

"I'll call him back."

"Yes, sir."

"The President," Balboa explained to Samson as the aide left. "Always looking for more information."

"What exactly is Whiplash?" asked Samson.

"Oh, Whiplash." Balboa made a face that was halfway between a smirk and a frown. "Whiplash is the name the Dreamland people use for their ground action team. They're air commandos. But the term is also the code word the President uses to deploy Dreamland assets—air as well as ground—around the world. The concept is to combine cutting-edge technology with special operations people. A few of us thought it would be a good idea years ago, but it's taken quite a while to get the kinks out. The line of communication and command—the National Security Advisor and the White House had their fingers in the pie, which twisted things around, as I'm sure you'd imagine."

"Of course."

"Well, that's finally been worked out. From this point forward, I think things will run much more smoothly. The concept—I fully support it, of course. But since I've been pushing it for so long, that's understandable."

Samson didn't know how much of what Balboa was saying to believe. Not only was the Chairman's disdain for the Air Force well known, but Balboa didn't have a reputation for backing either cutting-edge research or special operations, even in the Navy. Balboa loved ships—big ships, as in aircraft carriers and even battleships, which he had suggested several times could be brought back into active service as cruise missile launchers.

Or cruise missile targets, as some of Samson's friends at the War College commented in after-hour lectures. These sessions were always off campus, off the record, and far from any ears that might report back to the admiral. And, naturally, they were accompanied by studious elbow bending.

"As it happens," said Balboa, "Dreamland has been under the, uh, direction of a lieutenant colonel. Dog—what's his first name, uh . . ."

"Lieutenant Colonel Tecumseh Bastian," said Samson.

A decade younger than himself, Bastian had earned his wings as a fighter jock, a community unto itself in the Air Force, and so far as Samson knew, he had never met the colonel. But everyone in the Air Force had heard of Bastian and his incredible exploits at the helm of the EB-52 Megafortress.

"Presumptuous name," said Balboa. "Goes with the personality."

"A lieutenant colonel is in charge of Dreamland?" said Samson. He'd assumed Bastian was in charge of a *wing* at Dreamland, not the entire place. "I thought General Magnus took over after Brad Elliott."

"Yes, well, General Magnus did take over—on paper. For a while. The reality is, Bastian has been in charge. And while he has, I'm sure, points to recommend him . . ."

Balboa paused, making it clear he was struggling for something nice to say about the lieutenant colonel. Then he also made it clear he had given up.

"In the end, Bastian is a lieutenant colonel," said Balboa. "What Dreamland needs to reach its potential is a *commander.* A command general. You."

Samson sucked air.

"Of course, it's not just the base," added Balboa, obviously sensing a problem. "The Whiplash people, the Megafortresses—"

Samson cleared his throat. "I had been given to understand that I was to . . . that I was in line for Southern Command."

Balboa made a face. "That's not in the cards at the moment."

"When is it in the cards?"

"This is an important assignment, General. Weapons development is just *one* aspect of Dreamland. Important, but just part. We want to expand the capability—the Whiplash idea— we want to expand it exponentially. That's the whole point."

Samson felt his face growing hot. No matter how much sugar Balboa tried to put on the assignment, it was a major comedown. He was deputy *freaking* commander of the Eighth Air Force, for cryin' out loud. Not to mention former chief of plans for the air staff at the Pentagon. Base commander—with all due respect to other base commanders, fine men all, or almost all—was a sidetrack to his career.

Years before maybe, when he was still commanding a B-1B bomber wing, this might have been a step up. But not now. They had a *lieutenant* colonel in charge over there, for cryin' out loud.

And what a lieutenant colonel. No one was going to outshine him. The brass would be far better off finding a single star general a year or so from retirement to take things in hand quietly.

"Questions?" Balboa asked.

"Sir—"

"You'll have a free hand," said Balboa, rising and extending his hand. "We want this to be a real command—an integral part of the system. It hasn't been until now. We're going to expand. You're going to expand. You have carte blanche. Use it."

"Yes, sir."

Samson managed to shake Balboa's hand, then left the office as quickly as he could.

Air Force High Technology Advanced Weapons Center (Dreamland)
0630, 15 January 1998

JENNIFER GLEASON ROSE AND PUT HER HANDS ON HER hips, then began pacing at the back of the Command Center. She was due at Test Range 2B to check on the computer guidance system for the AIM-154 Anaconda interceptor missiles in a half hour. There had been troubles with the discriminator software, which used artificial intelligence routines to distinguish between civilian and military targets in fail-safe mode when the Identification Friend or Foe (IFF) circuitry failed. She had helped one of the engineers with the coding and agreed to sit in on today's tests of the missile to see if the changes had been successful.

But she'd agreed to do that weeks ago, before the trouble in India. Before her lover, Colonel Bastian, had deployed, before her friends had been shot down trying to save the world, or at least a big part of it.

Jennifer, though modestly altruistic, didn't really care about the world. She cared about Colonel Bastian. And Zen. And Breanna, though Breanna didn't particularly like her. And even Mack Smith, class A jackass that he could be.

"I truly wish you would stop pacing up and down," said Ray Rubeo. "Don't you have a test or something to supervise?"

Jennifer glared at him. Rubeo could be a difficult taskmaster—nearly all the scientists at Dreamland preferred dealing with the military people rather than him—but she had never felt intimidated by the tall, skinny scientist. Rubeo made a face, then touched his silver earring stud—an unconscious tic that in this case was a sign of surrender. He scowled and went back to his computer screen.

"All right, we have the missile trajectories," said one of the analysts nearby. "Do you want to see them, Dr. Rubeo? Or should I just zip the file and send it to the White House?"

"Hardly," said Rubeo, his witheringly sarcastic voice back in full swing. "Put it on the main screen and let me have a look at it."

"You think you know everything, Ray?" said Jennifer peevishly.

Immediately, she wanted to apologize. Sniping wasn't her style and she admired Rubeo. And he was brilliant.

Even if he was full of himself.

Rubeo ignored her, rising and walking toward the large screen at the front of the room. Adapting one of the test programs used at Dreamland, the analysts had directed the computer to show the likely path of the missiles that had been disabled by the T-Rays. Bright red ellipses showed the areas they were most likely to have fallen in; the color got duller the lower the probability.

A review of the launch data showed that the Indians had fired twenty nuclear missiles, the Pakistanis eight. All were liquid-fueled. Besides the guidance and trigger circuitry in the warheads, a number of engine parts were particularly vulnerable to T-Rays, including the solenoid valves and electronic level sensors necessary for the engines to function properly. Failure of these items in most cases would choke off the engines, causing them to fall back to earth.

The question was: Where? According to the computer, all but two had fallen in the Great Thar Desert, a vast wasteland between the two countries on the Indian side of the border.

Rubeo walked toward the large screen at the front of the room. Folding his arms, he stood staring up at the map, as if being that close to the pixels somehow allowed his brain to absorb additional information.

"Problem, Ray?" asked Major Catsman, who'd been absorbed in something on the other side of the room.

"Two warheads are not showing up," he told her.

"How can that be?"

"Hmmmph."

"Are you sure the launch count is correct?" asked Jennifer.

Rubeo continued to stare. The analyst manning the computer that controlled the display began reassessing the data.

"We can give them what we have and tell them there may be a problem in the data," said Catsman. "Better something than nothing."

"The difficulty, Major," said Rubeo, "is that the program doesn't seem to realize the missiles aren't there."

His sarcasm was barely masked, but Catsman either missed it because she was tired or ignored it because she was used to Rubeo.

"Well, we better figure something out."

"Hmmmph."

"I'll tell Colonel Bastian about it," Catsman added. "He's in the *Bennett*."

"He's in the *Bennett*?" said Jennifer. "I thought he went back to Diego Garcia."

"The search operations for the rest of our downed crewmen have been slow. He wanted to kick-start them."

Jennifer sat at one of the back consoles as Catsman made the connection. She looked away from the big screen when she heard his voice, afraid of what she might see in his face.

She wanted him home, safe; not tired, not battered, not pushed to his limit, as he always was on a mission.

She knew he would have scoffed at her, told her he wasn't doing anything any other member of the team hadn't done—anything that she hadn't done herself a hundred times.

"How could the computer lose the missiles?" she heard him ask Rubeo.

"If I knew the answer, Colonel, I wouldn't have mentioned the question," Rubeo replied. He explained that the most likely answer had to do with a glitch in the hastily amended software they used to project the landings. But it was also possible that the satellites analyzing the launch data had erred, or that the flight paths of different missiles had merged.

"There are a number of other possibilities as well," added Rubeo. "It will take some time to work things out."

"We're not the only ones doing this," said Catsman. "NORAD, the Navy, Satellite Command—they'll all have information. We can coordinate it and refine the projections. Once the U-2 is able to complete its survey of the area, things should be much clearer."

"The question for you, Colonel," said Rubeo, "is whether we should tell the White House what we have. They have tended to ignore our caveats in the past. Not always with the best results."

"Tell them," said Dog. "And keep working on it."

"As you wish," said Rubeo.

"What other information can you give us on the possible location of the *Fisher*'s crew?" Dog asked.

"We've already passed along everything we have," Catsman told him. "We're pretty confident of where they were when they bailed out, and where they would be in the water."

"Then why haven't they been found?"

When Catsman didn't answer, Rubeo did—uncharacteristically offering an excuse for the Navy.

"The *Abner Read* was distracted and too far from the area to be of much use at first," he said. "They're now coming south and the Werewolf should be able to help. The *Lincoln* is still quite far from the ejection area. Their long-range patrols can't stay on station long enough to do a thorough job. The odds should improve the closer they get. We computed the effects of the currents and wind on the crew and gave them to the Navy, as well as the U-2 surveying the region. That should help narrow the search."

"We'll find them, Colonel," added Catsman.

"I'm sure we will," said Dog. He paused for a moment, then asked for her. "Jennifer?"

She looked up. The large screen magnified his face to the point where she could see every wrinkle, every crease and blemish. He was pale, and his eyes drooped.

"Hi, Colonel."

The faintest hint of a smile came to his face.

"You were working on an updated search routine for the Flighthawks," Dog said, all business.

"It still has some bugs."

"Upload it to us anyway."

"Yes, sir."

For a moment it looked like he was about to say something else.

I love you, maybe. She wanted desperately to hear it. But he didn't say it.

"I'm here if you need me. Bastian out."

Jennifer felt a stabbing pain in her side as the screen blanked.

Oval Office, Washington, D.C.
0910

JED BARCLAY KNOCKED ON THE PRESIDENT'S DOOR BEFORE entering. President Kevin Martindale sat behind his desk, facing the window that looked out on the back lawn of the White House.

"I put together the latest data on the missiles, Mr. President," said Jed. "There's some disagreement between the CIA projections and Dreamland's. The Dreamland scientists say they have two missiles unaccounted for and that may indicate—"

"Can you imagine wanting to turn the earth into a nuclear wasteland, Jed?" asked the President, staring out the window.

The question took Jed by surprise. Finally he managed a soft "No."

"Neither can I. Some of the people in both India and Pakistan want to do just that." The President rose, but continued to stare out the window. "The reports are filled with misinformation this morning. I suppose we can't blame them. I didn't tell them exactly how we stopped the weapons, and there are a great many people who distrust us."

Jed hadn't seen any of the actual news reports, but had read the daily classified CIA summary before coming up to see the President. Martindale had said only that the U.S. used "new technology" to bring down the nuclear weapons launched by Pakistan and India; the news media, without much to go on, speculated that he was referring to antiballistic missiles launched from Alaska and satellite weapons that didn't actually exist.

What they couldn't quite understand was why power had gone off across the subcontinent. Some analysts had concluded that this meant at least a few of the nuclear weapons had exploded and created an electromagnetic pulse. Others simply ignored it. Given the President's desire to seize the warheads, ambiguity was definitely in their favor, and the

White House had issued orders forbidding anyone—including the official spokesmen, who actually knew very little—from addressing the matter.

Adding to the confusion was the fact that the T-Rays had wiped out communication with practically all of Pakistan and a vast swath of India. The media was starved for information, though obviously that situation wouldn't hold for very long.

"I hate sending people into war," continued the President. "Because basically I'm sending them to die. It's my job. I understand it. But after a while . . . after a while it all begins to weigh on you . . ."

His voice trailed off. Jed had never seen the President this contemplative, and didn't know what to say.

"We're going to recover the warheads," Martindale said finally.

He turned, walked across the office to the credenza that stood opposite his desk, and paused, gazing down at a bust of Jefferson.

"Some people call Dreamland my own private air force and army. Have you heard that, Jed?"

Having heard that said many times, Jed hesitated.

"You can be honest," added Martindale. "That's what I value about you, Jed. You're not involved in the political games."

"Yes, sir."

"Dreamland is too important a command to be run by a lieutenant colonel. The Joint Chiefs want it folded back into the regular command structure. And I have to say, they make good arguments."

"Yes, sir."

"We're going to appoint a general to take over. A two-star general for now—Major General Samson. He has an impeccable record. An enviable one."

"Yes, sir."

"What's your opinion of that?"

"I think whatever you want to do, sir—"

"I haven't used it as my private army, have I?"

"No, Mr. President, absolutely not."

"This has nothing to do with you, Jed," added the President. "Or with Colonel Bastian, for that matter. I still have the highest regard for him. I want him involved in the warhead recovery. Him and his people—they'll work with the Marines."

"Yes, sir."

"But it makes more sense—this whole mission has shown the real potential. We can double, maybe triple their effectiveness." Martindale looked at Jed. "General Samson will handle informing the Dreamland people. Understood?"

"I shouldn't tell them?"

"The news should come from the general, and the joint chiefs. That's the way I want it. We're following the chain of command. Dreamland is not my private army."

The joint chiefs—and especially the head of the joint chiefs, Admiral Balboa—had been fighting to get Dreamland back under their full control since early in Martindale's administration. With the end of Martindale's term looming—and the very real possibility that he would lose the election—the chiefs had won the battle. It certainly did make sense that Dreamland, as a military unit, should answer directly up the chain of command, rather than directly to the President through the NSC.

In theory, Jed realized, he was losing some of his prestige. But he knew he'd never been more than a political buffer. Part of the reason the President and the National Security Advisor used him as a liaison, after all, was the fact that he was young and had no political power base of his own.

"I'll do whatever job you want me to, sir," he said.

"Good. You have a bright future. Let's get through this crisis, get these warheads, and then maybe we'll have a chance to sit down and see how best you can serve your country."

"Uh, yes, sir."

The President went back to his desk.

"You can go now, young Jed. Forward these reports to Admiral Balboa, with copies to Admiral Woods on the *Lin-*

coln. Make sure he has everything he needs. Dreamland is working with the Marines, under Woods. We'll follow the chain of command."

"Yes, sir."

**Aboard the *Bennett*,
over the northern Arabian Sea
2100**

STEVEN L. BENNETT WAS A CAPTAIN IN THE U.S. AIR FORCE, assigned to the Twentieth Tactical Air Support Squadron, Pacific Air Forces, during the Vietnam War era. After completing B-52 training in 1970, Captain Bennett went about as far from strategic bombers as you could in the Air Force at the time—he trained to become a forward air controller, calling bombs in rather than dropping them, and flying in an airplane designed to skim treetops rather than the stratosphere.

By June 1972, Bennett was piloting an OV-10 Bronco, an excellent combat observation aircraft with only one serious flaw—it was almost impossible to crash-land successfully. The forward section of the two-seater would generally implode, killing the pilot, though the backseater could get out with minor injuries. Pilots quickly learned that it didn't make sense to try and ditch an OV-10; "hitting the silk," as the old-timers used to call ejecting, was the only way to survive.

On June 29, 1972, Bennett flew what was known as an artillery adjustment mission over Quang Tri Province in South Vietnam. His observer was a Marine Corps captain named Mike Brown. The two men pulled a three-hour sortie and were about to head home to Da Nang when they learned that their replacement was running behind schedule. Going home would leave ground troops without anyone to call on if they got in trouble.

Captain Bennett checked his fuel and decided to stay on station until the relief plane could get up. A short time later

South Vietnamese troops in the area called in for assistance; they were taking fire from a much larger North Vietnamese unit and were about to be overrun.

Bennett and Brown called for a tactical air strike, but no attack aircraft were available. They then requested that Navy guns bombard the attackers, but the proximity of the South Vietnamese to their northern enemies made that impossible.

So Bennett decided to do the job himself, rolling in on several hundred NVA soldiers with just the four 7.62mm machine guns in his Bronco's nose. After the fourth pass, he had them on the run. He came down again to give them another snoutful, but this time his aircraft was hit—a SAM-7 shoulder-launched heat seeker took out his left engine. His plane caught fire.

Bennett headed out over the nearby ocean to jettison his fuel and the highly flammable rockets used for marking targets. As he did so, an escort aircraft caught up with him and advised him that the fire started by the missile was now so severe that his plane looked like it would explode any minute. Bennett ordered Brown to get ready to eject; they'd punch out over the water and be picked up by one of the Navy ships or a friendly helicopter.

Brown agreed. But then he saw that his parachute had been torn by shrapnel from the missile that struck the plane.

Not a problem, said Bennett, whose own parachute was in perfect condition. Get ready to ditch.

And so they did. The OV-10 cartwheeled when she hit the water, and then sank. If Bennett was still alive after the crash, his cockpit was too mangled for him to escape as the plane went under the waves. Captain Brown, fortunately, managed to push his way out and was picked up by a rescue chopper a short time later.

For his selfless devotion to duty and his determination to save another man's life even at the cost of his own, Captain Steven L. Bennett was awarded the Medal of Honor posthumously. It was presented by then Vice President Gerald R. Ford to Bennett's widow and daughter two years after his death.

*   *   *

STEVEN BENNETT'S NAMESAKE, DREAMLAND EB-52 MEGA-fortress *Bennett*, had begun life as a B-52D. And, in fact, the aircraft had actually served in the same war as Captain Bennett, dropping bombs on North Vietnam during two different deployments. It remained in active service until 1982, when it was mothballed and put in storage. And there it remained until the spring of 1996, when it was taken from its desert storage area, gutted, and rebuilt as a Megafortress. The changes were many. Its wings and tail section were completely replaced, new engines and electrical controls were installed, a radar "bulge" was installed in a spine above the wing roots, and provision was made for the EB-52 to carry and launch robot aircraft. Much of the new gear was simply unimaginable when the B-52 was first built.

When the aircraft was flyable, she was taken by a special crew to Dreamland, where additional modifications were made to her frame. More equipment, including an AWACS-style radar for the bulge, was added.

The plane had completed final flight tests shortly before Thanksgiving, 1997. She'd received further modifications on Diego Garcia to make her systems impervious to T-Rays. Ironically, the work on those modifications had not been completed when the T-Ray weapons had to be used, and the *Bennett* remained on the ground. A subsequent glitch with her left outboard engine required her to turn back after being launched shortly afterward, much to her crew's consternation.

The *Bennett* was making up for it now, her engines pushing the airplane to just under the speed of sound as she raced northward in search of the crew of the stricken *Levitow*.

"We should be in the area where they ejected within the hour," Lieutenant Englehardt said as Dog looked over his shoulder at the situation map set in the middle of the dash. "So far we haven't heard the emergency beacons."

Dog nodded. The emergency PRC radios had a limited range. Like everyone else in the Air Force, the Dreamland fliers relied on PRC radios, which used relatively old technology. Better units were available, but hadn't been authorized for purchase because of budget issues. Dog suspected that if some congressman had to rely on one, money would be found for upgrades pretty damn fast.

"Incoming transmission for you, Colonel. This is from the NSC—Jed Barclay."

Dog dropped into the empty seat in front of the auxiliary airborne radar control. As soon as he authorized the transmission, Jed Barclay's face appeared on the screen. He was speaking from the White House Situation Room.

"Bastian. Jed, what's up?"

"Colonel, I, uh, I have Admiral Balboa on the line. He uh, wanted me to make the connection."

"OK," said Dog, puzzled.

"Stand by."

Balboa's face flashed onto the screen. Dog had spoken to the Chairman of the Joint Chiefs of Staff several times since taking command of Dreamland. Balboa didn't particularly like the Air Force, and Dog sensed that he didn't particularly care for him either.

"Colonel, how are you this morning?"

"It's nighttime here, Admiral."

"Yes." Balboa scowled. "The President has decided to recover the warheads. He wants you to work with the Marines from the Seventh MEU. Admiral Woods will have overall control of the mission."

Dog smiled. He knew Woods from exercises they'd had together—exercises where Dreamland had blown up his carrier several times.

"Problem with that, Colonel?" asked Balboa. The nostrils in his pug nose flared.

"Not on my side."

"Admiral Woods has no problems," said Balboa.

"What sort of support does he want?"

"Help him locate the missiles. He'll tell you what he wants."

"I'm going to need to gear up for this," said Dog. "We're down to one working Megafortress."

"Well, get what you need," said Balboa. "Has General Samson spoken to you yet?"

"Terrill Samson? No."

"Well, he will. We're reorganizing your command structure, Colonel. You'll be reporting to Major General Samson from now on. Got it?"

"Yes, sir."

"Good."

The screen blanked. Dog didn't know Samson at all. He'd had a Pentagon general to report to when he started at Dreamland, a good one: Lieutenant General Harold Magnus. Magnus had retired some months before after being edged out of the running for chief of the Joint Chiefs of Staff. Dreamland's official "position" on the Pentagon flowchart had been in flux ever since. Dog had known this couldn't last, and in some respects welcomed the appointment of a new superior: As a lieutenant colonel with no direct line to the Pentagon, he was constantly having trouble with even the most routine budget requests.

"Colonel, are you still there?"

"Yes, Jed, go ahead."

"You want to speak to Admiral Woods? I can plug you into a circuit with him and the Marine Corps general in charge of the Seventh MEU."

"Fire away."

"Bastian, you old bully—now what are you up to?" asked Tex Woods, popping onto the screen. Dog could only see his head; the camera didn't pan low enough to show if he was wearing his trademark cowboy boots.

"Looking for my people. They bailed out."

"Yes, and we're helping with that," said Woods. He was more enthusiastic than he had been the last time they'd spoken. "The admiral told you what we're up to?"

"Yes, sir."

"Good. Jack, you on the line yet?"

Marine Corps General Jack Harrison cleared his throat. Harrison was a dour-faced man; he seemed to personify the nickname leatherneck.

"General," said Dog.

"Colonel, I've heard a lot about you. I'm glad we're working together."

"We'll do our best."

"That's the spirit, Bastian," said Woods. "Your people are to coordinate the intelligence, the Marines will be the muscle. Aircraft from the *Lincoln* will fly cover. Everybody on the same page?"

Dog reached for his coffee as Woods continued. The specific operation plans would have to be developed by the Marine Corps officers.

"Your people would be very valuable, Colonel," said Harrison. "Your Whiplash crew?"

"My officer in charge of Whiplash is aboard the *Abner Read*," said Dog. "I don't—"

"We'll airlift him to the *Lincoln*," said Woods. "What other problems do I have to solve?"

"No problems," said Dog. Harrison remained silent.

"Good," said Woods. "Gentlemen, you have my authorization to do whatever it takes to make this work. This is the chance of a millennium. History will remember us."

I hope in a good way, thought Dog as the screen blacked out.

THE NEW SEARCH PROGRAM JENNIFER HAD DEVELOPED called for the Megafortress to fly in a path calculated from the weather conditions and known characteristics of the ejection seats and the crew members' parachutes. The flight path aligned the plane with the peculiarities of the survival radio's transmission capabilities; while it didn't actually boost its range, the effect was the same.

The program gave Englehardt the option of turning the aircraft over to the computer to fly or of following a path marked for him on the heads-up display projected in front of the windscreen.

"Which do you think I should do, Colonel?" the pilot asked.

"I'm comfortable with however you want to fly it," Dog said. "If it were me, I'd want the stick in my hand. But completely your call."

"Thank you, sir. I think I'll fly it myself."

"Very good."

Lieutenant Englehardt was one of the new wave of pilots who'd come to Dreamland in the wake of the Megafortress's success. Young enough to be Dog's son, he was part of a generation that had known things like video games and computers their whole lives. They weren't *comfortable* with technology—they'd been born into it, and accepted it the way Dog accepted his arms and legs.

Still, the fact that Englehardt would rather rely on himself than the computer impressed Dog. It was an old-fashioned conceit, but some prejudices were worth keeping.

Dog went over to the techie working the sea surveillance radar, Staff Sergeant Brian Daly. Aside from small boats anchored near the coast for the night, Daly had only a single contact on his screen: an Indian patrol vessel of the Jija Bai class. Roughly the equivalent of a small U.S. Coast Guard cutter, the ship carried two 7.62mm guns that could be used against aircraft, but posed no threat to the high-flying Megafortress.

"Two Tomcats from the *Lincoln* hailing us, Colonel," said Kevin Sullivan, the copilot.

"Say hello."

While Sullivan spoke to the pilots in the F-14 fighters, Dog looked over the shoulder of Technical Sergeant Thomas Rager, who manned the airborne radar. With the exception of the Tomcats, which had come from the *Lincoln* a good six hundred miles to the south, the Megafortress had the sky to itself. Neither Pakistan nor India had been able to get any flights airborne following the total collapse of their electrical networks, and the Chinese carrier *Khan,* now heading southward at a slow pace, had been damaged so severely that she appeared no longer capable of launching or recovering aircraft.

"Squids wish us well," said Sullivan, using a universal nickname for sailors. "They're on long-range reconnaissance for the carrier group. They haven't heard anything from our guys or seen any flares over the water. They'll keep looking."

"Thank them."

The weight of his fatigue settled on Dog's shoulders. He'd tried to sleep in the cot in the unused upper Flighthawk bay earlier but couldn't. He went to the back of the flight deck and pulled down the jumpseat, settling down, watching the crew at work.

He had to find his people. All of them, but Breanna especially.

He'd almost lost her twice before. Each time, the pain seemed to grow worse. Now it felt like an arrow the size of his fist, pushing against his heart.

Though they worked together, Dog couldn't honestly say they were very close, at least not if closeness was measured by the things fathers and daughters usually did together. Every so often they'd go out to eat, but he couldn't remember the last time they'd fished or biked or hiked. They didn't even run together, something they both liked to do.

And yet he loved her deeply.

He felt himself drifting toward sleep. He started to let himself go, falling down toward oblivion. And then a shout startled him back to consciousness.

"We've got them!" yelled Sullivan.

**Aboard the *Abner Read*,
northern Arabian Sea
2150**

"THIS IS THE BRIDGE? I FIGURED IT'D BE A LOT BIGGER. GOD, it looks like an amusement arcade."

Storm bristled but said nothing as Major Mack Smith surveyed the *Abner Read*'s bridge.

"Cool table. Moving maps, huh?"

"We call them charts, sir," said the ensign who'd been assigned as the Dreamland contingent's tour guide.

The rest of the Air Force people were crowding sickbay, but Major Smith claimed his sojourn in the water had left him refreshed. He certainly had a lot of energy, Storm thought.

"How does this work?" asked Mack, raising his hand above the holographic display.

"No, sir! No!" The ensign grabbed Mack's hand before the major could swipe it through the display.

"Hey, take it easy, kid. I wasn't going to touch anything."

"The ensign was trying to point out that in some modes, the holographic table accepts commands much like a touchscreen," said Storm stiffly. "So we look, don't touch."

"I get the picture." Mack smirked at Storm, then went over to the helm. "Almost like jet controls, huh?"

It must have taken the helmsman a monumental effort not to elbow Mack as he breathed over his neck, looking at the ship's "dashboard."

Pity he was so disciplined, thought Storm.

"I didn't think we'd be so low in the water," said Mack. "I mean, did you guys take a hit during the battle?"

"We took several," said Storm. "None of which were serious. The ship is designed to sit very low so it can't be seen by radar, or the naked eye for that matter, except at very close range."

"Wow. That's wild," said Mack. "It's weird, though, you know? I mean, it's a great boat and all. Don't get me wrong. Glad to be here. But it's low. What are we? Eight feet above the waves? Six?"

"I'm afraid that's classified, sir," said the ensign.

Storm decided the man would get shore leave and double beer rations for the rest of his life.

"*Sharkboat Two* is one mile north, Captain," said the helmsman.

"Very good. Prepare to rendezvous."

"Aye aye, Captain."

"Two more of your Dreamland people are aboard the Sharkboat, Major," added Storm. "Captain Freah and one of his sergeants."

"No shit. Man, it's like a regular reunion."

"Isn't it, though? Would you like to meet the captain on the fantail?"

"There or the bar. Whatever you got."

DANNY FREAH RESTORED SOME OF STORM'S GOOD HUMOR, modestly taking very little credit in the disabling of the Iranian minisub that had helped provoke the war between India and Pakistan. Storm had already heard a full report from his men in the Sharkboat and was well aware that Danny and his sergeant had nearly drowned while disabling the craft. Had it not been for the two Dreamlanders, the sub surely would have gotten away.

In Danny's account, however, the Sharkboat arrived just at the critical juncture. The Navy people saved the day, securing the craft and fishing him out of the water.

Storm was still soaking up the praises of his men when Eyes interrupted to tell him that several more downed Dreamland crew members had been found.

"They're from the *Levitow*," Eyes told him over the ship's intercom system. "They have six people in the water. They're not far from the coast. Eighty miles southwest of us."

"All right, we'll pick them up, too," Storm said. "Are the Chinese near them?"

"Negative. But there's an Indian ship in the area. A guided missile frigate."

"I'm not afraid of an Indian frigate," said Storm. He ordered the crew to plot a course to the downed airmen and set sail at top speed.

"I'd like to participate in the rescue," said Danny Freah after Storm finished issuing his orders.

"I'll tell you what, Captain. If my medical officer releases you to participate, you're welcome to help."

"Thanks, Captain."

"No, the pleasure's mine."

"The *Levitow* is Breanna Stockard's plane," said Danny. "She's the colonel's daughter."

"Bastian's daughter?" Storm hadn't realized Colonel Bastian had a child, let alone that she was in the Air Force and under his command. "Bastian doesn't seem old enough to have a pilot for a daughter."

"You'd have to take that up with the colonel himself, sir."

**Aboard the *Bennett*,
over the northern Arabian Sea
2151**

DOG GRABBED ONE OF THE HANDHOLDS ON THE AUXILIARY control panel of the surface radar station as the Megafortress plunged closer to the water, pushing into a low orbit around the tiny rafts bobbing about twenty miles from the Indian coast. A fitful splash of white blinked from three of the small boats, emergency beacons showing the *Bennett* where they were.

Captain Jan Stewart, who'd been the *Levitow*'s copilot, was on the radio with Sullivan, telling him that all six of the crew members who'd gone out together had been able to hook up. There were no serious injuries, said Stewart, and now that they saw the Megafortress's flares bursting through the cloud deck, they were in excellent spirits.

But the *Levitow* had been carrying eight people, not its usual six.

"Breanna and Zen went out after us," Stewart told the *Bennett*'s copilot. "They were going to jump through the holes left by the escape hatches. None of us saw their parachutes. We're sure they got out."

Her voice sounded almost desperate.

"Indian Godavari-class frigate, four miles due south," reported Sergeant Daly over the *Bennett*'s interphone circuit.

"Godavari is equipped with OSA-ME surface-to-air missiles. NATO code name Gecko SA-N-4. Radar guided; range ten kilometers. Accurate to 16,400 feet."

"How long before the *Abner Read* gets here?" Dog asked Sullivan.

The *Bennett*'s copilot told him that the ship had estimated it would take about two and a half hours.

"I'll bet the Indian ship saw their flares and is homing in on the signal from Stewart's radio," added Lieutenant Englehardt, the pilot. "They'll be close enough to see the beacons in a few minutes, if they haven't already."

"Let's find out what they're up to," said Dog. "Contact them."

He put his hands to his eyes. He was tired—beyond tired.

"Colonel, I have someone from the Indian ship acknowledging," said the copilot. "Ship's name is *Gomati*."

Dog pushed his headset's boom mike close to his mouth and dialed into the frequency used by the Indian ship. "This is Lieutenant Colonel Tecumseh Bastian on Dreamland *Bennett*. I'd like to speak to the captain of the *Gomati*."

"I am the executive officer," replied a man in lightly accented English. "What can we do for you, Colonel?"

"You can hold your position away from my men," said Dog. "We are conducting rescue operations."

The Indian didn't immediately reply. Dog knew he had a strong hand—the *Bennett* carried four Harpoon missiles on the rotating dispenser in her belly. One well-placed hit would disable the frigate; two would sink her.

And despite his orders not to engage any of the combatants, Dog had no compunctions about using the missiles to protect his people.

"Colonel Bastian," said a new voice from the destroyer. "I am Captain Ajanta. Why are you warning us away from the men in the water? We intend to offer our assistance."

"If it's all the same to you, we'd prefer to take care of it ourselves," Dog told him.

The Indian officer didn't reply.

"I think you insulted him, Colonel," said Lieutenant Englehardt over the interphone.

"Maybe." Dog clicked back into the circuit and took a more diplomatic tact. "*Gomati,* we appreciate your offer of assistance. We already have a vessel en route and are in communication with the people in the water. We request that you stand by."

"As you wish," replied the Indian captain.

"I appreciate your offer to help," said Dog. "Thank you."

**Indian Ocean,
off the Indian coast
Time unknown**

WITH HIS ARMS COMPLETELY DRAINED OF ENERGY, ZEN drifted along in the blackness, more flotsam than living being. He'd never been broken down so low, not even after he woke up in the hospital without the use of his legs.

Then all he'd been was angry. It was better than this, far better.

For the longest time he didn't believe what they told him. Who would? Doctors were always Calamity Janes, telling you about all sorts of diseases and ailments you *might* have, depending on the outcome of this or that test. He had never liked doctors—not even the handful he was related to.

So his first reaction to the news was to say, flat out, "Get bent. My legs are fine. Just fine."

He kept fighting. His anger grew. It pushed him, got him through rehab every day.

Rehab sucked. Sucked. But it was the only thing he could do, and he spent hours and hours every day—*every day*—working and working and working. Pumping iron, swimming, pushing himself in the wheelchair. He hated it. Hated it and loved it, because it sucked so bad it didn't let his mind wander.

Thinking was dangerous. If he thought too much, he'd remember the crash, and what it meant.

Breanna was with him the whole time, even when he didn't want her to be. He took a lot of his frustration out on her.

Too much. Even a little would have been too much, but he took much more than that.

The amazing thing was, she'd stayed. She still loved him. Still loved even the gimp he'd become.

Gradually, Zen realized he had two motivations. The first was anger: at his accident; at Mack Smith, who he thought had caused it; at the world in general.

The second was love.

Anger pushed him every day. It got him back on active duty, made him determined to pull every political string his family had—and they had a lot. It made him get up every morning and insist that he was still Major Jeff "Zen" Stockard, fighter ace, hottest match on the patch, a slick zippersuit going places in the world.

Love was more subtle. It wasn't until he got back, all the way back as head of the Flighthawk program, as a pilot again, as a true ace with five enemy planes shot down, that he understood what love had done for him: It had kept the anger at an almost manageable level.

Zen nudged against something hard in the water. He put his arm up defensively. The only thing he could think of was that he was being attacked by a shark.

It wasn't a shark, but a barely submerged rock. There were others all around. A few broke the surface, but most were just under the waves.

He stared into the darkness, trying to make the blackness dissolve into shapes. There were rocks all around, as if he were near a shore. He pushed forward, expecting to hit a rise and find land, but didn't. He dragged himself onward, the water too shallow to swim, expecting that with the next push he would be up on land. But the land seemed never to come, and when it finally did, it was more rock than land, somewhat more solid than the pieces he'd bumped over, but still rock.

He'd expected sand, a real beach. He wasn't particularly

fond of beaches, except that they gave him a chance to swim, which was something he'd liked to do even before it became part of his daily rehab and exercise. They also gave him a chance to watch Breanna come out of the sea, water dripping off her sleek body, caressing it.

He shook off the thought and concentrated on moving away from the water, crawling up a gentle incline about twenty or thirty yards.

Exhausted, he lay on his back and rested. A cloud pack had ridden in on a cold front, and as Zen closed his eyes, the clouds gave up some of their water. The rain fell strongly enough to flush the salt from his face, but the rest of him was already so wet that he barely noticed. The wind kicked up, there was a flash of lightning—and then the air was calm. In a few minutes, the moon peeked out from the edge of the clouds. The stars followed, and what had been an almost pitch-black night turned into a silver-bathed twilight.

Zen sat up and tried to examine the place where he had landed. There were no large trees that he could see, and if there were any bushes, they blended with the boulders in the distance. He groped his way up the hill, maneuvering around loose boulders and outcroppings until he reached the crest. There was another slope beyond, and then the sea, though it was impossible to tell if he was on an island or a peninsula, because another hill rose to his right.

He turned back to the spot where he had come in, perhaps a hundred feet away. The water lapped over rocks, the tops of the waves shining like small bits of tinsel in the moonlight. The sound was a constant *tschct-tschct-tschct*, an unworldly hum of rock and wave.

One of the rocks near the shoreline seemed larger than the rest, and more curiously shaped. Zen stared at it, unable to parse the shadow from the stone. He scanned the rest of the ocean, then returned, more curious. He moved to his right, then farther down the slope.

It wasn't a rock, he realized. It was a person.

Breanna, he thought, throwing himself forward.

**Indian Ocean,
off the Indian coast
0043, 16 January 1998**

DANNY FREAH CROUCHED AGAINST THE SIDE OF THE *ABNER
Read*'s boat, waiting for the chance to pluck one of the fliers
from the water. The boat was a souped-up Zodiac, custom-
made for the littoral warcraft that carried her. Special cells in
the hull and preloaded filler made the boats difficult to sink,
and the engine, propelled by hydrogen fuel cells, was both
fast and quiet. Danny decided he would see about getting
some for Whiplash when he got home.

Jan Stewart was the first of the *Levitow*'s crewmen to be
picked up. Her teeth chattered as Danny helped her in. One of
the sailors wrapped a waterproof "space blanket" around her
and gave her a chemical warming pouch. Dork—Lieutenant
Dennis Thrall, a Flighthawk pilot—was next. His face was
swollen and his lips blue.

Dork's hands were so swollen that he couldn't activate the
warmer. Danny took it from him and twisted gently, feeling
the heat instantly as the chemical reaction began.

"Thanks, Cap," said Dork in a husky voice. "Where's Zen?"

"Still looking."

"He and Bree were going out after us. They had to jump."

"Yeah, I know," said Danny.

"They should be south of us," said Lieutenant Dick "Bullet" Timmons, huddling next to Dork. Bullet had been the
Levitow's second-shift pilot. "We were flying west. They
would have bailed only a few seconds later."

"We'll find them," said Danny.

He glanced over his shoulder at the Indian frigate, sitting
in an oblong splash of moonlight a mile away. The Indians
had volunteered to help with the rescue, but no one knew
whether they could be trusted. It had been Indian missiles,
after all, that had shot down the *Levitow*.

"We were jumped by Indian MiGs and Sukhois on our way
to deploy the EEMWBs," Bullet told Danny. His voice was

rushed; he seemed to need to tell what had happened to them, to explain why they were down in the water. "They kept nicking us. The Flighthawks were gone because of the T-Rays. Then finally, one of the Sukhois got us with an AMRAAMski. Plane held together but there was too much damage to keep it in the air. Bree did a hell of a job getting us out over the water and just holding it stable enough to jump. Really she did."

"We'll debrief back at the ship," Danny told him gently. "It's all right."

But the pilot kept talking.

"She ordered everyone else to jump. She and Zen stayed behind. She was going to jump, though. Definitely. She was going out. Zen too. She knew she couldn't fly it back. And there was no way she was landing in India. The *Levitow* was shielded against the T-Rays. She wouldn't have let them have the plane, even if she could have landed it. No way."

"Relax," Danny said, grabbing another warmer for him. "We'll find them."

**Indian Ocean,
off the Indian coast
Time unknown**

ZEN KNEW BETTER THAN TO FLAIL AGAINST THE WAVES, BUT he did it anyway, throwing himself into the teeth of the tide, pushing and pulling and swimming and dragging himself to his wife.

It *was* Breanna. He knew it before he could see her face in the pale light, before he could make out the raft, or the horseshoelike collar she still wore. He just knew it.

What he didn't know was whether she was alive.

He fought against doubt, battering his arms against the rocks.

Ten feet.

But those last ten feet were like miles. The water rushed at him as if the ocean wanted to keep her for its own. Zen clawed and crawled forward, pushing toward her, until finally he touched the back of her helmet.

His fingers seemed to snap back with electricity. His guard dissolved. If she hadn't even taken off her helmet, how could she be alive?

"Bree," whispered Zen. "Bree."

His voice was so soft even he had a hard time hearing it over the surf.

"Bree, we have to get to land. Come on, honey."

Not daring to look at her face, not daring to take off her helmet, he reached into the raft, looped one hand gently around her torso, and began pulling her toward shore.

Dreamland
1112, 15 January 1998
(0043, 16 January, Karachi)

JENNIFER GLEASON FOLDED HER ARMS AS THE ARGUMENT continued over which weapons to ship to Diego Garcia.

"Anaconda missiles give the Megafortress pilots a long-range antiaircraft option," said Terrence Calder, the Air Force major who headed the AIM-154 program. "In addition, they can use them against land targets if necessary. You don't have to worry about the mix of Harpoons and AMRAAM-pluses. It's win-win."

"Not if the guidance systems don't function perfectly," said Ray Rubeo.

"They've passed most of the tests."

"There's that word 'most' again," said Rubeo. "Most means not all, which means not ready."

There was no question that the Anaconda AIM-154 long-range strike missile was an excellent weapon. A scramjet-powered hypersonic missile, it had a lethal range of nearly two hundred miles. It could ride a radar beam to its target, use its own on-board radar, or rely on an infrared seeker in its nose to hit home. For long-range or hypersonic engagements, the missile's main solid motor boosted it to over Mach 3. As it reached that speed, the missile deployed air scoops, turning the motor chamber into a ramjet, boosting speed to Mach 5. Its warhead could be fashioned from either conventional high explosives or a more powerful thermium nitrate, which was especially useful against ground targets.

The only knock against the missile was the fact that, as Rubeo pointed out, it still had not passed all of its tests. Like any new weapons system, the Anaconda had a few teething problems; in this case, they were primarily related to the target acquisition system and its interface with the Megafortresses' computer systems, which Jennifer had been helping fix for the past few weeks.

"I think we will err on the side of capability," said Major Catsman finally. "We'll ship the missiles to Diego Garcia and let Colonel Bastian make the final call."

Rubeo frowned. A smug look appeared on Calder's face.

Catsman looked frustrated. Unlike Colonel Bastian, who sometimes went out of his way to encourage dissent on military options, the major seemed frazzled by the differing opinions on how to help reinforce the Dreamland team. Since Colonel Bastian would have the final say on Diego Garcia, whether to send the Anaconda missiles or not was more a personnel issue than a weapons decision since sending the weapons would necessitate sending maintainers and techies to deal with them.

The real problem was the fact that only one radar-equipped Megafortress was available for deployment, and there was no answer to that; Catsman knew she couldn't flip a switch and speed up the refurbishment process. The EB-52 *Cheli,* just barely out of final flight testing, was already en route to Diego Garcia and would arrive shortly. The next radar version of the Megafortress wasn't even due to get to Dreamland from the refurbishment works for another month.

At least they had solved the problem of the two warheads that were missing from the projections. Rubeo found an error in the modifications that had been used to adapt the tracking program to its present use. But even that didn't satisfy the scientist. Rather than accepting congratulations gracefully, he answered with the question: "And what else did we miss?

"The new Flighthawks will give the Megafortresses better capability," said Rubeo, still not done arguing his point. "That's all they need."

"No, Ray, the matter is settled," said Catsman. "We'll send the Anacondas. And the new Flighthawks."

Similar in appearance to the original U/MF-3, the U/MF-3D had more powerful engines and a control system that would let it be piloted much farther from the Megafortress. While they, too, were in short supply, the aircraft had already passed their tests and were ready to deploy.

Jennifer found her mind drifting as the discussion continued. She couldn't concentrate on head counts and spare part contingencies; all she could think of was Dog.

He hadn't even looked at her, or asked how she was, when he briefed the Command Center.

And he looked like hell.

He needed her. She needed him.

"I'm going with the MC-17," she told Catsman as soon as the meeting ended. "I'll help the technical teams. The new Flighthawks may need some work."

"They don't need a nanny," said Rubeo.

Major Catsman just looked at her. Rubeo was right—the technical teams were self-contained. While she had worked on C³, the Flighthawk computer, her contributions were completed long ago.

"The Anaconda missiles also need work," she said.

"Another reason not to send them," said Rubeo. "And it's not your project."

"I've worked on them," said Jennifer.

"We need you to do other things," insisted Rubeo. "There is a great deal of work."

"If you think you should go," said Catsman, "then you should go."

"I think I should," said Jennifer. "And I am."

**Indian Ocean,
off the Indian coast
Time unknown**

ZEN CRADLED BREANNA IN HIS LAP AS HE PULLED HIMSELF up toward the peak of the slope. Finally he stopped, collapsing on his side. Breanna fell with him, her weight dead against his body. At first he was too exhausted to think, too wiped to feel anything. Then gradually he realized where he was and who was lying on top of him.

"OK, Breanna," he said. "Breanna? Bree?"

He lay on his back for a few minutes, an hour—it was impossible to tell how long. Clouds covered the moon then slowly slipped away. Finally, he shifted Breanna off him, sliding her weight away gently.

Far in the distance, he heard a groan.

The sound was so faint he wasn't even sure he'd heard it at first. Then he thought it was an animal. Then, finally, he realized it had come from his wife.

"Bree," he said, pushing up. "Bree?"

Zen rolled her onto her back, then undid her helmet strap, still not daring to look at her face. Without the ability to kneel, he had to shift himself around awkwardly until he was sitting and her head was resting on his thighs. He closed his eyes and removed the helmet, prying as gently as possible, cradling her head down to the ground.

Her face was badly bruised. Zen guessed she'd hit the plane going out, probably harder than he had.

She looked peaceful, except for the purple welts. She looked like she was sleeping.

Tears came to his eyes. He was sure he'd imagined the sound; sure she was dead.

Until her lips parted.

Cautiously, he pushed his face down to hers. She was breathing.

"Bree?" he said, pulling back upright. "Bree?"

She didn't say anything, but he thought she stirred.

"I'm here, baby," he said, leaning back down as close as he could. "I'm here."

**Aboard the *Bennett*,
over the northern Arabian Sea
0243, 16 January 1998**

"SEARCH PATTERN IS COMPLETE, COLONEL," ENGLEHARDT told Dog as the Megafortress completed the last orbit. "Nothing."

"The *Lincoln*'s search assets will be up within the hour," added Lieutenant Sullivan. "We've given them the flight projections Dreamland ran."

His men were subtly telling him that it was time to get on with the rest of their mission—finding the warheads. They had roughly six hundred miles to go before getting into the search area.

Dog pushed a long breath from his lungs.

"All right." Dog couldn't quite force enthusiasm into his voice; he had to settle for authority. "Mikey, get us on course. I'm going to take another shot at taking a nap. Wake me up when we're starting the search."

"You got it, Colonel."

Dog tapped the back of the pilot's seat and started for the upper Flighthawk bay. Daly put up his hand and stopped him as he passed.

"We'll find her, Colonel. Starship or someone will get her. And Zen. Don't worry."

Dog patted the sergeant on the shoulder.

"Thanks," he told him. "I know we will."

III

Finders Keepers

———

**Southeastern Iran,
near the coast
0200, 16 January 1998
(0300, Karachi)**

GENERAL MANSOUR SATTARI PACED THE LONG HALL OF THE
mosque's auxiliary building, waiting for word of his son.

That Captain Val Muhammad Ben Sattari had launched
the final phase of the elaborate plan, there could be no doubt.
India and Pakistan were at war, and had spent the day before
trading accusations at the UN that each had tried to annihi-
late the other. The American President had gone on television and claimed that the U.S. had prevented nuclear weapons
from exploding after the missiles were launched and would
now work for peace, but CNN also reported that the power
grids in both countries had been wiped out—a sure sign to
General Sattari that several nuclear weapons had exploded,
regardless of what the U.S. said. That meant his son had succeeded in his goal.

Now, if only Allah, blessed be His name, saw fit to carry
Val back to him unharmed. Then he would launch his own
goal—overthrowing the black robes who had ruined his life,
and his country.

The general continued to pace, his shoes squeaking on the
tile. He was alone in the building, and knew he would be for
several hours. This was good—he did not want others to see
his impatience as he waited for news from his son. He believed that a general must always maintain an image of calm
and control, even in the most trying times.

Unlike the prayer hall of the mosque, this building was nearly brand new, and while the architect had preserved the ancient style of the older structures, no expense had been spared on the lavish interior. The floors were marble from the best quarries in Italy. The walls were wood veneer taken from East Africa. Even the furniture, hand carved by Iranian craftsmen, was finely wrought.

General Sattari stopped his pacing as the music from the television in the assembly room suddenly blared, announcing another bulletin. He folded his arms and listened as an American anchorman began running down the "latest" on the situation. This turned out to be primarily a rehash of earlier reports, the only exception being the news that the U.S. President had sent an aircraft carrier to the region.

Sattari frowned. He considered going into the room and changing the channel to Sky News, the British network. But he'd done that twice already, only to realize that CNN's information was more up to date. And so instead he simply resumed his pacing, noting to himself that the fact that news was simply trickling in was an indication of how complete the destruction had been.

Aboard the *Abner Read*,
northern Arabian Sea
0310

THE MARINE CORPS OSPREY FLUTTERED LEFT AND RIGHT, ducking in and out of the spotlights as it descended toward the deck. At eighty-four feet counting the spinning rotors, the aircraft's tilt-wings extended well over the sides of the narrow-beamed ship, so it looked to Danny as if the Osprey would tip the *Abner Read* up from the stern when it landed. But the ship remained steady, and within a few moments two members of the crew had fastened restraints to the Osprey's body to keep it from slipping off the deck. When they were done, the forward hatch of the Osprey opened and two Marines stepped out.

"Dancer, we meet again," shouted Danny to the trim figure that led the way forward.

"I had a feeling you'd be in the middle of things," said Lieutenant Emma "Dancer" Klacker, shaking Danny's hand. "This is Major Behrens from the general's staff. He's the general's intel geek."

"Major."

"Captain Freah's the Dreamland crazy who helped stop the pirates a few months back in the Gulf of Aden," Dancer told her companion. "I told him another operation like that and we'd make him an honorary Marine."

"This may be his chance, then," said Behrens.

Danny led the way to the *Abner Read*'s Tactical Center, which the ship's captain had loaned them for the briefing. The holographic table at the center of the space displayed a three-dimensional map of northern India; Dreamland's map of the possible locations of the warheads had been superimposed on the layout. Danny quickly sketched out the situation.

The U-2 had spotted two missiles in a mountain valley south of the Pakistan-India border. Fired by India, the weapons had crashed in the high desert two hundred miles from the coast. The *Bennett* had identified another seventy-five miles to the northeast, closer to the border on lower land. The remaining warheads—twenty-five—were still to be found.

"This area has the most promise," said Danny, pointing to a spot in the southern Thar Desert. "You can see from the projections there may be as many as six here, all launched from Pakistan. The *Bennett* will look there next."

Danny explained that both countries lost their power grids, throwing them into chaos. Things were even worse in the wide swath of territory affected by the EEMWBs, where all electronics had been wiped out, even those that ran on batteries or could be connected to backup generators off the grid. It included all of the areas where the missiles were thought to have gone down. With the exception of three small radars on the west coast, the military installations in the rest of India were either using their radars intermittently or not at all because of power problems. The Indians had two phased-array, long-range warning radar aircraft. One had been wiped out by the T-Rays and crashed near Delhi. The other was patrolling the east coast of the country, helping to monitor a Chinese fleet there.

The Chinese, meanwhile, had ordered the stricken aircraft carrier *Khan* to return to port. It was still north, near Pakistan, preparing to go south. Even if it remained where it was, Danny said, it was in no shape to challenge their operations.

"Our real handicap right now is low-level reconnaissance. The Megafortress isn't equipped with Flighthawks. That should be remedied by this evening. Which brings me to another problem—we need to get our top Flighthawk pilot down to Diego Garcia so he can help out."

"Where is he?"

"Catching some z's in a rack," said Danny.

"He's aboard ship?" asked Dancer.

"He's been running the Werewolf and training the *Abner Read*'s crew to handle it themselves. We were hoping you could take him back to the *Lincoln* and fly him down to Diego Garcia. We can arrange refuels."

Dancer turned to Major Behrens. Danny stared at her face. She was a serious, serious temptation, even for a married man.

Especially for a married man.

He just barely managed to look away as Dancer turned back.

"I think the general can persuade the captain of the *Lincoln* to spare an airplane," said Behrens. "Or we can arrange something with Ospreys. We'll work it out."

"Good," said Danny. He sensed that Dancer was staring at him and kept his own eyes focused on the table. "How soon can you get people on the ground, and what's the game plan?"

"Major, Lieutenant, I'm sorry I was busy when you arrived," said Storm, striding into the room unannounced. "Welcome aboard."

Danny stepped to the side, thankful for the interruption. He *was* married, he reminded himself. And this was work.

But damn, Dancer looked even more gorgeous than he remembered. The Marine camo uniform somehow accented her dusky rose face, and it didn't hide her trim hips. She wore her black hair in a tight braid that looked part Amazon warrior, part beauty queen.

"We're happy to host you," continued Storm. "Make us your operations center."

"Thank you for your hospitality," said Major Behrens, "but we've already set up temporary ops on the carrier. Our ship is on her way; she should be close enough to handle full operations in fifty-six hours."

"You'll be done by then," said Storm gruffly.

Danny kept his smile to himself. Storm liked to be in the middle of the action.

"Hopefully," agreed Dancer. "In the meantime, Captain, we'd be grateful of any support you can give. This is one of the best ships in the Navy," she added, turning to Behrens. "It's the future. I've seen the crew in the action. They're very good."

"What about you, Captain Freah?" Storm asked, pretending to ignore the compliment—though he'd shaded slightly. "Where are you going to be?"

"You're coming with me and the assault team, aren't you, Captain?" asked Dancer.

"Wherever we're needed," said Danny, holding her gaze for the first time since she'd come on board.

It felt good—too good, he knew. But he didn't break it, and neither did she.

DANCER'S UNSOLICITED COMPLIMENT ABOUT THE *ABNER Read* didn't lift Storm's mood. Having shot off all his missiles in combat, he found himself nearly impotent just when things were going to turn hot again. True, he had torpedoes, but they were intended primarily for use against submarines and had nowhere near the range of Harpoons. Nor would they be much good against airplanes.

And the more he thought about it, the more he was sure he was going to face airplanes very soon. Not from the Indians, but from the *Khan*.

The master of the Chinese ship resented the fact that they had picked up his pilot. Storm could tell from the brief communication he'd sent, almost a blowoff, when they'd shipped the man out in the Sharkboat. And the *Khan* was still north, clearly planning something.

"Captain, you have a minute?" asked Eyes as he started for the bridge.

"Sure," he told his exec.

"In private?"

Storm nodded, then followed Eyes forward to the galley, a short distance away.

"Coffee, sir?"

"No, I've had my fill," said Storm. "What's up?"

"I'm wondering if we're going to have an option on what port we put into, and if so, I'd like to make some suggestions," said Eyes.

"Port?" sputtered Storm.

"Aren't we going to get—"

Storm didn't let him finish. "We're not going into port. Not now. Do you understand what we're in the middle of?"

"We've done our part," said Eyes. "Between the action earlier—"

"What's gotten into you, Eyes?"

"What do you mean, Storm?"

"You don't want to quit, do you?"

"Quit?"

"You're talking about going home."

"Captain, we have no more weapons. We have to replenish."

"We have plenty of fuel."

Eyes frowned. "I'm just trying to get the men the best place for R and R."

"You're talking about shore leave at a time when we should be fighting," said Storm. He felt his whole body growing warm. "You need to be coming up with a plan to deal with the *Khan*. Their captain is up to something."

Eyes put his coffee down on the table. "We have no more Harpoons, Storm. Or Standard missiles. We have no fresh vegetables. The ship has been at sea for over a month. That's twice as long as we'd planned."

"Don't be a defeatist. We'll get resupplied once we meet the *Lincoln*."

Eyes frowned. "Yes, sir." The lieutenant commander picked up his coffee and started to leave.

"Were are you going, mister?" snapped Storm.

"I was just going back to my duty station, sir."

Storm wondered if he should relieve Eyes. He couldn't have someone with a negative attitude as his number two.

No, he thought. His exec was just tired. He hadn't been to sleep for a day and a half, at least.

"Go get yourself some rest, Eyes," Storm told him. "You've been pushing yourself too hard."

"I feel fine, Captain."

"That was an order, mister."

Eyes stared at him for a moment. "Aye aye, Captain," he said finally. "Aye aye."

**Aboard the *Bennett*,
near the Pakistan-India border
0400**

"COLONEL, IF I CAN MAKE A SUGGESTION?"

"Absolutely, Mike," Dog told Englehardt.

"If I drop the Megafortress to five hundred feet and walk her as slow she'll go, the low-light video camera in the nose will get us an excellent picture."

Ordinarily, Dog would have readily agreed—the jagged terrain was making it hard for the radar to "see" what was on the ground. But they had spotted a Pakistani ground unit to the north just as he came back from his brief nap.

"How close are the Pakistanis?" Dog asked.

"Two miles almost directly north," replied the pilot. "They're on that east-west road just over the rise, right on their side of the border. We can get down and then away before they even know what's going on.

"There are just two deuce-and-a-half troop trucks," he added, using the American slang for a multipurpose six-by-six troop truck. "Worst they're going to have is a shoulder-launched missile. It's not going to be much of a threat."

"That's not what I'm worried about," Dog said. "I don't want them coming over to see what we're interested in. Or radioing for help."

"Wouldn't their radios have been fried by the T-Rays?" the copilot, Kevin Sullivan, asked. "We haven't heard any transmissions."

"Maybe, maybe not. The EEMWB that knocked out the missile was detonated farther south," said Dog, who had helped design and implement the detonation plan. "They may have driven into the area afterward. We can't count on them having been affected."

"We can take them out with the Harpoons," said Sullivan. "Not going to be a problem."

"Firing on them is a last resort," Dog told him.

"Let's fake them out," said Englehardt. "Make it look like we're interested in them, buzz them, then look for the warhead on the way out."

"Maybe."

Dog examined the ground radar plot on Sergeant Daly's screen. The two trucks were in the middle of the road. It occurred to Dog that the vehicles themselves might have been disabled by the T-Rays. Even if that weren't the case, they might have strict orders not to go over the border—though the line was marked here only on maps, not on the ground.

What would he do if they made a move to get the missile?

The admiral had made it clear that he could use whatever force he needed to protect his people, and to recover a warhead once it was spotted, but as usual, the orders couldn't cover everything. It seemed clear that he wasn't permitted to fire on them in this case, before the warhead had been identified and at a moment when they posed little threat. But what if they moved toward it? Could he fire then, even though he hadn't ID'd the missile?

"Colonel, what do you want to do?" asked Englehardt.

"Take another nap," laughed Dog. Then he got serious. "Hold this orbit and continue to monitor the Indians. I'll talk to Danny and the Marines. When they're close enough to come for the warhead—if it is in fact a warhead—we'll make our move."

"That may be an hour at least, Colonel."

"By my calculations, your coffee will hold out for at least another six," said Dog. "We can wait until then."

"Careful on that coffee, sir," said Sullivan. "That's our backup fuel supply."

**Indian Ocean,
off the Indian coast
Time unknown**

IT STARTED TO LIGHTEN. DAWN APPROACHED, STALKING over the ocean behind a cover of clouds.

Voices echoed in Zen's head, murmurs and echoes that he couldn't quite decipher. He thought he heard birds, then a cow, then a dog barking. Finally he was sure that someone was calling to him. But the island—more an oversized rock with a pebble and sand beach punctuated by black hunks of igneous stone—remained empty.

Breanna was alive. That he was sure of. What he didn't know, and couldn't, was how badly she was injured. She was unconscious, her breathing shallow. From what he could tell, she wasn't bleeding anywhere, and her bones seemed to be intact. He assumed she was in shock, and maybe suffering from hypothermia.

He could do almost nothing for her. He propped her head up, took off the survival vest and the rest of her gear. Her flight suit was sopping wet, but he thought she'd be warmer in it.

Zen was cold and wet himself. He decided that when the sun finally rose, he'd strip to his underwear and lay his clothes out on the rocks to dry.

He had his personal Beretta and two sets of small "pencil" flares. He had four candy bars and four granola "energy" bars, which were basically cereal pressed together with fruit and sugar. He had a survival knife. He had fishing line and a small poncho.

His matches and lighter were gone. So were the extra bullets for his gun. And his med kit.

Breanna's radio was in her vest, along with her med kit, which had a small Bic-style lighter in it. He left her weapon strapped in its holster, but took her extra clip.

Zen turned on the survival radio and monitored the rescue frequency or "Guard band" for a few minutes, trying to see if anyone was around. The "spins"—times when he was supposed to broadcast—had been set at five and thirty-five minutes past the hour. But the routine was useless without a working watch.

Breanna had one. He leaned over her, then slipped it gently from her wrist. It was four minutes past the hour.

Close enough.

He switched the dial on the radio to voice and broadcast, nearly choking over the phlegm in his throat.

"Zen Stockard to any nearby aircraft. Zen Stockard to any American aircraft—can you hear me?"

There was no reply. He tried a few more times, then put the radio down.

Zen looked down at his wife. He slid his thumb over to her wrist, feeling for her pulse, and began counting the heartbeats, but stopped after ten.

What the hell was he going to do if it was beating slow? Or fast? What the hell was he going to do, period?

He was going to get someone on the Guard band and get the hell out of here, that's what.

The clouds had passed to the east, but there seemed to be more coming from the west. He needed a shelter to keep Breanna dry if it rained again.

He could turn the poncho into a tent. There weren't any sticks handy, but he could rig something by piling the rocks on either side. There were certainly enough of them.

It was something to do, at least. He patted his wife gently, then began crawling toward the nearest loose stones.

**Aboard the *Bennett*,
near the Pakistan-India border
0540**

DOG DIDN'T KNOW WHERE EXACTLY TO PUT HIMSELF. He felt like he should be in the pilot's seat, running the show, but he was far too tired to be at the stick. The jumpseat at the back of the flight deck was too far from the action to see what was going on. And sitting at either of the auxiliary radar operator seats made him feel as if he was looking over the operators' shoulders.

So he ended up more or less pacing around the flight deck, in effect looking over *everyone's* shoulders and making them all uncomfortable.

His body, meanwhile, felt as if it was tearing itself in two. He'd had so much of the high octane coffee Sullivan brewed that his stomach was boiling. Fortunately, the Megafortress upgrades included an almost comfortable lavatory, because he was visiting it often.

"Incoming from Captain Freah," reported Sullivan.

"Great," said Dog.

Sergeant Daly stiffened as he sat down next to him at the

auxiliary ground radar station. Dog plugged in his headset and flipped into the Dreamland channel.

"Bastian."

"Hi, Colonel. Good to talk to you again, sir."

"It's good to talk to you too, Danny. What's your status?"

"We're twenty minutes from our target area, P-1. What's going on?"

"There's a Pakistani army unit, two trucks, about two miles north of the possible warhead marked as P-3 on the Dreamland map," Dog told him. "They haven't moved, but they're close enough to get over there in a hurry. We haven't gotten low enough to verify that there is a warhead there."

Dog explained that he wanted to check the site, and if it was a warhead, have Danny land there first.

"I got you," said Danny. "You think they don't know it's there at all."

"Exactly. The only way we can check it is by getting very low, and they're likely to realize something's going on. If they call for reinforcements, they might have a pretty good-sized force up here in a few hours."

"Stand by."

Dog furled his arms and leaned back in the seat, brushing against Daly as he did.

Dreamland's present configuration scheme rarely called for all four stations to be occupied, but when the Megafortress went into service with regular Air Force units, all the stations would be filled. It occurred to Dog that another six or eight inches of space between the two stations would make things much more comfortable for the operators. There was room too, though it would call for a few modifications to the galley.

A small thing, maybe, but important to the guys on the mission.

"Colonel, this is Danny."

"Go ahead, Captain."

"We're going to change course. We're maybe thirty minutes from point P-3."

"We'll scout it and give you a go, no-go, when you're ten

minutes away," Dog told him. "What do your rules of engagement say about deadly force?"

"To defend ourselves and the weapon."

"Good. If they make a move toward you, we're going to use our Harpoons. Bastian out."

Dog switched over to the interphone, sharing Danny's information with the rest of the crew.

"I can get us over the warhead exactly thirty seconds before they hit their mark," Englehardt promised.

"Excellent," said Dog.

"No action from the Pakistanis," said Daly. "They don't seem to know we're here."

"They will," said Dog.

**Aboard the USS *Abraham Lincoln*,
the Arabian Sea
0600**

FEELING DISORIENTED, STARSHIP FOLLOWED HIS GUIDE through the bowels of the aircraft carrier to the squadron ready room. He had heard carriers described as miniature cities floating on water, but the *Lincoln* seemed more like the underbelly of a massive football stadium. It smelled like one too, ten times worse than the locker room in Dreamland's gym.

He thought he was somewhere in the maze of rooms below the flight deck and hangar—the playing field, to follow his metaphor—but how far down and where exactly, he had no idea. He'd gone down three flights of stairs—known to the Navy as a ladder, for some inexplicable reason—and through several hatchways—actually doors, though they looked like hatches to him. He had also learned the meaning of "knee knockers"—the metalwork at the base of watertight openings.

"Ensign Watson reporting with Lieutenant Andrews," said his guide as they entered a cabin about half the size of the closet in Starship's Dreamland apartment.

"Lieutenant Bradley," said the balding man on the cot. "Friends call me Brad." He rose and shifted his coffee cup to shake Starship's hand.

"People call me Starship."

"Starship?" Bradley laughed. "You Air Force guys have the weirdest nicknames and call signs. You got a Buck in your outfit, I bet."

"Uh, no Buck. A Dork."

Bradley began to howl with laughter. But something about his smile made the laugh inoffensive.

"So, I hear you need the fastest sled ride to Diego Garcia that you can find," said Bradley.

"Yeah."

"You've come to the right place. Come on, let's get you some coffee and gear, then go preflight."

Starship wasn't sure why a passenger would need to take part in a briefing, but figured that Bradley was just being accommodating for a visitor. His confusion grew as Bradley mentioned he'd need to know his hat size for the trip, meaning they were going to find him a helmet.

"Jeez, I didn't think you guys took Osprey flights so seriously," said Starship finally.

"Osprey?"

"We're flying down on a V-22, right?" said Starship.

"Hell, no. You wanted to get there *fast,* right?"

"Well, yeah, but—"

"Admiral Woods arranged for you to backseat my Super Hornet, Lieutenant," said Bradley.

"What's a Super Hornet?"

"A toy you can't have." Bradley laughed. "The admiral says you need to be there fast. This is the fastest thing we can spare. Don't worry. Just keep your hands inside the car at all times and you'll be fine."

THE SUPER HORNET—OFFICIALLY, AN F/A-18F—WASN'T your run-of-the-mill swamp boat. An upsized version of the all-purpose F/A-18, this Super Hornet was one of three being tested by the Navy before the aircraft entered full production.

Designed to replace the Navy's heavy metal, the Grumman F-14, the new Hornet shared very little components with its look-alike predecessor and namesake. From the engines to the wings to the tail surfaces, the designers had reworked the aircraft, making it bigger, faster, and stronger. Close in size to an Air Force F-15C, it incorporated a number of low-radar section strategies, making it less noticeable to enemies at long range. It could carry about a third more munitions half again as far as the standard F/A-18s lining the *Lincoln*'s side.

As Starship buckled himself into his seat, Bradley gave him a quick rundown of the instruments and multifunction displays. Then the Navy pilot hopped into the front seat and got ready to rumble.

Engines up, the Super Hornet's computer tested the control surfaces, recording the status of the aircraft equipment on the multifunction display.

"You ready for this, Starship?" asked Bradley.

"Good to go."

Even though he had braced himself, the shot off the carrier deck jolted Starship. He felt like a baseball that had been whacked toward the bleachers. It took a good four or five seconds before he could breathe and relax; by then the Hornet had her nose pointed nearly straight up.

They climbed rapidly through the sparse cloud cover, the newly risen sun a giant orb below. Bradley turned away from the carrier's airspace and began rocketing south.

"What do you think of the view?" asked Bradley.

"Very nice," said Starship. Like the F-15, the backseater—technically an RIO, or radar intercept officer, in the Navy—sat in a clear bubble cockpit with a good view to the sides.

"So, you think you could handle this baby?" asked Bradley.

"Could I?"

"That's my question."

Starship scrambled to find the volume button to turn down the sound of Bradley's laugh.

"I think I can handle it," said Starship. He'd told Bradley earlier that he had flown F-15s.

"Take a shot," the Navy aviator told him, and he gave the stick a little waggle.

Starship treated the aircraft as if it were a baby carriage, holding it gently level and perfectly on course.

For about five seconds.

Then he gave the stick more input and snapped into a right aileron roll. He came back quickly—the Super Hornet seemed to snicker as she pushed herself neutral, as if asking, *Is that the best you can do?*

The aircraft was very precise, and while the stick required a bit more input than the Flighthawk's, it felt sweet.

"So do you have your hand on the stick yet, or what?" asked Bradley.

Starship did a full roll, then another. He nudged himself into an invert—a little tentative, he knew—and flew upside down for a few miles before coming back right side up.

"So you do know where the stick is," said Bradley, laughing.

"Can I go to afterburners?"

"Knock yourself out."

Starship lit up the power plants. The dash through the sound barrier was gentler than he expected; he did a half-stick 360 aileron roll, then recovered, starting to feel his oats.

"Better ease off on the dinosaurs or we may end up walking to the tanker," suggested Bradley.

"Sorry."

"It's all right. I know exactly how you feel. Nice plane, huh?"

"I could get used to it."

"Beats flying robots, I bet."

"They have their moments," said Starship, pushing his stick left and taking about four g's as he got on course. "But there's a lot to be said for sitting in the cockpit yourself."

**Aboard the *Bennett*,
near the Pakistan-India border
0600**

SHE WAS LIKE A THOROUGHBRED RELEASED FROM THE chute, flicking her mane back as she bared her teeth and charged down the track. She put her head down and galloped, hard and proud, determined to hit her marks.

The Megafortress charged 150 feet over the Pakistani trucks at about 500 knots, loud and low. Looking like startled spectators at a horse race after a thoroughbred jumped the fence, the half-dozen Pakistani troops dove for cover.

"P-3 object dead ahead, one mile," said Englehardt as the Megafortress continued toward their target.

"No offensive action from the ground troops," said Sullivan, watching the rear-facing optical video. "Look more startled than anything."

Dog stared at the screen in front of him, which was projecting the forward video camera view. The desert rose up then fell off into a slope. In real time, the ground was a blur; Dog had trouble separating the rocks from the shadows.

Englehardt pushed the nose of the aircraft down to get closer to the terrain, then counted off his turn, beginning a wide, almost leisurely bank to the east.

"Paks are still doing nothing," said Sullivan. "Scratching their heads, probably."

Dog hit the preset for the video screen replay, showing what the camera had seen in the past thirty seconds. He slowed the action down, freeze-framing the ground they had flown over.

"This looks like it might be it," he said aloud, zeroing in on a gray mound on the left side of his viewer. The shape seemed a little jagged, but there was a line behind it, as if the object had dug a trench as it skidded in.

The more he looked at the image, though, the less sure he became. Where was the body of the missile? Why would it have come in on a trajectory that would allow it to ski across the landscape before stopping?

"Dreamland, I need your opinion on this," he said, tapping the button to make the image available over the Dreamland channel.

"I don't know, Colonel," said Englehardt, who'd brought it up on one of his screens. "Looks like a rock to me."

"Definitely a warhead," said Sullivan. "Skidded in and landed nose up in the sand. Look at it."

"Dreamland Command?" said Dog.

"We are examining it, Colonel," said Ray Rubeo. "We will have something definitive in a few minutes."

Dog glanced at his watch. Danny and the Marines would be at the go/no-go point in exactly thirty seconds.

"You want another run, Colonel?" asked Englehardt. "I can come in from the opposite direction."

"No," said Dog. "But let's let the Pakistanis see us orbit to their north. If they're going to get curious, let's have them get curious in that direction."

He took one last look at the screen, then pressed the preset on the radio to talk to Danny.

**Aboard Marine Osprey *Angry Bear One*,
over northern India
0610**

THE TONE IN HIS HEADSET ALERTED DANNY FREAH THAT they were five minutes from the landing zone. Tucking the M16 the Marines had loaned him under his arm, he twisted his body left and right, stretching his muscles in anticipation.

Had they been in a Dreamland version of the Osprey, he would have been able to switch the view in his smart helmet so he could see the terrain in front of them. Then again, he thought, had he been in a Dreamland bird, he'd also be leading the mission. Right now he was basically a communications specialist, relaying information from Dreamland and the *Bennett* to Dancer, her sergeants, and the pilots of the three Marine Ospreys on the mission.

Once on the ground, Danny would work with two Navy experts to determine if the warhead was armed and could be moved. The men had been trained to handle American "broken arrow" incidents, cases where U.S. nukes had been lost or otherwise compromised. Besides his own training, he'd had experience disarming a live nuke two years before in Brazil.

"Danny Freah to Colonel Bastian. Colonel, what's the status?"

"The experts are looking at the image right now. Shouldn't be long."

Danny turned and signaled to Dancer that they should go into a holding pattern. She'd just leaned into the cockpit when Dog came back on the line.

"It's a warhead," said the colonel. "Proceed."

"Roger that." He tapped Dancer and gave her a thumbs-up. The Osprey, which had just barely begun to slow down, picked up speed once more.

"What about the trucks?" shouted Dancer over the whine of the engines.

"I'm checking," said Danny.

He had Dog describe the layout. The two trucks looked to have about six men in them. They were two miles from the warhead and maybe another half mile from the landing area. It looked as if they'd been ordered to the road and told not to leave it, but there was no way of knowing for sure until they landed.

"First sign of trouble," added Colonel Bastian, "and we'll fire a pair of Harpoons at them."

"Acknowledged. Thank you, Colonel. We're two minutes from the landing zone."

Danny tapped Dancer on the shoulder and relayed the information. She gave him a thumbs-up. Her face was very serious, eyes narrowed, cheeks slightly puffed out, the shadow of a line—not a wrinkle, just a line—visible on her forehead.

"Marines! Make your mothers proud!" shouted Dancer as the Osprey touched down.

Danny went out with the corpsman and one of the bomb experts, toward the end of the pack. By the time he reached the warhead, the Marines had set up a defensive perimeter around it.

The scent of unburned rocket fuel was so strong, his nose felt as if it were burning. He'd run the whole way, and now had to catch his breath by covering his face with his sleeve. For a moment he thought he might even have to resort to the protective hood and contamination gear the Navy people had brought—gear that he knew from experience was so bulky he'd never be able to actually work on the bomb.

The warhead and upper end of the missile had buckled and split off from the body when they came to earth, skidding along the ground and making what looked like a shallow trench littered with rocks before stopping. On closer inspection, it was clear that the rocks were actually bits and pieces of the missile that had fallen off along the way. The warhead itself looked like a dented garbage can half submerged in the sand. The protective nose cone had been cracked and partly shredded, but the framework that covered the top portion of the missile remained intact. The black shroud of the bomb casing was visible below a set of tubes that had supported the cone section and the battered remains of instruments, electrical gear, wires, and frayed insulation.

Danny's smart helmet was equipped with a high definition video camera, and he used it now to send images back to Dreamland Command.

"You getting this, Doc?" he asked, scanning the crash site and then bending over the warhead.

"I keep telling you, Captain, I'm not a doctor," replied Anna Klondike a bit testily. "I wouldn't associate with Ph.D. types."

"I'm sorry, Annie. I thought I was talking to Ray Rubeo."

"What Dr. Rubeo doesn't know about nuclear weapons would fill a very large book."

"How are you, Annie?"

"Cranky without my beauty rest. Please get closer to the base of the warhead," she said, quickly becoming all business. "Scan down the body. Our first step here is to confirm that this came from a Prithvi SS-150."

It took several minutes before the scientists were satisfied that it was indeed a Prithvi SS-150. The Prithvi family, derived from the Russian SA-2 surface-to-air missile, were all single-stage liquid fueled missiles; they differed mostly in terms of range and payload, though the family's accuracy had also improved as the weapons evolved. The 150 could deliver a thousand-kilogram payload 150 kilometers.

As nukes went, the egg-shaped bomb Danny and the Marines were standing around was relatively small; its theoretical yield was fifteen kilotons, though members of the Atomic Energy Commission had told the Dreamland scientists its effective yield was probably ten to fifteen percent lower.

The difference meant the weapon's blast would obliterate everything within 0.569 kilometers rather than, say 0.595. Since most people within 1.5 kilometers of either weapon would be burned or fatally radiated anyway, the difference was largely academic.

As he continued to pan the weapon, Danny could hear the scientists discussing the system among themselves in the background, sounding like they were looking over a new Porsche before it went on sale.

"So is this thing safe to move or what?" he finally asked.

"Please, Captain," Klondike said from Dreamland Command. "This is going to take a little while. We've never seen a real Indian nuke before."

"You're not filling me with confidence, Annie."

"You think you've got it tough?" she replied. "Ray Rubeo made the coffee."

Aboard the *Bennett*,
near the Pakistan-India border
0625

"PAKISTANIS ARE USING THEIR RADIO," SULLIVAN TOLD
Dog. "They're reporting helicopters and fighters in the area."

"No points for accuracy," quipped Englehardt.

"Yes, but at least now we know they have a radio," said
Dog, standing behind the two pilots. "Are they getting a response?"

"Negative."

"How are we doing down there, Danny?" Dog asked over
the Dreamland Command line.

"We have to start checking the circuits to make sure it's
dead," Danny replied. "Then we can get it out of here."

"You have an ETA on when you'll be done?" Dog asked.

"Working on it, Colonel."

Dog flipped off the mike.

"Paks may be scrambling aircraft from Faisal," said the
airborne radar operator, Sergeant Rager. "Have two contacts
coming up. Distant."

"Types?" asked Englehardt.

"Hmmmph." Rager adjusted something on his console.
The computer identified aircraft at very long range by comparing their radar profiles with information in its library;
depending on the distance, the operators used a number of
other comparison tools to narrow down the possibilities.

"Old iron," said Rager finally. "F-6. Pair of them.
Bearing . . . looks like they're making a beeline for the
trucks."

"Farmers, huh?" said Sullivan, since the F-6 was a Chinese version of the Russian MiG-19 Farmer, a venerable Cold
War fighter.

A two-engined successor to the famed MiG-15 of Korean
War vintage, the design had proven surprisingly robust.
Reverse-engineered and updated by the Chinese, the plane

was exported around the world. The Pakistani versions had been retrofitted with Atoll heat-seekers, and could not be taken lightly, especially by a Megafortress flying without Flight-hawk escort.

Which was just fine with the *Bennett*'s pilots. While neither had seen combat, their basic Megafortress training included extensive simulated combat against F-6s, as well as more capable aircraft.

"Scorpions," Englehardt told Sullivan. The long-range AMRAAM-plus missiles could knock the F-6s out of the air before they got close enough to use their heat-seekers. "I'm going to slide north."

"Hold your course," Dog told the pilot. "The Pakistanis are our allies. Let's see what they're up to before we start thinking of shooting them down."

"Yes, sir," said Englehardt, clearly disappointed.

Great Indian Desert
0630

THE FINAL ARMING CIRCUITRY ON THE INDIAN NUCLEAR WAR-head appeared to use a two-stage process, detonating the weapon only after it had traveled for a specified period of time and passed back through a designated altitude. The altimeter had been fried by the T-Rays and crushed in the crash, rendering the warhead inert.

Probably. The weapons people at Dreamland were worried that the nanoswitches that initiated the explosion might have survived the T-wave bombardment and the crash, and could be activated by a stray current. Since they didn't know enough about the weapon to rule that out, they decided to take further steps to disable it.

"The odds against some sort of accidental explosion are very long," said Anna Klondike, trying to reassure Danny. "Much worse than hitting the lottery."

"So are the consequences," said Danny. "How long will it take to disassemble?"

"We're still working on what we want to do," she said. "In the meantime, please treat the weapon as if it were live."

"You don't have to worry about that," said Danny.

A beeping signal indicated that Dog wanted to talk to him, and switched to another channel on the Dreamland network.

"Freah."

"Danny, we have two Pakistani aircraft approaching from the north. When are you getting out of there?"

"Unknown at this time," he said, and explained what Klondike had told him.

"This could take a while, Colonel," added Danny. "The scientists don't want to make any guesses about the weapon."

"Nor should they. Bastian out."

An atoll off the Indian coast
Date and time unknown

ZEN KNEW THAT HIS JURY-RIGGED PUP TENT WOULDN'T BE featured in *Architectural Digest* anytime soon, but it did cover both him and Breanna and would keep them *almost* dry if it rained. There was no way to keep warm, however, and though he thought the temperature was probably in the seventies, he felt a decent chill coming on.

If he'd had the use of his legs . . .

The idea was poison. He pushed it away.

The best way to warm up would be to start a fire. He decided he would explore. He made three broadcasts on the emergency channel, close together; when no one responded, he tucked the radio under Breanna's arm, then bent over and kissed her on the back of her head.

"I'll be back, baby," he told her, crawling up the shallow hill behind them to survey their domain.

Aboard the *Bennett*,
near the Pakistan-India border
0632

"BROADCAST ON ALL FREQUENCIES," DOG TOLD THE *BEN-nett*'s copilot. "Let's make sure they hear this."

"Ready for you, Colonel."

"Dreamland EB-52 *Bennett* to Pakistani F-6 pilots vector-ing south from Faisal. We are conducting a Search and Res-cue mission for a downed U.S. pilot in the border area. We have located the airman and are attempting to recover."

Dog waited for a response. The Pakistani planes were about 120 miles away, moving at just over 400 knots. That would bring them in range to use their air-to-air missiles in roughly fifteen minutes.

"Nothing, Colonel," said Sullivan finally.

"Anything from the ground units?"

"Negative."

"Let's give it another try," said Dog.

He repeated his message, again without getting an answer. The Megafortress was flying a lazy-eight pattern over the Marines, riding around and around at 15,000 feet. The Paki-stani trucks were at the northeastern end of their racetrack, still sitting in the middle of the road doing nothing.

"We may be out of range of their radios," suggested Rager from the airborne radar console.

"Maybe," said Dog.

"Just about in Scorpion range, Colonel," added Sullivan.

"We can take them," said Englehardt. "They'll never know what hit them."

Dog got up from the auxiliary radar station and walked up to the front of the cockpit, looking over the pilots' shoulders.

"Open the bomb bay doors," he said. "Let's make it easier for them to find us."

Englehardt glanced over his shoulder, then passed the or-der to Sullivan.

The aircraft shuddered as the doors swung open. The open

bay increased the Megafortress's radar cross section, increasing the range at which the aircraft could be seen. Dog plugged his headset into the auxiliary console on the airborne radar side.

"Pakistan F-6s flying from Faisal, this is Colonel Tecumseh Bastian in Dreamland *Bennett*. I'm conducting a Search and Rescue mission over Indian territory. Are you authorized to assist?"

"Dreamland flight, please identify yourself," said a voice in heavily accented English.

The transmission was weak but unbroken. Dog repeated what he had just told them.

"Dreamland USA—you are operating in Indian territory?"

"Affirmative. We have the situation under control at this time," Dog added. "Be advised that we spotted two Indian aircraft to the southeast approaching Pakistan territory approximately zero-five minutes ago. We tentatively ID'd them as Su-27s. They are no longer on our radar. I can provide our last contact."

The Pakistani pilots didn't reply. Possibly they were checking with their ground controller.

"F-6s are turning," said Rager. "Going east. Roughly on an intercept."

"Dreamland USA—do you require assistance?" asked the Pakistani pilot.

"Negative. We are in good shape," said Dog.

The Pakistani pilot requested the Indians' last position and their heading. Dog gave them coordinates that would take the interceptors well to the east.

The Pakistanis acknowledged.

Sullivan began laughing as soon as the conversation ended.

"Good one, Colonel," said the copilot. "I wouldn't have thought they'd fall for it."

"Neither did I," said Dog.

"I'm not sure they did," said Rager. "They've extended their turn—looks to me like they're trying to sweep around and come at us from the east."

Aboard the *Abner Read*,
northern Arabian Sea
0640

"I DON'T CARE WHAT CAPABILITIES YOU HAVE, STORM. YOU have orders. And you . . . will . . . follow them."

Admiral Woods's face grew redder with each word. Storm, sitting in his quarters and addressing the admiral through the secure video communications hookup there, squeezed his fingers into a pair of fists behind his back.

"Admiral, if the *Khan* is moving south, I should move with her. We should be prepared for anything she does. The Chinese—"

"We are prepared for anything she does," said Woods. "The *Decatur* will trail her. And if she makes any aggressive move—"

"A Chinese frigate fired missiles at one of the Dreamland aircraft. That's *damn* threatening."

"Storm, we've been through this. You yourself said that was the result of a misunderstanding."

"I believe I was wrong."

"Based on what evidence?"

Storm had no evidence, but he had strong feelings. He strongly regretted arranging the trade for the Chinese pilot— he could have engaged the frigate with his torpedoes and deck gun.

"I'm just convinced," he told the admiral. "I'm convinced they're going to try something."

"Then the *Decatur* and the *Lincoln* will deal with her. In the meantime, you have no weapons and must replenish."

"So let me replenish off the *Lincoln*. All I need are a dozen Harpoons."

"The *Lincoln* has only enough ammunition and stores for its own task force."

"But if I have to go all the way to Japan, I might just as well head to San Diego. The ship is due back there for full evaluation in three weeks. By the time the contractors get everything together—"

"You . . . have . . . your . . . *orders!*"

The admiral reached toward his screen, and the image on Storm's video disintegrated into a tiny blue dot.

The admiral was jealous, thought Storm. Woods couldn't stand the idea that he and his ship had made history.

Storm decided that Woods must be sending the *Decatur* to trail the stricken *Khan* because he was convinced the Chinese weren't done. The *Decatur* was a conventional destroyer; if it finished off the *Khan*, it would take some of the shine off his own accomplishments.

Storm went out into the conference room next to his cabin to pace and consider his orders. The admiral hadn't ordered him out of battle—he'd ordered him to replenish. Logically, if he could find another way to replenish, he could stay in the fight.

There was a replenishment ship about two days sail to the south, steaming toward the *Lincoln* task group, and another off the coast of Africa. But the radical design of the *Abner Read* called for special handlers to load its forward weapon pods, and neither ship was equipped with them. The alternative was to hand-load the littoral destroyer. This would involve taking the missiles from the containers they were transported in, slinging them across the open sea, and then manhandling them—gently, of course—into their launch boxes.

Doable, but not easy, and sure to require higher approval before proceeding. Higher approval meant talking to Woods, and Storm knew how that would go.

There had to be other sources.

Dreamland used Harpoons, didn't they? Where did they get the missiles?

Diego Garcia.

Storm called his procurement officer, an ensign who told him he'd already checked with Diego Garcia; no Harpoon missiles were available there.

"You're telling me there are *no* missiles on that base?"

The answer involved a lengthy explanation of the Navy's supply system. Storm was in no mood to hear it.

He needed to put a chief petty officer in charge of keeping them armed and supplied, he thought. Someone who knew his way around the regulations, not someone who spouted them to him.

He was about to switch channels when the ensign offered a suggestion: "The Dreamland people may have some to spare. Maybe we could try them."

The Air Force did use Harpoon missiles, but Storm wondered whether they were compatible. He knew that the ship-launched weapons contained a booster that the air-launched weapons lacked, but wasn't sure what other differences there might be. It took him nearly fifteen minutes to determine that the missiles should work in the *Abner Read*, provided they were properly mated with the booster units.

The *Abner Read* carried six spares.

Storm clapped his hands together, then punched the com unit on his belt. "Communications, get me Colonel Bastian, would you?"

Aboard the *Bennett*,
near the Pakistan-India border
0640

DOG WATCHED THE TWO PAKISTANI JETS AS THEY SWUNG IN toward them from the east. The aircraft were now about ten minutes away.

"What do you think, Colonel?" asked Englehardt. "Do we take them down or not?"

"They haven't challenged us yet," Dog told him.

"Respectfully, sir, if they have bombs, they could do some decent damage to the Marines before we can shoot them down."

"I don't intend on letting them get into a position to do that," said Dog. "They're not flying an attack profile. Change your course so we can go out to meet them. Plot an intercept so we can come around on their tails. Get us a little more altitude."

Dog wanted to get the Megafortress close enough so he could see what the diminutive fighters had under their wings before they were in a position to threaten the Marines. But he knew that would make the Megafortress more vulnerable.

Bending over the center power console, he peered through the Megafortress's windscreen. The two Pakistani planes looked like white pocketknives in the distance as the *Bennett* began her turn.

"Communication from the *Abner Read*, Colonel," said Sullivan. "For you personally."

"Not now."

"They claim it's urgent."

Dog snapped into the frequency. "Bastian."

"Colonel, this is Storm. I was wondering—"

"I'm just about to confront a pair of F-6 fighters here, Storm—make it damn quick."

"I'm looking for some Harpoon missiles," answered Storm.

"I haven't got time—"

"Listen, Bastian—"

Dog switched to the Pakistani frequency.

"Dreamland *Bennett* to Pakistani F-6s. Did you find those Indian Sukhois?" Dog asked, watching the two planes approach.

"Negative, Dreamland USA. You are over Pakistan territory."

"Acknowledged," said Dog. "Our operations are to the southwest, over Indian land. We thought it would be prudent to fly over friendly territory as much as possible."

"They're trying to transmit the information back to their base," said Sullivan when the fighters didn't immediately respond. "Having trouble. The backup generators at the base seem to be giving them fits."

The two Pakistani fighters spread slightly as the Megafortress turned. Dog watched the God's eyeview screen on the dash closely—if the planes had any hostile intent, one would attempt to close on the *Bennett*'s tail, where a shot from the heat-seekers would be difficult to defend against.

"Coming up outside our wings," said Sullivan.

Dog heard Englehardt blow a large wad of air into his oxygen mask. He'd undoubtedly been ready to flick the stick and call for flares—standard response to a missile launch.

"Pakistan F-6s, this is Dreamland *Bennett*. Are you free to assist? If so, we would welcome a high CAP," said Dog, asking the aircraft to patrol above them and protect against high-flying fighters.

"Dreamland USA, we are not at liberty to assist you at this time. We are on the highest state of alert."

"Acknowledged. Appreciate your taking the time to check on us," said Dog.

"We just going to let them overfly the missile area?" Englehardt asked.

"At this speed and altitude, they're not going to see much," Dog told the pilot. "The Ospreys could be doing anything. We'll stay with them as they make the pass."

"No air-to-ground missiles," said Sullivan, inspecting the aircraft with the Megafortress's video.

"Power back a bit in case we have to get in their way," Dog told Englehardt.

"Ready."

But it wasn't necessary. The F-6s began a turn northward well before they reached the area where the Ospreys had landed. Clearly, they were under orders to stay out of Indian territory.

"Dreamland USA, you're on your own," said the lead pilot. "Radio if you require further assistance from enemy fighters."

"Roger that, Pakistan F-6. Thanks much."

Aboard the *Abner Read*,
northern Arabian Sea
0645

EVERY TIME STORM PERSUADED HIMSELF THAT BASTIAN wasn't a bastard, a jerk, and worse, the flyboy colonel did something to show him how right his original opinion was.

Here, he had saved his *people,* just gotten them off the boat, for cryin' out loud, and all the Dog-haired colonel could do was hang up on him.

Storm waited for his fury to subside, then told his communications specialist to get him the colonel again.

"Bastian."

"What do you want me to do, Dog? Grovel?"

"What's up, Storm?"

"I find myself short of Harpoon missiles. I'm told that the Air Force versions can be made to work with my ship's weapons systems without—"

"Why don't you resupply off the *Lincoln*?"

"It's not quite that simple. Unfortunately, Harpoons are in short supply. I only need six."

Storm hated the tone in his own voice—weak, pleading, explaining. He was about to snap off the communication in disgust when Dog answered.

"We have some. Have your people check with Captain Juidice on Diego Garcia. I'm not sure how we'd ferry them there; maybe one of the Whiplash Ospreys."

"I won't forget this, Dog," gushed Storm. He could feel his face flush. "I won't forget it."

"Bastian out."

Great Indian Desert
0655

DANNY GLANCED AT THE TWO NAVY EXPERTS BESIDE HIM, then slid his hand down below the bomb casing to the nest of wires.

"Keep the probes away from the wires," Klondike repeated.

"Yeah, they're away."

"I want you to cut them in this sequence. Black, pure red, red with two black stripes—"

"Hold on, all right?" The wire casings were color coded for easy identification. But there were so many different codes that it wasn't easy to tell them apart.

"I need another flashlight," Danny said.

He took a breath, then pushed back close to the weapon. One of the sailors was already shining a beam on the wires; it just didn't seem bright enough.

Danny felt as if someone was squeezing his neck.

"Here you go," said the Navy expert, turning on another flashlight.

He located the first wire, nudging it gently from the rest of the pack, picked up the pliers with his right hand, pushed the nose toward the wire, then backed off and switched hands.

"How's it going?" asked Lieutenant Dancer from behind him.

Her voice steeled his fingers and he began cutting, working methodically. Klondike had him move on to the fusing unit.

"What we think is the fusing unit," she said, amending her instructions as she told him how to remove it.

He could have done without the note of uncertainty in the description, but when he was done, the scientists decided that the bomb was safe enough to move.

Which presented them with the next problem—they wanted time to study it before bringing it aboard the *Lincoln*.

"Why?" asked Danny.

"Just in case it blows up," said Klondike dryly.

"So it's all right to blow us up," Dancer said sarcastically, "but not the squids."

"Probably more worried about their delicate airplanes," said one of her sergeants.

"Well, I'm all for getting the hell out of here," Danny told them. "Given that the Pakistanis are two miles away."

"We'll just keep the weapons with us at P-1 for the time being," said Dancer, "since we're setting up camp there anyway."

Meanwhile, a harness and a set of titanium rods were dug into place under the warhead. A pair of hydraulic jacks with balloon-style wheels lifted the rods up so the warhead could be set into another jack and gingerly rolled over to the Osprey. It took considerable grunt work, but within a half hour the nuclear weapon was being rolled up into the aircraft's hold, where it was set into a veritable nest of inflatable stretchers and strapped to the walls so it couldn't move. Danny, one of the Navy bomb people, and two Marine riflemen sat in the rear of the aircraft with the weapon; everyone else flew in the other two rototilts.

"This'll be a story to tell our grandkids, huh?" said the Navy expert as the Osprey revved its engines.

"If it's declassified by then," replied Danny.

Aboard the *Bennett*,
near the Pakistan-India border
1215

"POSITIVE ID ON THE LAST OF THE PAKISTANI WARHEADS," Major Catsman told Colonel Bastian.

"Good," said Dog. He glanced at Sergeant Daly, sitting next to him. The radar operator's eyes had narrowed to slits, his brows sagging toward the puffy skin below. "I think we're about to call it a day here."

"When was the last time you slept?" Catsman asked.

Dog changed the subject, going over the arrangements Catsman had made for handling communications with the U-2s and Marines recovering the nukes on the ground. Then he checked in with Danny, who was helping set up the warhead recovery base in a hilly section of the desert between India and Pakistan. So far, four Indian and two Pakistani warheads had been recovered, all without incident.

"Any word on Major and Captain Stockard?" asked Dog, trying to sound as unemotional as possible.

"Negative."

"Alert me if there are any new developments," he told Catsman. "I'll check back with you when we land at Diego Garcia."

"Roger that. Get some rest."

"I will, Major. Thanks for the advice."

**Base Camp One,
Great Indian Desert
1800**

BY THE TIME DANNY FREAH HAD A CHANCE TO STOP AND catch his breath, night had begun stealing into the rugged hills around him, casting long shadows over the temporary camp the Marines had hastily erected. Over fifty Marines guarded the perimeter, with additional sentries located to the north and south and a Marine Pioneer unmanned aerial vehicle orbiting overhead to provide constant surveillance. Flights of F/A-18s from the *Lincoln* were being rotated north to provide air support if any was needed.

For the moment, things were quiet, and neither the Indians nor the Pakistanis seemed to know they were there. The closest Indian troops were border patrol units nearly two hundred miles to the south.

Admiral Woods had decided that the warheads would be transferred to the USS *Poughkeepsie*. Laid down in the 1960s and designated as an LSD or "landing ship dock," the

Poughkeepsie had a long helicopter deck and could accommodate over two thousand tons of cargo, the ostensible reason for its selection—though the Navy experts told Danny the ship was so old no one in the Navy would care if the nukes took her down, unlike the *Abe.*

The *Poughkeepsie,* en route from maneuvers off Africa, was not expected to be in range for more than twenty-four hours. By then, it was hoped, all of the warheads would be recovered and the Marines ready to end their operations.

Danny ambled down the narrow path to the tent area, the fatigue of the long day slowing every step. It was a good kind of tired, he thought, the kind that came from a tough but successful mission. On the other hand, tired was tired.

Dancer met him as the trail gave way to the narrow plain where the Marines had established their command area.

"You look like you could use a good home-cooked meal," she told him.

"If you're cooking, I'm eating."

"This way."

Danny tried thinking about his wife Jemma. But she was far away, and they hadn't been getting along too well anyway, and—and Dancer was right in front of him, just begging to be touched.

Somehow he managed to keep his hands to himself as she led him into the mess tent.

"Pot roast," said Dancer. "Just like mom used to make. Of course, my mom was in the Army."

She pointed at a tray of squished plastic packages containing vacuum-sealed meat and gravy—a Meals Ready to Eat version of pot roast.

"I thought you were cooking," Danny said, laughing.

"Oh, I am," said Dancer. She picked up one of the packages and dropped it into a tray of simmering water nearby.

"Lieutenant, I'm surprised at you," he said, grabbed a set of tongs and fished the package out of the water. "That's going to give it that plasticky taste. Come on. Let me show you how it's supposed to be done."

He picked up two of the packages and four metal plates, then went outside.

"Most important thing you have to do," he told Dancer as he walked away from the tents, "is find the proper location."

Danny picked a spot with a scattering of small and medium-sized rocks. He squatted down and quickly created a miniature fireplace. He made covered casserole dishes by covering a plate's worth of food with another plate and placing them over the hearth, securing the tops with small stones.

"You forgot the charcoal," said Dancer.

Danny smiled and took a pencil flare from his tac vest.

"No," said Dancer.

"Learned this in high school," he told her. He lit the flare, then set it under the pans. He arranged the rocks to help channel the heat to the food. "I was with the local ambulance squad. We used to do this when we were on standby at football games."

"You seem more like you would have been playing football than waiting for someone to get hurt."

"Couldn't play football that year," said Danny. "Bad knee. That's why I became an EMT."

"How can you parachute if you have bad knees?"

"That was my junior year. They got better."

Danny had gone on to play—and star—as quarterback the next year, and even played in college, albeit for a Division III school. But he didn't mention this to Dancer; it would sound too much like bragging.

The food had already been cooked before it was packaged, and long before the flare died out, the scent of warm meat and gravy filled the air.

"Only thing we need now is wine," he said, pulling the pans off the fire.

"Wait!" said Dancer. She turned and trotted to the mess tent.

Now he did think of Jemma—how mad she would be if

she saw him at that moment, ready to jump Dancer's bones.

If she loved him so much, why wouldn't she give up her job in New York, or at least spend more time visiting him at Dreamland?

And why didn't Jemma want kids? She wouldn't even talk about it anymore.

"Here we go," said Dancer, returning. "Best I could do."

She held up two boxes of grape juice.

"From the north side of the vineyard, I hope," said Danny.

"Nineteen ninety-eight was a very good year for concord grapes." Dancer tossed him a box. "The vintage has aged especially well since it's been boxed."

Danny laughed.

"This is good. Hot, but good," said Dancer. "The flare definitely adds something."

Before he could think of a witty reply, a sergeant approached and told them the *Lincoln* wanted to know what sort of supplies they'd need for the night.

"As much as we can get," said Dancer, getting up. "Let me go talk to them. Hate to eat and run, Captain."

Danny watched her go, unsure whether he was glad or sorry that they had been interrupted.

An atoll off the Indian coast
Date and time unknown

ZEN'S ISLAND WAS SHAPED LIKE THE SOLE OF A SHOE. HE AND Breanna had come ashore near the toe. Roughly fifty yards wide, it was crowned by a large bald rock. It was cracked and pitted severely, but porous enough that the rain that fell soon after he arrived had drained away from the narrow holes.

The rock was the high point of the island, about twelve feet above sea level. Perched atop it, Zen could see more land in the distance to the east. Whether this was another island or part of the mainland, he couldn't tell. Nor was he sure how far off it was. He guessed it was four or five miles, though it might just as well have been fifty since they were in no shape to swim it.

The heel of the atoll looked like a rock pile that had been disintegrating for decades, tumbling toward the middle of the island. It resembled a swamp, but one made of loose stone. Rocks parceled the saltwater into irregular cavities, none deeper than two feet.

Seeing some large pieces of wood on the northern shore, Zen began crawling toward them. By now his hands were covered with small scrapes and cuts. The grit on the rocks ate at his skin as he went, and he had to stop every few minutes to gather his strength and let the stinging subside.

The first piece of wood was too well wedged in the rocks for him to pull away, and he had to settle for some smaller pieces, sticks actually, that had landed nearby. He wedged them in his flight suit and crawled along the shoreline to a piece about as long as he was. There was another piece, thicker but shorter, beneath it. All of the wood was bleached white and appeared to have been there a long time.

The sun had begun to set. Zen decided it would be faster and easier for him to swim back. He dragged the wooden sticks with him but soon realized he couldn't hold it and swim at the same time. Returning to shore, he sat himself upright and reached down to his pants leg, thinking he could tear off some of his flight suit to use as a crude rope. But the flight suit was too strong to rip, so he had to resort to his knife, poking it gently against his calf and auguring a hole.

His lower leg had turned deep purple, covered almost completely by bruises.

The color shocked him. He couldn't feel anything there, but thought his legs must have been badly damaged in the crash. Deciding they needed whatever protection they could get, he pushed the pant leg down and instead undid the top portion of his flight suit so he could use his T-shirt. This was easy to rip, and he soon had the sticks tied to his wrist.

Swimming on his back, he had no trouble at first; the heavy eastward current was mitigated by a long length of stone that

jutted from the atoll and formed a protective arm. But as he
tried to turn toward the west beach where he'd left Breanna, he
found the current hard to fight. Within seconds he was being
pushed away from the island. Turning over, he began swimming with all his strength, pushing through the swells as they
beat rhythmically against his face. He managed to push himself back to the edge of the island, clinging to a rock until he
recovered enough strength to pull himself up onto shore.

By now the sun had set. In the fading twilight, he dragged
himself up the hill, trailing the wood behind him. He'd gotten no farther than halfway before it was pitch-black and he
could barely see in front him. But he wasn't about to stop. He
felt his way forward, pushing up slowly and trying to be
gentle on his legs.

It seemed to take hours before he found himself moving
downhill. The sticks made a scratching sound that was almost funny, or at least struck him that way.

Tchchhhh, tchchhh, tchchhh—a witch's broomstick dragging along the ground because she was afraid of heights.

Tchchhhh, tchchhh, tchchhh—the Jolly Green Giant, rip-
ping his pants as he walked.

Tchchhhh, tchchhh, tchchhh—the sound seemed outra-
geously funny, and he began to laugh. He was still laughing
when he reached the rocky part of the atoll, where the shadows made it almost impossible to see where the tent was. He
stared at the darkness, hoping to find some hint of the spot
before pushing down. Thinking he finally spotted it, he set
out, only to reach the water ten minutes later. He dragged
himself back up in a diagonal without any better luck.

"Bree!" he called before starting a third pass. "Bree—hey,
babe, where's our tent?"

There was no answer. Though he hadn't expected one, he
felt disappointed.

"Bree? Bree!"

Nothing.

Zen resumed his crawl. The sticks tumbled and occasionally snagged alongside him. They were no longer amusing, and he even thought of letting them go. But he kept dragging them, and finally found the pile of rocks he had set at one edge of their shelter.

Breanna was still unconscious inside. He put his head next to her face, close enough to feel her breath on his cheek. He thought she was breathing better, more deeply.

"Hey, Bree. You awake?" he whispered.

She didn't answer.

Zen laid the wood out near them. It was wet from having been in the water, and he was too tired anyway to try and start a fire; he'd do it in the morning. He made a broadcast on the radio but got no response. He repeated it again and again, but still no one answered.

It was amazing how long it had taken him to get the wood. He thought about it, trying to analyze what he might have done faster and better. Exhausted, he tried another broadcast, then crawled under the shelter, curled himself around his wife, and fell asleep.

**Southeastern Iran,
near the coast
1800 (1900, Karachi)**

"THE UNITED STATES AND SEVERAL OTHER MEMBERS OF the United Nations have launched a massive diplomatic effort aimed at both sides, trying to convince them the futility of war—"

General Mansour Sattari flipped off the television. Somehow, the Americans had actually succeeded. The Indian and Pakistani nuclear weapons had not exploded. The Americans had vaporized them without a trace!

The end of war—or so the idiotic news commentator said.

"It is good that you turn that drivel off," said someone behind him.

Surprised, Sattari turned and found Jaamsheed Pevars standing in the doorway. Pevars's face was ashen.

"I don't trust the western media," Sattari said. "It is full of lies."

Pevars waved his hand, as if warning the general away from something. Then he turned and walked from the room. Sattari followed.

Jaamsheed Pevars was the country's oil minister, and usually a most happy fellow—but then who wouldn't be if he could divert a portion of Iran's oil revenue to his own accounts? While he served the black-robed imams who ran the country, Pevars was enough of a maverick to back several alternatives, including Sattari.

The fact that the two men had gone to school in England together was, to Sattari's way of thinking, more a coincidence than a help, but it had made a certain level of intimacy possible between them.

"The American super weapon will change everything," said Pevars when they reached the small but luxuriously furnished office he kept near the front of the building. "The black robes are quaking in their shoes."

"What?"

"How does one go to war with a nation that can pulverize your weapons in midair?" Pevars shook his head. "One of the imams has already asked if you were involved."

"Me?"

Pevars shrugged. "Perhaps word of your son's operation leaked."

Sattari knew there was only one possible source of the information—Pevars himself. Undoubtedly, he had leaked word out when things looked to be going well, hoping to capitalize on the connection. Now his braggadocio and conniving meant trouble.

Not for Pevars, though. He was able to slither out of everything.

"How did the black robes find out about this?" demanded

the general. "What do they know? The submarines? The aircraft?"

"Who knows what they knew? They seem to have heard . . . rumors."

Sattari felt his anger growing. Rumors? Pevars was the only possible source.

"If the Americans have a weapon like this," Pevars continued, "the balance of power will shift again. The Chinese—*pffft*, they are nothing now."

"I would rather die than join an alliance with the Americans," said Sattari.

"Who said anything about an alliance? An alliance? No, that is not possible. Peace, though—that is a different story."

Sattari choked back his anger, trying to consider what Pevars had said. Peace with America—what did that imply? An oil agreement possibly, the sale of petroleum at some guaranteed rate.

Pevars would not be concerned about that.

Did the black robes intend to offer someone up as a chip for a new business agreement?

"I have information from the fisherman," added Pevars.

"Finally," said Sattari. The "fisherman" was one of their spies. "But why did he not send word directly to me?"

Pevars grimaced. "The submarine was captured. Two men were taken prisoner. All the others perished."

"Which others?"

Pevars did not answer.

"The fisherman said all this?"

Pevars nodded.

Was that possible? The fisherman worked for him, not Pevars.

"You're lying," said Sattari.

"No. He was afraid to tell you because it involved your son."

"You're working with the Americans, aren't you?"

"General, take hold of yourself. I know the loss of your son is a great blow. But surely he is in paradise now."

General Sattari had realized this as soon as Pevars mentioned the submarine, but the words severed the last threads of restraint on his emotions. He threw himself at Pevars, launching his body at the other man as if it were a missile.

Pevars was slight, barely over 120 pounds, and much of that weight was concentrated in a potbelly. The general weighed twice what he did, and while no longer young, his daily regimen of exercise, along with the hardships he'd endured with his soldiers over the past decade, had kept his body tough and fit. He began pummeling the oil minister, smashing his head against the thick rug and lashing it again and again with his fists. If Pevars offered any resistance, it had little impact on Sattari. He punched the oil minister over and over, beating him as a hurricane beats the shore.

Blackness filled the room. It was not darkness but the opposite—a light so harsh that it blinded Sattari. He continued to flail at Pevars, emptying decades worth of rage from his body.

When the rage lifted, Sattari found himself sitting in the hallway, his hands and clothes covered with red blood.

"The Americans did this to me." Sattari's words echoed through the marble hall. "The Americans."

He would find them, and take his revenge.

IV

New Sheriff in Town

———

Dreamland
1600, 16 January 1998

EVEN FOR A MAJOR GENERAL, GETTING TO DREAMLAND WAS not an easy task. General Samson had to first fly to Nellis Air Base, and from there arrange for a helicopter to ferry him several miles to the north. A pair of Dolphin helicopters— Americanized versions of the Aerospatiale Dauphin—were tasked as Dreamland "ferries" and used regularly by personnel trekking to the base. But Samson couldn't make the trip with the assortment of engineers and other riffraff who used the Dolphins. So a helicopter had to be found for him and the three staff members traveling with him. The chopper, in turn, needed a crew. Much to Samson's surprise, it turned out that not just any crew could be used to fly to the base; Dreamland's security arrangements were so tight that only personnel with a code-word clearance were allowed to land at the base's "dock."

The official reason for this was that planes had to cross two highly classified testing areas to get to the dock. But since clearance came from the colonel's office at Dreamland, Samson was convinced that the actual reason had to do with a personal power play on Lieutenant Colonel Bastian's part. He simmered while a crew with the proper clearance and training were found.

The idea that a lieutenant colonel—a *mere* lieutenant colonel—could effectively hold up a major general fried Samson's gizzard. He knew Bastian wasn't at the base, of course, but that was irrelevant. The lieutenant colonel undoubtedly knew that he had a good thing going here and had instituted a series of bureaucratic hurdles and practices to keep anyone from getting too close a look.

Samson's mood deepened when the helicopter ferrying him to the base was ordered to halt about fifty meters over the perimeter. And halt meant halt, not hover—the helo pilot was told to put his chopper down on the desert floor and await further instructions.

"What the *hell* is going on?" demanded Samson as the old Huey touched down.

"Orders, sir."

Samson was about to express his opinion concerning the validity of the order with several expletives when he spotted a jet making what looked like a bombing run in the distance. At first he thought the aircraft was very far away. Then he realized it was actually a miniature aircraft. It carried diminutive bombs—125-pound so-called "mini-munis" being developed to help ground soldiers in urban settings where larger bombs might cause civilian casualties.

The attack aircraft was a sleek, wedge-shaped affair, with air intakes on the top of the body and what looked like fangs at the front. These were apparently some sort of forward wing or control surface, and Samson guessed that they accounted for the airplane's twisting maneuver after the bombs were dropped—the jet veered almost straight up, dropped suddenly, and ended up backtracking on the path it had taken to the target area.

Remarkably, it seemed to do this without a noticeable loss of speed. Samson knew this was probably mostly an optical illusion—the laws of physics and aerodynamics made it impossible to completely change direction like that without losing speed—but even allowing for that, the airplane was several times more nimble than anything he had ever seen.

"General?"

Samson turned his attention back to the front of the Huey just as a mechanical voice broke into the helicopter's interphone system.

"Huey 39, you are ordered to follow Whiplash Osprey 5. No deviation from your flight path will be tolerated."

"What the hell?" said Samson. "I thought we were cleared."

"We were, but it's the way they do things," said the pilot. "Security is tight."

"Tight security is one thing—" Samson began, but before he could say anything else, a shadow descended over the front of the aircraft and their path was blocked by a black Osprey.

This was Whiplash Osprey 5, which differed from standard-issue Ospreys in several respects. Besides the black paint scheme, most noteworthy were the twin cannons mounted under the rear of the fuselage, pointed ominously at the Huey's cockpit.

A second Osprey zipped in from the rear, pulling alongside the Huey just long enough for Samson to see that it had heat-seeking missiles on its wing rails.

"Follow him," snapped Samson, folding his arms angrily.

Base Camp One,
Great Indian Desert
0600, 17 January 1998

DANNY FREAH PUSHED BACK THE SOFT CAMPAIGN CAP THE Marines had loaned him and surveyed the base area. In less than twenty-four hours the makeshift camp had swelled from a few tents in the rocky hills to a small city. Six Ospreys sat in formation on the nearby plain. Across from them, three sideless tents housed the fifteen warheads that had been re-covered thus far. Two different teams of scientists and military experts were going over the weapons, examining them before crating them for transport to the USS *Poughkeepsie*. The ship was still a good distance away, but making decent speed. Present plans were to start shipping the warheads around midnight, though there were contingencies for an earlier evac if necessary.

The nuclear devices represented a variety of technologies. Pakistan's eight were all of similar design; according to the experts, they were relatively straightforward and not large, as nukes went, though fully capable of leveling a city.

The rest of the weapons were Indian, with warheads ranging in yield from five kilotons—very small, as nukes went—to 160 kilotons, roughly the same class of explosive power as the W62 on the U.S. Minuteman III ICBM. The discovery of the latter surprised the experts; until then, it was believed that India's biggest warhead was in the fifty to sixty kiloton range.

"Penny for your thoughts," said Lieutenant Dancer as Danny contemplated how many lives the warheads would have claimed had they gone off.

"I usually get a whole dollar," he told her.

"Have to wait for payday for that." Dancer smiled at him, then shaded her eyes from the sun. Her skin looked as soft as a rose petal's. "We have the last two Pakistani warheads secured. The Ospreys are en route. Any sign of activity to the south?"

"Negative," said Danny. "Radio traffic is picking up, though."

"Mmmmm," said Dancer. She gazed toward the coast, probably thinking it would be a good thing to get the warheads out as soon as possible.

He was thinking about other things—none of which were military.

Dancer unfolded a small sketch map with an X drawn at each of the verified warhead locations. Four more warheads, all Indian, had been spotted; Dancer reviewed their locations, pointing to two at the very northern edge of her map. Six more missiles had to be found.

"The warheads at I-6 and I-8 are going to be much harder to retrieve," she told Danny. "I wonder if you'd lead that team."

"Be glad to."

The warheads she'd referred to had crashed about two hundred miles to the east in Pakistani territory. The Pakistani army had a decent-sized military post less then thirty miles away, and the Indians had an unmanned listening post ten miles south. The electronic surveillance equipment there was thought to have been fried by the T waves, but a truck was spotted in the area, and it was suspected that the Indians were working hard to get it back on line.

"You coming with us?" asked Danny.

"I have my work cut out for me here," Dancer told him. "And hopefully we'll be launching another mission as soon as the other warheads are found."

"Shame," said Danny, feeling as if he'd been turned down for a date.

White House Situation Room
2010, 16 January 1998
(0610, 17 January, Karachi)

MOST OF THOSE IN THE SITUATION ROOM REGARDED Robert Van Houton as little more than a political hack, and so eyes glazed over when he warned that China would be extremely interested in the nuclear warheads the U.S. had punched out of the sky. It didn't help that his monotone voice made it sound as if he was simply repeating vague concerns others had voiced earlier in the meeting. Even Jed Barclay, not a dynamic speaker himself, realized Van Houton wasn't coming across very well as he briefed the cabinet members on the latest developments.

"We're not going to attack the Chinese," said Defense Secretary Chastain finally.

"I'm not suggesting that," said Van Houton defensively. "What I'm saying—"

"I've spoken to Tex Woods," said Admiral Balboa. "He concurs that there's no need to get into a conflict with the Chinese. The aircraft carrier *Khan* is out of it—they can't even launch aircraft. Of course, if they attack our people, we'll defend ourselves."

"Um, it's not the *Khan* we h-h-have to worry about," said

Jed. "The Ch-Ch-Chinese may be helping terror groups."

"Not that old bugaboo," said the Secretary of State. "With all due respect, Jed, every time there's a conflict somewhere, you guys bring up terrorists. Thank you, but the Pakistanis and Indians are quite capable of blowing up the world on their own."

"There have been interceptions from the NSA," said Jed's boss, National Security Advisor Philip Freeman. "There is talk going on between some of the radical Sunni groups and the Chinese. Some of this involves the bin Laden group."

"Nonsense," said Balboa. "Navy intelligence says that's impossible. The Pakistanis think the weapons were destroyed. The terrorists take their lead from them."

"Not entirely."

"Iran is the country we have to worry about when it comes to terrorism," said Balboa. "Tell the NSA to find some evidence from that direction, and we'll bomb Tehran back to the stone age."

Vice President Ellen Christine Whiting rolled her eyes. She was chairing the meeting while the President flew to New York to address the UN.

"Anything else, gentlemen?" she asked, looking around. "The warhead removal mission is continuing, and we should have most of the warheads out by noon our time tomorrow?"

"Yes," said Jed and Balboa simultaneously.

Jed felt his face turn red. Balboa's scowl made it clear that he resented him even being here; there were no other aides at the session.

"I'm sure the President will be very pleased with this update," said Whiting. "Gentlemen, thank you for your time."

Diego Garcia
0630

IN SOME WAYS, DIEGO GARCIA WAS A HAVEN FROM THE world at large, a beautiful gem dropped in an azure sea. Palm trees swayed ever so slightly on a soft breeze, and the sand and sky made the place look more idyllic than Tahiti.

Of course, if she was going to be on an island paradise, Jennifer Gleason thought, she would have preferred being alone with her lover, rather than sharing him with a force that now topped two hundred. She also would have greatly preferred that he paid more than scant attention to her.

Her C-17 had beaten Dog's Megafortress to the island by several hours, which made it possible for her to greet him when he arrived. But instead of the joyful hug she'd envisioned—or even a lousy peck on the cheek—Dog merely grunted a hello and went off to bed.

Alone.

Now, roughly twelve hours later, he seemed more irritable than ever. He was holding court in his room, growling rather than speaking to the crews of Dreamland *Bennett* and the *Cheli*, the recently arrived EB-52.

"We don't know how long their defenses are going to be knocked out, so we have to make the most of the time we've got," said Dog. He looked up and saw her at the door. "Ms. Gleason, can we help you?"

"I brought you some coffee, Colonel."

"Thanks, I already have some."

Dog turned his attention abruptly to the others. Jennifer felt as if she'd been slapped in the face.

"I have a lot to do," she said. She squatted down and placed the cup on the floor, then walked away.

EVEN THOUGH HE HAD SLEPT FOR MORE THAN TEN HOURS after getting back to Diego Garcia, Dog felt anything but rested. He certainly had more energy, but it was an unsettled energy, vibrating wildly inside him. At the same time, his body felt as if it were a heavy winter coat wrapped tightly around him, making it harder to move.

"The rest of the missile sites are believed to be in the east," he told the others. "We'll have two missions. Number one, attempt to verify the remaining sites using the Flighthawks for low-level reconnaissance. And number two, we'll be providing air cover for the teams operating to the west of Base Camp One. The Navy planes can back us up, but they're a little too far from the *Lincoln* to stay on station around the clock. Everybody got it?"

The pilots and crewmen nodded.

"Sparks, brief us on the Anacondas," Dog said, turning the floor over to Captain Brad Sparks. The Megafortress pilot had worked extensively with the missiles during their development and testing.

"Hardest thing about using them," said Sparks, "is pressing the button."

Everyone laughed. Sparks was a bit of a cowboy and an occasional ham, but he was playing to a friendly audience.

As the briefing continued, Dog found his thoughts drifting to Breanna and Zen. They still hadn't been found. Given how much time had passed since they went out, things didn't look good.

No debris from the wreck of the plane had been found, but the Navy had investigated two slicks on the waves in the search areas. It was possible that the stricken EB-52 went straight under. But it was also possible that the plane crashed farther west of the search sites. If so, Breanna and Zen might still be alive. Dog knew that all he could do was hope for the best.

"All right," he said as the briefing broke up. "Let's get dressed and do a preflight at the hangar. We want to be in the air very quickly," he added. "So come ready to roll."

He got up from his chair, signaling the end of the meeting. As the others were filing out, he asked Lieutenant Englehardt to stay behind.

"What's up, Colonel?"

"Mike, I'm going to take the pilot's seat on the *Bennett* today."

"That's my spot."

"You slide over. Sully gets bumped," said Dog. He meant that Englehardt would sit in as copilot, with Sullivan remaining behind.

"Listen, Colonel, if you have a problem with me—"

"Why are you flying off the handle, Mike?"

"I'm not flying off the handle," said Englehardt, his voice giving lie to his words. "It's just that I figured I'd be flying this mission. I earned it."

"You're acting like a two-year-old."

"I can pilot that plane, Colonel."

"I didn't say you couldn't."

"Everybody's going to take it that way, like this is a demotion, like I'm not good enough."

"If you're so concerned about that, maybe you shouldn't be flying for Dreamland at all. Tell Sullivan he's bumped. I'll meet you at the plane."

"The hell with this."

Englehardt's face had turned red. Dog sensed the pilot knew he'd made a mistake and wanted to find a way out gracefully. Maybe on another day he might have found a way to help the younger man; he thought Englehardt was a good pilot, and though at times tentative, had a bright future. But he wasn't in a helping mood.

"You have a problem, mister?"

"Maybe Sullivan should fly instead of me, then," said Englehardt.

"Good," said Dog. He grabbed his small flight bag and strode from the room.

An atoll off the Indian coast
Time and date unknown

ZEN SLEPT LIKE A BABY, EVERYTHING AROUND HIM MUFFLED, his body surrendering to unconsciousness. He had no dreams that he could remember, and the rocks that made up his bed had no power to jab him or stick in his ribs. The makeshift tent covered him like a grave, keeping him not just from the elements, but from worries.

And then he woke.

His body felt as if it were tied up, bound in heavy cable.

He heard his wife next to him, her breaths shallow and sounding like moans.

He patted her gently, then crawled from the tent, his stomach rumbling for food.

The wood he'd brought back sat nearby, a pathetically small assortment of bleached branches and sticks. He flipped them over, hoping the sun would dry the bottom parts out better. Then he tried the radio.

"Major Stockard to any American force," he began. "Stockard to American force. I'm a crewman from Dreamland EB-52 *Levitow,* lost over the Indian peninsula, lost in the Indian Ocean."

Zen continued, giving what he thought their approximate position had been when they jumped. He repeated his message several times, pausing to hear a reply, but none came.

Was it possible that their attempt to stop the war had failed? If so, much of India and surely all of Pakistan would have been wiped out by nuclear attacks. Very possibly the U.S. and China were at war right now. And if that was true, who would hold back?

The possibilities were too awful to contemplate.

Zen knew the EEMWBs had worked; they'd lost contact with the Flighthawks the moment the missiles exploded. But he had no idea what happened afterward.

Hope for the best, plan for the worst. But what was the plan now? He was an invalid on a bleak island, alone with his unconscious, possibly dying wife.

He could give in. He could throw himself into the tide and let himself be swept away. He could give in.

But he knew that instead he'd start the fire in a few hours, once the sticks dried in the sun a bit. And try and figure out something for food in the meantime, something more filling than the few bars he'd salvaged from their survival vests.

There might be fish in the shallow water near the pinched middle of the atoll, Zen thought. If so, he could spear them with his knife, or better, kill them with rocks. He'd get a bunch of little fish and fry them in the fire.

Zen leaned back into the tent, checking on Breanna. Had he examined her for injuries when they landed? He couldn't remember now. He must have—but he couldn't remember, and so he checked again, gently loosening her flight suit, still damp, and running his hands over her skin. It was clammy and cold, sticky; it seemed to belong more to the sea than to Breanna.

There were bruises, but he didn't see any gashes, and if bones had been broken, the breaks weren't obvious.

"I'll be back," he told her after zipping her back up. "I'll be right back."

Aboard the *Abner Read*
0700

STORM PRACTICALLY DANCED A JIG AS THE OSPREY appeared over the horizon.

"All right now, men! Look alive! Jason, Josh—clear the deck there. Look alive! Look alive!"

The Osprey—a black, cannon-equipped Dreamland special operations version—swept in over the forked tail of the *Abner Read,* her arms steady. The craft matched the ship's slow pace, then began to rotate. The helipad on the *Abner Read* was tiny, and the Osprey had to face toward the stern so its cargo could be off-loaded.

The aircraft lurched to port as she descended. Storm's heart lurched with it. But the pilot quickly got it back under control, setting down on the narrow confines of the *Abner Read*'s deck.

"Very good! Very good," shouted Storm as the rear hatchway opened. "Look alive! Look alive! Let's get those missiles assembled and into the bow tubes!"

"Captain?"

Storm turned. His executive officer was standing in the portal to the robot helicopter shed, which had been cleared as a temporary loading and work area.

"Eyes. How are you feeling?"

"I'm fine, Captain."

"Ready for full duty?"

"Yes, sir."

Eyes looked like he was going to say something—an apology probably. Storm held up his hand. "No explanation necessary. We're all burning the candle at both ends."

Storm stepped back as a work crew brought the first missile crate out of the aircraft.

"What exactly are we planning to do next, Captain?" asked Eyes.

Surprised that Eyes hadn't gone back to work, Storm turned around. "Next? That's up to the Chinese."

Eyes didn't reply.

"Well, get back to your station," said Storm. "Get down to Tac. Go."

"Yes, sir."

Dreamland
1800, 16 January 1998
(0700, 17 January, Karachi)

BECOMING A CHIEF MASTER SERGEANT IN THE AIR FORCE—or achieving a similar rank in any of the services, for that matter—requires an unusual combination of skill, knowledge, hard work, and determination. A man or woman who becomes a chief arrives at that position with an impressive range of information at his or her fingertips.

Part of this is the result of sheer longevity and experience; it can accurately be said that a chief master sergeant doesn't just know where the bodies are buried, but buried a good number of them himself.

Another part is due to the network of friends, informers, and other hangers-on an enlisted man builds during his career. And, of course, initiation into the rites of chiefdom brings a new chief into contact with the elder members of the tribe, who view each new member as an important link in the chain that holds the Air Force together. Chiefs may not necessarily get along, but they can always be counted on to rally to the side of a fellow chief master sergeant in matters both large and small, aware that the cause is greater than any personal animosity.

Dreamland's administrative side was run by a chief among chiefs, Sergeant Terence Gibbs. Ax, as he was universally known, had served as Colonel Bastian's right-hand man since prehistoric times. The colonel thought he had pulled strings to get Ax transferred to Dreamland with him when he took over the command, but in truth it was Ax who pulled the string that needed to be pulled. Letting Colonel Bastian believe otherwise was a strategy Ax had taken from page one of the chief's handbook.

Though only at the base for two years, Ax knew more about Dreamland than anyone, with the possible exception of Greasy Hands Parsons, who was, after all, a fellow chief.

Ax's intelligence network extended far beyond Dreamland and even the Air Force. Information was a chief's currency, in many cases as valuable as money or even tickets to the Super Bowl—several of which Ax managed to procure and distribute each year. There was generally not a facet of Air Force life that Ax did not know once he decided it was important. He'd put considerable effort into building an efficient early warning system, capable of alerting him to the slightest pending move that would affect him or his command.

So it was amazing—dumbfounding, even—that when Major General Terrill "Earthmover" Samson (aka Terrill the Terror, in some circles) was appointed to be Dreamland's new commander, Ax did not know it until several hours after the fact. Worse—far worse, as far as he was concerned—he didn't know that Samson had decided to forgo protocol and play a surprise visit to the base several days ahead of schedule until Samson was well on his way.

In fact, Ax learned this so late that he didn't arrive at the helicopter landing strip until the general and his staff were stepping out of their helicopter under the watchful eyes of the base security team. It was an intelligence failure of monumental proportions, though Ax would not be at leisure to contemplate its implications for several hours.

"General Samson, good to see you sir," he shouted loudly. "You're, uh, several days ahead of schedule."

"I move on my own schedule," growled Samson.

"Yes, sir. Major Catsman is waiting for you." Ax stiffened and pumped a textbook salute, as stiff and proper as any he had delivered in the past ten years—which was damning with faint praise, since he had perhaps saluted twice.

Samson returned it with a scowl.

"Why isn't the major here herself, Chief?" demanded the general.

"Begging the general's pardon, but there's a Whiplash action under way. Things get a little—hectic."

Samson frowned. Ax smiled ever so faintly in response, then turned his head toward the two airmen he had shanghaied to carry the general's bags. Within a few minutes he had the security team placated and the general and his people en route to the Taj Mahal, the nickname for the base's administrative center.

Samson's arrival at the Taj caused another stir. In order for him and his aides to tour the base, biometric measurements and readings had to be taken from all of them. Samson balked, saying it was a waste of his time.

"Only about ten minutes per person," said Ax. "It's standard procedure."

"Do you get major generals visiting this base often?"

"We've had a few," said Ax.

Samson started for the elevator that stood at the center of the lobby. He got in, as did his aides. Ax stayed in the lobby.

"The thing is, sir, if you're not in the computer, it won't allow you access. You can get in the elevator car, but it won't go down. And now that you're in there, it won't move until you're out. I can get this straightened out."

Samson didn't believe Ax until he had pressed all of the buttons and nothing happened.

"It will only take a few minutes," said Ax. "If you'll just come over to the security station . . ."

Samson stalked over to Security, nearly as angry as he'd been at the landing dock. His aides followed.

Or attempted to.

"I'm afraid—and no offense, sirs," said Ax, making sure to spread one of his better chief's smiles across the arrayed majors and captains, "under a Whiplash order, you're supposed to be confined to the non, um, technical parts of the base. Strictly speaking, you shouldn't even be here in the Taj. We can do some temporary passes, but your access is going to be limited."

"What the hell kind of rule is that?" said Samson.

"Begging the general's pardon, but it would be a similar situation if somehow a busload of visitors had deposited themselves into his F-111 cockpit during his mission over Hanoi as a captain. Or when he personally led the squadron over Panama. The general would have been so busy dealing with the enemy, that even the presence of well-meaning onlookers, no matter their rank, would have been a distraction."

Samson frowned. For a moment Ax wondered if he had found the proverbial exception to the old chiefs' rule that it was impossible to lay it on too thick for a general.

"All right," said Samson finally. "Let's get the lay of the land for now," he added, speaking to his entourage. "Stay wherever you're supposed to stay."

The men nodded in unison, as if their heads were connected by hidden wires.

"As for this other thing, though," said the general, to Ax again, "I don't see the purpose."

Ax finally realized why Samson was objecting to the biometric recordings.

"The process, General, is pretty straightforward. You step into a small booth and the computer takes its readings. No human intervention. The information is encrypted right away, and isn't even accessible to the operator. Security precaution, in case someone was trying to duplicate your biometrics."

"Well, let's get on with it, then," said Samson.

"Step over this way, sir," said one of the security sergeants, leading Samson to a spot on the floor where a laser and weight machine would record his measurements.

Lieutenant Thomson pulled Ax aside.

"Why'd you say that about the operator? He can see the measurement. What would be the sense of hiding it?"

"General's getting sensitive about his weight," whispered Ax. "Too many nights on the chicken and peas circuit."

**Aboard Dreamland *Bennett*,
over the Indian Ocean
0800**

NO MATTER HOW MUNDANE THE MISSION, HOW ROUTINE THE flight, flying an aircraft always gave Dog a thrill. It was the one thing he could count on to raise his heartbeat, the jolt that pushed him no matter how straight and slow the flight. Whether it was a Cessna or an F-22 Raptor, simply folding his fingers around the control yoke of an aircraft filled Tecumseh Bastian with a quiet passion.

He was going to need it. He sensed that the crew resented his replacing their captain. They were too well disciplined and professional to do anything to jeopardize their mission, of course, and Dog knew that he could rely on them to do their best when and if things got hot. But the quick snap in their voices when he asked a question, the forced formality of their replies, the lack of takers when he offered to get coffee and doughnuts from the galley—a thousand little things made it clear that he might have their respect and cooperation, but not their love.

Then again, in his experience, love could be overrated.

"Flighthawks ready to start their pass," reported the co-pilot, Lieutenant Sullivan.

"Roger that. Flighthawk leader, proceed."

"Thanks, Colonel," said Starship downstairs. "I hope we'll find something."

"Me too."

They had laid out their course north through the search area where Breanna and Zen were thought to have parachuted, hoping to put the long leg to some use.

It had been Englehardt's suggestion.

"Flighthawks are at fifty feet, indicated," said Sullivan. "Ocean appears empty, as indicated by radar."

Was Breanna really gone? Dog struggled to push away the feeling of despair. He had a job to do. He couldn't afford a moment of weakness.

"How are we looking, Airborne?" he said, trying to focus on his mission.

"Only friendlies, Colonel," said Sergeant Rager at the airborne radar.

"Very good," said Dog.

"Waymarker in zero-one minute," said Sullivan, noting they were approaching a turn that would take them away from the search area. "Colonel, you want to extend the search?"

For the first time since they'd boarded the plane, Sullivan's voice sounded almost normal.

"Much as I'd like to, Sully, I'm afraid we have other business," said Dog. "Starship, we're coming up to our turn."

Dreamland
1930

"GENERAL, I'D HEARD YOU WOULD BE VISITING SOMETIME next week."

"You heard wrong," snapped Samson. He frowned at the scrawny major, then looked past her toward the massive screen at the front of the room. According to the legend, the display showed a swath of land in Pakistan as it was being surveyed in real time by one of Dreamland's Flighthawks.

The scale and clarity were unlike anything Samson had ever seen, even at the Pentagon. He could literally count blades of tumbleweed, or whatever the desert vegetation was called.

"This is part of the search for the disabled warheads," added the major. "We're providing assistance to the team assembled by the Seventh Fleet."

"Yes," said Samson. He turned his attention to the rest of the situation room, which the Dreamlanders called Dreamland Command. Workstations were set up theater style, descending down both sides of a center ramp toward the screen. Each desk was big enough for five or six operators, though in no case were there more than two people working at them. Most had a single person. With only two exceptions, the operators wore civilian clothes, appeared less than kempt, and were clearly not military—including a gorgeous blonde Samson had trouble taking his eyes off of.

No wonder Bastian wanted to keep this all to himself, he thought. The place was the military equivalent of the world's biggest entertainment center.

"With all due respect, sir," said a tall, skinny man in a tone that suggested exactly the opposite, "I'd request that you didn't look too closely at the displays or question the scientists."

"You'd request what?"

"Frankly, you shouldn't be in this room at all, not during a mission."

"Who the hell are you?"

The man fidgeted, his fingers moving up to his earlobe nervously. Samson was startled to see that he had an earring there.

An earring!

And *he* was trying to kick *him* out?

"Who are you?" demanded Samson again.

"Ray Rubeo. I'm the head scientist. And I'm afraid that while your security clearance may allow you to observe the operations themselves, it does not cover the specific weapons that are being tested as part of the operations. As a result—"

"Weapons tests?"

Rubeo frowned at him. "General, you really should leave. This is not a good time."

"Now listen, mister—" began Samson.

"That would be *Doctor*."

"I don't give a shit if you're a brain surgeon." Samson turned to Catsman. "Major, what the hell is this?"

"Ordinarily, no one is permitted inside Dreamland Command during an operation," she said.

"I'm your new commander. Do you understand what that means?"

"I didn't mean—"

"If you're interfering with the mission," said Rubeo, "you're going to have to leave. The President controls Whiplash missions once the order is given, not the Air Force."

"Who made that rule up? Bastian?"

"The procedures predate him," said Rubeo testily. "Check Presidential Order 92-14."

Samson turned to Catsman, whose face had turned crimson.

Samson folded his arms, trying to control his anger. He was tempted—sorely tempted—to have the room cleared. But interfering with the mission was the last thing he wanted to do—especially since he could then be blamed for anything that went wrong. He forced himself to be silent, and stayed just long enough to keep his dignity and authority intact. Then with an abrupt "Carry on," he left the room.

An atoll off the Indian coast
Date and time unknown

THE SHALLOW WATER AT THE WEST OF THE ATOLL DIDN'T seem to hold any fish. As he moved toward the southern end of the atoll, Zen spotted some seaweed growing a few feet from the sand. He pushed into the water and got a surprise— one of the rocks began to move.

It was a turtle, about two feet long, with a brown and white oval-shaped shell. Zen froze for a moment, unsure what to do. By the time he had unsheathed his knife, the turtle was gone.

There must be more turtles here, he thought. Or maybe some fish this one was feeding on.

Zen stopped moving and focused on the water. When he was sure there was nothing in front of him but seaweeds and rocks, he moved to his left, pushing through the water gingerly.

Nothing.

The most difficult part of being a fisherman was patience. Zen had the patience of a fighter pilot—which was to say, none.

He slid onto his side, pushing along in the water. Something moved to his right. He leaned over toward it.

Another turtle, this one only twelve or fourteen inches.

Zen swatted at it with his knife, but the creature dove away. Mud and rocks swirled up in a cloud. He fished in the water, then pulled back as the turtle's beak suddenly appeared.

The turtle squirted away. Zen lunged and managed to get his left hand under it. He flung it upward, sending it crashing against a group of rocks closer to shore.

Pulling himself through the rocks and water as the turtle flailed upside down, he raised his knife, then stopped, paralyzed by the small creature's struggle. Then his own instinct for survival took over and he plunged the knife straight down into the underside of the turtle's shell.

The blade penetrated, but the turtle continued to struggle. It snapped its beak wildly, cutting the air as if it were its enemy.

Zen tried to pull the knife from the turtle but it was stuck. Unsure what to do, he let go of the knife. When he did, the creature slipped off into the water. Zen grabbed the handle of the knife as the turtle sank and threw the creature, blade and all, onto the rocks. It landed sideways, propped there, still struggling when he reached it.

Dazed and confused, its life ebbing, the turtle craned its neck in the direction of the water. Zen circled behind the animal, then took hold of its leg, dragging it farther ashore. The leg felt slimy and cold. It was a live thing, pushing against him, and once again Zen was paralyzed.

But he had to eat, and so did Bree. He picked up the leg and dashed the turtle against the rocks, smacking it so hard the shell cracked open. Then he grabbed a nearby rock and pounded it on the hilt of his knife, driving the weapon into the animal. Finally the creature stopped struggling, its life over.

Exhausted, Zen let the rock drop from his hand. Then he turned his attention back to the water, wondering if it might be possible to swim back to the pup tent rather than crawl.

As he did, something caught his eye.

A small boat was approaching, less than a hundred yards away.

**Dreamland
1945**

MAJOR CATSMAN AND THE SMILING CHIEF MASTER SERGEANT tried to placate General Samson, suggesting he try dinner in the VIP dining room, but Samson wasn't buying the bullshit they were selling. He was filled with rage toward the arrogant and ignorant scientist who'd threatened to have him booted—*booted!*—from Dreamland Command.

Undoubtedly this had been done at Colonel Bastian's behest, Samson thought, since it was inconceivable that a mere civilian scientist would have the audacity.

What really irked him, however, was the fact that the military people hadn't intervened. The world had truly turned upside down here.

Samson had thought that there might be room for Bastian under his command. Clearly, that was not going to work. The incident in Dreamland Command aside, Bastian's outsized ego was on clear display when Samson entered his office.

It was outfitted with well-polished cherry furniture fit for a king.

"When I was a lieutenant colonel," muttered Samson to his aides as he surveyed the office, "I had a tin desk."

"Begging the general's pardon," said Ax. "The colonel inherited this from the last commander, who was a major general. Rather than—"

"He's disinherited. As of now, this is my office."

"You're moving in?" said Catsman.

"Major, what did you think my purpose in arriving here today was?" said Samson. Catsman was also high on his list of people to be replaced.

"Sir, we were under the impression—"

"Which impression is that?" thundered Samson.

Catsman seemed lost for words. "General Magnus, when he was in your position—"

"General Magnus had many things on his plate," said Samson. "I am not him. Dreamland is my baby now. I saw no reason to wait several weeks before coming out here."

"Well no, sir. I wouldn't expect you to."

Samson turned to Ax. "Find some men to move Bastian's things to a secure location."

"Uh . . ."

"How long have you been a chief master sergeant, Mr. Gibbs?"

"We'll get right on it, General."

Maybe he can stay, thought Samson. Having someone around who knew where all the latrine keys were kept might be handy.

WHILE IT WAS OFTEN SAID THAT THE WHEELS OF GOVERNMENT moved slowly, Major General Terrill Samson did not. Even though it was nearly midnight back in Washington, he got on the phone and did what he could to kick the paperwork into gear to move the transition forward and, most important, update the Whiplash order so it named him personally.

Then he decided to call the National Security Advisor personally to discuss his new command. If Bastian could work closely with the White House, so could he.

Thinking he would simply leave a message with the overnight staff, Samson was surprised to find that Freeman was working. But as soon as he was put through, he was met with more questions than answers.

"How many warheads have been recovered?" demanded Freeman. "What's the status?"

"I'm not up-to-date on all of the operational details," said Samson, caught off guard. "Generally, I let my people in the field—I give them full rein."

"Well, when are we getting an update? I realize Colonel Bastian is busy, but the President needs to know. He's addressing the General Assembly at the UN first thing in the morning."

"Understood."

"The President wants every warhead recovered. We want that accomplished before news of the operation leaks. It has to proceed quickly."

"Of course," said Samson. "I can assure you we're working on it. We're going to do it."

"Good."

"There is one thing," said Samson. He told Freeman, as delicately as he could manage, that some "legal types" had advised him that Whiplash orders should be directed to him so that the proper chain of command could be followed. This would facilitate the process—"speed up the operation," said Samson.

"Why is that an issue at this moment?" said Freeman.

"It's not an issue," said Samson quickly. "Legal types, though—you know the red tape that can get involved."

"Dreamland is about avoiding red tape."

"Exactly."

"I'll look into having the order reissued," said Freeman. "If it's necessary."

"I'm told it is. The lawyers—if you could have my name there specifically, instead of Bastian's . . ."

"I'll have someone work on it," said Freeman.

Aboard Dreamland *Bennett*,
over the Indian Ocean
1100

"*HAWK TWO* REFUELED," STARSHIP SAID, PULLING THE RObot aircraft away from her mother ship.

As far as the pilot was concerned, the differences between the first generation and the upgraded U/MF-3D Flighthawks were generally subtle. The increased controllable range was the most noticeable change; depending on the altitudes, and to a lesser extent the atmospheric conditions, the Flighthawk could now operate at full throttle two hundred nautical miles from the Megafortress. The autonomous programming had also been improved, allowing the pilot to tell the computer to attack an opponent beyond the controllable range, then rendezvous along a vector or at a specific GPS point. The Flighthawk's ground attack modes had also been upgraded, as had its capacity to carry small bombs and ground-attack missiles, a capability jury-rigged into the earlier models.

But it was still a robot. As Starship steered his two Flighthawks over the Indian desert toward their designated search area in Pakistan, he found himself longing to be behind the stick of a *real* airplane, like the F/A-18 he'd flown down to Diego Garcia in.

Robot planes were the future of the Air Force. But they just didn't give you the same kick in the pants the heavy metal did.

He brought *Hawk Two* down through a thin deck of clouds, accelerating as he pushed toward a thousand feet. They were nearing the northern edge of a search zone designated as

I-17, after the warhead that supposedly had crashed here. He was over Pakistan, and though marked on the maps as desert, the area was far from uninhabited. He saw a cluster of small houses on his left as he leveled off. There was no activity, however; he was in the zone affected by the T-Rays.

Starship checked quickly on *Hawk One*, which was flying an automated search pattern to the west. That area was much more desolate, without even a highway in sight as the Flighthawk trundled along at five hundred feet, moving at just under 200 knots.

Unlike Zen, Starship preferred controlling the Flighthawks from the standard control panels rather than using one of the flight helmets. He could see more at a glance, and had no trouble zoning out the rest of the noise around him.

He punched a preset to flip his main screen back to *Hawk Two,* then nudged the joystick to nose the aircraft downward. Just as he dropped through six hundred feet he spotted what looked like a large skid mark in the earth about five hundred yards to his right. The computer flagged it as well, sounding a tone in his headset.

Starship leaned *Hawk Two* gently onto her right wing, dropping his speed as he headed for the end of the ditch. He was moving too fast, however, and before he could get a good look was beyond his target. He came back around, lower and slower, and this time saw what looked like a garbage can half wedged in the earth.

"Colonel, I have something."

"Roger that, Flighthawk leader. Give us the GPS points."

Starship tapped the object on the screen, locking the data into the computer before transferring it. He put *Hawk Two* into an orbit around the warhead, then took control of *Hawk One* to begin a new search.

"Looking good, Starship," said Dog a few minutes later. "Dreamland Command confirms that's warhead I-17. One down, five to go."

On the ground in southeastern Pakistan
1120

"WE'RE JUST ABOUT WRAPPED UP HERE, COLONEL," SAID Danny, using his portable mike pack instead of bothering with the smart helmet. "We should be leaving for I-8 in about thirty minutes."

"We've found I-17," Dog told him. "It's a little farther north than the projections show. There are some settlements nearby."

Danny checked the paper map as well as his global positioning device. The device had been found about twenty miles outside of the projected landing points, the first time the projections had been wrong.

It looked to him as if the villages could be easily avoided. However, there was a highway just a mile northwest of the site; they'd be in full view when they landed.

Danny debated whether they could afford to wait until nightfall, when villagers would be less likely to interfere. Weighed against that was the possibility that the warhead might be discovered before they got there.

Since it was close to the village, it seemed likely that someone had already seen it. The area was in the zone affected by the T-Rays, and isolated to begin with. Maybe the villagers had no one to tell.

"I think we're best off sticking with the present plan, and go after I-17 at dusk," Danny finally told the colonel. "Would it be possible to keep it under surveillance in the meantime?"

"Doable."

"One other thing, Colonel—I'm wondering if we could bring up a few more men from the Whiplash detail, along with more of our gear. The Marines are great, but they're stretched kind of thin. Admiral Woods wants everything found and out ASAP."

"We only have three men to run security at Diego Garcia as it is," said Dog.

"The only thing they're doing there is watching the lizards."

Dog knew that it wasn't quite the no-brainer Danny made it out to be. While Diego Garcia was among the most secure bases in the world, some of the gear the EB-52s carried was so classified the Navy security people would not be authorized to enter the hangars. While the chances of a problem were remote, any resulting security violation would have severe consequences for the commander.

"All right," said Dog finally. "Get them up there."

"Thanks, Colonel."

An atoll off the Indian coast
Date and time unknown

THE BOAT WAS SURPRISINGLY SMALL, MORE LIKE A LOG IN the water than a canoe. Zen flattened himself on the rocks, watching as it made its way across the shallow lagoon toward the area where he'd spotted the first turtle. Whoever was in the boat didn't seem to notice him.

He considered slipping into the water but decided that he'd make too much noise. There was no way to escape—unless he was extremely lucky, eventually he would be spotted.

He'd never done very well depending on sheer luck to get by. And maybe he wanted to be found. He needed to get help for Breanna. No one was answering his radio hails; the person in the boat was the only alternative.

The Megafortress had been attacked by Indian planes and missiles, but maybe they thought they were going after a Chinese or Pakistani aircraft. The military wasn't necessarily antagonistic toward Americans; on the contrary, the Indians had often helped U.S. forces, at least before this conflict.

Maybe the person in the boat would be friendly. Maybe the Indians didn't hate Americans and this Indian could be persuaded to contact someone without telling the authorities.

But he knew it didn't matter, because Breanna was going to die if he didn't get help.

She might even already be dead.

Zen shook his head, chasing the idea away. Then he stood.

"Hey!" he yelled, waving his hand. "Hey! Over here!"

The figure in the boat turned his head in Zen's direction, but the boat kept moving, crossing in front of him.

"Hey," repeated Zen. "Help," the word "Help" coming from his mouth as a bare whisper.

He was too proud to ask for help, too proud to admit defeat.

Breanna would die because of his ego.

"Hey!" Zen yelled. *"Help! Help!"*

The boat slowed, then began to turn in his direction. The oarsman was short, small—young, Zen realized, a teenager or even younger.

Zen pushed himself around and sat, arranging his useless but bruised and bloodied legs under him. They seemed to ache ever so faintly. He hadn't experienced the phenomenon in quite a while. He'd been told it had to do with reflex memory stored deep in his brain and nerve cells.

The boat was so shallow it got within a foot or two of the shoreline before beaching. A boy of perhaps nine or ten knelt in the bottom. His oar looked more like a battered stick than a paddle. He stared silently at Zen, perhaps five yards away.

"Hello," said Zen. "Can you help me?"

The boy looked at him quizzically.

"Do you speak English?" asked Zen. He'd assumed that everyone in India did, though this was not actually true. "English?"

The boy nudged his stick against the rocks but did not reply.

"I'm American," said Zen. "USA."

"Sing sons?" asked the boy.

Zen didn't understand.

"I'm a pilot. My plane had trouble and crashed," he said. "I—there's another pilot. We need to contact our base."

"Singsons? Simsons."

"You mean the TV show?" asked Zen. *"The Simpsons*?"

"You know Simpsons?"

"Bart Simpson?"

The boy's eyes grew wide. "You know Bart Simpson?"

"Watch him all the time."

"Bart?"

"We're good friends," said Zen. "Can you help me?"

The young man looked at Zen suspiciously, then jabbed his stick against the rocks and quickly pushed away.

"Hey, come back," said Zen. "Don't go. Don't go."

But the kid had already turned around and was speeding away.

"Well, that worked," muttered Zen. "Maybe I should have told him Homer was my uncle."

Dreamland Command
2300

RAY RUBEO GOT DOWN ON HIS KNEES SO HE COULD GET closer to the computer screen.

"You're sure this is where they discovered warhead I-17?" he asked.

"That's the GPS reading from the Flighthawk," the operator told him. "I verified it off the Megafortress."

"You look like you're praying, Ray," said Major Catsman, coming down the ramp toward him.

"I may be, Major." Rubeo frowned at the map. "We've found one warhead outside of the search parameters."

"And?"

Rubeo sighed. There was no explaining things to some people.

"It's not possible for it to be outside of the search area," he told Catsman, rising.

"Well, obviously it is."

"Yes. That's my point," said Rubeo. "What we have here is all math—Newton's laws applied. We know exactly where the missiles should have fallen if the T-Rays worked as we think they did. So the only possible conclusion is that the T-Rays did not work in that manner. The T-Rays must not have disabled all the systems on the missing missiles. My guess is that the engines didn't shut down when we believed they did."

"Are you sure?"

"It will be useful to examine the missile at I-17," said Rubeo. "Maybe there is some shielding of some components and not others. Perhaps the T-Rays do not work as we believe they do. There is always a distance between theory and reality, Major. The problem is to measure that distance."

"What do you suggest?"

"I'd like one of our people to look at it closely." Rubeo picked at his earlobe.

"Danny Freah will be securing it."

"With all due respect to Captain Freah, I don't believe his expertise lies in the area of electronics. I was thinking of Ms. Gleason. She is twiddling her thumbs on Diego Garcia. She would be of more use there."

"All right." Catsman folded her arms. "Did you have to piss General Samson off so completely, Ray? Couldn't you have been just a little more polite?"

"I don't do polite."

"You should learn," said Catsman, turning away.

Diego Garcia
1300

JENNIFER GLEASON TAPPED GENTLY ON THE SMALL LAPTOP as she rose. Wires snaking from the computer connected to a missile a few feet away. Tom Crest, one of the weapons engineers on the Anaconda team, looked up from one of the circuit boards in the warhead assembly.

"Still?" he asked.

"The anomaly is still there," said Jennifer. "Even though the circuit checks out at spec on the bench, you're getting some sort of error that has to be coming from the hard-ware."

"I'll be damned if we can find it. It doesn't come up more than one time out of a thousand." Crest got up from the missile. "Jeez, it's hot. You mind?"

He put his thumbs under the bottom of his T-shirt, gesturing.

"Go ahead and take it off," said Jennifer. "If you don't think you'll get sunburned."

"Nah." Crest pulled his shirt off, revealing a surprisingly tan and fit torso. For an engineer, Jennifer thought, he was pretty good-looking.

Not that she was looking.

"I wonder if maybe one of the software revisions on the microcode was done erroneously," she said. "You've checked everything else."

"That was checked weeks ago."

"Maybe the check was wrong. You've looked at everything else."

"Looking at it again could take a couple of days."

Jennifer shrugged. She was about to volunteer to do it when the trill of a bike bell caught her attention. She turned around and saw Sergeant Lee Liu approaching on one of the Dreamland-issue mountain bikes the Whiplashers were using to patrol the area.

"Jen, Major Catsman needs to talk to you right away."

"Really? OK." Jennifer shaded her eyes. "Any word on Zen and Breanna?"

Liu shook his head. "Sorry. Hop on and I'll give you a ride to the Command trailer."

"Where am I going to get on?"

"You can sit on the handlebars."

Jennifer eyed the bike dubiously.

"Only take us a few minutes," said Liu.

"All right. But look out for the bumps."

RAY RUBEO, NOT MAJOR CATSMAN, GREETED JENNIFER when she arrived at the Dreamland Command trailer.

"I hope you are enjoying your South Pacific sojourn," said Rubeo testily.

"Fun in the sun, Ray. Wish you were here."

"We have a real job that needs to be done."

Rubeo explained what had happened with the warhead located at I-17, and its implications.

"Twenty miles is only a four percent error," said Jennifer. "That's not off that much."

"The search areas are twenty-five percent larger than the formulas calculated," said Rubeo. "Which means that the missile traveled *considerably* farther than should be possible. It is far beyond the likely error rate."

"Maybe the formula's wrong."

"Don't you think I considered that possibility?"

It was a sharp response, out of character even for Rubeo.

Jennifer asked what was wrong. The scientist's frown only deepened. Instead of answering, he changed the subject.

"The Whiplash team is going to recover the weapon in a few hours. It needs to be examined by someone with expertise," said Rubeo.

"I'll get up there as soon as I can."

"When?"

"Soon, Ray. Relax."

"That does not seem possible," he said, and the screen blanked.

Jennifer got up from the communications desk and walked over to Sergeant Liu in the trailer's common area. "How soon will the Whiplash Osprey be back?" she asked.

"Not for several hours," said Liu. "What's up?"

"I need to get up to the border area between India and Pakistan to look at a weapon with Captain Freah. I'd like to be up there in a couple of hours."

"Couple of hours can't be done," said Liu. "But I do know how you can get up there just after nightfall. If you're willing."

"Tell me."

"The ride will be a little, er, bumpy."

"It can't be as bad as the bike ride," said Jennifer. "I'm all ears."

An atoll off the Indian coast
Date and time unknown

ZEN DIDN'T KNOW WHAT SORT OF FISH LIVED IN THIS PART OF the ocean, but he did know that sharks were spread out across the globe. He knew too that they had an incredible sense of smell, and would come from miles away to strike bloodied prey.

He also knew that with the sun sliding low in the sky, there was no way he'd make it back to the tent before it got too dark to see, if he crawled over land. Swimming might take an hour at most; it was a risk he was going to have to take.

He pulled the knife from the turtle's shell and held it in his teeth, ready to use. Then he pushed his way down to the water. Positioning himself at the edge of the water, he took a breath and started to swim. He held the turtle in his left hand, closest to the open sea, and stayed in water as shallow as possible. At times he felt his legs dragging against the rocks.

Except, of course, he didn't. Because he couldn't feel anything in his legs.

He pushed as well as swam, stopping several times because the knife made it difficult to breathe. He was nearly back to the tent where he'd left Breanna when he heard the voice calling to him over the waves.

"Friend! Friend of Bart! Where are you?"

He stopped paddling for a moment, listening as the voice called for him again.

Should he go back? Was it a trap?

Unsure, he decided his first priority was getting the dead turtle back to the tent. He took a few more strokes, then beached himself for good, crawling out of the water with the turtle, a little worse for wear but still intact. Even as he pulled the animal onto the rocks, he worried a shark would rise up and snatch it from him, *Jaws*-style.

Zen slipped the knife in his belt and pushed up the rocks toward the tent. He had to stop twice, exhausted, to gather his breath. Finally, when he was about twenty feet from the tent, he looked up and saw a figure standing next to it.

"Bree!" he shouted.

Then he realized the figure was too skinny and short to be his wife. It held up a stick.

"Who are you?" he demanded, sliding his hand down to the knife.

"Whoareya?" said the figure.

"Simpsons?" asked Zen.

The figure took a step closer, coming out of the shadow. It was a kid, though not the same one he had seen earlier. He was older, a little bigger. He held the stick out menacingly, as if it were a spear.

"Who are you?" asked the youth.

"Hey, where's your friend?" Zen asked. "The Bart Simpson fan?"

The boy didn't say anything.

"Did he tell you I know Bart Simpson?"

There was a shout from behind Zen. He whirled, the knife out and ready.

It was the boy he'd seen earlier.

"You *do* know Bart Simpson?" said the kid.

"My best friend."

The other kid shouted something and pointed. It took Zen a few seconds to realize he was pointing at the turtle.

"Food," said Zen, gesturing at the dead animal. "I'm going to start a fire."

Both kids started talking at once, first in a language he couldn't recognize, then in English. Gradually, they made him understand that they had come to the island to hunt for turtles and wanted his.

While the two kids spoke English, Zen had trouble understanding their accents.

"The turtles have to be bigger," said the younger boy.

"We take," said the older boy.

"I don't think so," Zen told him.

The boy came down and grabbed at the turtle. Zen pulled it toward him. The kid started talking rapidly, and Zen couldn't understand.

"We need," said the younger boy finally. "You give."

"Why do you need it?" asked Zen.

He couldn't understand the answer. The turtle had been difficult to capture and kill, and Zen was hardly confident he could get another. But simply turning the boys away would be foolish.

"If I give it to you, can you bring me a cell phone?" said Zen.

Now it was the boys who didn't understand.

"Phone," said Zen. He mimicked one. "T-r-rring-ring."

"Phone," said the younger boy.

"Yes. Can you bring me one?"

"Phone."

"I give you the turtle, you give me a phone."

"Phone, yes," said the older boy.

It seemed to be a deal. By now it was getting dark, and the boys managed to explain to him that they had to leave. They told him that they would be back the next day.

Or at least he thought that's what they said.

As soon as he gave them the turtle, they lit out for the eastern side of the island, where they had apparently left their boats. Zen immediately regretted the deal, sensing he'd been gypped. But there was nothing he could do about it now. He checked on Breanna, still sleeping fitfully, then retrieved the stick the older boy had tossed aside, and with it and the driftwood he'd gathered the day before he managed to start a small fire.

A strong foreboding overcame him as he went to Breanna, intending to pull her a little closer to the fire. He closed his eyes as he crawled the last few feet, fearing he would find her dead.

She was still breathing, more rhythmically it seemed to him.

"Can you feel the fire here?" he asked her.

She made no sign that she heard.

"Come on down with me a little. It'll warm you up a bit. Just a bit."

He cradled her upper body on his lap and pushed closer to the fire. It wasn't much, but he could feel the warmth, and hoped she could too.

Zen told his wife about the boys. "Funny that they know the Simpsons, huh? I told them I'm Bart's best friend. Maybe they'll come back for an autograph."

He remembered the radio. He hadn't broadcast all day.

He reached into his pocket for Breanna's watch to check the time, but it wasn't there.

Had he put it in his other pocket? He swung his body around and reached to his left.

It wasn't there either. He began to search feverishly, sure it was somewhere in his flight suit—then not sure. Had he left it in the tent? Given it back to Breanna? Where was it?

Where the hell was it?

It's the little things that make you crazy.

Zen heard the voice, but he knew it was only in his head— a snatch of a memory, part of a lecture someone had given during his survival training. The point had been: Don't obsess over things that aren't important.

He didn't need a watch. Time was irrelevant. They'd be listening for him around the clock.

Zen went to the radio and made several calls, but there was no answer, and even the static sounded far away.

Tired, he poked at the fire. It was dark, and with the embers glowing a faint orange, he huddled around his wife and drifted off to sleep.

Southeastern Pakistan
1900

DANNY FREAH STUDIED THE IMAGE FROM THE I-17 LANDING zone in his smart helmet, mentally plotting the Ospreys' ingress into the site. They had just swung south of the nearest village and were about ten minutes from the landing area.

"When you make your cut north," he told the Osprey pilot, bending down over the console that separated the two aviators at the front of the aircraft, "you have a straight run to the target. There's a slight rise to the road. It looks like there's a high spot overlooking it and the missile as well."

Unlike the Dreamland birds, the Marine Ospreys weren't set up to receive the video image. Once they got close, though, their forward looking infrared radar would provide a good view.

The pilot put up his hand, gesturing to Danny that they were now five minutes from the landing zone.

"Clean," said Danny.

Behind him the Marines got ready to hit the dirt. Even though this was the third warhead they'd recovered today, the men still tensed as they gathered near the door. Danny could smell the sweat as their adrenaline picked up and they got ready to go.

The Ospreys bucked slightly as they pitched toward the ground. The rear ramp opened and the Marines swarmed over the desert, anxious ants swarming an abandoned picnic basket.

Danny had Starship give him the widest possible view of the area from the Flighthawk; after making sure it was clean, he tapped the pilot on the shoulder and went to join the men as they took control of the area. Two fire teams ran full throttle to the highway, moving in opposite directions so they could observe and stop any traffic if necessary. Four men went toward the village, setting up a post where they could watch for anyone approaching them.

"Secure, Captain," said the ranking Marine NCO, a gunnery sergeant named Bob McNamera, who, like gunnery sergeants throughout the Corps, was called Gunny. "Ready to take a look at our Easter egg?"

"Let's get a look," said Danny, starting toward the warhead.

It was larger than the last two. Much of the fairing was burnt, and the ground around it was scorched. Bits and pieces of rocket were scattered behind it in an extended starburst pattern.

"This one's a different missile than the others," Danny told Dreamland Command as he scanned the area with his smart helmet's built-in camera. "Bigger."

"Very good," replied Ray Rubeo over the satellite connection.

"Different procedure for disarming?"

"We're determining that right now, Captain. What exactly is the ETA of Ms. Gleason to the site?"

"Huh?"

"When is Ms. Gleason expected to arrive?"

"Ms. Gleason *isn't* expected to arrive."

Rubeo cleared his throat, then explained that Jennifer Gleason was en route with the rest of the Whiplash ground team.

"Are you kidding?" Danny said. "They're supposed to parachute into our camp in India an hour from now."

"It would be useful for Ms. Gleason to join you at the scene," said Rubeo. "Sooner rather than later."

"Who told her she could do a night jump?"

"Who tells Ms. Gleason she can do anything?"

**Aboard MC-17 *Quickmover*,
over northwestern India
1955**

"CHANGE IN PLANS, JEN," SAID SERGEANT LIU AFTER HE clambered down the ladder from the cockpit area. "We're going to go out a bit farther north than originally planned."

"OK," she answered, gripping her jump helmet. She was sitting with the other Whiplashers on a row of plastic fold-down seats at the side of the large cargo hold. The big aircraft was empty except for a small pallet of gear that would be dropped with the team.

"You sure you don't want to hitch up?" Liu asked.

"I hate tandem jumps," she said.

"It's a high altitude jump at nighttime."

"I'm Army qualified, Sergeant."

Liu gave her a dubious look, but it was true. A year before, she had suffered the ignominy of a tandem jump into Iran. She liked the excitement of parachuting, but didn't like being tethered to someone else. So she'd gone to the trouble of completing a parachute course with a former Army Ranger and master combat jumper.

"Qualified" was a relatively low standard—a soldier could earn the basic Army parachutist badge with five jumps, only one of which was at night. Liu and his men would do five jumps in a single day just to stay sharp. And HALO jumps— high altitude, low opening—weren't even part of the program.

"I've had three night jumps, all with more gear than I'm carrying now," added Jennifer, sensing Liu's objections. "And I've done thirty jumps, including three HALO. OK? So I don't need a keeper."

"Hey, I jumped with her, Nurse," said Sergeant Geraldo "Blow" Hernandez. Blow was also the team jumpmaster. "She's got the goods."

"Thank you, Sergeant."

"It's gonna cost you," said Blow.

"Not if I hit the ground first."

Southeastern Pakistan
2010

"GLOBAL HAWK SHOWS A CAR COMING, CAPTAIN. DRIVING from the east."

Danny couldn't believe the bad timing. The Whiplash team had just gone out of the aircraft.

"How fast?"

"Hard to tell," said Gunny. "Ground team can't see him yet. You want us to nuke him?"

Danny knew what the sergeant meant, but it was still a poor choice of words.

"Let's see if he goes fast enough to miss them," Danny told the sergeant. "Better for all of us if he just drives on."

"Your call," said the Marine, his tone leaving no doubt that he disagreed with Danny's decision.

Danny waited for the car to come into view. If only the Whiplash team had jumped, he could have told Liu and the others to change their landing spot to avoid being detected. But he felt that was too much to ask of Jennifer.

She really shouldn't have been on the mission at all.

"Guy's a slowpoke," said Gunny, who was watching the car with a set of night glasses.

Danny glanced toward the sky. The team would be opening their chutes just about now.

"We may make it," said Danny hopefully.

"Your call."

"Yes, it is."

THE SHOCK OF WIND AS SHE HIT THE SLIPSTREAM BELOW the jet sent a chill through Jennifer so severe that her legs shook. Even with the Dreamland night-vision technology embedded in the smart helmet, all she could see was black.

"Damn," she told herself.

That was as close as she would come to admitting that she'd bit off a little more than she could comfortably chew. She pulled her arms and legs back closer to her torso, shaping herself into a frog position as she plummeted downward. The altimeter in the smart helmet was somewhat distracting— the default display flashed large numerals in blue as the jumper descended—but she did like the infrared night view, which bathed the world in a warm green glow.

It didn't feel like she was falling. The sensation was more of flying, sailing through the air at a tremendous clip. For all her intellectual skills, Jennifer loved to push her body; running and rock climbing were regular pursuits. Skydiving wasn't quite as much fun—there was too much prep involved, which meant she had to plan quite a bit with her schedule. But it was definitely a rush.

The smart helmet showed her where she was compared to her designated landing zone. She tilted her arm and left leg, leaning back to the right spot.

A tone sounded. Jennifer yanked the ripcord, and within moments the loud hurricane rush transformed into something gentler. This wasn't the lullaby of a bassinet slowly lulling a newborn to sleep: she had to work, checking her canopy with the aid of a wrist flashlight and then steering according to the cues given by the helmet. The parachutist and her parachute were a miniature aircraft, capable of flying literally miles before touching down.

Jennifer didn't have to go quite that far. With her chute and lines looking good, her course set, she enjoyed the view. There were small huts in the distance, a car on a road, the Osprey and work team.

The digital altimeter counted down her altitude: 200 feet . . . 150 . . . 100 . . .

The helmet blacked out.

Her legs locked. She tried to relax them, tried to relax everything, taking a deep, long breath.

The ground grabbed her before she could exhale. Jennifer tumbled hard to her right, skidding ignobly and twisting completely around three times before coming to a stop against a pile of very hard rocks.

DANNY FREAH SAW THE FLASH OF THE BRAKE LIGHTS JUST as the first Whiplash trooper sailed across the landing zone toward his touchdown. The auto was a mile away, and slightly ahead of the parachutist as he landed, but Danny decided he just couldn't take a chance.

"Nab him," he told Gunny. "As gently as possible."

"Will do," said the Marine cheerfully.

Danny turned his attention to the team landing around him. Suddenly, the night was filled with the sound of a woman cursing her head off—Jennifer Gleason had come in hard twenty yards away from him. Danny ran over and found her rolling up her parachute.

"Hey, Jen, you keep that up, the kids are going to learn a whole bunch of new words," he said.

"Stinking fucking helmet."

Danny couldn't help but laugh.

A fresh string of expletives exploded from her mouth. "It's not funny, Freah," she told him. "The stinking helmet blacked out just before I landed."

"Did you have it in default mode? If so, it reverted to standard view five seconds before you landed. You should have set it to a custom mode if you wanted it to continue counting."

Jennifer expanded her vocabulary to include a description of what could be done to default mode. The description defied the laws of physics, though Danny made it a point never to argue science with a scientist.

"Where is the stinking bomb at?" she said finally.

"This way," said Danny.

She seemed to be limping as she followed.

"You want an ice pack on that knee?"

"Just show me where the son of a bitch is."

Danny got Jennifer over to the warhead, then went to check on the rest of his team. Liu and the others had landed about a quarter mile away, shading away from the car.

"Good to see you, Cap," said Blow. "How's Boston doing?" he asked, referring to Sergeant Ben Rockland. Boston had been hurt, though not seriously, apprehending the Iranian commandos who instigated the Indian-Pakistani nuclear exchange.

"He's going to be OK," said Danny. "Listen, there was a car stopped up the road."

"We saw it coming in," said Liu.

"Run up there and see if you can help the Marines with the language," said Danny. "Link back to Dreamland and use their computer translators."

"On it," said Liu.

A few minutes later Sergeant Liu, Gunny, and two Marine privates returned with a skinny Pakistani man who looked as if he'd seen a ghost.

"You gotta hear his story, Cap," said Liu. "Claims his wife is pregnant and he's going to fetch her mother."

"They don't have doctors in Karachi?"

"Doesn't live in Karachi," said Liu. "Lives about five miles up the road. She sounds like she's in serious labor, Captain. Kind of like that breeched birth we had on the Iranian mission?"

"You guys deliver babies?" asked Gunny.

"We do all sorts of things, Sergeant," said Danny.

Aboard Dreamland *Bennett*, over Pakistan 2100

DOG TURNED THE STICK OVER TO HIS COPILOT AND GOT UP to stretch his legs. The crew's resentment had diminished a bit, but he knew he still wouldn't win any popularity contests.

Not that it mattered. He walked to the galley and started a fresh pot of coffee in the Zero Gravity Mr. Coffee. The sealed coffeemaker, which worked as advertised, was still rated by most of the technical people as their biggest contribution to mankind.

"Hey, Colonel, you got Ray Rubeo looking for you," said Sullivan.

"Thanks, Kevin."

Dog poured himself a half cup of the steaming java, then made his way back to his seat. Rubeo's familiar frown was frozen on the screen.

"One of these days, Ray, you're going to smile," said Dog.

"It won't be today. We've done some new calculations based on Ms. Gleason's findings," said the scientist, launching into an explanation of why the five missiles still missing had not been found. They all belonged to a subtype of the Prithvi family that had not been previously identified. According to Rubeo, solenoid valves that controlled parts of the engine had been shielded sufficiently so they had not been destroyed by the T-Rays.

As Rubeo's discussion veered toward the technical, Dog cut him short.

"Do we have new projections of where they came to earth?"

"We're working on them, Colonel. There are several variables involved. At a minimum, we believe that all of the missiles went much farther north."

Rubeo had a map ready. The search areas included Kashmir and the borders of Afghanistan and China.

"Ray, this map has to cover a hundred thousand square miles."

"It's 225, 963." Rubeo's scowl deepened. "We are working on reducing it. We don't entirely understand why the solenoid valve—and it was only one—on the missile at I-17 wasn't affected. We should have this quantified in a few hours, depending on how quickly Jennifer works."

"I'm sure she'll work as quickly as possible," said Dog. "What did she do? Set up a simulator in the Command trailer?"

"No, we've done the simulations. She provided the measurements and electric readings. I would have preferred—"

"Wait a second. Are you telling me Jennifer Gleason is on the ground in Pakistan?"

"Yes. I assume she checked with you before going . . . or is that an invalid assumption?"

Southeastern Pakistan
2115

DOG'S VOICE WOULD HAVE SHATTERED DANNY'S EARDRUMS if it weren't for the special volume reducer built into the smart helmet's headset.

"Why the hell did you let Jennifer jump into a battle zone?" demanded Dog.

"I didn't let her do anything. Rubeo told me she was on the way. I thought you told her she could go."

"Let me talk to her. *Now.*"

Danny walked over to the missile assembly. Jennifer was peering into the ruined and burned skeleton, examining bits of circuit boards with an oscilloscope.

"Colonel wants to talk to you," Danny told her. "He's hot. Real hot."

"WHAT EXACTLY IS YOUR OBJECTION?" JENNIFER ASKED.

"You know very well what my objection is. You're in a combat zone."

"There's no combat here. *And* I've been in combat zones before. We needed a specialist. I was available."

"We have other experts. You're a scientist, damn it."

"I'm not made out of paper."

"You're more valuable back at the base," said Dog. "You shouldn't have gone to Diego Garcia in the first place."

She could practically feel his anger in the long breath and pause that followed. Jennifer felt her own anger rise.

"I should have said something to you then," Dog told her. "I was wrong not to send you back. But this—"

"Colonel, is there anything else?" she demanded.

"The next time . . ."

She waited for him to finish the sentence. Instead, he signed off.

Jennifer looked at one of the Marines standing nearby, a young private barely out of high school.

"Officers," she said, shaking her head.

"Know what you mean," said the man, nodding.

THE PAKISTANI WAS SO EXCITED, AND SO DISTRAUGHT, that Danny decided his story *had* to be true. The question was what to do about it.

According to the man, his house had been without electricity, telephone, or running water for several days. His wife had gone into labor and he'd left her to get her mother, who lived in the nearby village.

The man practically hopped up and down, pleading that he be let go so he could get his mother-in-law. He interspersed his English with long sentences in Punjabi, convinced that Danny would understand if he spoke slowly and distinctly. He seemed to take the appearance of the Americans in stride, as if they belonged there; Danny thought it better not to press the issue.

But what should he do with him? Releasing him was too dangerous. On the other hand, it seemed that if they did nothing, the baby and its mother might die.

"Ya don't even know if this woman he's going to get can help her," said Gunny.

Danny nodded.

"We can deliver the baby," said Liu. "We've done it before. The woman could die without medical attention."

"We're not exactly a maternity ward," said Danny. "We have other things going on here."

He turned around and walked down the hill toward the rutted area where the missile had come to rest. A set of tarps had been erected to shield the work lights from the roadway. Jennifer Gleason was hunched over a mangled part of the body and the engine in the first third of the debris field.

"How's it going, Doc?" Danny asked.

"Slow, Captain. I'm not an expert on these systems."

"I thought you knew everything, Jen."

"Ha ha."

"How much longer do you need?"

"Two or three hours at least," she said. "Are we in a hurry?"

"I want to be out of here before daylight."

"Then let me alone."

Danny went back to the Pakistani and Liu. Gunny was standing with them, trying to engage the Pakistani in a conversation about what was going on in the country. The man wasn't interested in anything but his wife.

"Sergeant Liu, grab Blow and Jonesy and take this guy back to his house. Assess the situation and report back."

"You got it, Cap."

"Excuse me, Captain," said Gunny.

"What's up, Sergeant?" asked Danny, already suspecting the problem.

"Hey, no offense here, but, uh, sending those guys out there—you really think it's a good idea?"

"It's the best alternative."

"I don't know about that. For one thing, he may be lying."

"I don't think he is."

"For another thing, Captain, what are you going to do if she is in labor? We going to deliver the baby?"

Danny shrugged. "Those guys have done it before."

The Marine sergeant shook his head.

"Look, we're not at war with these people," Danny told him. "On the contrary, they're our allies."

"I don't think I'd trust them much."

"You don't have to," said Danny, turning to go check on the Osprey crews.

Dreamland
0815, 17 January 1998
(2115, Karachi)

SAMSON FLATTENED THE PAPER ON THE DESK, SPREADING his large hand across its surface. For all its high-tech gizmos, the Dreamland commander's office still relied on a fax machine that used thermal imaging paper.

The letters were a little faint and the image crinkled, but he didn't care. He could see what it said: The Whiplash order had been reissued, directed to Major General Terrill Samson, rather than Colonel Bastian.

Just in case.

He'd keep Rubeo through the deployment—being too vindictive would only hurt the mission. But once it was over, the egghead was history.

Samson got up from the desk. Bastian—or his predecessor, if the chief master sergeant was to be believed—had good taste in furniture, he decided. But the place was a little cluttered with chairs and files. The first thing he had to do was have them cleared out. He'd put them in the conference room next door, which he would now use as an office annex—a library.

He didn't need a conference room. He wasn't planning on doing much conferring.

"Begging the general's pardon," said Ax, still standing near the doorway, "but was there anything else this morning?"

"Yes, Chief, there is. I need a memo telling all department and section heads, all heads of testing programs, everyone from the head scientist to the janitor, that Dreamland's entire agenda is now open for review. *My* review. Top to bottom. I want something that will convey urgency. I want it to sound . . ."

Samson drifted off, unsure exactly how he wanted it to sound.

"Like if they don't do a good job you'll sack them?" asked Ax.

"That's it, Chief. Exactly." Ax would definitely stay, Samson decided. "Have it on my desk before lunch."

TECHNICALLY SPEAKING, CHIEF MASTER SERGEANT TERence "Ax" Gibbs was a bachelor. But in a very real sense, Gibbs was as married as any man in America. It's just that his wife—his children, his relatives, his home, his family, his friends, his pets, his entire existence—was the U.S. Air Force.

But now it was time for a divorce. So as soon as he finished writing Samson's memo—it took all of three minutes, and had a much more balanced tone than the general wanted—he went online and obtained the appropriate paperwork to initiate a transfer back to his home state of Florida, in anticipation of a separation from the service in a few months. And just in case Samson objected—Ax sensed he would, if only on general principles—the chief sent out a handful of private messages lining up support. Among the recipients were two lieutenant generals and the Air Force's commanding general, giving him a full house to deal with any bluff Samson might mount.

He had worked for people like Samson at numerous points during his career. But he'd been young then. Age mellowed some people; for others, it removed their ability to stand still for bullshit. He fell into the latter category.

Lieutenant Colonel Bastian wasn't the perfect boss. He was occasionally given to fits of anger; however well justified, fits of pique in the long run could be counterproductive. The colonel also insisted on keeping things at Dreamland streamlined, which for Ax meant that he had to make do with about a tenth of the staff he would have at a "normal" command. But Dog respected, trusted, and related to his people in a way that Ax knew Samson never would.

But this wasn't about Samson. It was about Terence "Ax" Gibbs. If he worked things out properly, he would arrive in the civilian world just after Florida's high tourist season. Prices on charter boats would be reduced, and he would be able to use a small portion of his tidy Air Force nest egg to set himself up as a boat operator.

Tough getting used to all that sun after decades of working indoors, but everyone needed a challenge, especially in retirement.

Aboard the *Abner Read*
2200

HAVING OBTAINED THE HARPOONS, STORM ENDEAVORED TO get into position to use them. He remained on a southerly

course toward the Indian Ocean. The Chinese aircraft carrier *Khan,* meanwhile, was heading in roughly the same
direction, presumably intending to go around the southern
tip of India and head home.

In the days when wind powered a sailing ship, a captain
had a great deal of autonomy and could easily set a course
that would bring him against an enemy; it was how many a
master had won the accolades of triumph and treasure. Even
a captain in the early Cold War era often had leeway to sail
more or less where he pleased; there was simply no way for
the admirals to keep complete track of him.

But Storm belonged to a different time.

"Why is your course paralleling the *Khan*'s?" demanded
Admiral Woods over the secure link.

"We're just remaining in a position to be of use if necessary," said Storm.

"The *Decatur* is more than prepared to do the job," said
Woods. "The *Los Angeles* will meet it near Ceylon. Together they will trail it to its home port. You are to proceed
to resupply."

"I have resupplied," said Storm. "I have Harpoon missiles
and my ship is ready for combat."

"Where did you get the missiles?"

"Dreamland gave them to me," he said.

The admiral's face turned even redder.

"We don't have a full complement, but I have more than
enough to sink the *Khan,*" said Storm.

"You will *not* sink the *Khan.* Storm, have you lost your
mind?"

"I meant—"

"Let me talk to your executive officer."

"But—"

"Now!"

Storm felt his legs tremble beneath the small desk where
he was sitting. He knew the video camera was showing
Woods everything he was doing, so he moved as deliberately
as possible, picking up the handset on his desk and calmly

asking Eyes to his cabin. When he returned the phone to its cradle, he looked at the screen, trying to narrow his eyes in a show of concentration and sincerity. It wasn't a lie; he was being both focused and forthright. But he wanted his face to match what he felt.

"Admiral," said Storm, "let me make my case. I simply want to be nearby if—"

"There is no case to be made, Storm. No ifs. No anything. Your ship is not to engage the *Khan*."

"I'm talking about making sure the *Khan* leaves the area without being a threat," said Storm.

"Flight operations from the *Khan* have stopped. They are no longer capable of even providing their own air cover," said Woods. "I am not going to risk an international incident with them."

"They've already shot at our planes."

"Not in two days. And for all we know, Bastian egged them on," said Woods. "Is that why he gave you the missiles? Are you two trying to start a war?"

"That's unfair. We carried out orders—"

"Then carry out these."

Storm clamped his teeth together, knowing that if he said one word he'd say a dozen, and if he said a dozen he'd say a hundred, each an expletive.

There was a knock at the cabin door. Storm got up and opened it.

"You wanted to see me?" Eyes asked.

Storm pointed to the video screen. Looking a bit bewildered, the executive officer sat down in Storm's extra chair.

"Lieutenant Commander Eisenberg," said Admiral Woods. "If Captain Gale makes an aggressive move toward the Chinese aircraft carrier *Khan*, you are to immediately relieve him of command. Is that understood?"

"I, well, uh—"

"Is that understood?"

"Yes, sir."

"These are your orders, gentlemen. Since you have found a

way to resupply and do not wish to rest, you are to sail to the area of the Cherbani Reef and act as a picket ship for any of our vessels moving toward the *Lincoln* task group. You are to go no farther south than twelve degrees longitude, and you are not to engage any ship—Indian or Chinese—without my explicit permission. Under any circumstances. Is that understood?"

"What if we're fired on?" blurted Storm.

"Then you badly screwed up."

"I have to be able to defend myself."

"You better not be in a position where you need to."

Eyes glanced at Storm. "Admiral, I'm not sure—"

"What is it that you're unsure of, Commander? Following orders?"

"I can follow orders, Admiral."

"Then do it."

The picture dissolved into black.

Southeastern Pakistan
2200

SERGEANT LIU BELIEVED THE MAN WAS TELLING THE TRUTH, but he'd learned long ago that belief and reality were sometimes different things. He pulled the car off the road a half mile from the man's house and sent Blow and Sergeant Kurt Jones up the road to check out the house. Ten minutes later Jonesy checked in over the short-range Whiplash channel.

"House is clear—this lady is about to drop an egg any second, Liu. Better get the mojo on."

Jones hadn't been exaggerating. By the time Liu and her husband got inside, the woman's grunts were shaking the small two-room house. The only illumination came from a small kerosene lantern on a dresser set at the side of the room.

Jonesy's flashlight, shined on the small bed where the wife was giving birth. "I can see the head, Sarge. A lot of hair," he added. "I think Blow's the dad."

"Har har."

Liu set down his medical bag and dropped to his knees. As he did, the baby's head and upper torso appeared, along with a gush of meconium, the greenish liquid waste and birth fluids. The baby's eyebrows appeared, then disappeared as the mother's contractions starting to tug it back inside.

"You have to stay with us, little one," said Liu, starting to grab for the newborn.

Just as he got his hands down, the mother's body gave one last shudder. Her new son slid out into Liu's arms. Jones reached in and cut the cord with his knife.

"Towels, swabs—we got to clean his face. Can't let him eat this crap," said Liu, cradling the infant in his arm so he could wipe the meconium from the infant's mouth.

"It's turning blue, Nurse," said Blow, pointing as he handed over a towel.

The baby wasn't breathing. Liu gave the child a gentle smack, but that didn't seem to have an effect. He placed it down on the floor, bending over to try mouth-to-mouth resuscitation.

As he did, the father began to scream and started pounding Liu on the back. Blow grabbed him and threw him against the wall. Then the mother started to scream too. Jonesy dropped down to hold her arms.

The only people in the room who were quiet were the baby and Liu. The sergeant struggled to get the infant to breathe. The infant seemed to gasp, but then gave up. The sergeant kept trying.

"Come on, kid!" shouted Blow.

"Let me try, Sarge," said Jonesy.

Liu ignored them, working steadily though he was starting to give up hope.

The baby's heart wasn't beating. He started CPR.

"I'll respirate," said Blow, dropping down beside him.

They worked together, desperate, for more than ten minutes, long past the point that there was any chance of the baby surviving. Finally, tears streaming from his eyes, Liu put his hand out to Blow, signaling that it was time to stop. He looked up at the father, who shrieked and ran from the room.

"Damn," said Blow, jumping up to get him.

Just as he reached the door, automatic rifle fire lit up the front of the house.

**Aboard Dreamland *Bennett*,
over Pakistan
2255**

DOG LOOKED AT THE LATEST PROJECTIONS OF WHERE THE remaining missiles had landed. There was just too much territory to cover.

"You're going to have to narrow this down, Ray," he told the scientist. "You're including Afghanistan and half of China."

"That's an exaggeration, Colonel," said Rubeo.

"Not by much."

"We're working on it. We have a theory on the solenoid valves. We think that rather than surviving the T-Rays, some of them may have locked the engines open. Ms. Gleason is still gathering data."

Dog frowned but said nothing.

"If we could find a second missile and examine it, we could narrow the projections down considerably."

"Is there any projection you're surest of?" Dog asked.

"Statistically, they're all the same," said Rubeo. "But there is one where the geography makes the search easiest. Unfortunately, it's the farthest from the U-2's present track.

"Then we'll take it," said Dog.

"It is I-20, northeast of Siakor on the border."

Dog looked at the long finger marked on the map as the search area. It was at the extreme southeastern end of Pakistan, roughly 450 miles from the base camp Danny and the Marines were using in the desert.

"Colonel, has Major Catsman had a chance to speak to you about General Samson?" said Rubeo.

"I'm sorry, I haven't had a chance to talk to Major Catsman about that. I assume you've heard he's replacing General Magnus."

"That's not exactly how it's going to work," said Rubeo. "He's here. For the duration."

"The duration?"

"It's not going to be like the arrangement with Magnus. He's taking over your job, Colonel. They're going back to the arrangement that existed under Brad Elliott."

Dog wasn't surprised. Under ordinary circumstances, a base the size of Dreamland—let alone one of its importance— would be run by a general, not a lieutenant colonel. When he'd been assigned, everyone assumed he was there to close the place down.

Everyone except him. He'd fought for the Whiplash concept—a fighting force working closely with the developers of cutting-edge technology. The idea had proven itself long ago. And now the bureaucracy was catching up, folding Dreamland back into the regular hierarchy.

It was going to be a tough transition for a lot of people. Including himself.

"General Samson was making a distraction of himself in Dreamland Command," continued Rubeo. "I nearly had him removed."

"You *what*?"

"I can give you the entire sordid tale if you wish, Colonel, but I assume you have better things to do. In any event, it's irrelevant. I'll be handing in my resignation at the end of this mission."

"What?"

"Yes, Colonel. It's been a pleasure working with you too."

"Ray—"

"You'll excuse me, Colonel. I have work to attend to."

The screen blanked. Dog stared at the black space on the

dash in disbelief for nearly a full minute before turning to
Sullivan and telling him to prepare for the course change.

Southeastern Pakistan
2255

STRUCK POINT-BLANK IN THE CHEST BY THE BULLETS,
Blow fell back into the room. Liu scrambled to pull his Beretta from its holster and get out of the line of fire at the same
time. A barrel appeared, then flashed. Liu brought up his
pistol and began to fire. Before he realized it, he'd emptied
the magazine into the Pakistani father.

Jones and Blow had both been shot by the father. Fortunately, they were wearing lightweight Dreamland body armor. Blow's left ribs had been seriously bruised and possibly
broken, but otherwise he was not seriously wounded. Jones
had taken two bullets in the side, where neither did any
damage; a ricochet had splintered some wood, which flew
into his arm, cutting him, but that was the extent of his injuries.

The same could not be said for the Pakistani's wife. Two
of her husband's bullets had struck her in the face, and another hit her heart. Any one of the wounds would have been
fatal.

"This sucks," groaned Jones. "This wasn't supposed to
happen. We were helping them, damn it."

Liu paced the small room, not quite in a state of shock but
not quite in full control of his senses either. The kerosene
lamp flickered, casting its dim yellow shadows around the
wretched scene. The dead infant lay nearby, its body splat-
tered with blood as well as the green meconium it had been
bathed in at birth. Blow had loosened his vest and was gingerly touching his side.

Jones suddenly rushed at the dead man and began kicking
him. "You jackass. We didn't kill your son. We were trying
to help him."

Liu grabbed him and pulled him out into the night. "It wasn't our fault," he said to Jones. "It wasn't."

"This sucks," said Jones again. And then he started to cry.

DANNY LISTENED GRIMLY AS LIU RECOUNTED WHAT HAD happened over the radio.

"Should we bury the bodies?" Liu asked.

"No," said Danny. "Use the smart helmets to take as much video of the scene as possible. Leave things the way you found them. Leave the car. Come back by foot."

"Take us about forty minutes, Cap."

"Make it thirty. We're just about ready to leave."

Aboard Dreamland *Bennett*,
over Pakistan
2310

DOG HAD NEVER HEARD DANNY'S VOICE TREMBLE BEFORE.

"I take full responsibility for what happened, Colonel. I should never have sent them."

"It was a tough call," said Dog, not knowing what else to say.

"They're on their way back now. They videotaped the scene. I told them to leave it the way it was," said Danny. "They're pretty broken up. I'll evac them as soon as I get a chance."

"We have to inform Admiral Woods," said Dog.

"That's my next call, Colonel."

"They're going to need to be debriefed."

"I know, Colonel."

There was nothing else to say, and nothing for Dog himself to do at this point.

No. He'd have to tell Samson. *That* was a conversation to look forward to.

Danny gave Dog a quick update on the warhead, then signed off. Before Dog could punch into the Dreamland channel and ask for Samson, Sergeant Rager sounded a warning.

"Colonel, I have two contacts at 250 miles, headed in our direction," said the airborne radar operator. "Computer says they are Mikoyan MiG-31s."

"Chinese?"

"Affirmative. They may be homing in on our radar," Rager added. "They're adjusting to our course. Looks like they're going to afterburners. Colonel, these suckers are headed in our direction in a *serious* hurry."

V

Long Day's Night

———

THE MIG-31 HAD BEEN CREATED DURING THE HEIGHT OF
the Cold War with one goal in mind: shoot down B-52s.

On a spec sheet, it was an awesome aircraft. Its twin Solo-
viev D-30F6 power plants could push the plane over 1,600
knots at 60,000 feet; the aircraft was capable of breaking the
sound barrier even at sea level. A two-seater, the Foxhound
came standard with so-called look-down/shoot-down radar,
allowing it to defeat the ground-hugging tactics of bombers
and cruise missiles, which ordinarily took advantage of radar reflections from the ground to pass invisibly at very low
altitude toward their target.

But the MiG-31 had one serious drawback: While it
could go very fast in a straight line, it was about as maneuverable as a heavy freight train on a sheet of ice. The faster
it went, the wider its turning radius; if a nimble aircraft
like the F/A-18 could be said to turn on a dime, the Foxhound needed ten thousand quarters.

As built, the B-52 wasn't known for cutting X's in the sky
either, but the aircraft responding to Dog's pulls had been
radically transformed before joining the Dreamland flock. He
pushed his left wing down, trading altitude for speed as he
pirouetted away from the intercept the MiG jocks had plotted.

"They're changing course," said the copilot, Kevin Sullivan. "Range is now 175 miles. Still closing."

"Looks like they insist on saying hello," said Dog.

"I have two launches," said Rager at the airborne radar. He gave the location and bearing—the missiles were coming from the aircraft.

"They launched from that range?" said Dog.

"No way—those planes don't even have their weapons radar activated," said Sullivan, monitoring the Megafortress's radar warning receiver. "And we'd be too far for them to lock onto even if they did."

"Computer IDs missiles as Vympel R-27s, based on radar profile," said Rager.

"Gotta be wrong," said Sullivan.

While potent, the missile's range was roughly 130 kilometers, or seventy miles, half what it had been fired at. The R-27—known to NATO as the AA-10 Alamo—came in several different "flavors," defined by the guidance system used to home in on its target. By far the most popular version used a semiactive radar, following guidance from its launch ship. For that to have been the case here, the radar in the Foxhound would have "locked" on the Megafortress; the characteristic pattern was easily detected, and a warning would have sounded had it occurred.

"Definitely missiles in the air," insisted Rager. "Heading for us."

"ECMs, Colonel?" asked Sullivan.

"Not at this distance," said Dog. "Those missiles will crash long before they're a real threat."

Hawk One was covering Danny's ground operation, while *Hawk Two* was conducting the search for warhead I-20. Dog told Starship to keep the Flighthawks where they were; the Megafortress could deal with the MiGs on its own.

The Chinese pilots he'd encountered in the past ranged from very professional to serious cowboys. None, however, had wasted missiles by firing them at such long range.

So what were they up to?

"Stand by for evasive maneuvers," said Dog, pushing the Megafortress into a sharp turn, then dropping her toward a mountain range he'd seen earlier. He swung the Megafortress so it would beam any radar aboard the MiGs—flying parallel to the waves, which made detection more difficult.

"MiGs are changing course," said Sullivan. "So are the missiles."

"All right. They have passive detectors," said Dog. "They're homing in on our radar."

"Why'd they launch so early?" asked Sullivan. "We're well out of their range."

"We should be," said Dog.

Dog took another turn, lengthening the distance the missiles had to travel. The missiles stayed with the Megafortress, and corrected once more as he took another leg south.

"They're approaching what should be the limit of their range," said Sullivan, tracking them.

"Kevin, broadcast on the Chinese frequency. Tell the MiG pilots that if they continue their hostile action, they will be shot down."

"Kind of late for that, don't you think, Colonel?"

"Broadcast it anyway."

"No acknowledgment," reported Sullivan a few seconds later. "Missiles are now fifty miles and closing. They should have crashed by now."

"Target the missiles with the Anacondas," said Dog.

"Targeted. Locked."

"Open bay."

The aircraft shook as the bomb bay doors opened.

"Fire," said Dog.

Most missiles, even the sophisticated Scorpions, clunked when they left the bomb bay dispenser, dropping awkwardly for a few seconds before they fired up their motors and got under way. But the Anacondas leapt from the aircraft, lit up and ready for action. They made a distinctive *whooosh* as they sped away, the missiles shooting directly under the fuselage and then veering upward.

"Foxfire One," said Sullivan, employing the time-honored code for a radar-guided missile launch. "Missile one away. Missile two away."

"The MiGs have fired two more missiles," warned Rager.

Dog started another turn, pushing the Megafortress so he could put the Megafortress head-on to the Chinese aircraft. He knew from experience that in a two-on-one matchup, Chinese pilots would typically go in opposite directions as they closed, aiming to take wide turns to get on their target's tail. While the strategy made sense in many two versus one encounters, it wasn't particularly effective against a Megafortress, which could use its Flighthawks to fend off one of the aircraft at long range while concentrating on the second plane.

These pilots, however, moved closer together as the Mega-fortress came to their bearing, the wingman looking to protect the lead's tail as they approached. While it might just have been coincidental, Dog concluded that they knew how Megafortresses fought and were trying different tactics.

"Target the bandits," said Dog.

"Locked."

"Fire."

STARSHIP STRUGGLED TO REMAIN FOCUSED ON THE FLIGHT-hawk screen as the Megafortress jerked through a series of evasive maneuvers. Reconnaissance was an important mission, surely, but he felt as if his real duty was fifty miles away, taking down the Chinese fighters.

They were a lot faster than the Flighthawk. That was a serious advantage, and the first thing the remote pilot had to do was decide how to counter it. Starship—who had fought against MiG-31s only in a simulator, liked what he called the in-your-face attack: He'd fly the Flighthawk on a course that crossed in front of the MiG at very close range, close enough for the aircraft to seem to shoot out of nowhere. Success depended on the Flighthawk being invisible until the very last moment, which was possible because the radars in the export versions of the MiG-31, like most aircraft, couldn't see the U/MF until it was in extremely close range.

The downside of such an attack was that there was only a very small window to fire. You had to be right on the cannon as you came in, then swerve hard and maybe, maybe, get a chance at another burst as the aircraft moved away.

Starship was daydreaming so much about what he would do that he almost missed the computer cue as it flashed in his screen: POSSIBLE SEARCH OBJECT SIGHTED.

He tapped the boxed highlight, then turned the Flighthawk to the north to get a better view.

"MISSILE ONE HAS OBLITERATED ENEMY MISSILE," REPORTED Sullivan. "Two—enemy missile two is gone."

The second missile was so close to the first that shrapnel from the exploding Anaconda missile had taken it out.

"Retarget Anaconda Two for one of the other missiles," said Dog calmly.

"Roger that. Retargeting. Missiles three and four are on course—Chinese aircraft starting a turn to the west, coming for our tail, I bet."

Dog was already tracking the aircraft on his own screen. The MiGs had slowed down somewhat but were traveling at nearly twenty miles a minute. They launched two more missiles—and then Sullivan practically leaped from his seat.

"*Knockdown, knockdown!* We got *Bandit One. Two!* We got *Two!* Oh wow! Holy shit. *Holy shit!*"

Dog pushed the Megafortress closer to the nearby mountain peaks, aiming to drop as close as possible to a jagged pass. Even though it was nighttime, the aircraft's computers synthesized a crisp view before him, detailing the nooks and crannies in the peaks nearby. Dog pushed the aircraft toward the rocks, pitching hard on his left wing to get as close as possible.

A proximity warning sounded, telling him he was within one hundred feet. He ignored it.

"Missile three is off the screen," said Sullivan. "Anaconda is targeting missile four."

Rager gave him some ranges and speeds on the other two missiles. Again they all appeared to be passive radar homers.

"Target the last two missiles with Anacondas," Dog told Sullivan.

"Two more aircraft, at long range, Colonel," said Rager. "ID'd as Shenyang J6s."

"Hold that thought, Sergeant," said Dog. "Sullivan, take out those missiles."

STARSHIP WALKED THE FLIGHTHAWK OVER THE RECTANGU-lar slice of earth marked out by the search program, moving toward the highlighted box the computer claimed contained the warhead. All he could see was a square shadow at the edge of much rounder shadows. Freeze-framed and enlarged, it still looked pretty much like a shadow.

He took the Flighthawk around for another pass, dropping his forward speed to just over 110 knots, about as slow as he could go. But the image was not much better; it might be part of a missile control surface, like a tailfin, he decided, but it could also be ten or twenty other things.

He pulled up, circled around, and tried to replicate the course a missile would have taken getting there. Flying a straight line from the base it had been launched from revealed nothing. Then he realized that the theory that placed the missile here called for it to have veered off course sharply when the T-Rays hit. Dreamland Command hadn't given him the course, but it wasn't difficult to approximate, since the original projections showed where the missiles were when the EEMWBs went off.

Starship's first plot was a straight line, angling sixty degrees from the point where the T-Rays hit the missile. Even as he swooped toward the ground, he realized that the missile wouldn't have gone in a straight line; most likely it veered in some sort of elliptical curve. But he flew the vector anyway, passing just to the west of the squarish shadow and continuing over a rocky valley. The boulder suggested another theory—the missile had buried itself in an avalanche after it crashed.

As he circled back, he saw what looked like a gouge in the side of a rock peak opposite the first missile part. Starship did a 180, swinging back around and flying beyond the rocks.

The computer's search program began IDing pieces of metal on a plain just beyond the rockslide.

"Flighthawk leader to *Bennett*. Colonel, I think I've got something."

"Good, Starship. I'll get back to you."

An atoll off the Indian Coast
Date and time unknown

THE CHOKING SOUND SHOOK ZEN AWAKE, PULLING HIM from a twisted dream of dark shapes and roiling winds. He grabbed at Breanna next to him, not sure what to do or how to help her, only that he had to.

Her body heaved against his. She must have something stuck in her throat, he thought, and he reached his arms and hands down, fishing for her stomach and diaphragm so he could perform the Heimlich maneuver.

He pulled once, violently jerking his fists against her organs. He'd done this in a first aid class years ago, but it felt nothing like this. He was amazed at how empty his wife felt, her body offering no resistance to his pressure.

She coughed and he pushed his hands up again. A gasping squeal replaced the cough, then Breanna began to wheeze. She shuddered, and Zen shuddered with her.

He held her as he had when they were first sleeping together, completely wrapped around, so close that every movement she made registered in his own body.

Breanna breathed normally again. Gradually, Zen began to wonder what had happened. She couldn't have been choking on something, he thought; she'd had nothing to eat. She hadn't vomited. But he hadn't imagined or dreamed it.

Gradually, he forced his mind to drift away from the possibilities of what had happened and focus on one thought— whatever had happened, she was still alive. He drifted for a time in a silver space between fatigue and dream before finally losing consciousness.

Aboard Dreamland *Bennett*,
over Pakistan
2320

"HAVING TROUBLE LOCKING ON THAT LAST MISSILE, COLO-
nel. I'm looking at it, but the computer refuses to accept it."

"Keep trying," Dog told Sullivan calmly. He got ready to
turn the Megafortress around, intending to swing his tail toward the missiles so they could use the Stinger air-mine
weapon in the tail.

Not to be confused with the shoulder-launched missile of
the same name, the Stinger air mines were essentially large
explosive disks that detonated near their target. When they
ignited, they sent shards of tungsten into the path of a pur-
suer. Generally much more effective against aircraft, recent
upgrades to the targeting radar and an increase in size had
made them useful against missiles, but only as a last resort.

"Bandit missile four is down," reported Rager. "Five and
six still pursuing."

"Sullivan?"

"Lock on Bandit missile six. Firing."

The moment Dog heard the whoosh, he threw the *Bennett*
into the turn.

"Stinger up," he told Sullivan. "Get ready in case the Anaconda misses."

"Missile five is down. Missile six is closing to ten miles."

Dog's turn slowed the Megafortress, but even had he been
going in a straight line, there was no chance of outrunning
the remaining enemy missile. At 1,400 knots, it was traveling more than twenty miles a minute.

"Stinger ready," said Sullivan, breathing hard.

"Arm autodefense," Dog told him.

"Stinger autodefense."

The sky flashed white.

"Our Anaconda took down the last missile," said Rager.
"Wow."

Brian Daly, who'd been silently manning the ground radar station during the entire incident, let out a whoop.

"All right, guys," Dog told them. "We still have two more aircraft to worry about. Let's stay on our game."

STARSHIP SURVEYED THE AREA OF THE CRASH, THE VIDEO camera in the nose of the Flighthawk recording the roughly two-mile swath where the missile had crashed. He could make a reasonable guess about what had happened. The missile had scraped against the side of the mountain peak, slammed across the second, causing an avalanche, and then landed—in pieces—on the small plain in front of him.

But where was the warhead? The debris trail petered out at the edge of a solid plain.

He'd already pulled his nose up when he realized that the plain wasn't a plain at all—it was a small lake.

He also realized something else—people were crouched at the far end, watching the Flighthawk as it zipped by.

They weren't just admiring the black shape as it sailed past the full moon either. Something flared from the ground as he passed—a shoulder-launched missile, aimed not at the U/MF, but at the Megafortress almost directly above.

"STINGER MISSILE!" SAID SULLIVAN, PRACTICALLY SHRIEK-ing over the interphone.

"Flares," said Dog. "Prepare for evasive maneuvers."

Dog had dealt with shoulder-fired missiles dozens of times before, but even he felt his heart begin to race as the decoys showered behind the Megafortress.

The FIM-92 Stinger shoulder-launched missile was designed as an easy-to-use, no-hassle-to-maintain antiaircraft weapon that could be fired by soldiers in the field with minimal training. There were several variants, but this was almost certainly an original FIM-92A model, the type given to mujahideen rebels in Afghanistan to use against the Russians there, and then later sold to terror groups around the world.

Once launched, the missile homed in on the heat source its nose sensor had locked onto, flying over the speed of sound and able to climb to about three miles. At 2.2 pounds, its explosive warhead was relatively small, but nonetheless deadly. The fuse worked only on impact, which made the use of decoys less effective. On the other hand, it also meant that the weapon had to actually strike something to go off.

The Megafortress's four turbojets were sexy targets for the missile's seeker, red hot magnets that pulled it onward. The *Bennett*'s altitude was its one advantage; while the airplane was almost directly over the man who had fired the missile, the aircraft had been at 10,000 feet, the very edge of the Stinger's lethal envelope. Dog mashed the throttle, knowing he'd need every ounce of power to get away. As the decoys bloomed behind him, he twisted sharply, taking roughly five g's and trying to cut as close to 180 degrees as possible.

The turn and flares made it hard for the Stinger to sniff its target, and by the time the Stinger realized it had to turn, it was too late. The rocket propellant in its slender chassis spent, the missile tumbled back to the ground.

"Starship, you see who fired at us?"

"Got a glimpse, Colonel."

"They Chinese troops?"

"Negative. Look like guerrillas, some sort of irregulars. Dressed, you know, kind of like natives, farmers or something."

"Pretty clear they're not farmers," snapped Dog.

"Maybe they're growing missiles," said Sullivan.

The rest of the crew laughed—more to release tension than because the joke was funny. But it was a good sign, Dog thought; they were starting to get used to dealing with combat.

It wasn't, however, a time to relax.

"Two Sukhoi-27s, early models, flying straight for us," said Rager, summarizing the situation for Dog. "Two hundred nautical miles from us. From the northeast. Chinese. They're subsonic, 500 knots, 23,000 feet. Behind them there are two helicopters, 10,000 feet. Type ID'd as Harbin Z-5 Hound. Troop carriers."

"Flighthawk leader, do you have the exact location of the warhead?" Dog asked Starship.

"Negative, Colonel. Looks like it's in a lake. I haven't confirmed it's there."

"Get on with Dreamland Command. See if the scientists can pin it down."

"Roger that."

The territory they were flying over was Indian but heavily populated by Muslims, and there were a variety of separatist groups active in the area. Some were suspected to be allied with Islamic terrorists, and even those that weren't would find a ready market for a nuclear warhead. The question in Dog's mind was what was China's interest. Were they protecting their nearby border, or working with the people on the ground?

"*Bennett* to Danny Freah. Whiplash leader, what's your status?"

Danny Freah's tired face came onto the com screen. The camera in the smart helmet was located at the top of the visor, and the image had a fish-eye quality to it. It exaggerated the puffiness under his eyes, so the captain looked like he had two shiners.

"Freah. We're about ready to bug out, Colonel."

"We think we found the I-20 warhead. There are two problems. One, it may be underwater. Two, we have what look like local guerrillas on the ground, and the Chinese seem to be interested as well."

Because of the location, it would take several hours for a fresh group of Marines to come in from the gulf. By then the guerrillas and/or the Chinese might have recovered the weapon.

Danny got hold of the Osprey pilots and discussed the situation. They could send one of their Ospreys with troops east; it would take roughly an hour and a half to reach the site. Reinforcements could include another bird, which would refuel them.

Assuming Dreamland Command could pinpoint the warhead and that divers could then find it, the Osprey could be used to lift it from the water. There was another problem, however: Of the twenty Marines and the handful of Navy technical people Danny could bring, only Danny was qualified as a diver.

And the three Whiplashers who had been at the Pakistani house.

"Admiral Woods's chief of staff wanted all three of our guys sent over to the *Lincoln* ASAP," said Danny. "In the meantime, they were to stay on the sidelines if possible."

"It's not possible," said Dog. "Take whoever you need with you. I'll clear it with the admiral. Assuming our guys are OK."

"I don't know about Jonesy or Blow," said Danny. "They were both shot. The gear protected them, but they're pretty, uh, you know . . . mentally, with the kid—"

"What about Liu?"

"I think he's OK."

"All right. As long as he can carry out the mission. Use your best judgment."

There was a time, before Dreamland, before he ever engaged in combat, that Dog would not have asked whether his subordinates could carry out a mission he knew they were physically capable of. But having been through combat, he'd learned how it could wear at you over time. More important, he'd also learned that a good percentage of people didn't realize the toll it took, and that most of the others would ignore that toll because they felt their duty was to perform the mission. His job as a commander was to make the call for them, insisting that they sit down when sitting down was the best thing for them, and the best thing ultimately for the mission.

Were they at that point? Seeing a baby die, seeing a husband self-destruct up close—these were somehow different than deaths in combat, however horrific. Having people you were trying to save turn on you at a tragic moment—how much more terrible was that than killing a sniper at long distance?

"Get over there, then, as fast as you can," Dog told Danny. Then he killed the transmission and called the *Cheli* to back him up. He'd talk to Admiral Woods—and General Samson—as soon as he had the situation under control.

Aboard Dreamland *Cheli*,
over northwest India
2320

THOUGH SHE HAD BEEN FINISHED ONLY A FEW WEEKS AFTER the *Bennett,* the EB-52 *Cheli* incorporated a number of improvements both subtle and significant. Like her mate, the Megafortress had been rebuilt from an earlier incarnation, in this case a Model H that had once served with the Nineteenth Bomb Wing at Homestead Air Force Base in Florida. She was optimized for radar work and included the latest upgrades to both the airborne and ground search and surveillance radars, as well as software that allowed the bomber to target missiles launched by other sources. Like most Megafortresses, there were two Flighthawk bays, upper and lower. Unlike the *Bennett*, the upper Flighthawk bay was operational; instead of bunks, there were two more Flighthawk control stations, allowing the aircraft to control a total of eight robots, though for now she was equipped only with two. The *Cheli*'s uprated engines allowed her to take off with a full load without tapping the engines of the four Flighthawks she could hold under her wings.

The aircraft's ECM suite had been updated as well. While not as comprehensive as the ELINT, or electronic intelligence, versions of the Megafortress, which could listen to as well as jam a wide range of communications, the *Cheli* could suppress antiaircraft fire from ground and aircraft by scrambling radar and command signals the way the now retired Wild Weasels once had. Dreamland's wizards had studied recent encounters with the Chinese and updated the electronics to do a better job against their weapons. They had also added transcripts of the air battles to the computers that helped fly the plane, providing the Tactics section with better information on what to expect from the planes they encountered.

Her pilot, Captain Brad Sparks, was in some ways also a new version of the breed. Sparks had been at Dreamland as a lieutenant three years before, working briefly on the Megafortress project, where, among other things, he had helped perform a feasibility study on using the aircraft as a tanker. He'd transferred out just before Dog arrived, promoted to a captain and assigned to a B-1B squadron.

When Dreamland began getting involved in operational missions, Sparks realized he'd made a mistake and started angling for a comeback. He'd arrived two weeks before, and already he could tell it was the best decision he'd ever made in his life.

"Colonel Bastian for you," said his copilot, Lieutenant Nelson Wong.

"Colonel, how goes it?" said Sparks, snapping his boss's image on his com screen. The EB-52's "dashboard" was infinitely configurable, but like most Megafortress pilots, Sparks kept the communications screen at the lower left, just below a screen that fed data and images from the Flighthawks.

"We've located another warhead, very far north," Dog told him. "It's in a lake. Looks like the Chinese are interested in it as well."

"Hot shit."

"Excuse me?"

"What do you need us to do, Colonel?"

"These are the coordinates of the site. The *Bennett* will go north and try and divert the Chinese. I'd like you to back us up and help provide cover for the ground unit; they should be there inside of ninety minutes. How soon can you get up here?"

"Thirty minutes," said Sparks, though he knew he was being optimistic—the *Cheli* was nearly five hundred miles away."

"Be advised that the Chinese used long-range radiation-seeking missiles against us. They look like AA-10 Alamos but have at least twice the range. We took them down with Anacondas. We have two Su-27s approaching, and we're unsure how they're armed."

"We're on it, Colonel."

"Alert me when you're within ten minutes." The screen went blank.

The cavalry to the rescue, thought Sparks before telling the rest of the crew what was going on. Getting back to Dreamland was the best thing he'd ever done.

Aboard Dreamland *Bennett*,
over Pakistan
2345

DOG'S GOAL WAS SIMPLE—KEEP THE HELICOPTERS FROM landing at the site. They were well within range of his Anaconda antiair missiles, but he had only two left. If he used them against the helicopters, he'd have only the Flighthawks as his defense against the Su-27s.

A much better option was to engage the fighters first, get them out of the way, and then deal with the helicopters. After telling Starship what was up, Dog turned the Megafortress in the Sukhois' direction.

Unlike the MiG-31s, the Sukhois hadn't followed him through his course changes. There was no question in his mind that they were heading toward the warhead site and had to be considered hostile, but he wasn't sure if they were carrying long-range weapons like the other planes. He decided he couldn't take the chance. His only option was to take them out before they were close enough to use their weapons.

"Range on *Bandits Three* and *Four*," he said to Sullivan.

"Just coming up to 180 miles."

"Stand by the Anacondas," Dog told Sullivan.

"Standing by."

"Target them and fire."

The missiles whisked away from the Megafortress. Dog held his course, watching the MiGs continue to approach, clearly unaware of their impending doom. Only at the last second did they realize their danger, jerking desperately to the east and west as the missiles bore in.

It was far too late. The Anacondas exploded only a few seconds apart, obliterating the Sukhois so completely that neither crew could eject.

"The helicopters are all yours," Dog told Starship. Then he dialed into the fleet satellite communications channel to tell Woods what was going on.

THE HARBIN Z-5 HOUND WAS A CHINESE VERSION OF THE Russian Mil Mi-4, a 1950s-era transport that typically carried fourteen troops and three crew members. Though the Chinese versions were improved somewhat, the basic design remained the same, a thick, two-deck fuselage beneath a massive rotor and a long, slim tail. The aircraft were pulling 113 knots, close to their top speed, flying twenty feet over the landscape.

They were easy prey for the Flighthawks. Starship kept the two U/MFs in a trail and took control of the first aircraft, flying a head-on attack against the lead helicopter. On his first pass he raked the cockpit and the engine compartment immediately behind it with 20mm cannon fire, decapitating the aircraft. There was no need for a second pass.

The other chopper tried to get away by twisting to the west, through a mountain pass. But the pilot miscalculated in the dark. By the time Starship turned *Hawk One* in its direction, the aircraft was burning on the side of the mountain, its rotors sheered off by a collision with the side wall of the canyon.

"Choppers are down," Starship told Colonel Bastian. "I need to refuel."

"Roger that," said Dog.

Dreamland Command
1100

TO SAMSON'S GREAT DISAPPOINTMENT, RAY RUBEO HAD left Dreamland Command to supervise some tests in another part of the complex.

Samson didn't intend to fire him—not yet, anyway. Given the administration's interest in the missile recovery operation, there was no sense doing anything that might possibly derail it.

Or give critics something to focus on if the mission failed.

But he did want to put Rubeo in his place. And he would, he promised himself, as soon as possible.

"I'm not here to interfere," Samson told Major Catsman. "I want you all to proceed as you were. But let's be clear on this—I am the commander of this base, and of this mission. The Whiplash order is issued in my name. Understood?"

"Yes, sir."

Samson detected a note of dissension in Catsman's voice, but let it slide. A bit of resistance in a command could be a good thing, as long as it was controllable.

"Update me on the process, please. Where specifically are our people? How many missiles have yet to be recovered? All of the details. Then I want to speak with Colonel Bastian, and finally Admiral Woods."

"There is a bit of a time difference between Dreamland and the area they're operating in," said Catsman.

"I'm sure Colonel Bastian won't mind being woken to brief me."

"It wasn't him I was thinking of, sir. Colonel Bastian is already awake, and on a mission. Admiral Woods, on the other hand . . ."

Samson smiled. He had tangled with Woods several times while deputy commander of the Eighth Air Force, and owed him a tweaking or two.

"Tex Woods and I go way back," Samson told Catsman.

"Disturbing his sleep would be one of life's little pleasures."

Catsman gave him a tally of the warheads that had been recovered and a rundown on the overall situation; her briefing was, in fact, extremely thorough. And when she turned to tell a civilian at a console to make the connection to Bastian, the colonel came on almost instantaneously, his half-shaven face filling the main screen.

"General, I need to update you on a serious situation," said the colonel from the cockpit of his Megafortress.

"Very good, Colonel. Fire away," said Samson, noting the serious and, he thought, slightly subservient tone. Bastian was getting the message.

"We've engaged Chinese fighters," Dog told him.

Samson felt his jaw lock as Colonel Bastian continued, explaining everything that had happened. The engagement surely was necessary—the alternative was to be shot down—but as Colonel Bastian freely admitted, it went against the standing orders not to engage the Chinese.

And then Bastian told him about the incident at the Pakistani farmhouse.

"Jesus, Bastian! What are your people trying to do?" bellowed the general. "Do you know how that's going to look? Can you imagine when the media gets hold of this? My God!"

Dog explained that they had video of the incident that would back them up. Samson felt as if a sinkhole had opened beneath his feet.

"Admiral Woods knows about the incident," Dog added. "He's ordered our men back to Base Camp One. But I needed one to help check the lake where the warhead is."

At least it's not just my orders he disregards, Samson thought.

"That's our situation," said Dog. "Things are a little busy here, General. If you don't mind I'm going to get back to work."

"Yes," said Samson, not sure what else to say.

"Admiral Woods for you, General," said Catsman as the

screen changed back to a large-scale situation map. "He's a little piqued at being woken. I told him you wanted to give him an important update."

"I might as well talk to him now," said Samson sarcastically. "While he's in a good mood."

**Aboard Dreamland *Bennett*,
over Pakistan
2357**

STARSHIP TOOK TWO QUICK PASSES OVER THE GROUP AT the lake to get an idea of how many men were there and what other surprises they might have.

There were nine. He could see Kalashnikovs and one grenade launcher, but no more Stinger missiles. Two or three pack animals—from the air they looked like camels, though the pilot suspected they were donkeys—were tied together a short distance away.

Starship pushed the Flighthawk closer to the earth as he widened his orbit, trying to find supporting units that might be hiding in the jagged rocks nearby. There were no roads that he could see, and if there was a warm body in the neighborhood, the infrared scan couldn't find it.

The mountains were as desolate as anyplace on earth, emptier even than the desert where most of the warheads had landed. The nearest village looked to be a collection of hovels pushed against a ravine about five miles to the east. A road twisted about a mile below the settlement; Starship spotted two paths connecting them but found no one on them.

"Should I take these guys out, Colonel, or what?"

"Let's wait until the Osprey is a little closer," Dog told him. "They may pull the warhead from the lake and save us some work."

"Roger that."

* * *

DOG DECIDED IT WAS PRUDENT TO KEEP THE *BENNETT* WELL above the ground, establishing an orbit around the area at 40,000 feet, high enough that the black Megafortress could neither be seen nor heard from the ground. With the Osprey still about an hour away, he had the two radar operators take short breaks, sending Sullivan back to monitor their equipment while they got some coffee and relaxed for a few minutes. It wasn't much of a break, but it relieved the monotony a bit and let them know he was thinking of them. They were warming to him slightly, but he still wouldn't have gotten many votes for commander of the month.

The Dreamland Command channel buzzed with an incoming message from General Samson.

"Colonel Bastian, good morning again."

"It's just about midnight here, General."

"Woods is not particularly pleased, but I think he'll accept the fact that you had no choice but to shoot down the Chinese. What the hell are they up to?"

"I'm not sure. I haven't spoken to Jed Barclay about it. He may have an opinion."

"Jed Barclay?"

Dog explained who Jed Barclay was and how he liaisoned with the different agencies involved in operations.

"Well, I'll see what he knows," said Samson.

"There's one other thing," said Dog, sensing that Samson was about to sign off.

"Well?"

"We still have two crewmen missing. The Navy has been doing the search but—"

"Where are they missing?"

"The mid-Indian coast. I'd like to supplement that. I'd like to dedicate one of our radar surveillance planes full-time to the mission."

"Recovering the warheads takes precedence. The President wants that done. That's where your efforts have to be concentrated."

"They're our people, sir. No offense meant to the Navy."

Samson frowned. "I'll talk to Woods. We'll get a better effort out of them."

"I don't mean that they're doing a bad job," said Dog. "Just that we can help them do a better one."

"I told you I'll take care of it," said Samson. "Keep me updated."

The screen blanked.

"Nice to talk to you too," said Dog.

**Aboard Marine Osprey *Angry Bear One,*
over western Pakistan
0130, 18 January 1998**

JENNIFER GLEASON BALANCED THE LAPTOP BETWEEN HER legs, squinting at the close-set type as she continued her doctorate-level briefing in rocket science.

Or more specifically, rocket-guidance electronics, and how they interacted with T waves.

While the T-Rays had fried most of the missile's circuitry, one of the solenoid valves and two electronic level sensors— parts used in the rocket motor itself—had apparently escaped damage. The experts at Dreamland theorized that something had inadvertently shielded these pieces. Jennifer hadn't spotted any sign of deliberate shielding, she could not see a difference between the unaffected solenoid valve and another unit that had failed.

The first reaction at Dreamland was that she must have missed something, and they forwarded her reams of technical data. Having now read six different papers explaining how the systems worked, she had enough background to be as confused as the experts.

One of the T-Ray experts believed that whatever had shielded the parts simply vaporized during the crash. This seemed plausible, especially if what shielded the components had actually been part of something else, such as a temperature monitor for one of the fuel tanks. The shields used by the Megafortresses were not thick pieces of lead or other heavy metal, but a thin mesh of wires that ran current when the T-Rays hit. The shields were "tuned" to catch the radiation in the way a sound-canceling machine "caught" or neutralized sound; the shield's trough effectively neutralized the T-Ray's mountain peak. A thin-wire temperature sensor, or perhaps a radio antenna, might have accidentally provided a partial shield.

Jennifer thought it more likely that there wasn't enough information about how the T-Rays worked, and that they were interacting with something else. If this were the case, it could take years before the problem was actually solved. In any event, she had to gather as much data as possible.

The Osprey jerked as it hit a bit of turbulence, and the Marine sitting next to her brushed against her. Jennifer shot him a glance. His eyes were fixed on the mesh deck between his combat boots. He looked young, nineteen or twenty at most, and very tired.

None of the men aboard the aircraft—she was the only woman—had slept much in the last forty-eight or seventy-two hours. Even Captain Freah, who ordinarily never looked tired, seemed beat.

She knew there was a good chance she looked as tired as they did. She brushed back a strand of hair from her ear, then turned her attention back to the laptop, bringing up another technical paper to read.

Sergeant Liu glanced around the cabin, nervous for the first time in as long as he could remember.

The sergeant didn't consider himself a particularly brave man. On the contrary, he thought of himself as prudent and careful, not much of a risk taker. While others might view his job as exceedingly risky, in Liu's view, working special operations was a good deal less hazardous than most combat jobs in the service. He continually trained and practiced, and worked with only the most qualified people. Missions were generally carefully planned and laid out. As long as you remembered your training and did your job, the odds were in your favor. There was no reason to be scared.

But he was nervous tonight, very nervous.

The image of the little kid being born stayed in his head. Possibly—probably—the child was dead before he was born, but he had no way of knowing.

Why had God sent them to the house if He intended on letting the child and its parents die?

A Catholic Chinese-American, Liu had always felt some solace in his faith, but now it seemed to raise only questions. He knew what a priest would tell him: God has a plan, and we cannot always know it. But that didn't make sense in this case—what plan could He accomplish by letting a child die? Why go to such extraordinary lengths to send help to the baby, then snuff its life out? And the lives of its parents?

Liu looked up. Captain Freah was staring at him.

"You ready, Nurse?" Danny asked.

"Ready and willing," said Liu, shrugging.

**Aboard Dreamland *Bennett*,
over Pakistan
0201**

WHEN THE OSPREY WAS TEN MINUTES FROM THE LANDING zone, Dog gave Starship the order to take out the guerrillas on the ground.

Starship had the two Flighthawks moving in figure eight orbit over the lake. He took them over from the computer and brought them down so they could make their attacks from opposite sides, catching the men on the ground in the middle. With a split screen and left and right joysticks, he felt briefly as if he were two people, each a mirror image of the other.

Green sparkles flashed on the screen of *Hawk Two*—tracers, fired by someone on the ground unit reacting to the sounds of the airplane.

The targeting box on the screen for *Hawk One* began to

blink, indicating that the computer thought he was almost close enough to shoot. Starship held off for another few seconds, then opened fire just as the tracers turned in his direction.

The effect was brutal and efficient, lead pouring into the men who'd tried to shoot him down little more than an hour earlier. Only two of the men on the ground seemed to escape the first pass, running to the north and throwing themselves on the ground as the Flighthawks passed east and west.

Starship cleared both of the robot planes upward, circled them around, and then pushed into a new attack, this one with the two aircraft in a staggered trail, so that *Hawk Two* flew a bit behind and to the right of *Hawk One*.

"Ground attack preset mode one," he told the computer. "*Hawk Two* trail."

He handed *Hawk Two* off to C^3, allowing the computer to fly as his wingman. In the preset, *Hawk Two* would act like a traditional wingman, primarily concerned with protecting the leader's tail and only firing after *Hawk One* had ended its attack.

Starship nudged his stick gently right, moving *Hawk One* on target. The Flighthawk did not use pedal controls like a manned fighter; instead, the computer interpreted inputs from the stick and took all of the necessary actions. Even so, Starship jabbed his feet against the deck, working an imaginary rudder to fine-tune the approach. He could have been an old-time Skyraider driver, jockeying his A-1A into the sweet spot as he looked for his enemy.

As good as the Skyraider was, it could never have turned as quickly back to the left as he did when he finally saw his targets hiding near a rock formation. He let off a pair of long bursts, then rocketed upward, getting out of the way for *Hawk Two*. As soon as the nose of the aircraft tilted up, Starship changed seats, so to speak, swapping control of the planes with the computer.

The targeting box was flashing red, but Starship couldn't

find the soldiers. Finally, he saw something moving at the very left edge of the target reticule. He kissed the stick gently with his fingers, holding his fire even though the computer declared he couldn't miss.

When he finally did shoot, the nose of his plane was about a half mile from his targets. He walked the bullets left and then right, pulverizing the rocks as well as the men who'd tried to hide in them.

"Hawk leader to *Bennett*. Enemy suppressed, Colonel. You can tell the Osprey it's safe to land."

"Roger that, Hawk leader. Good going, Starship."

Aboard Marine Osprey *Angry Bear One*,
northern India, near China
0206

DANNY FREAH LEAPT FROM THE OSPREY AND RAN BEHIND the Marine pointmen as they raced toward the men the Flighthawk had gunned down a few minutes before.

Twenty millimeter shells did considerable damage to a body, and even battle-hardened Marines didn't linger as they surveyed the dead.

If they had been farther west, Danny would have thought the mangled bodies belonged to Afghan mujahideen. He had briefly worked as an advisor with mujahideen fighting the Russians a few years before, instructing them at a small camp in northern Pakistan. Some of those same men, he believed, were now sworn enemies of the U.S. They or their brothers had participated in a number of attacks against the U.S. military, including a suicide bombing of the USS *Cole* in the Persian Gulf.

"Looks like they were using sat phones to communicate," he told Colonel Bastian after the remains had been searched. "I have two of the phones. One of them is pretty shot up, but maybe the CIA can get something off of them."

"Anything else?"

"Negative," said Danny. "I'd sure like to know if they're working with the Chinese."

"For the moment, we have to assume they are," said Dog. "Did Dreamland Command give you possible search coordinates?"

"Northeastern quadrant of the lake. We're on it, Colonel."

Aboard Dreamland *Bennett*,
over Pakistan
0210

"BIG PACKAGE COMING FOR US COLONEL," WARNED Sergeant Rager at the airborne radar station. "I have six Su-27 interceptors, Chinese, on their way from the north, 273 miles. Two aircraft, currently unidentified, behind them. Large aircraft," he added. "Maybe transports, maybe bombers. Can't tell."

Dog keyed the Dreamland channel to contact the *Cheli*. Despite its pilot's optimistic prediction earlier, the Megafortress was still about ten minutes away.

"Dreamland *Bennett* to *Cheli*. Brad, looks like the Chinese want to crash the party."

"Roger that, Colonel. We're ready."

Dog scowled, now a little suspicious of Captain Brad Sparks's overarching optimism. He told Sparks that he wanted him to take the *Cheli* north and intercept the Sukhoi at long range.

"Shoot them down with your Anacondas," Dog said. "Use them at long range, in case the Chinese have more passive radiation seekers. The MiG-31s fired at about 140 miles."

"Roger that, Colonel. You told me. We're good. Copy everything."

"Get the lead out, Sparks," Dog added. "Our people are sitting ducks on the ground there."

Karachi, Pakistan
0210

GENERAL MANSOUR SATTARI PULLED HIMSELF FROM THE rear of the Mercedes and stepped into the chilly predawn air. Gravel crunched beneath his feet as he walked down the dark path toward a squat cement building in one of Karachi's poorer districts. Like most of the rest of the country, power had not yet been restored, and the only light came from the dim reflection of the moon, peeking from behind a veil of thin clouds.

The door of the house opened as Sattari approached.

"General, my general, how good to see you," gushed the tall man who stood on the threshold. "I received word two hours ago—an honor."

"Thank you, Razi," said Sattari. "May I come in?"

"Of course, of course. My manners."

Razi was the size of a bear, and awkward in his movements; he pushed back and knocked into a small table as he made way for his guest. Two chairs were set up in the front room, with an unlit candle between them; Razi gestured for Sattari to sit, then bent to light the candle. The light made small headway against the room's dimness.

"How are you, General? I was sorry to hear about your son."

"Yes."

"I am assured that the burial was prompt and proper," said Razi, reaching to the floor and picking up a large manila envelope. "The location is on a map. The people who discovered the body were devout Shiites."

Sattari nodded. He opened the envelope and looked inside. He could see that there were two photographs, intended to seal the identification. He hesitated, then pulled them out, determined to confront the bitter reality.

His son's face was bloated from the water, but it was definitely him. Sattari slipped the pictures back inside the envelope.

"I greatly appreciate your service," the general told Razi. "You have done much for me."

Razi nodded. Now the second in command of the Iranian spy network in Pakistan, his father had served with Sattari in the days of the shah. Not quite as tall as his father, who had been a true giant, he had inherited his hard gaze.

"And so, what are the Pakistanis up to?" Sattari asked, changing the subject.

"In chaos, as usual. Some want to make peace with the Indians. Some want to continue the war. They are so disorganized. They have not even been able to mobilize to recover the missiles that the Americans disabled."

"Can they be recovered?"

"The Americans are already hard at it. That is what we have heard, anyway. There is no reason to doubt it—the Americans are everywhere."

"Yes," said Sattari.

"The Chinese are doing the same thing, we believe," said Razi. "They are very, very busy. They have made an alliance with the bearded one, the Saudi. An alliance with the devil."

Sattari had nothing but disdain for the Saudi, a Sunni fanatic who had built a terror network by giving money to every psychotic madman in the Middle East. The Saudi hated Shiites, and hated Iran.

Still, there was a saying: The enemy of my enemy is my friend.

"What is the Saudi doing?"

"He has offered money for the recovery of a weapon, that much we know. And, from the two camps he had in the Baulchistan, some followers were sent north. They must be looking for it. Perhaps the Chinese helped him. Rumors . . ." Razi was silent for a moment. "The Pakistani army actually tried to stop them, but after a gun battle they slipped away."

"The Chinese are helping him?"

"It is not clear," said Razi. "One of my people works at the Chinese consulate, the headquarters for the Chinese spy operations. There was a meeting a day ago, with a representative of the Saudi. After that, more activity. Their cryptologists were so busy they could not go home. The consulate is one of the few places in the city with its own power and satellite dishes," he added. "Even the local government has asked to use them."

"Do they know where the missiles came to earth?"

"The Pakistanis do not. The radars tracking them were wiped out by the American weapons."

"The Chinese must," said Sattari. "That is why the Saudi is working with them."

"Or perhaps they just want his money."

Sattari leaned back in his chair, thinking. Here was his opportunity after all.

Perhaps.

"I would like to go to Islamabad," he said, making up his mind. "Is this possible?"

"Anything is possible, General."

"Are there men there who can be counted on?"

"Yes." Razi looked up, and their eyes met. "There is one thing, though."

"What is that?"

"The oil minister was found dead in a mosque complex yesterday."

"The Pakistani oil minister?" said Sattari, feigning ignorance.

"Our minister. Jaamsheed Pevars."

"I had not heard that."

The two men's eyes were locked.

"My superior was a friend of Pevars," said Razi.

"No one is closer to the oil minister than I," said Sattari. "Are you sure that he is dead? I saw him myself just a few days ago."

"Very sure. His murderer should be brought to justice."

"As quickly as possible."

Razi grinned faintly, then rose. "For myself, I did not like Pevars. Too corrupt. Come, let me give you the name of a man who might help you in Islamabad. You should leave immediately."

An atoll off the Indian coast
Time and date unknown

THEY MOVED TOGETHER IN A DANCE, THEIR BODIES SO CLOSE
together they seemed to be welded, his leg between hers, her
back nestled against his stomach. They rolled on the bed in a
timeless trance, restless but peaceful in sleep, so used to the
other's movements that even their breaths were in sync.

Then something gripped him and he began sliding away,
pulled back by a force greater than gravity, yet slower, more
painful. He tried to cling to her but could not, found himself
twisting in hot wind. An intense heat enveloped his head. His
throat became parched, then burned. He was alone and felt
empty, thirsty, for water and for her.

Alone.

Zen pushed himself away, rising on his chest in the darkness before twilight. He was sure that Breanna was gone.

But she wasn't. He heard her breathing before he saw her,
saw her before he felt her. He let himself slip back against
her, trying to reassure himself that what he had felt was just a
misshapen remnant of a bad dream induced by thirst and
nothing else.

He was very thirsty but they had to conserve their water.

Perhaps this was what had caused his nightmare.

Thirst.

Zen wrapped his arm gently around his wife, cupping her
breast. He tried to remember the first time he'd done that,
concentrating not on the day or the time but the sensation,
the way it had felt the first time to be in love. That was what
he wanted to remember. He slid closer to Breanna, pressing
his body on hers, huddling against the pain until the faint
memory of falling in love lulled him to sleep.

Northern India,
near the Chinese border
0220

THE WATER WAS AS CLEAR AS A POOL. LIU MOVED HIS WRIST light around, playing it in front of him as he slid downward. The large rocks at the bottom were smooth and shiny white, as if they'd been polished.

A piece of jagged metal lay on the floor of the lake to his left. He paddled to it slowly, still getting his bearings. The water wasn't quite as cold as he'd thought it would be, but it was far from warm. The scuba gear stored on the Osprey was standard Navy gear, without the heating circuits that were part of the Dreamland equipment.

The metal twisted into a C, the curved end pointing toward a shallow ravine twenty feet away. Liu swam toward it, guided by the light from Captain Freah's wrist as well as his own. The captain pushed ahead of him, then moved to his right. As Liu began to follow, a shadow emerged from the rocky bottom.

The baby. Not breathing.

It wasn't the baby. Liu knew it wasn't, but he had a hard time clearing the notion from his mind. He forced himself to look away, but the idea persisted, as if the ghost had managed to get inside his skull.

Danny Freah was waving at him. He'd found the warhead.

Liu pushed up to the surface, grateful to get away.

"Here!" he yelled to the others. "Here!"

JENNIFER WATCHED FROM THE SHORELINE AS THE OSPREY settled over the spot where Liu and Danny had surfaced. A metal chain and strap dangled from its belly; the strap would be connected to a hastily rigged harness that Danny and the sergeant had put on the warhead.

The noise from the Osprey was so loud that Jennifer almost didn't hear Danny's smart helmet beeping with an incoming communication. She put the helmet on, cleared the transmission, and found herself talking to Dog.

He stared at her for a moment, clearly taken off guard. Jennifer felt an overwhelming urge to kiss him—but of course she couldn't.

"There's a fresh wave of Chinese fighters on their way," said Dog. "Two other aircraft as well. May be transports with paratroops; they're a little too far away right now. What's your situation?"

"We've located the warhead in the water. They're rigging the Osprey to pull it out now."

"How long before you get it out of there?"

"It'll take a couple of hours at least. Safing it is an hour-long procedure."

"Move it along as quickly as you can," Dog said.

"Tecumseh, I know you're mad, but I only did—"

"This isn't the time. Bastian out."

**Aboard Dreamland *Cheli*,
over northwest India
0235**

NAILING THE SUKHOIS WAS AS EASY AS PRESSING A BUTTON.

Or should have been. The targeting system was having trouble locking.

"I can't lock number three, Brad," said Steve Micelli, the *Cheli*'s copilot. "It just won't lock."

"Yeah, keep trying," snapped Sparks. The pilot put his hand on the throttle glide, urging more power from the turbos.

"Targets are at 160 miles," said the airborne radar operator, Tom "Cheech" Long.

"Yeah yeah, Cheech, I know," said Sparks. "Come on, Stevie. Get the missiles locked and away."

"Targeting *Bandit Three*," said the copilot finally. "Locked. Firing missile."

The Anaconda whipped away, sailing out from under the

Megafortress's nose. Two more followed in quick succession.

Then more problems.

"Lost *Bandit Six* entirely," said Micelli.

"Steve, I'm going to get up and slap you on the side of the head if you don't stop screwing around," said Sparks. "And I'm only half joking here, dude."

"I'm trying, Brad. I'm trying."

Sparks glanced at his sitrep plot, which showed his position and that of the other aircraft in the sky. The Sukhois were moving at him from the northwest; he was nose-on with their leader, *Bandit One*, at 150 miles.

"Missile launch from *Bandit One*. Missile launch from *Bandit Two*," warned the radar man.

"Steve?"

"Yeah—got it. ECMs."

"Stand by for evasive maneuvers."

As soon as the Anaconda missile was under way, Sparks threw the Megafortress into a hard turn south.

"Missiles are tracking us," said Cheech. "Must be passive homers, just like Colonel Bastian said."

"The ol' Dog knows his stuff," said Sparks, starting another turn, this one to the west. "Kill ECMs."

"Moving at 2,000 knots," said Cheech. "Coming for us. Both of them."

"I only want to hear good news from you, Cheech."

Sparks had turned the aircraft around so the missiles were now following him; he hoped to outrun them. The problem was, he didn't know if it was possible, since he had no data on the missiles' range. They were moving roughly 33 miles a minute to his ten.

"Hey, Flighthawk leader—you staying with me or what?" Sparks asked.

"With you," said Lieutenant Josh "Cowboy" Plank. "We running away from these assholes?"

"Bite your tongue, Cowboy," said Sparks. "This is merely a strategic retreat."

Unlike the *Bennett*, the *Cheli* was only escorted by one

Flighthawk; Cowboy didn't have enough experience yet to handle two at a time, and there was no second Flighthawk pilot available.

"Missile one—bull's-eye!" said Micelli. "Nailed him! Missile two—hit."

Sparks listened with satisfaction as the copilot tallied the score—five Sukhois down.

"What happened to *Bandit Four*?" said Sparks.

"Still there. Missile is off the screen."

Sparks had other things to worry about at the moment— the two missiles that had been launched at him were now just thirty miles from his tail. He began a series of hard jinks, pushing the Megafortress sharply left and right in the sky, hoping the trailing missiles would have a difficult time following.

"Stinger air mines," he told Micelli. "Get ready."

"Ten miles," warned Cheech.

The air mines had a very limited range, and to make it easier for his copilot, Sparks had to hold the plane as steady as possible. Unfortunately, that would also make it easy for the missiles.

"Five miles. Stinger ready."

"Well, shoot the bastards down!"

A *chit-chit-chit* sound erupted from the back as the air mines were launched. Sparks put his hand on the throttle, urging the power plants to give him a few more knots.

Sixty seconds later he realized they'd made it.

"Missile is off the scope," said Cheech. "Gone."

"I shot it down! I got it!" yelled Micelli. "I got them both. Yeah! *Yeah!*"

Sparks turned the Megafortress back in the direction of the Sukhoi and the two larger aircraft. They had altered their courses slightly, but were still moving toward the area where the warhead was being recovered.

"Computer is IDing those two aircraft as Fokker F27 airliners," said Cheech.

"Go away," said Micelli. The encounter had given him a

serious adrenaline rush, Sparks thought, as if he could fly home without the airplane.

"No shit, that's what it says," said Cheech. "Two Airbus airliners."

"You queried them?" asked Micelli.

"Computer did and it confirmed."

"Bullshit. Try it again."

"We're too far right now. You think it's going to be different?"

"All right boys, settle down," said Sparks. "Flighthawk leader—yo, Cowboy, I want you to rustle on over there and scout those aircraft out. We'll take the *Suck*-hoi."

"Roger that, *Cheli*."

**Northern India,
near the Chinese border
0250**

THE OSPREY'S HEAVY ROTOR WASH PUSHED DANNY FREAH downward as he waited for the aircraft to get close enough so he could attach the lifting chain. Liu treaded water near him, pushed the spray from his face while rubbing his face so hard Danny thought he was going to poke his eyeballs out.

Unlike their Whiplash-issue diving gear, the borrowed Navy sets didn't have radios. A spotter stood on the shoreline, radioing to the pilot of the Osprey, who was also relying on two crewmen in the rear to help guide him.

His first attempt was way off, the chain closer to the shore than to them. As the Osprey moved sideways, the chain began to swing like a pendulum. Danny made a swipe, only to have the heavy strap at the bottom smack the back of his hand so hard he thought for a moment he'd broken a bone.

Liu lunged at it, grabbing the loop and wrapping his body around it. The Osprey's momentum pushed him several feet through the water. Danny seized him as he began to twirl around, pulling him to a stop.

"This is almost funny!" yelled Danny.

The roar of the V-22's engines overhead made it impossible to hear if Liu replied. Danny let go of him and, his hand still hurting, plunged beneath the water and retrieved the harness lead from the warhead a few feet below. They hooked the lines together, then swam backward to get out of the way.

As they did, Liu disappeared beneath the roiling surface of the lake. Danny glanced to his right, getting his bearings, then looked back, expecting to see Liu. But he wasn't there.

He stared, waiting for his sergeant to reappear. Three or four seconds passed, then ten, then twenty.

Where was he?

IF IT WAS GOD'S WILL THAT THE BABY AND HER FAMILY DIE, thought Liu, what is His will now? If I just let myself sink beneath the waves, will He let me drown?

Pushed under by the rotor wash, Liu let his body drift down, toward the smooth rocks and shadows he'd seen before, toward the ghost that he knew waited here.

How easy it was to just let go, to just give up and die.

He took his breather away from his face. Almost immediately his lungs began to scream for water.

Liu drifted, expecting the baby to appear. He closed his eyes, then opened them. There were shapes in the water, strange shapes, but he recognized them all—the warhead being lifted, Captain Freah's feet in the distance, some of the metal casing to the missile that they'd discarded earlier.

No ghosts. No easy way out.

If he stayed underwater until his lungs burst, then he would never know why it had happened. He would never know if it was part of another plan, if it was meant to push him toward something or if God had merely extracted some awful toll and wanted him as a witness to His power.

Did he really want to know?

Yes, answered Liu, pushing back to the surface.

* * *

JENNIFER STARTED TO TROT TOWARD THE WARHEAD AS THE Marine Osprey set it down on the beach.

"The Chinese are coming," she told Danny, explaining what Dog had told her.

"All right. We'll pack it into the Osprey and take it back to Base Camp One."

"We have to make it safe first," she said.

"That'll take far too long. There's a plane full of Chinese paratroopers on the way," said Danny. "No. I'll do it in the Osprey."

"You're crazy."

"We have to get out of here."

"I'll safe it," said Jennifer.

"In the Osprey," said Danny, kicking off his flippers.

Not having an alternative, Jennifer nodded.

**Aboard Dreamland *Bennett*,
over northwest India
0303**

ACCORDING TO COLONEL BASTIAN'S SITREP DISPLAY, THE three aircraft approaching the warhead recovery area included one Sukhoi fighter and two Xian Y-14 transports. The Y-14s were Chinese versions of the Russian An-24 "Curl," military transport aircraft that he guessed were carrying paratroopers.

The screen also showed that the *Cheli* had moved far west during the encounter. Though it was hard to criticize the results of the air battle—five aircraft shot down—Sparks and his crew had put the *Cheli* in a poor position to deal with the other aircraft.

But that's why the *Bennett* was backing him up.

"*Cheli,* what's your situation?" Dog asked.

"Hey, Colonel. We have one bandit, two bogies heading in."

"What do you mean bogies?" Dog said, cutting him off. The slang term meant that the aircraft were unidentified;

"bandits" were airplanes that were ID'd as bad guys, as these should have been. "Those are Xian Y-14 transports."

"Computer is disagreeing with you there, Colonel. We're showing them as Fokker F27s. Cowboy is on his way to check it out. I'm going to handle the other Sukhoi."

Experience alone told Dog that the IDs were wrong; civilian transports did not travel in twos, much less behind a fighter escort.

"You're not in position to make an intercept on that Sukhoi, let alone the transports."

"We will be in five minutes."

"Too long. I've got them," said Dog. "Swing back toward the recovery area."

"Colonel—"

"Swing back toward the recovery area."

"Yes, sir."

STARSHIP PULLED UP THE VIEW FROM THE UNDERSIDE camera of *Hawk One* as the aircraft swung around the recovery area, watching the Osprey straining to pull the warhead from the water. The V-22 seemed to stand dead still, a bodybuilder hunched over a barbell. The aircraft started up slowly, moving toward the northern end of the mountain lake as it went. Starship could see a ripple of waves on the water, but the warhead itself hadn't appeared as the Flighthawk passed by.

"Flighthawk leader, I need you to intercept those two Chinese transports," said Dog over the interphone. "You see them?"

"On it, Colonel."

Starship checked the sitrep, discovering that the airplanes were less than seventy miles away. He pulled back on his stick, automatically taking *Hawk One* from the computer's control.

"The *Cheli*'s radar system is claiming that the aircraft are Fokker airliners," added Dog. "We have them as Y-14s. Verify them visually."

Starship touched the talk button for his mike, allowing him to give a voice command to the computer. "Trail *one*," he said, ordering the computer to fly *Hawk Two* behind the other Flighthawk.

"What do you want to do with that Sukhoi?" Starship asked.

"That's mine. You concentrate on the transports."

"Roger that."

**Aboard Dreamland *Cheli*,
over northwest India
0324**

"WE JUST SHOT DOWN LIKE FIVE AIRPLANES—*FIVE!*—AND Bastian's mad at us?" said Micelli.

"I wouldn't call him mad," Sparks told him. "Just not happy."

"It's Cheech's fault," retorted the copilot. "We have bullshit IDs on those transports. Everybody knows they're not civvies."

"Hey, screw you, Micelli," said the airborne radar operator. "The radar says what the radar says. They're *not* identing," he added, using slang for using the automated identification gear. "What can I tell you?"

"Relax, guys," said Sparks sharply. "We went too far west getting out of the way of the Chinese missiles. Just play it the way it lays."

Sparks pushed the Megafortress south toward the warhead recovery area.

"You with us, Flighthawks?" he asked.

"Roger that," said Cowboy. "Got your six, big mother."

Aboard Dreamland *Bennett*,
over northwest India
0330

"MISSILE LAUNCH!" SHOUTED SULLIVAN, THE *BENNETT*'S copilot. "Two—FD-60s. Pen Lung Dragon Bolts."

"ECMs."

The FD-60 was a medium range semiactive radar homing missile similar to the Italian Aspide, which by some reports had been reverse-engineered to create it. Unlike the missile they had dealt with earlier, Dog had considerable experience with the Dragon Bolt, and was confident the electronic countermeasures would sufficiently confuse it.

"Range is forty miles," said Sullivan. "Sukhoi is changing course."

As soon as it fired its missiles, the Chinese plane swung eastward. Dog held his own course steady, figuring the Sukhoi was looping around to get closer to the transports.

"He may be running away," said Sullivan as the Sukhoi continued to the east.

"No, he's going to swing back and protect the transports. Where are those missiles?"

"Missile one is tracking. Missile two is off the scope."

"Keep hitting the ECMs."

"We're playing every song the orchestra knows, Colonel."

THE LEAD TRANSPORT WAS A SMALL GRAY BLIP IN THE SIMU-lated heads-up display screen at the center of Starship's station. According to the computer, the aircraft had turboprop engines, was moving at 320 knots, and was definitely a Xian Y-14. But Starship knew he couldn't trust the computer's ID; he had to close in and get visual confirmation.

But the computer was so integrated into the aircraft he was flying that even a "visual" was heavily influenced by the computer's choices. The image he saw wasn't an image at all, it was constructed primarily from the radar aboard the Mega-fortress. The computer took the radar information, along with data from other available sensors, weighed how much each was worth under the circumstances, and then built an image to the pilot that represented reality. Even at close range, when he was ostensibly looking at a direct image from one of the Flighthawk's cameras, the computer was involved, enhancing the light and steadying the focus. So where did you draw the line on what to trust?

The two aircraft were flying single file, headed directly toward the lake. They were descending at an easy angle, coming down through 20,000 feet above sea level—relatively close to some of the nearby peaks, which topped 12,000. The lake and the valley it was in were about 5,000 feet.

Starship was approaching the lead plane just off its right wing. At ten miles he switched the main screen to the long-range optical view, but all he could see was a blur, and a small one at that.

Within five seconds he had closed to inside five miles. The starlight-enhanced image showed a dark gray plane with no civilian markings. It was a twin turbojet, high-winged, with its engines close to the fuselage. Admittedly, it looked a lot like the reference pictures of a Fokker that he had pulled up from the Tactics library. But the wing area was larger, and the angle of the fuselage near the tail just a bit sharper—according to the computer, which modeled the image against the references for him.

But the key for Starship were the passenger windows—round on the An-24, and round on the airplane in front of him. The Fokker's were rectangular.

All aircraft carried an IFF—Identification Friend or Foe—system, designed to distinguish between civilian and military aircraft. While the Megafortress had tried ident earlier, Starship instructed the computer to query the airplane again. The transponders in the two planes failed to respond.

"*Bennett,* I have the lead turbojet aircraft in sight," said Starship. "I confirm visually that it is an An-24. Be advised, its ident does not respond."

"Roger that. Take it down."

"Copy, *Bennett*."

THE SU-27 BEGAN A TURN BACK TOWARD THE TRANSPORTS when it was about fifty miles from the *Bennett*, a little later than Dog hoped. His plan was to get close to the Su-27 and then spin in front of him just within range of the Stinger air mines.

He'd have to wait two whole minutes now before he'd be close enough to make the turn, and a lot could happen in that time. Including getting hit by the Sukhoi's first missile, which was still tracking them.

"Missile one is still coming at us," said Sullivan. "Ten miles."

"Chaff. Crew, stand by for evasive maneuvers," said Dog, even as he jerked the aircraft onto its wing. The chaff was like metal confetti tossed into the air to confuse targeting radars. The Megafortress dropped downward, away from the chaff, in effect disappearing behind a curtain. Dog pressured his stick right, putting the EB-52 into a six g turn.

The missile sailed past. Apparently realizing its mistake as it cleared the cloud of tinsel without finding an aircraft, it blew itself up—not out of misery, of course, but in the vain hope that its target was still nearby.

By this time, however, the *Bennett* was swinging back to the north. The Su-27 was approaching her nose from about two o'clock. The Chinese fighter pilot wanted to do exactly what Dog wanted him to do—get on his tail and fire his heat-seekers. Quicker and with a much smaller turning radius than the Megafortress, the Chinese pilot undoubtedly felt he had an overwhelming advantage.

Dog had flown against Chinese fighter pilots several times. They had two things in common: They were extremely good stick and rudder men, and they knew it. He was counting on this pilot being no different.

What he wasn't counting on was the PL-9 heat-seeker the pilot shot at his face as he approached.

"Flares," said Dog. He tucked the Megafortress onto her left wing, sliding away as the decoys exploded, sucking the Chinese missile away.

The Su-27 pilot began to turn with the Megafortress, no doubt salivating at the sight—the large American airplane was literally dropping in front of him, its four turbojets juicy targets for his remaining missile.

"Stinger!" said Dog. "Air mines!"

Sullivan pressed the trigger, and the air behind the Megafortress turned into a curtain of tungsten.

"Launch! Missile launch! He's firing at us!" shouted Sullivan.

Dog throttled back hard and yanked back sharply on his stick, abruptly pulling the nose and wings of his aircraft upward. The aircraft's computer barked out an alarm, telling him that he was attempting to "exceed normal flight parameters"— in layman's terms, he wasn't flying so much as turning himself into a brick, losing all of his forward momentum while trying to climb. The Megafortress shook violently, gravity tugging her in several different directions at once.

Down won. But just as it did, Dog pushed the stick forward and ramped back up to military power on the engines. This caused a violent shudder that rumbled through the fuselage; the wing roots groaned and the aircraft pitched sharply to the right. Dog eased off a bit, grudgingly, then finally saw what he'd been hoping for—two perfect red circles shooting past.

They were followed by a much larger one. This one wasn't simply red exhaust—the edges of the circle pulsed with a violent zigzag of orange and yellow. Not only had the Sukhoi sucked a full load of shrapnel into its engine, but one of the exploding air mines had started a fire.

"He's toast!" yelled Sullivan. A second later the canopy of the Chinese jet flew off and the pilot bailed, narrowly avoiding the tumult of flames as his aircraft turned into a Molotov cocktail.

* * *

STARSHIP STRUGGLED TO KEEP HIS FLIGHTHAWK ON A steady path as the Megafortress jerked and jived through the air. This was the most difficult part of flying the robot planes: making your hand do what your mind told it to do, and not what its body wanted. The disconnect between what was happening on the screen—an aircraft in straight, level flight—and what was happening to his stomach was difficult to reconcile.

Starship put both hands on the control and lowered his head, leaving the Megafortress behind as he willed himself inside the little plane. He took *Hawk One* in a wide turn to his left, away from the military transport he'd just passed. *Hawk Two*, trailing by a little over two miles, followed. He thought of switching planes—*Hawk Two* would have had an easier shot—but the Megafortress's shuddering sounds seemed to promise more heavy g's to come, and he decided to stay where he was.

By the time he came out of his turn, the lead aircraft had made a turn of its own to the east. Its companion was following suit.

"Colonel, my contacts are heading away," said Starship. "Should I pursue?"

"Stand by, Flighthawk leader."

The *Bennett* leveled off. Starship checked the position of his airplanes on the sitrep; he was about eighty miles northeast.

"What's the situation, Starship?"

"Looks like they've broken off and are heading home," said Starship. "I'm not sure if they saw the Flighthawks or not—*Hawk One* was definitely close enough for a visual."

"Save your bullets," said Dog. "We're out of Anacondas and we may need them for the ride home."

VI

Borrowed Time

———

White House basement
1500, 17 January 2006
(0600, Karachi)

"So I hear Rocky Balboa finally got his mitts on Dreamland," Margaret McGraw said when she called Jed to brief him on the latest round of NSA intercepts related to the warhead recovery mission.

"How's that?"

"Oh, don't give me the I'm-above-all-the-infighting line, Jed. I know you know what's going on. Admiral Balboa pulled a coup."

"Dreamland is being folded back, um, um, into the c-c-command structure."

"There's a positive spin for you. What are they going to do with you?"

"What do you mean?"

"They're not kicking you out too, are they?"

"N-N-Not that I know."

"Kissing up to Balboa, huh?"

"No."

McGraw laughed. She was a section leader in the NSA analysis section. Jed had met her only once or twice in person, but had spoken to her several times a week for more than a year.

"To work," she said. "There's a definite connection between the Kashmir guerrillas and China. They're going *crazy* looking for the gadget."

"Gadget" was McGraw's way of saying warhead. She summarized a set of NSA intercepts and decrypted messages, then told Jed that the CIA had somewhat similar information from "humanint"—human sources, or spies.

"Word is, though, DIA and Navy intelligence are poo-pooing it," added McGraw. "They think China is neutral."

"Why?"

"Because the words 'Navy' and 'intelligence' don't go to-gether?" McGraw laughed. "Did I ever tell you what DIA stands for?"

"Like twenty times," said Jed.

"Aw, ain't that cute—you're turning red." McGraw chuckled.

"How do you know that?" said Jed, who was.

She laughed even harder.

"The Ch-Ch-Chinese have been firing on Dreamland air-craft," said Jed.

"Absolutely. But, see, it hasn't happened to a Navy ship, so they still think China's neutral," said McGraw. "I'm forward-ing you a report on what we have. We have traffic back and forth, but the encryptions are good. We haven't broken them."

"When will you?"

"Don't know. Not my department. It's immaterial," McGraw added. "What do you think they're talking about? The price of tea?"

"Uh, no."

"Good. Well, let's wrap this up, hon. I don't want to keep you from any hot dates."

An atoll off the Indian coast
Time and date unknown

ZEN WOKE THIRSTY, HIS ENTIRE BODY ACHING FOR WATER. For a second he thought he was home, and he reached his hand toward the small table at the side of the bed, where by habit he usually kept a bottle of springwater. But of course he wasn't at home, and instead of finding water, his hand swung against the side of his makeshift tent, collapsing it.

The struggle to fix the shelter took his mind off his thirst for a few minutes, but the craving soon returned. His lips felt as if they had shriveled into briquettes of charcoal. His throat had turned to rock, his tongue to sand.

There was about a half liter left in the bottle from his survival pack. How long could he make that last?

Grudgingly, Zen pulled himself to a sitting position and picked up the bottle. Two sips, he told himself. Small ones.

The first was small, but on the second his parched lips took over and he caught himself gulping.

Enough, he told himself, capping the bottle.

If he was thirsty, Breanna must be even more so.

"Hey, are you awake? Bree? Bree?"

He touched her gently, brushing away her hair. Then he moved his hand to her shoulder and pushed more firmly, as if she'd overslept the morning of a mission.

"Bree, come on now. Come on. Got some water. Let's go."

She didn't move. She was breathing, but still far away.

Was she even breathing?

Zen uncapped the bottle and dripped some of the water onto his fingers, then rubbed it onto her lips, his forefinger grabbing at the chapped flesh. It didn't seem like enough—he cupped his hand in front of her mouth and dribbled it from the bottle, pushing it toward her mouth. But she didn't drink, and the water slipped away to the ground.

"Come on, Bree. We can't waste this!"

For a moment he was angry at her, mad as he hadn't been in months, years—since his accident, when he was mad at everything and everyone, at the world.

"Damn it, Breanna. Get the hell up. Don't leave me! Don't leave me!"

He balled his hand into a fist and pounded his own forehead. The anger disintegrated into fear. Slowly, he recapped the bottle. Tucking it away, he sucked the remaining moisture from his fingers, then crawled out of the tent to see what the new day would bring.

Aboard the *Abner Read*
0600

STORM STOOD ON THE DECK, IGNORING THE SPRAY AS THE ship's low-slung bow ducked up and down in the waves. In order to provide the smallest possible radar signature to an enemy, the *Abner Read* was designed to sit very low in the water, which meant the deck of its tumble-form hull was always wet. It was not exactly a good place to stroll, even on the calmest of days.

Storm liked it, though; standing on it gave you the feeling that you were part of the water. The salt really was in the wind, as the old cliché had it, and that wind rubbed your face and hands raw. It flapped against your sides, scrubbing the diseases of land away, rubbing off the pollution of politics and bureaucratic bullshit.

Should he defy Woods? The admiral was wrong, clearly wrong—even if the Chinese weren't preparing the *Khan* for an attack, even if they had no intention of breaking the truce, wasn't it in America's best interests to sink her?

Especially since she had a nuclear weapon aboard.

Sink her. It would take less than a half hour now.

The opportunity was slipping through his grasp. The *Khan* would be out of range in a few hours.

A gust of wind caught him off balance, nearly sending him off his feet.

Storm steadied himself. He would follow his orders, even if they were misguided. It was his job and his duty. Besides, Eyes would never go against the admiral. He would have to lock him up.

No, that was foolishness. Woods had taken his moment of glory away out of jealousy, and Storm knew there was nothing he could do about it but stand and stare in the *Khan*'s direction, knowing that somewhere in the future they would meet again.

**Base Camp One
0600**

LIEUTENANT DANCER WAS WAITING FOR DANNY WHEN THE Osprey touched with its water-logged load at the Marine camp in the Indian desert. The sun was just starting to rise, and it sent a pink glow across the sand, bathing the woman in an ethereal, angel-like light. It was a good thing Jennifer was with him, Danny thought, because he wouldn't have trusted himself otherwise.

"Captain Freah, welcome back," said Dancer, stepping forward and extending her hand. "Glad you're in one piece."

"Never a doubt," said Danny. "How are you, Lieutenant?"

Dancer gave Jennifer a puzzled look. "How did you get here?"

"We needed an expert to look at some of the wiring and circuits on the missiles," said Danny. "And Jen was available. She jumped in with the Whiplash team."

"You're qualified to jump?"

"Jumping's the easy part," said Jennifer. "It's the landing that's tough."

Dancer turned back to Danny. "Captain, we have to talk. What happened out there?"

Danny explained about the stillborn baby and the disaster that had followed its birth. Dancer had already heard a similar version of the story from the Marines who were on the mission—including Gunny, who had made it a point to say that he'd advised against sending the men.

"He did," said Danny. "I take responsibility for my men."

"The general is worried about how it will look public-relations-wise," said Dancer. She seemed to disapprove as well, though she didn't say so.

"Nothing I can do about that."

Dancer nodded grimly. "I'm sorry."

"Not your fault," said Danny.

"I have to talk to the pilots," said Dancer. "I'll be back."

"Sure."

Danny watched her trot away. His attraction toward her hadn't faded, though it seemed to him she could have been more supportive.

"Lieutenant Klacker's a pretty unique Marine," said Jennifer.

"How do you mean?"

"Oh, it's OK, Danny. I know."

"Know what?"

She laughed. "Nothing."

"No, seriously, Jen. Know what?"

"Nothing . . . You have a crush on her, that's all."

"No, I don't."

Jennifer laughed even harder.

"I'm married," said Danny, wondering if he was talking to Jennifer or to himself.

Jennifer smirked, then changed the subject. "Where do you think I can find something to eat around here?"

"There's a temporary mess tent in that direction," said Danny, pointing. "They may not have anything hot."

"As long as it's edible."

"That may be pushing it as well," he said.

"WHAT'D HE SAY?" DEMANDED BLOW AS SOON AS HE SAW Sergeant Liu.

"What do you mean?" Liu asked his fellow Whiplasher.

"Did Captain Freah say something about what happened?"

Jonesy, silent, stared at them from a nearby stool. The sun had just come up, and Liu found its harsh light oppressive, pushing into the corner of his tired eyes.

"You know Cap," said Liu. "He said what he was going to say already. Case closed."

"It ain't closed, Liu. We're going to be up to our necks because of this." Blow shook his head and made the loud sigh that had earned him his nickname. "Man, I don't know."

"There wasn't anything we could have done differently," Liu told him. "I believe that."

"Is anybody else gonna? We shoulda kept quiet about it. Shit."

"No, we did the right thing," said Liu. "God has a plan."

"God?" said Jones.

"Yeah."

Jones continued to stare blankly toward him. Liu wanted to tell him—both of them, but Jones especially—what he had felt in the water, what he'd realized, but he couldn't put it into words. He'd passed some sort of line, not in understanding, but in trusting—but how did you say that? The words would just sound silly, and not convey a tenth of the meaning. He couldn't even tell himself what had happened.

"I don't know," said Blow. "I think they're going to court-martial us. There'll be an investigation."

"Colonel Bastian will understand," said Liu.

"He's not going to be in charge of it. We're supposed to go to the aircraft carrier to talk to Woods. The admiral. You know what that will be like."

"We know what happened," said Liu. "And the smart helmets will back us up."

"Nobody's going to believe that's the whole story."

"They'll just have to."

"It really went to shit, didn't it?" said Jonesy.

Dreamland
1730

LESS THAN FORTY-EIGHT HOURS INTO HIS COMMAND, AND already he was scheduled for a tête-à-tête with the National Security Advisor, Defense Secretary, and Secretary of State—not bad for someone whom the Chiefs of Staff had obviously decided to shunt aside, General Samson thought, checking his uniform.

Of course, he also had three men who might be charged with a war crime. Even if he could blame that on Colonel Bastian, the stain might spread to him. Samson had decided he'd have to handle the issue with kid gloves. Certainly he'd defend the men, especially if there was evidence that they weren't to blame. But if push came to shove, three sergeants weren't worth jeopardizing his career over.

"They're ready for us, General," said Major Catsman.

"How do I look, Natalie?" Samson asked, presenting himself.

"Very good, sir."

Samson smiled appreciatively. Use a woman's first name, defer to her judgment on aesthetics, and they'd follow you anywhere.

Catsman could be salvaged, as long as he surrounded her with enough of his own people. He needed a good staff officer, someone who knew the place well, so he could avoid the land mines while reshaping the place.

Catsman led Samson down the main hallway to the elevator. Inside, they had to wait for the security devices to take their measurements.

"We're getting rid of that thing," said Samson impatiently.

"General?"

"The biometric thing or whatever the hell it is that's wasting our time."

The elevator jerked the doors closed, as if it had overheard. Samson wondered if maybe it had—there was no telling what the eggheads had concocted here.

The video conference had already begun by the time Samson arrived. Colonel Bastian's red-eyed, stubble-cheeked mug filled the center screen.

"The aircraft were definitely Chinese," Colonel Bastian was saying. "Absolutely no doubt."

"Were you over their territory?" asked Secretary of State Jeffrey Hartman.

"Not for the better part of the engagement."

"Which means you were at one point."

"After we attacked, certainly."

"Before then?" asked Hartman.

"I'd have to review the mission tape. The border there is tricky."

"Do these new weapons pose a threat?" asked Secretary of Defense Arthur Chastain.

"We can neutralize them now that we realize they exist," said Dog. "We'll use radar-emitting decoys."

"What weapons is he talking about?" Samson asked Catsman.

He thought he was whispering, but his voice was picked up by a nearby microphone and transmitted over the network.

"Good evening, General," said the Secretary of Defense. "We're speaking of the radiation homing missiles the Chinese used against the *Bennett*."

"I see," said Samson. Had he been briefed on this earlier? He didn't think so, but then he'd spent the day listening to so many reports about weapons systems that he couldn't be sure.

"The missiles aren't the major threat," said Bastian. "As more of the power comes back and the military in both India and Pakistan turn their attention back to their borders, it's going to be difficult for us to operate up there all. The Marines and our Whiplash people are operating very far from the coast—too far. We have to wrap it up quickly."

"I'm of the opinion that we wrap it up now," said the Secretary of Defense.

"There are only three warheads left," said the Secretary of State. "If we don't get them, someone else will. Terrorists, most likely."

"The Ch-Ch-Chinese are helping them," said a young man Samson didn't recognize.

"Who is that?" Samson asked Catsman. "He has a terrible stutter."

Again, Samson thought his comments were private. But the session was conducted with open mikes, and everyone on the line heard. The young man—Jed Barclay—turned beet red.

"NSC liaison," said Catsman.

"Navy intelligence has a different view," said Admiral Balboa. "They don't see a link. The Chinese actions can be explained by their own internal needs. And you were over their territory, Bastian. You shouldn't have fired."

"I was under fire already," said the colonel. "I did what I had to defend myself and complete my mission."

Samson felt torn. Bastian was surely correct, and one of his people; the general felt he should stick up for him. But on the other hand, Balboa was the head of the Joint Chiefs, and the lieutenant colonel's tone was hardly respectful.

"And then there's the matter of that baby," said Balboa. "Wait until the media gets a hold of that. Al Jazeera, or whatever that damn Arab television station is—they'll crucify us."

"I take responsibility, Admiral," said Bastian.

That was just what Samson wanted to hear. The colonel explained the circumstances, adding that the entire incident had been caught on video.

"So we've heard," said Balboa. "I, for one, haven't seen it."

"As tragic as it was," said Admiral Woods, "it does appear to have been an accident. The Dreamland people uploaded some of the digitalized recording of the event. Obviously, I still want to speak to the men, but from what I've seen—"

"I'm looking into it personally myself," said Samson, protecting his territory. "I'm going to speak to them. I'll make a full report."

Woods frowned. There would be a question of jurisdiction and priority—the men were under Samson's command but had been operationally controlled by him. Who took precedence?

As far as Samson was concerned, he did. He prepared for a fight, but before he could say anything else, the Secretary of State changed the subject.

"Where are the other warheads?" asked Hartman. "How long before they're found?"

"Colonel Bastian is the best source on that," said the admiral.

"We're not sure," said Bastian. "Probably in the far border areas around western Pakistan and northern India, near the Chinese border. The scientists are still refining the estimates.

Additional U-2s and Global Hawk drones have arrived in the area and are flying at night, using infrared and low-light sensors. The scientists are tweaking some of the image reading data to make them more effective. Dr. Rubeo can give you the technical information on the search plots and everything related to them."

"Thank you, Colonel," said Ray Rubeo.

Rubeo was sitting quietly at a front console on the right, head stooped down as if he were one of the engineers and techies monitoring systems—so low-key, in fact, that Samson hadn't noticed him until now. The general kept his displeasure in check as the scientist flashed a brief presentation on the screen showing the possible locations of the three missiles. The presentation was brief and professional, but it still angered Samson—he should have seen it first.

"We are still developing theories on what happened," added Rubeo. "I can bore you with the technical details, or we can move on."

His voice dripped with arrogance, but none of the others peeped.

"Until the President orders otherwise, we have to proceed with the operation," said Chastain. "But it can't go on indefinitely."

"Indeed," said Rubeo. "I would note that the power grids in the affected countries have now been offline for twenty-four hours more than our original projections predictions. We may be living on borrowed time."

Diego Garcia
0930

THE TIRED CHATTER OF THE *BENNETT*'S CREW AS THEY walked toward their quarters irked Michael Englehardt more than he could say. It wasn't just that they were talking about a mission he should have been on; it was the fact that they were talking about Colonel Bastian in such glowing terms.

*Ol' Dog did this, and then he said that . . . Could you be-
lieve how he got the ship to stand still in the air? He sucked
that Sukhoi right into the Stinger air mines . . . I've never
seen anything like that . . . Can't teach an old Dog new
tricks—he knows them all . . .*

And on and on and on until Englehardt thought he would
puke.

It was his fault. He should have been on the mission himself, at least a copilot. He'd acted like a jerk. Bastian had
blindsided him, taking over the plane, but still, he should
have kept his mouth shut.

Not that it was fair. But now his days at Dreamland were
probably numbered.

"You shoulda been there, Mikey," said Sullivan as they
entered the dormitory-style building they'd been given for
personal quarters. "What a wild night."

"I wanted to be there," said Englehardt.

"Yeah." Sullivan immediately turned away.

"Next time," said Englehardt, trying but failing to sound
optimistic.

COLONEL BASTIAN RUBBED HIS EYES AND STARTED TO GET
up from the communications console in the Dreamland Control trailer.

"Hold on there, Tecumseh," said General Samson, his voice
vibrating the speakers over the unit. "Where are you going?"

"I thought we were done," said Dog. "I was thinking—"

"There are a few things I wanted to speak to you about in
private."

"I'd really like to catch some sleep," Dog told Samson. "I
just got back from my mission."

"That's number one—what the hell are you doing flying
missions?"

"What?"

"You have plenty of pilots out there now. Put them to good
use. Yes, I understand the need for a commander to lead
from the front," added Samson, his voice somewhat more

sympathetic. "But you're spending far too much time in the air to actually do your job—your real job—of supervising the men. All the men, not just one plane crew."

Dog was too tired to argue—and Samson didn't give him much of an opening, moving right on to his next subject.

"I want full reports on all of the programs Dreamland is conducting. And a personnel review. How long will it take you to get that all together?"

"As soon as I get back I can—"

"I want you to start working on it immediately."

"I have a mission here to run."

"Devote as much time as possible to it. If you're not flying, you'll have more time. Those Whiplash men—I want to talk to them before they talk to Admiral Woods. Do you understand? They're part of my command. I talk to them first. Not as a Navy admiral. Now do you understand?"

"Sure."

"And another thing . . ."

Samson paused, obviously for effect. Dog felt so tired he thought he would teeter toward the floor.

"Briefings will now be done through me," said the general finally.

"Which briefings?"

"Briefings with administration officials," said Samson. "That's my job. You provide the information to me. I interface."

"Anything you want, General," said Dog.

He reached over and hit the button to kill the communications. Then he got to his feet, suddenly feeling ten times more tired than when he'd come into the trailer, and he'd been pretty tired then.

"Bedtime," he muttered, going to the door—where Mike Englehardt practically knocked him over.

"Colonel, can we talk?" said Englehardt.

"What is it, Mike?"

"Colonel, I want to, uh—apologize. I was a—I mean, I—"

"Yeah, yeah, don't sweat it, Mike."

Dog started to push past. Englehardt grabbed his shoulder. Surprised, Dog looked the pilot in the eye.

"I'm sorry," said Englehardt. "I really want to fly. Pilot, copilot, whatever you say. As long as I'm in the cockpit."

"Well, that's good, because you're going to take the *Bennett* on its next mission. Now let go of my arm so I can go get some sleep, all right?"

An atoll off the Indian coast
Time and date unknown

THE DAY WAS WARMER THAN THE ONE BEFORE, BUT LESS humid, and if not for their extreme circumstances, he might have considered the weather perfect. Trying not to think of his thirst, Zen made several radio calls and rearranged the rocks that helped support their tent so a bit more sunlight fell on Breanna. Finally he began moving down to the water, intending to swim back to the spot where he'd caught the turtle the day before. He was just getting into the water when he heard a shout.

One of the boys was back, paddling his small boat.

"Bart Simpson!" called the youth. It was the youngest one, the first one he'd spotted.

"Hey, Bart!" Zen yelled back. He did his best to hide his surprise that the kid had returned.

The wooden hull of the boy's boat skidded against the shore and he climbed out, pulling a pack with him.

Zen's heart jumped.

"You brought a phone?" Zen asked. "Cell phone?"

"Phone? No."

The boy dropped to his knees in front of him, plopping the bag between them.

"Eat for you," said the kid, pulling a fist-sized package from the bag. It was wrapped in brown paper. A strong odor announced it was fish. The flesh looked purple.

"For me?" asked Zen.

"You."

Zen devoured it. The fish tasted like bad sardines drenched in coconut and vinegar, but he would have eaten ten more handfuls had the boy brought them. He was so hungry he licked at the paper.

"So," he said finally. "No phone, huh?"

"Why do you want phone?"

"I want to call my friends."

"No phone. Who are you? Not Bart?"

Zen guessed that the boy had been quizzed by his parents or other adults when he went home with the turtle. They might be waiting for his answers now, to decide what to do.

He had no idea what was going on in the world beyond this atoll. He wondered if the Chinese had managed to use their nuke, and if so, if the Indians would blame them for the destruction.

"Is there a war?" Zen asked the boy, not sure how to phrase his question.

"War?"

"Did people die?"

The boy looked at him blankly. He was old enough to know what war was, but maybe his village was so isolated he had no idea.

"Where do you live?" Zen asked the child.

"Where do you live, Bart?"

"Where do I live? Las Vegas," said Zen. "Near there."

"Vegas?"

"Slot machines. Casinos. Las Vegas."

"Springfield?"

Springfield was the fictional setting for *The Simpsons* television show.

"That's not a real place, kid," blurted Zen. "I live near Vegas. That's real."

The boy's face fell.

"You know that's a television show, right? Make believe?" asked Zen. He realized he'd made a mistake, a bad mistake, but didn't know how to recover.

The kid started to retreat.

"Hey! Don't go!" yelled Zen. "No. Don't."

But it was too late. The boy pushed the small boat into the water without looking back. Lying across the shallow gunwales, he stroked back toward the sea, turning right and quickly fading from Zen's view.

Base Camp One
1500

DESPITE A TWO-HOUR NAP, JENNIFER WAS STILL FEELING groggy when she sat down with Danny Freah and Dancer to review the situation with the experts at Dreamland Command. The possible locations for the three remaining warheads had now been narrowed down to approximately five-mile rectangles. New data from a pair of U-2s and a Global Hawk scouring the region near northern India and northeastern Pakistan would be available by nightfall.

"Tonight may be it," said Colonel Bastian, coordinating the briefing from Diego Garcia. "Power is coming back all through the subcontinent, and both countries are pushing their militaries to resume patrols. And then there's the Chinese."

They were participating in the briefing via an external speaker and microphone hooked into Danny's smart helmet. Jennifer couldn't see Dog's tired face as he spoke, but she knew what it would look like—thick, sagging bags beneath his eyes, taut lips, hollowed out cheeks.

He'd have shaved before he came on duty. He wouldn't have waited for hot water, just scraped his chin clean as quickly as possible.

But thorough. He had a system that he never deviated from.

"Any word on Zen and Bree?" Danny asked as the briefing came to an end.

Dog paused a second longer than normal before answering, and that half of a half second told Jennifer everything. She could almost feel his chest expanding in the next moment as he took in a breath—a stabilizing breath—before answering.

"Nothing yet," said Dog.

"They'll find them."

"Yup."

And then he was gone, without even saying anything to her.

It took Jennifer a minute or two to return her thoughts fully to the operation. By then Danny and Dancer had drawn up a plan for dividing the Marines into three groups and retrieving the warheads once they were located.

"Wait," she told them as they started to get up from their camp chairs. "Who am I going with?"

Dancer glanced at Danny, then said to her, "You're staying here, aren't you? There are more tests you have to do."

"The tests are a waste of time," Jennifer replied. "I can help disable the weapons."

"I don't think we need you, Jen. No offense," said Danny.

"I'll go with Dancer," she said.

"I have one of the Navy guys," said Dancer, referring to the members of the nuclear team. "The other will be with Gunny on the third team."

"So who's going with you?" Jennifer asked Danny.

"Just me," he told her. "I've done this a couple of times now."

"What if you get hurt? You have no backup."

"Yeah, but—"

"I'm going to get something to eat," she told him. "I'm ready to go whenever you are."

An atoll off the Indian coast
Time and date unknown

TWICE, ZEN THOUGHT HE SAW AIRCRAFT CROSSING THE sky. Not wanting to carry anything that would make it difficult for him to swim back, he'd left the radio back at the tent. All he could do was stare at the sky, trying to make the wisps of clouds form into something tangible.

He had no luck with turtles. Perhaps he had found the only

two on the small atoll yesterday, or maybe the one that escaped had somehow alerted the rest of the species. He sat for
a while in the shallow shelf, staring at the water around him,
and then just staring, wondering what to do next.

Sooner or later someone would hear one of his broadcasts.
They'd track them down and then come for them. There was
no place on earth so desolate that someone somewhere
wouldn't come across you.

But what if the unthinkable had happened, if he and Bree,
and the kids they'd seen yesterday, were the only people left?

He couldn't get the idea out of his mind.

Tired, and convinced that there were no more turtles, he
pushed his way back to the sea. He turned his head so the
side of his face barely touched the water and began gently
stroking back to Breanna.

HE DIDN'T SEE THEM UNTIL HE WAS ONLY A FEW YARDS AWAY,
and then all he saw were their legs, brown and scarred.

Zen's heart jumped. He raised his body, pushing his gaze
upward until he could see their backs and then their heads.
There were three of them—boys. They were arrayed in front
of the tent, standing a few feet away from it in a semicircle. If
they'd had sticks or any sort of other weapon, he would not
have been able to control his rage. As it was, he just barely
managed to stay calm.

"Hey guys, what's going on?" he yelled.

The three kids turned around. The one on the right was
the older boy who'd come yesterday. The others were about
his age.

"So what's happening?" Zen asked. He pushed himself up
the incline toward the tent, then pulled himself into a sitting
position so he sat near their legs. "One of you guys bring a
phone?"

"You're American," said one of the boys. He had a light
birthmark on his cheek, as if someone had pressed a thumb
to his face at birth.

"Yeah. That's right. Where are you from?" Zen asked.

The boy gestured. "Here."

"I didn't see your house."

The kid laughed again, then said something to the others, probably sharing the joke.

"I was wondering if you guys could help me get in touch with my friends," said Zen. "I need some sort of phone."

He wasn't sure if what he said was too colloquial or too fast, or if the boys simply didn't want to help him. In any event, they didn't respond, still talking among themselves. Zen felt his pulse quickening, his apprehension suddenly stoked. The kids might not have weapons, but there were rocks all around.

The gun was in the tent.

"So what do you guys do?" he asked loudly, trying to break through their conversation and gain some sort of control over the situation. He pushed himself to the right, angling a little closer to Breanna. "What's school like?"

"School?" said the young man who'd been there the day before.

"Well, you guys speak English pretty well. I'm sure you go to school."

"Where do *you* go to school?" asked the boy with the birthmark on his face.

"Actually, I'm done," said Zen. "Stanford University. I studied engineering. You ever hear of it? Stanford? California?"

When they didn't respond, Zen asked if any of them wanted to be engineers when they grew up.

"You are a pilot, not an engineer," said the boy with the birthmark. He said it quickly, with a bit of anger—he thought Zen was trying to trick him somehow.

"That's right, I am. But usually you study something else too. Flying is one thing, and you want to learn other things. People study all kinds of things. Literature, sometimes. A lot of engineering and science. Math. Fun stuff. For me."

The boy made a face.

What did he think of when he was twelve or thirteen? Zen wondered. He needed to make conversation, to say something that would make a connection. He didn't want to sound desperate, though clearly he was.

"Do you guys like to fly?" he asked.

"Fly?" said the boy from yesterday. "We can't fly."

"In planes. When I was your age, that was all I thought about. Flying."

"How did you get here?" demanded the boy with the birthmark. His tone was more aggressive than before.

"Our plane was shot down," Zen said. "The Chinese and Pakistanis were going to attack your country. We got in the way."

"The Muslims are scum," said the boy with the birthmark. The others began speaking with him in their native language. They seemed to be vying with each other to make the strongest denunciation of their enemy.

"Was there an attack on your village?" asked Zen.

The young men ignored him. Their conversation had shifted; the boy who had been silent gestured at Zen, telling the others something.

Zen slid closer to the tent. He had no doubt that he could fight them off if they piled on him, but if they were clever, if they picked up rocks, if they attacked Breanna instead of him, he wasn't sure what would happen.

"Can you guys get me a phone?" he asked. "A cell phone? I can call my people."

They ignored him, and started walking up over the hill.

"Water?" Zen asked. "Can you bring us some drinking water?"

They made no sign that they heard him, and within minutes were out of sight.

Northeastern Pakistan
1500

MONEY DIDN'T HELP VERY MUCH IN THE FAR NORTHERN reaches of Pakistan. Knowing people did.

Fortunately for General Sattari, he knew people.

A distant cousin of Sattari's ran a madrassa religious school in the foothills about a hundred miles north of Islamabad. Though not a spy himself, the cousin had helped Iran establish a spy network here, and in turn the Iranian government had helped his school, supplying texts and a small stipend that paid for about a dozen students at a time. They shared space with an assortment of farm animals, including chickens and goats, in a small, white brick compound tucked into the hillside.

"I am honored to help you," said his cousin when Sattari arrived. "You should have given me more notice."

"Had it been possible, I would have," said the general, following him into a small sitting room at the front of the building. "But your lights are out. How did you get my message?"

"There are no power lines here." His cousin gestured to the candles. "This is how we see all year round. I have a generator in the back," he added. "It supplies what we need for the computer, and to charge the satellite phones. We are not like the Saudis. They are the ones with the money to burn. So much that it makes them foolish."

The Saudis were Sunni teachers who ran schools throughout northern Pakistan and southern Afghanistan. Many were aligned with men like bin Laden, who used them to help train supporters sworn to wage holy war against the West. While Sattari did not much mind the results, he considered bin Laden and his ilk amateurs incapable of inflicting real damage.

"I've heard the Saudis have been active here," said Sattari. "There are rumors they have made a pact with the Chinese."

"Yes. They are looking for fallen aircraft parts," said his cousin. "They offer a good reward."

"I'm looking for something myself," said Sattari. "And I can pay more than the Saudis. But it is imperative that I get to it before they do."

A young man entered the room with a tray of tea. He placed it on the table in front of them, then poured them both a cup. Neither Sattari nor his cousin spoke. When the young man left, Sattari's cousin closed his eyes and bent his head, reciting a silent prayer of thanks.

Sattari bowed his head out of respect for his cousin.

"I think we may be able to assist you," said his cousin, lifting his cup. "Warm yourself, and then we will talk."

Dreamland Command
0400

THE MORE HE THOUGHT ABOUT IT—AND UNABLE TO SLEEP at 4:00 A.M., it was *all* he thought about—the more Samson realized Dreamland was not big enough for both him and Lieutenant Colonel Tecumseh "Dog" Bastian. And the more he thought about that, the more he realized that he was better off dealing with the problem sooner rather than later, and in person.

But Bastian was also on to something, leading from the front. Being out there in Diego Garcia, where the action was—that was the secret of his success. Dreamland's high-tech communications gizmos kept him in touch with what was going on back home. Then when the big shots wanted to talk to him, where did they see him but in the thick of things? No wonder he had such a sterling rep.

He could do that himself, Samson thought. He had to do that himself.

And now. Right now. Before Bastian was too big to deal with. He'd go directly to Diego Garcia and assert his personal control.

It would mean leaving someone else in charge at Dreamland while he was gone. The only practical choice was Major Catsman; the few staff officers he'd brought with him were still working out where the restrooms were. She would no doubt be ineffective in dealing with Rubeo, who, despite having toned down his antagonism, showed no sign of actually coming to heel. But Bastian was the bigger problem, Samson decided; once he was dealt with, the other dominos would fall.

The general sat down at the desk in the small VIP apartment he'd commandeered and pulled out the base directory. At a good-sized command, the directory would be a substantial phone book listing the various officers, their responsibilities, and contact information. The Dreamland directory, by contrast, was barely twenty pages long, and most of the listings were for civilian scientists and supervisors.

That was going to change, ASAP. They were seriously undermanned. He needed money, he needed head count, and he was going to get both.

Samson found the officer responsible for scheduling and assigning flights and, despite the hour, called him at home.

"This is Samson," he said when the groggy captain picked up the phone. "What's the status of our VIP aircraft?"

"What VIP aircraft, sir?"

"What does Bastian use to get around? Where is it?"

"The colonel doesn't have a VIP aircraft. Generally on a Whiplash deployment he would be one of the pilots, and is assigned to that aircraft."

"What about a *nondeployment*?"

"Well, it would depend, I guess—"

"How would he get to Washington, Captain?"

"Commercial flight."

Samson shook his head. "I need a plane that can get me to Diego Garcia, and I want it ready immediately. Understood?"

"Sure, General. What sort of plane do you want?"

"One that is waiting for me on the runway no more than two hours from now," said Samson, and hung up. Then he put a red X next to the captain's name in the directory.

**Diego Garcia
1700**

DOG STOOD ON THE CEMENT APRON JUST OUTSIDE THE Dreamland Command trailer, watching as the *Cheli* took off. The Megafortress looked like a vulture in the red light of the horizon-hugging sun. In addition to a Flighthawk beneath each wing, she carried a pair of radar decoys; Sidewinder antiair missiles were loaded at the wingtips.

Two additional warhead sites had been tentatively identified about a hundred miles apart in the area north of Jamu, technically in India though the border was in dispute. The *Cheli* and the *Bennett* would each support a separate recovery mission. If the third warhead was positively located, whichever aircraft was closer would swing over to cover that recovery.

Power had been restored in about a third of southern India in the past few hours; even if the third missile wasn't found, Dog feared this would be the last mission they would undertake.

"Feared" because when the mission was over, the search for Breanna and Zen would end as well.

While the search for the two pilots was continuing, an unspoken adjustment had already been made. While no one said so, the mission had become more a recovery than a rescue. This long after a bailout, the odds of finding either alive was very slim. The searchers, of course, knew that, and would make subtle adjustments, no longer pushing themselves to the limit.

Dog wasn't quite ready to make the adjustment himself. But neither could he pretend that it was likely he would see his daughter or son-in-law alive again. All he could do was stare at the *Cheli,* watching it disappear into the purple sky.

Jamu
2100

DANNY FREAH PUSHED UP THE VISOR ON HIS SMART HELmet as he clambered down to the missile, deciding there was enough light from the moon to see without using the night-vision shield. The weapon seemed to have skidded to a landing as if it were a disabled aircraft, perhaps after a glancing blow against a nearby cliff as it descended. Aside from a large gash at the side of the housing below the warhead assembly, much of the missile was still intact.

A light flashed as Jennifer Gleason snapped a photo of the overall location before descending to examine the warhead.

"You want to take a look at this, Captain!" yelled one of the Marines near the warhead.

"Hey, Jen, something's up," yelled Danny, starting to trot down the embankment. About a third of the way, he tripped over something and began to slide on his back, sledding down the hill until his foot caught on a large boulder.

Cursing, he got up and stalked to the missile. He expected some good-natured ribbing from the Marines gathered around the warhead, but they were silent, staring at the banged-up metal.

One of the access panels on the warhead had separated from the rest of the skin just enough to let light shine through from the inside.

Light. The internal works had not been completely fried.

Jennifer knelt down in front of the panel without saying a word. Danny watched as she took a star-head screwdriver from her small pack of tools and gingerly unscrewed the panel. A bank of LEDs on the circuit board were lit.

"Huh," she said.

Danny reach to the back of his helmet for the communications button.

"You see this, Dreamland?"

"Yes," said Anna Klondike. "Stand by. And please tell Ms. Gleason not to touch anything."

Aboard Dreamland *Bennett*
2130

DURING THE WHOLE FLIGHT, PILOT MICHAEL ENGLEHARDT felt out of sync, as if he'd stepped into a movie moving about a half frame faster than he was.

It was ironic. He'd been *so* keyed up for the sortie before it happened, so ready to go—and so mad at Dog for taking him off the last mission—but now everything just seemed wrong. Or he seemed wrong, almost out of place. The crew didn't respond to him the way they used to. In the space of twenty-four hours, less, they'd become strangers. And so had the plane.

"Indian radar site just powered up," said his copilot, Kevin Sullivan. "Shouldn't be able to see us from this distance, but it may catch the Osprey on the way out. We'll have to alert them."

"Yeah, roger that."

"You want me to do that?"

"Yeah, jeez, come on, Kevin. Do it."

"Two aircraft from the southeast," announced Sergeant Rager, the airborne radar controller. "At 250 miles. MiG-29Bs. Must be out of Adampur."

Englehardt's heart began to pound, and suddenly his throat felt dry. He checked his position on the map, then double checked, basically stalling for time.

What was he supposed to do?

He'd been in situations like this dozens, maybe even hundreds, of times—in simulations. He'd always handled it then.

Now?

Now he was still moving a step behind. What was going on?

"Flighthawk leader to *Bennett*—you want me to send *Hawk Two* out that way?" asked Starship, downstairs in the Flighthawk bay.

"Roger that," he said. "Check them out. Copilot—Kevin, they challenge us?"

"Negative."

"Radar, continue to track. If they continue on course, we'll ask their intentions. If they show hostile signs, we'll shoot them down."

His voice cracked as he finished the sentence. Englehardt winced, hoping no one else would notice. Then he reached for the water bottle he kept tucked in his pants leg, his throat bone dry.

Jamu
2143

JENNIFER GOT DOWN ON HER BELLY SO SHE COULD SEE THE interior of the weapon better, then pushed the electronic probes toward the two points at the far end of the circuit board. The narrow, needlelike probes felt as if they were frozen solid. Anna Klondike had assured Danny that taking the measurements would not cause the weapon to explode. But Jennifer had had too much experience with integrated circuits gone bad to feel completely at ease.

"OK," she told Danny as the needles made contact. "Take the reading, please."

"Zero."

Jennifer pulled the probes back, then straightened.

"Well? What did they say?"

Danny put up his hand. He was wearing his smart helmet, visor up, listening to the experts at Dreamland.

"They say there's about a twenty percent chance that it's armed," he told her. "If that's the case, it can go off at any time."

"No way."

"You want to talk to them?"

"Yes."

Danny pulled off his helmet and put it on Jennifer's head. It felt heavy, and she had to steady it with both hands.

"This is Jennifer Gleason."

"And this is Ray Rubeo," said the scientist. "Why am I talking to you?"

"This bomb is armed?"

"There is a possibility."

"If it was armed, it would have exploded by now."

Rubeo snorted.

"Don't you think?" Jennifer added, slightly less sure of herself.

"The fail-safe circuitry is dead," said Rubeo. "Now is that a good thing or a bad thing?"

"You have the experts there. What do they think?"

"They are divided. We have steps for you to take."

"Is it going to blow up if I do the wrong thing?" Jennifer asked.

"It may. It may very well go off if you do the *right* thing."

"I wish you had a sense of humor, Ray. Then I would think you were joking."

Aboard Dreamland *Bennett*
2150

STARSHIP CORRECTED SLIGHTLY AS THE INDIAN MIG TACKED gently to the north. The MiG was still on a dead run for the Megafortress, about a hundred miles away. The two planes were closing in on each other at a rate of about seventeen miles a minute.

"*Bennett,* this is Flighthawk leader. I'm about two minutes from the MiGs. What's your call?"

"Let's find out what their intentions are," said Englehardt. "Sullivan, see if you can contact them."

The pilot's voice sounded a little shaky. Starship had flown with him once or twice, not long enough to form an opinion. He seemed tentative, but then the prospect of combat could do that the first time you faced it. Starship remembered his first combat sortie—he'd emptied his stomach as soon as they landed.

"Indians don't answer our radio calls," said Sullivan.

"Try again," said Englehardt.

The Indians called the MiG-29 "Baez"—Eagle. The models coming toward the *Bennett* were the initial version produced by the Mikoyan Opytno-Konstruktorskoye Byuro in the 1980s. A twin-engined, lightweight fighter-bomber, the MiG-29 was an extremely maneuverable aircraft, and generally came equipped with a pair of medium-range R-27 Alamos and four shorter range R-73 Archers. The MiG was considerably faster than the Flighthawk, but had one serious disadvantage—its N019 coherent-pulse Doppler radar could not see the Flighthawk until it was in extremely close range.

The attack pattern Starship mapped out took advantage of

that; it was unlikely that the MiG driver would know he was there until the first bullets began smashing through his fuselage.

Assuming Starship got the go-ahead to fire. While the MiGs had not answered the calls from the *Bennett* to identify themselves, they hadn't made any overtly aggressive moves, either.

Hawk Two was now a minute away.

"*Bennett,* how are we proceeding here?" Starship asked.

"Just hang on a minute, Flighthawk leader," said Englehardt.

"Roger that," said Starship, throttling back.

ENGLEHARDT COULDN'T BELIEVE THIS WAS HAPPENING TO him. He just couldn't think.

A voice inside his head seemed to be screaming at him: *Don't blow it!*

I won't.

Don't!

"Still nothing," said Sullivan in the copilot's seat. "They obviously know we're here."

"Their attack radars on?"

"Negative."

Not answering their hails was provocative, Englehardt thought, but not threatening. His orders of engagement were pretty clear that he was to fire only if threatened.

On the other hand, if he let these planes get much closer and they did turn on their attack radars, it might be too late to get away.

"*Bennett,* this is Flighthawk leader. What do you want me to do?" asked Starship.

A good, legitimate question, Englehardt thought. And his good, legitimate answer was—he didn't know.

"I don't see these planes as a threat to us at the moment," he told Starship.

"What if they're carrying dumb bombs and are going to use them on the recovery team?" asked Sullivan.

He wants us to take them down, Englehardt thought. Maybe he's right. Better safe than sorry.

"I have a suggestion, *Bennett*," said Starship.

"Make it," said Englehardt.

"Let's move our orbit away from the ground team. See if they follow. I'll keep *Hawk Two* near them, ready for an intercept."

Good, Starship, good.

Englehardt wondered why he hadn't thought of it—it was a simple, obvious move.

"Good. Let's do that," he said. "Sully, we're going east."

"Hey, I got something on the ground, on the highway that runs to the valley," said Sergeant Daly, working the ground radar. "Four trucks, Humvee-sized. Moving through the passes. Real hard to get these suckers on radar with these mountains and vegetation. Yeah, all right—they're about ten miles from the recovery area. Four of them."

"Tell Captain Freah," said Englehardt, the screech creeping back into his voice.

Jamu
2153

"NOTHING," SAID DANNY FREAH. "ZERO. NO CURRENT."

"Very good, Captain," said Klondike. "Now we're going to try the oscilloscope readings."

Danny passed the information on to Jennifer, who sighed and sat back from the warhead, fluttering her fingers as if trying to get rid of a cramp.

"Can we take a short break?" Danny asked.

"As long as you need."

Before Danny could acknowledge, there was a buzz on the line, indicating that someone else on the Dreamland network wanted to talk to him. He switched over to channel two, where Kevin Sullivan, the copilot of the *Bennett*, warned him about the ground units.

"They're about ten miles south of you," Sullivan warned. "Coming up that road that cuts back and forth through the valley. They're hard to track because of the terrain and trees."

"Copy that."

Danny yelled to the Marine sergeant in charge of the detail, telling him to pass the word about the trucks. Then he switched back to Dreamland Command.

"How much longer before the warhead is safe to move?" he asked.

"Three more steps," said Klondike.

"How long will it take?"

"Five minutes, maybe. But first we have a series of tests. If we get the wrong result—"

"We have ground troops moving in our direction," Danny told her. "If I can get the hell out of here before they arrive, I'd be a very happy man."

"Stand by."

Danny flipped back to the *Bennett*. "How fast is that ground unit moving?"

"Not very fast," replied Sullivan. "Maybe fifteen miles an hour. That road takes a lot of turns and switchbacks."

"Can you give me a visual from *Hawk One*?"

"Affirmative. Stand by."

"No, I'm going to have to get back to you," said Danny. "I'll talk directly to Starship."

He ducked down to Jennifer and pulled off the helmet. "We have troops coming up the road in our direction. Find out the quickest way to get this thing ready to move. Then give me the helmet back, OK?"

She bit her lip, then nodded and took the helmet.

Aboard Dreamland *Bennett*
2155

STARSHIP TURNED *HAWK TWO* AWAY FROM THE MIGS, THEN took over *Hawk One*. Slipping down toward the unit the ground radar had spotted, he cut between a pair of 3,000 foot cliffs and shot into an open valley.

The jagged road twisted and turned across what looked like a dry streambed. A dozen men were riding on the backs or tops of the four vehicles, which had their lights out.

"Starship, you with me?" asked Danny Freah.

"Yeah, here we go, Captain. This is a live feed." He banked, and took another run up the road, this time from the rear of the column. "Four trucks, a dozen guys or so hanging on them. They're moving pretty slow. About forty minutes away from you, maybe a little more."

"Yeah, listen, take a run all the way up that road for me again, OK?"

"On it."

Starship tucked the Flighthawk through a nearby canyon, then back up and over the low mountain before falling into the valley the road ran through. One of the passes was so narrow that the computer gave him a proximity warning as he shot through. Starship ignored it, tucking the Flighthawk to the right to stay with the trail.

He took a quick look at *Hawk Two*. The MiGs were about thirty seconds from overtaking it. So far they hadn't changed course or acknowledged the *Bennett*'s repeated attempts to contact them. He notched up the Flighthawk's speed, then jumped back into *Hawk One*.

"You see that ledge on my side of that tight pass?" Danny asked as Starship climbed over the recovery site.

"I think I know which one you mean."

"Any chance you could get some rocks into it?"

"You mean start an avalanche?"

"That's it."

"Let me take another look."

Starship brought the airplane around and swooped toward what looked like a sheer, solid cliff. He wasn't sure the relatively small missiles the Flighthawk held would do much.

Now that he had the idea planted in his head, however, he started hunting for a place where it might work.

"There's a spot about two miles south of you where a bunch of boulders are piled against the side of the road," he told Danny. "There are some small trees holding them back, but I think if I put the missiles there we'd get something on the road. Downside is, if it doesn't work, I won't have any missiles to use against the trucks."

"Give it a shot," Danny told him.

"Roger that."

"INDIAN FIGHTERS ARE PASSING THE FLIGHTHAWK, STILL coming for us," said Daly at the radar.

"Let's move farther north," said Englehardt. "Let's see how far we can bring them."

"Should we target these guys or what?" asked Sullivan. "They're just about in range to fire at us."

Englehardt started to say no, then reconsidered. If he let them fire first, could he avoid their missiles *and* fire the Anacondas?

He started to reach for the radio to ask for instructions, then stopped. His rules of engagement covered the situation— avoid firing except to protect the mission, and himself. He didn't need authorization from anyone, or advice.

If he called Dreamland Control, he'd look weak, wouldn't he? That's what he was really worried about.

So what was he going to do? Was there a threat or not?

Colonel Bastian had been right to bump him the other day. He couldn't make a decision.

Screw it.

Just make a decision. Either way. Do it.

He took a breath.

"Hold off on the Anacondas," he said. "If they get hostile, we have a bunch of things we can do."

"Roger that," said Sullivan, not sounding particularly convinced.

THE COMPUTER HELPING STARSHIP FLY THE FLIGHTHAWK beeped at him when he boxed the rocks at the side of the cliff on the weapons screen, asking if he was sure he knew what he was doing.

"Confirm target," said Starship.

The computer replied by turning the small aiming reticule red. Starship pressed the trigger button at the top of his stick and began dumping lead into the pile of rocks. They disappeared in a cloud of dust.

A fine mist of dirt still covered the area when he swung back, and even the Flighthawk's radar couldn't see whether the road had been blocked or not. Starship continued past, moving down the road toward the Indian column a few miles away. Apparently they'd heard the commotion; the trucks had stopped and the men were crouched around them and in the nearby rocks.

As Starship turned to come back north, the computer warned him that the MiGs were past *Hawk Two.*

"*Bennett,* what are we doing with those MiGs?" he asked.

"We're going to lead them away from the ground party," replied Englehardt.

"Well, yeah, roger that, but they're inside fifty miles."

"I know where they are, Flighthawk leader."

Starship changed course, angling in the direction the *Bennett* was taking. The MiGs had slowed down but were still about three miles ahead, out of range of sure cannon shot for the robot aircraft.

He went back to *Hawk One,* bringing it up the road. The cloud of dust had cleared. The road was blocked—but only partially.

"You seeing this, Danny?" he asked Captain Freah.

"Roger that," said Danny.

"Good enough?"

"It'll have to do."

Jamu
2200

JENNIFER JERKED BACK AS THE LEDs ON THE LARGER OF the two circuit cards in front of her began to flash.

"Danny, I need the helmet right now!" she yelled, still staring at the lights.

Danny plopped the helmet down on her head, catching her ear in the process.

"Ray, I have blinking lights here," she said, trying to make her voice sound calm. "What does this mean?"

"Move the helmet a bit so we can see," said Rubeo.

He sounded real calm, she thought. But of course, why wouldn't he?

"Jennifer, locate the green wire with the white striping at the left, and snip it."

"Snip it? You told me five minutes ago we weren't cutting anything."

"The thinking has changed."

"Why?"

"Ms. Gleason, there comes a time when you have to let the pilot fly the plane. Just cut the wire."

Jennifer leaned over, took the narrow-headed wire cutters from the blanket where she had laid it out, and moved her hand carefully beneath the circuit board. Gingerly working her fingers against the strands, she separated the wire from the bunch. Her hand shook slightly; she steadied the cutters against their target with the forefinger of her other hand and snipped.

Then began promptly cursing, because she had caught her finger as well.

"Jennifer?" asked Rubeo.

"The lights are out," she said, looking at the tiny balls of blood that seemed to percolate up from the red line on her finger where she'd caught it. "The LEDs are out."

"Very good. One more step and the warhead can be moved."

"How good an electrical conductor do you think blood is?" she said as the small spheres turned to a large drop and oozed off her finger.

"Surprisingly good," replied Rubeo. "I wouldn't test it."

* * *

THE TERRAIN WAS SO RUGGED TO THE SOUTH THAT THE Marines manning the observation point there couldn't even see the landslide. Sergeant Norm Ganson, in charge of the landing team security, didn't trust the eye-in-the-sky assessment and sent two men down to assess the damage.

"Four vehicles, a dozen guys—we can hold them off, no sweat," the Marine sergeant told Danny.

"Hopefully it won't come to that," Danny replied. He trotted back to Jennifer, whom he found squatting next to the bomb, her left forefinger in her mouth.

"Jen?"

"We can move the warhead now," she said, rising.

"What happened to your hand? It's bleeding."

"It got in the way. Can you spare anybody to attach those straps, or should I do it myself?"

An atoll off the Indian coast
Time and date unknown

IT WAS THEIR WEDDING, BUT NOT THEIR WEDDING. BREANNA danced in her long white dress, sailing across the altar of the church, into the churchyard, the walls and roof of the building vaporized by Zen's dream. She floated on the air and he followed, alone in a white and brown world, stumbling on the rocks. The band played in a large, empty fountain, arrayed around a cement statue of a forgotten saint, his face chipped away by centuries of neglect. Every time he held his hand out to his wife, she danced farther away, moving through the air as easily as if she were walking. She lay herself down on a bench, holding her arms out to him, but when he arrived, she floated off, just out of reach.

A bird passed overhead, then another, then a flock. Breanna looked at them and started to rise. She was smiling.

"Bree," he called. "Bree."

As she glanced down toward him a look of sorrow appeared on her face, her sadness so painful that it froze him in place. He felt his heart shrivel inside his chest, all of his organs disintegrating, his bones pushing inward suddenly. He wanted to say more but her look stopped him, her sadness so deep that the entire world turned black.

And she was gone.

Aboard Dreamland *Bennett*
2202

ENGLEHARDT KNEW HE COULD BEAT THE MIGS IF THEY fired. He saw in his mind exactly what he'd do: jive and jab and zigzag while Sullivan hit the ECMs. He'd drop low, then come up swinging—fire the Anacondas at point-blank range.

The question was: What would he do if they didn't fire?

"Still coming at us," said Rager. "Slowing."

Englehardt checked his position. The *Bennett* was close to the Chinese border—another problem, he thought; if he went over it, the Chinese might send someone to investigate as well.

That might be a good idea. He could duck out of the way and let the two enemies go at it.

"MiGs are thirty miles and closing," said Sullivan.

Englehardt once again thought of radioing for instructions. But there was no point in that—he'd only be told to use his judgment.

That was the Dreamland way, wasn't it? You were on your own, trained to make the call. A Megafortress flying alone wasn't "controlled" by an AWACS or even a flight leader—its pilot was on his or her own. If he wasn't up to the responsibility, he didn't belong in the cockpit in the first place.

So do it. Just do it.

And yet he balked, inherently cautious.

"Are they talking to anyone?" Englehardt asked.

"If they are, we're not hearing it," said the copilot.

Englehardt flipped over to the Dreamland Command channel to speak to Danny Freah.

"Captain, we have a couple of Indian aircraft up here taking an interest in us. Are you ready to get out of there?"

"We need ten more minutes."

"I'm going to lead these planes away from the area. When you take off, have the Osprey stay low in that mountain valley. The MiGs shouldn't be able to see them on radar."

"Good. Copy."

He had it figured out now: he'd fool the Indians, diverting their attention while the Ospreys got away.

Was that the smart thing to do? Or was he wimping? Maybe he should shoot them down.

"I'm going to try talking to those bastards myself," said Englehardt. "I'm going to broadcast on all channels and see what the hell they're up to."

"Take your shot," said Sullivan.

Englehardt identified himself and the ship, saying they were on a Search and Rescue mission and asking the Indians' intentions. Once again they didn't answer.

"Ten miles," said Sullivan. "Still closing."

"Get ready on the Stinger air mines."

"Yeah," said Sullivan.

The two MiGs had widened their separation as they approached. They flanked the Megafortress, then slowly began drawing toward her wings, still separated from her by a mile or so.

"American EB-52," said one of the Indians finally. "Why are you over Indian territory?"

"I'm on a Search and Rescue mission for American fliers," said Englehardt. "Why didn't you answer my earlier radio broadcasts?"

The Indians once more chose not to answer. The Megafortress's radio, however, picked up a succession of squeals and clicks, indicating they were using an encrypted radio system to talk to someone.

"Gotta be talking to their ground controller," said Sullivan. "What do you think? Did he just tell them to shoot us down or leave us alone?"

* * *

BY SLOWING DOWN TO MATCH THE MEGAFORTRESS'S SPEED, the MiGs allowed *Hawk Two* to catch up to them. Starship angled *Hawk Two* toward the tail of the closest MiG, which was aiming itself roughly toward the *Bennett*'s right wing. The Flighthawk's faceted body and absorbent skin gave it a radar profile about the size of a flying cockroach, and the black matte paint made it hard to pick up in the night sky. But even if it had been daylight the Flighthawk would have been nearly impossible for the MiG pilot to see; Starship had the plane exactly behind his tailfin.

"Computer, hold position on aircraft identified as *Bandit Two*."

"Hold position."

Starship took over the controls for *Hawk One*, still circling low over the recovery site. The Indian ground unit had stopped about a mile south of the landslide. The Americans, meanwhile, were getting ready to bug out.

This is going to work out, he thought. The Osprey was going to sneak away, and then the Megafortress would head over to Pakistan and go home without the Indians knowing exactly what was going on.

Then he noticed a flicker in the lower corner of *Hawk One*'s screen.

He pushed his throttle slide up to full.

"Hawk leader to Whiplash ground team—Danny, there are helicopters trying to sneak in up that valley behind the Indian ground units."

Jamu
2205

STARSHIP'S WARNING CAME JUST AS THE WARHEAD WAS secured and the Marines had been ordered to return from their lookout posts. Danny needed a second to work out in his head where everyone was. Then he jumped in the back of the V-22, slipped through the nest of lines and straps holding the warhead in place, and ran to the cockpit.

"Helos coming up that road," he told the pilot. "Can you get us out without them seeing us?"

"No way, Captain," said the pilot. "I have to clear that ridge ahead or go right past them. Either way, they'll see us."

"All right. Go over the ridge as soon as we're secured back here." He switched his radio on. "Starship, see if you can slow those guys down a bit. We want to exit to the north."

Aboard Dreamland *Bennett*
2207

STARSHIP TOOK *HAWK ONE* STRAIGHT AT THE LEAD INDIAN helicopter, a large Mi-8 Hip troop carrier. He got so close to the chopper that if he'd tipped his wing down he could have sliced through its rotors.

He cut over the second chopper—another Hip—then circled around for another pass. If either helicopter pilot had seen him, they didn't let on; both aircraft continued flying through the valley. They were doing about seventy knots, flying so low that their rear wheels, which hung on struts off the side of the fuselage, couldn't have been more than a foot off the ground.

"This time I'm going to get your attention," said Starship. He pulled into the valley ahead of the helicopters, jammed his stick back and let off a bunch of flares, climbing into the night like a giant Roman candle. Both helicopters immediately set down. Their rotors continued to spin, and the sandstorm that had been following them caught up.

"Helicopters are down, Whiplash," said Starship. "Get out of there while you can."

"AMERICAN MEGAFORTRESS! WHY ARE YOU FIRING ON OUR helicopter?"

"We're not firing at all," said Englehardt. "You're sitting right with us."

"Cease your fire!" repeated the Indian.

"MiGs are dropping back," said Sullivan. "Getting into position to fire heat-seekers at us. Air mines?"

Yes, thought Englehardt. Then no.

Anacondas?

He was way out of position for that. He'd have to use the Stinger.

They still hadn't fired.

"Wait until they activate their weapons radars," he told Sullivan.

"They don't need their weapons radars," said the pilot. "Hell, they can hit us with spitballs."

"Starship, where are you?" asked Englehardt. He could feel sweat running down every part of his body, and his colon felt as if it was about to jump through his skin.

"*Hawk Two* is right behind *Bandit Two. Hawk One* is back with Indian helicopters."

"Did you fire at them?"

"Just used my flares to get their attention. It worked."

"Marine Osprey *Angry Bear* is up," said Sullivan.

"Cover the Osprey, Starship."

"Yeah, roger, circling back to cover them."

"American Megafortress, you will leave the area," said the Indian pilot.

"I intend to," answered Englehardt. "Be advised that we are over Chinese territory."

"They're talking to their controller again," reported Sullivan. "They're saying a lot of something."

"As long as they're talking, not firing, we're fine," replied the pilot.

Aboard Marine Osprey *Angry Bear One*,
over northern India
2215

GRADUALLY, DANNY FREAH LOOSENED HIS GRIP ON THE strap near the bulkhead separating the Osprey cockpit from the cargo area. Finally he let go and looked at his palm. The strap's indentations were clearly visible.

"We're OK?" asked Jennifer Gleason, sitting on the bench next to him.

"Yeah. We're good. The MiGs are following the Megafortress to the east. We're out of here."

Danny followed her gaze as she turned and looked at the warhead, snugged in the middle of the Osprey's cargo bay. It seemed almost puny, sitting between the Marines and their gear.

"Funny that such a small thing could cause so much destruction," Danny said.

"I was just thinking it looks almost harmless there," said Jennifer. "Like part of a furnace that needs to be overhauled."

"I guess."

A tone sounded in his helmet. Danny clicked into the Dreamland channel.

"Freah."

"Danny, a Global Hawk with infrared sensors just located the last warhead," said Dog. "It's fifty miles north of you."

"OK, Colonel. Team Three is waiting at Base Camp One. They can be airborne inside of ten minutes. Take them about sixty to get there."

"I'm afraid it'll be too late by then," said Dog. "The Global Hawk has spotted a pair of pickups near the site, and four or five men nearby. Looks like another two trucks are on their way."

"Give me the GPS point," Danny replied.

VII

No Chance to Survive

———

THE MIGS STILL HADN'T MADE A THREATENING MOVE.
Englehardt locked his eyes on the sitrep, sizing up the situation. The lead aircraft was about three miles behind the
Megafortress. He was in the Stinger's sweet spot—but then
again, the *Bennett* would be right in the sights of a heat-
seeker or the MiG's cannon.

The Stinger needed about twenty seconds to "warm up"
once activated. Englehardt didn't want to turn it on until he
meant to use it; he reasoned that the Indians didn't know it
was there, and were thus more vulnerable to it.

The Dreamland channel buzzed.

"Go," said Englehardt, opening the communication line.

"Mike, the last warhead has been found," said Colonel
Bastian. "Danny and the Marines are on their way. We want
you to cover them."

"Be happy to, Colonel, but I have a complication."

Englehardt explained his situation. The colonel winced. But
if Bastian thought he'd done the wrong thing, he didn't say.

"They're not hostile?" he asked.

"Annoying, definitely," said Englehardt.

Dog continued to frown.

"Should I shoot them down?" Englehardt blurted. "The
rules of engagement—"

"Take the MiGs south with you," said Dog. "I'll have the

Cheli go northwest to cover Danny in *Angry Bear.* Have Starship escort the Osprey until they arrive."

"Colonel, if—"

"Bastian out."

**Aboard Dreamland *Cheli*,
over the Great Indian Desert
2240**

BRAD SPARKS SMILED AS THE MARINE LIEUTENANT GAVE AN update on the ground team, which had just secured its warhead and was en route to Base Camp One. She had the sexiest voice he'd ever heard on a military radio.

"Did you copy, Dreamland *Cheli*?" she demanded.

"Just daydreaming up here, Dancer," Sparks told Lieutenant Klacker. "Anyone ever tell you you have a sexy voice?"

"Your transmission was garbled," responded Dancer coldly. "I suggest you do not repeat it."

"Hey, roger that," chuckled Sparks. "All right, I have your ETA at Base Camp One at fifteen minutes. Those Osprey drivers agree?"

"Good. Copy."

Sparks leaned back against the Megafortress's ejection seat, arching his shoulders. As soon as the Osprey reached the base camp, the Navy boys from the *Abe* would take over; most likely they'd be free to go home. It had been a long, dull night, nowhere near as entertaining as their last go-round. But maybe that was what his crew needed. Their energy was off; no one was even laughing at his jokes.

Day on the beach at Diego Garcia might change that. Day on the beach with that hot little Navy ensign he'd spotted on the chow line the other morning would definitely boost his morale, at least.

The Dreamland channel buzzed. Sparks keyed the message in and found himself staring at Colonel Bastian.

"Hey, Colonel, what's up?"

"Brad, we've found the last warhead. I need you to go north to cover the recovery team."

"Kick ass, Colonel, we're ready," said Sparks. "Feed me the data."

Near the Chinese-Pakistani border
2240

GENERAL SATTARI PUT THE NIGHT GLASSES DOWN.

"The mujahideen are there now," he said, speaking not to the men who'd helped him but to himself.

Sattari pushed the binoculars closer to his eyes, watching the men walk through the wreckage. They didn't seem to realize that the warhead had already been taken. Most likely they didn't know what they were looking for. Most if not all were ignorant kids, lured from their homes in Egypt and Yemen and Palestine by the promise that they'd be someone important.

"Helicopter," said one of Sattari's men.

The general didn't hear it for a moment. Then he heard the deep rumble reverberating in the distance. It wasn't a chopper that he was familiar with, yet he had definitely heard the sound before.

An Osprey—an American Osprey.

"Quickly. It is time to go," he said loudly in Urdu, walking to the truck.

Aboard Dreamland *Bennett,*
over India
2335

STARSHIP TOOK *HAWK ONE* AHEAD OF THE MARINE OS-prey, scouting the site where the warhead had been located. Even with the live infrared image from the Global Hawk orbiting above to guide him, he had trouble pinpointing the missile wreckage; to him it looked more like a slight depression in the landscape than anything else.

The pickup trucks, on the other hand, were clearly visible.

Starship slid *Hawk One* down through 10,000 feet, plotting the most efficient approach to the pickups. Almost immediately the piper in his gun sight screen began to blink red, indicating that he had his target. As the small reticule went solid red, he pressed the trigger.

While almost everything else in the Flighthawk represented cutting-edge, gee-whiz technology, the aircraft's cannon was ancient; the M61 Vulcan 20mm Gatling hadn't been cutting edge since before the Vietnam War. But sometimes the old iron was the best iron.

The first few shots went wide left and low, but Starship held his stick steady, riding the stream of 20mm lead across and into the rear of the first pickup truck. As the vehicle exploded in flames, his bullets hit the cab of the second truck. He flicked right, perforating the engine compartment before his momentum carried him clear of the targets. He started to turn, moving a little faster than he wanted to, but couldn't find anything or anyone in front of him, so he pulled up for another run.

He checked *Hawk Two*—still riding behind the MiGs shadowing the *Bennett*—then rolled *Hawk One* into a second attack. As he did, the Flighthawk's computer warned that he was within ten miles of losing its connection to the mother ship. Starship glanced at the sitrep and realized he couldn't complete the attack before losing the connection.

"*Bennett,* I need you to get closer to *Hawk One*," he said. "I'm going to lose the connection."

Englehardt didn't answer. The Flighthawk and her mother ship were moving away from each other at close to a thousand miles an hour—or sixteen a minute.

"Disconnect in fifteen seconds," warned the computer, using an audible message as well as the text on the screen.

"*Bennett!* Need you north!"

Starship felt the Megafortress lurch beneath him.

"We're on it," said Englehardt.

Near the Chinese-Pakistani border
2340

DANNY FREAH SQUATTED TO ONE SIDE OF THE PASSAGEWAY between the Osprey's cockpit and cargo area, watching as the aircraft headed toward the landing zone. He could see the Flighthawk's red-yellow tracers arcing across the sky. Small bursts of green rose up toward the spray—ground fire.

"What do you think, Captain?" asked one of the pilots.

"I think we're going in, if you can make it."

"We can make it."

Danny turned around and yelled to the landing team. "LZ is hot. Show these bastards what the Marine Corps is made of."

Aboard Dreamland *Bennett*,
over the Chinese-Indian border
2343

"MIGS ARE TALKING TO THEIR BASE AGAIN," SULLIVAN TOLD Englehardt. "I'm betting they don't like our course change."

"How close is the *Cheli*?"

"Their nearest Flighthawk is still ten minutes off."

Ten more minutes. Englehardt worked his tongue around his mouth, trying to generate a little more moisture for his throat.

"They're dropping off," said Sullivan.

For a moment Englehardt felt relieved. The Indians must be low on fuel by now, he thought, and were backing off and going home.

Then he realized that wasn't the case at all.

"Evasive maneuvers. Give me flares!" he shouted, a second before the missile-launch warning buzzed on the cockpit dash.

STARSHIP WAS JUST ZEROING IN ON A CLUSTER OF SMALL arms flashes at the landing zone when the Megafortress seemed to plunge beneath him. He kept his hand steady, staying with his target and ignoring the urge to jump back into *Hawk Two* and battle the MiGs.

The key thing to remember when you're flying two planes, Zen always said, *is to finish one thing at a time.*

Zen.

Starship lit the Flighthawk's cannon. The ground in front of the aircraft began to percolate, dirt and rocks erupting from the landscape as the bullets hit. He gently wagged the stick back and forth, stirring the mixture of lead and rock into a veritable tornado.

He let off on the trigger and pulled up. He didn't see any more tracers from the ground. If there were more guerrillas there, they'd taken cover.

"*Hawk One* orbit at 15,000 after targets are destroyed," he told the computer. "Danny, landing zone is as clean as it's going to get."

ENGLEHARDT PUSHED HARD ON THE STICK, THROWING HIS whole body against it. The Megafortress twisted herself hard to comply, jerking to the right and pulling her nose up.

Between the sharp maneuvers and the cascading decoys exploding behind the plane, the heat-seeking missiles the MiGs had fired flew by harmlessly, exploding more than two miles away.

Now it was his turn.

His turn. His brain stuttered, as if it were an electrical switch with contacts that weren't quite clicking.

"Stinger air mines," he said. "Sullivan?"

"Targets out of range."

"Fuck."

Everyone on the circuit seemed to be hyperventilating. Englehardt turned his eyes toward the sitrep screen on the lower left portion of his dash. His position was marked out in the center—where were the Flighthawks and the MiGs?

A tremendous fireball flared in the corner of the windscreen—a partial answer to his question.

* * *

STARSHIP BROUGHT UP THE MAIN SCREEN OF *HAWK TWO* just in time to see the robot turn away from the MiG it had destroyed.

"Good work, dude," he told the computer. "I'll take it from here."

The second MiG had turned to the east after firing its missiles. Now about twenty miles from the Megafortress, it was banking through a turn that would leave it in position to launch its AMRAAMskis.

"*Bandit Two* is getting into position to attack," said Starship over the interphone. "I'm not going to be able to close the gap before he fires."

"*Bennett,*" acknowledged Englehardt. Even with the one-word reply, his voice had a tremble to it.

"You want me to get him or are you going to use the Anacondas?" prompted Starship.

"He's ours," said Sullivan, the copilot.

"Yeah, we got him," said Englehardt. "Anacondas. Take him, Kevin."

Near the Chinese-Pakistani border
2350

JENNIFER GLEASON SNUGGED HER BULLETPROOF VEST tighter as Danny and the Marines fanned out from the Osprey. Automatic rifle fire rattled over the loud hush of the rotating propellers. She had a 9mm Beretta handgun in her belt, and certainly knew how to use it. But she also knew that it wasn't likely to be very effective except as a last resort.

She wasn't scared, but standing in the bay of the aircraft with no way of making a real contribution made her feel almost helpless. A single Marine corporal had stayed behind with her, guarding the defused warhead; everyone else was taking on the guerrillas outside.

A bullet or maybe a rock splinter tinged against the side of the Osprey. Jennifer jumped involuntarily, then put her hand on the pistol.

Two or three minutes passed without anything else happening. No longer hearing any gunfire, she took a step toward the door.

The Marine caught her shirt. "Excuse me, miss. The captain said you are to stay inside until he gives the OK."

"It's safe."

The corporal frowned. "Sorry, ma'am. His orders."

"Would you go outside?"

"Not the question."

"Well what the fuck is the question?"

The Marine frowned but didn't let go. He swung his other hand up and pushed the boom mike for his radio closer to his mouth. Jennifer folded her arms, waiting while the corporal called for permission.

"Captain says proceed with caution."

"Caution is my middle name," said Jennifer. She rushed down the ramp and curled behind the aircraft, staying low. She could see clusters of Marines on both the left and right; they were standing upright.

Jennifer trotted across the rock-strewn field of scrub and dirt, heading toward a jagged piece of metal that stood straight up from what looked like a dented garbage can. She knelt near the damaged missile part; it looked as if it were part of one of the oxidizer tanks located at the top of the weapon just under the warhead section.

"Where's Captain Freah?" she asked a nearby Marine.

"That way." He pointed across the field in the direction of the two trucks destroyed by the Flighthawk. "Careful, ma'am. We're still mopping up. Those suckers were hiding in the rocks and grass."

"I'll be careful."

Jennifer began walking across the moon-lit field, the grass and weeds gray in the light. There were pieces of metal strewn on the ground. Bits of wire and paper and plastic were bunched like fistfuls of confetti dumped by bystanders grown tired of waiting for the parade to pass. She caught a whiff of burnt metal and vinyl from one of the trucks that was still smoldering up ahead.

She found Danny near one of the trucks.

"Where's the warhead?"

"That way. Hang on a second—one of the Marines thinks he saw some movement up near those rocks. We're checking it out."

A guerrilla lay perhaps twelve feet away, his torso riddled with bullets. Jennifer stared at it, waiting while Danny talked to other members of the team.

"All right," he said finally. "But you stay next to me."

"I intend to."

"By the way—the corporal's mike was open in the Osprey," added Danny. "Anybody ever tell you you curse like a Marine?"

"Most people say worse."

**Aboard Dreamland *Bennett*,
over the Chinese-Indian border
2355**

THIRTY SECONDS AFTER THE ANACONDAS LEFT THE *BEN-nett*'s belly, the MiG launched its own missiles. Englehardt had anticipated this and turned the plane away, hoping to "beam" the radar guiding the missiles.

"ECMs," he told Sullivan.

"They're on. Missiles are tracking."

"Chaff. Stand by for evasive maneuvers."

He put the Megafortress on her wingtip, swooping and sliding and dropping away, just barely in control. He pushed back in the opposite direction and got a high g warning from the computer, which complained that the aircraft was being pushed beyond its design limits. Englehardt didn't let off, however, and the airplane came hard right.

There was a loud boom behind him. A caution light popped

on the dash. For a moment he thought they'd been hit. Then he realized that engine one had experienced a compressor surge or stall because of the change in the air flow rushing through it.

The compressor banged, then surged a second time. Easing off on the stick, he reached to the throttle, prepared to drop his power if the engine didn't restart and settle down on its own.

"Missile one is by us," said Sullivan.

Englehardt concentrated on his power plant. The exhaust gas temperatures jolted up, but the power came back. He babied the throttle, moving his power down and steadying the aircraft.

"Splash the MiG!" said Sullivan as their Anaconda hit home. "Splash that mother!"

Englehardt felt his pulse starting to return to normal. He slid the throttle glide for engine one up cautiously, keeping his eye on the readouts. The engine's temperatures and pressures were back in line with its sisters'; it seemed no worse for wear.

"What happened to that second missile the MiG fired?" he asked Sullivan.

"Off the scope near the mountains," said the copilot. "No threat."

"Rager, what's near us?" Englehardt asked. His voice squeaked, but it didn't seem as bad as earlier.

"Sky is clear south," answered the airborne radar operator.

"Starship, what's your situation?" Englehardt asked.

"*Hawk Two* is a mile off your tail. *Hawk One* is orbiting the recovery area. Both aircraft could use some more fuel."

So could the Megafortress, Englehardt realized.

"*Cheli,* this is *Bennett*. What's your position?"

"Our Flighthawks are just reaching the recovery area," said the *Cheli*'s captain, Brad Sparks. "We're right behind the little guys."

"All right. I have to tank. We're heading out."

"Roger that. Word to the wise—the Indians have been powering up their radars all night. We ducked one on the way to the Marine site. I wouldn't be surprised if their missiles are back on line."

An atoll off the Indian coast
Time and date unknown

THE NIGHT DRIFTED ON, MELTING AWAY EVERYTHING BUT Zen's stoic shell. His thirst, his anger, all feeling and emotion vanished as the hours twisted. He woke, and yet still seemed to be sleeping. As if in a dream, he pushed himself up on his arms and crawled from the tent, cold, an animal seeking only to survive.

He'd strapped his gun to his belt before going to sleep. It dragged and clung against the rocks as he moved, part of him now. He reached the remains of the driftwood where he'd made the fire the other night and pushed up, sitting and staring at the darkness.

There was a plane in the distance.

Zen took a slow, measured breath.

The aircraft was very far away.

He took another breath, yogalike, then leaned back and took the radio from the tent.

"Major Stockard to any aircraft. Dreamland *Levitow* crew broadcasting to any aircraft."

He stopped, pushed the earphone into his ear mechanically. All he heard was static.

Why even bother?

Zen set the radio down. He pulled himself farther down the beach, staring at the edge of the ocean and the way the reflected moonlight on the tip of the waves seemed to grab at the air, as if trying to climb upward.

It was a vain attempt, a waste, but they kept trying.

If only I had that strength, he thought, continuing to stare.

**Aboard Dreamland *Bennett*,
over India
0015, 19 January 1998**

STARSHIP WAS JUST ABOUT TO TURN *HAWK TWO* OVER TO
the computer for the refuel when the *Bennett*'s radar officer
warned of a new flight of Indian jets, this one coming at them
from east.

"MiG-21s. Four of them. Coming from Hindan," said Sergeant Rager.

The MiG-21s were somewhat outdated, and certainly less
capable than the planes they'd just dealt with. But they
couldn't be ignored either.

"What do you want to do, *Bennett*?" Starship asked.

"Continue the refuel," said Englehardt. "I think we can
tank one of the U/MFs before we need to deal with them."

"Roger that," said Starship, surprised that the pilot sounded
confident, or at least more assured than he had earlier.

Starship set up the refuel, then turned the aircraft over to
the computer. He swung *Hawk One* toward *Bennett*'s left
wing, then began pushing in so it could sip from the rear fuel
boom as soon as its brother was done.

"Radar warning," said Sullivan. "We have a SAM site
up—SA-2s, dead ahead."

Now things are going to get interesting, thought Starship,
checking on *Hawk Two*'s status.

ENGLEHARDT FELT THE BLACK COWL SLIP BACK OVER THE
edges of his vision. The *Bennett* was about three minutes
from the antiaircraft missile battery.

Three minutes to decide what to do.

Plenty of time not to panic, though his heart was pounding
again and his stomach punching him from inside.

The MiGs behind him complicated his options. He didn't
want to go in their direction anyway—he wanted to get to the
coast. But turning south to avoid the SAMs might make it
easier for them to catch up.

So? Use the Anacondas on them.

Hell, he could use the Anacondas against the SAMs.

His orders were to attempt to avoid conflict. But he'd already been fired on. Did that give him carte blanche? Or was the fact that he was no longer protecting the ground units rule, meaning he should do what he could to get away.

The first. Definitely.

God, he was thinking too much. What was he going to do?

"All right, let's skirt the SAM site," Englehardt said. "Turn to bearing one-eight—"

"If we go south, not only will we go closer to the MiGs but we'll have more batteries to deal with," said Sullivan, cutting him off. "There are a dozen south of that SA-2 site."

"I know that," said Englehardt sharply. "Just do what I say."

In the silent moments that followed, he wished he'd been a little calmer when he responded. But it was out there, and apologizing wasn't going to help anything. They set a new course; he moved to it, staying just on the edge of the SA-2s' effective range.

What if they fire anyway? he wondered. What do I do then?

And as the thought formed in his brain, he got a launch warning on his control panel—the SAMs had been fired.

Near the Chinese-Pakistani border
0015

THE FIRST THING JENNIFER THOUGHT WAS THAT THE WARhead section had broken into pieces when it landed, and that the bomb had somehow managed to bounce away from the conical nose and the metal superstructure that held it above the propellant section. But as she stared at the wreckage, she realized that couldn't be the case—there were cut screws on the ground, and the pieces of metal had been torched and hacked away.

She looked back for Danny Freah and waved to him.

"Somebody took the warhead," she told him when he ran up. "It's gone."

"You're sure?"

"They hacked it out. Look. See?"

"All right, look—the *Cheli* says there are Chinese helicopters headed in our direction. We have to get out of here, quick."

"I want to take some of the electronic controls from the engines," said Jennifer. "There's some circuitry that they left behind. And pictures of the missile and damage. It'll only take a minute."

"You have only until the Marines start pulling back. Keep your head down."

"Will do."

**Aboard Dreamland *Bennett*,
over India
0019**

"COUNTERMEASURES," ENGLEHARDT TOLD HIS COPILOT as the SA-2s climbed toward the *Bennett*.

"Already on it."

"OK, OK." Englehardt pushed his stick left, instinctively widening the distance between his aircraft and the missiles coming for him.

"MiGs are going to afterburners," said Rager, monitoring the airplanes that were chasing them at the airborne radar station.

The MiGs had pulled to seventy-five miles from the Megafortress. Englehardt realized that they probably intended on firing medium-range radar missiles as soon as possible—in roughly two minutes, he calculated.

Huge amounts of time, if he kept his head. He'd be by the SA-2s by then and could cut back east as he planned.

God, did this never end? It was twenty, thirty times worse than a simulation. His brain felt as if it were frying.

"Stay on course," he said aloud, though he was actually speaking to himself.

"You want me to target those MiGs with the Anacondas?" asked Sullivan.

"I have a feeling we're going to need them when we get toward the coast," Englehardt said. "Better warn the *Cheli* and Danny Freah that we're attracting a lot of attention. They may get the same treatment."

"Mobile missile site up! Akash missiles," said Sullivan.

Unlike the SA-2, the Akash was a modern missile system guided by a difficult-to-defeat multifunctional radar. Developed as both a ground and air-launched missile, it could strike targets at two meters and 18,000 meters, and everything in between. But because its range was limited to about thirty kilometers, or roughly nineteen miles, Englehardt knew he could get away from it simply by turning to the west.

But that would bring him closer to the MiG-21s.

Which would be easier to deal with, the planes or the missiles?

The MiGs, he decided, starting the turn.

"Mike, what are we doing?" asked Sullivan.

"We're going to avoid the Akash battery."

"They haven't launched."

"Neither have the MiGs."

"Sooner or later we're going to have to deal with some of these bastards," said Sullivan. "And we're getting farther from where we want to go. We have to get out over the water."

"I am dealing with them," snapped Englehardt.

He pulled back on the stick, aiming to take the Megafortress high enough so he wouldn't have to worry about any more Akash sites.

"Starship—Flighthawk leader. Set up an intercept on those MiGs," said Englehardt. He was angry now; he felt his ears getting hot.

"I still have to tank *Hawk One*," said Starship. "They'll be in range to launch before I can get to them."

"Do it now, then tank."

* * *

STARSHIP CURLED *HAWK ONE* AWAY FROM THE MEGAFORTRESS, then unhooked *Hawk Two* from the refueling probe, its tanks about seven-eighths full. The EB-52's maneuvers to avoid the radar were becoming so severe that he couldn't have continued with the refuel anyway.

He slotted the two ships into a loose trail as he sized up his opponents. If the MiGs kept coming for the Megafortress once they fired their missiles, he'd be in a good position to take on *Bandits Three* and *Four*, the northernmost planes. He plotted the intercept for the computer, telling it to take *Hawk Two* while he rode *Hawk One* onto the lead plane of the element, *Bandit Three*.

He'd just started his turn to get the Flighthawk on its intercept when the Indians began launching their missiles, medium-range R-27s, known to NATO as AA-10 Alamos. Each plane fired two, then immediately turned away. Starship broke off the attack; there was no sense chasing the planes now.

"We have two Mirage 2000s coming up from the southeast," said Rager, identifying a pair of advanced fighter-bombers he'd just spotted on the radar scope.

"I have them," said Starship, changing course.

OF THE EIGHT MISSILES LAUNCHED AT THE MEGAFORTRESS, two took immediate nosedives, either because they were defective or because they had been launched incorrectly. The Megafortress's electronic countermeasures soon confused three more; they, too, disappeared from radar.

The last three climbed with the Megafortress, moving nearly three times as fast as she could. As they went to terminal guidance, closing in on their target, Englehardt called for chaff and began jinking through the sky, pulling a series of hard turns that left the missiles sucking air. When the last one blew itself up in confusion, he turned back westward.

All right, he told himself. *Let's get the hell out of here.*

"Flighthawk leader, what's your status?"

"Zero-two minutes from an intercept on those Mirages,"

said Starship. "I'm going to be cutting it close on *Hawk One* fuelwise."

"We're going to fly to the coast. Should be plenty of chance for you to tank."

"Yeah, roger that."

Englehardt ground his teeth together. They had more than a thousand miles to go before they cleared the Indian defenses; he had only six Anacondas left, and his own fuel supply was beginning to dwindle.

Time to get home. No more dancing, just go.

THE LEAD MIRAGE PICKED UP *HAWK TWO* ON ITS RADAR when the two aircraft were about five miles apart. The pilot's reaction was to pull back on his stick, attempting to outclimb *Hawk Two*.

That might have worked had Starship been flying the earlier model U/MF. The Mirage had an extremely powerful engine—it could outclimb an F-15—and would have been able to get over the robot plane before Starship was in a position to fire. But the improved Flighthawk could best the Mirage's 285 meter per second climb by about fifteen meters; he had no trouble staying with his enemy. Instead, his main concern was to fly himself out of a firing solution as the Mirage began twisting left in the climb. He couldn't get his nose down quickly enough as the Mirage slid left, swooping eastward. Starship tucked his right wing and managed a quick shot as the Mirage turned sharply across his flight path. While the Indian's maneuver seemed counterintuitive, it put him so close to *Hawk Two* that Starship couldn't turn quickly enough to stay on his tail. It was the first time he had ever been outturned while flying a U/MF.

Not counting the simulated battles he'd flown against Zen.

So what did Zen say the solution was?

Don't follow. That's what I want—I've cut my speed and all I have to do is wait for your engine outlets to show up in my screen. It's a sucker move, totally a psychout, to throw you in front of me.

Starship pushed the Flighthawk the other way, figuring that once the Mirage caught on, it would think it had an easy shot from behind. But that was his own sucker move—he slammed into a dive and then looped over, throwing the enemy plane in front of him as it started to pursue.

Sure enough, a thick delta wing materialized in front of him. Now the Mirage's maneuvers cost it dearly—the hard turns had robbed it of flight energy, and even its powerful engine couldn't get it out of the gun sight quickly enough.

Starship got a long burst in, more than five seconds, long enough to see the bullets tear a jagged line in the wing. As he broke off, the Indian pilot pulled the ejection handles and was shot skyward. His plane spun furiously, a dart aimed at the ground.

Hawk One, meanwhile, was pursuing the other Mirage as it climbed through 40,000 feet, twisting and turning as it went. Starship took over from the computer, knowing that the Indian was close to his top altitude. The Indian rolled out and then managed to put his nose practically straight downward. The maneuver was executed so quickly and perfectly that after a few seconds Starship realized he wouldn't be able to keep up. Instead, he broke off, banking northward, trying to get his bearings.

And to check his fuel. He was at bingo; he had to go back to the Megafortress.

Until now the Indian had outflown both the computer and Starship; he should have called it a day. But instead he pushed his Mirage around and fired a pair of heat-seeking missiles at the Flighthawk.

As soon as he got the launch warning, Starship hit his flares and pulled hard on the stick to tuck away.

"Computer, return *Hawk One* for refuel," he said, switching planes.

The Mirage continued to move in *Hawk One*'s direction, trying to close for another shot. Either his radar had completely lost *Hawk Two* in the scrum or the pilot just didn't pay attention to his scope, because the Flighthawk was driving hard toward the Mirage's tail. Within twenty seconds Starship had it lined up for a cannon shot on the Indian plane's wing. He pressed the trigger.

The bullets tore a jagged line up the middle of the Mirage's right wing. The canopy of the French-made jet burst upward, its pilot ejecting almost before Starship could let go of the trigger.

"Flighthawk leader to *Bennett*. Mirages are down. *Hawk One* is coming in to tank. What's our game plan?"

"Looks like every SAM from here to the coast is going to take potshots at us," said Englehardt. "We're heading west and not stopping."

"Roger that."

Near the Chinese-Pakistani border
0025

"CLAIMS THEY DIDN'T GET ANYTHING, CAPTAIN. HE SAYS WE got here just a few minutes after they did."

Danny Freah looked from the Marine to the prisoner. He was a kid, maybe seventeen, probably younger. He didn't look very threatening, or determined to die for his cause. But bitter experience had proved that looks could be deceiving.

"You're lying," Danny told the guerrilla. "Why are you lying?"

The Marine translated the words into Arabic. The guerrilla got a pained look on his face. He shook his head violently, then began to speak.

"He comes from Egypt," said the Marine. "He joined what he calls the Brotherhood. He was going to fight against the infidels in Kashmir. He says he's not a terrorist. He only fights soldiers."

"That's nice," said Danny. "Get some plastic cuffs on him."

* * *

JENNIFER PICKED UP THE LAST PIECE OF METAL AND HANDED it to the Marine helping her.

"We're good to go," she told him, and started walking back toward the landing area. As she did, an AK-47 barked up on the ridge.

Jennifer dropped to one knee and pushed the helmet she'd been given down against her head as the Marines began to answer. She saw someone moving on the ridge, then a white flash, followed by an explosion and more gunfire. The weapons sounded furious, rattling the air with a beat that crescendoed with another explosion.

Then, silence.

The Marine she'd been walking with rose slowly. Two other Marines trotted over, making sure she was all right.

"I'm OK, it's OK," she said, getting up. "Let's go."

She watched them for a few minutes, then began walking toward a small ravine at the side of the plain, planning to get out of the way of the Osprey. As she did, she felt a bee sting her in the ribs. The next thing she knew, she was falling on the ground, lying on her back, her knee, head, and chest howling with pain.

What hit me? she wondered, then blacked out.

THE OSPREY'S ROAR DROWNED OUT THE GUNFIRE. THE sniper had taken at least two shots before Danny saw the muzzle flash.

He threw himself to the ground and peppered the rocks with his assault rifle. Dust and dirt sprayed around him as the Osprey passed overhead. He pushed himself up and began running toward the sniper's position.

A gun barrel appeared between the rocks; Danny flew forward, barely diving out of the line of fire. He tried to roll to his right to get into a ditch, but found his way blocked by a fresh hail of bullets.

Crawling on his belly, the Whiplash captain managed to get behind a pair of boulders about knee high. He burned the rest of his magazine, then reloaded. Two Marines had started to fire at the sniper from the north, pinning the gunman down. Danny jumped up and ran toward a line of rocks that jutted from the enemy position, making it just before the sniper turned his attention and rifle back in his direction.

Hunkering down beneath the stones, splinters and dirt flying around him, Danny waited for the man to shoot through his ammunition. The firing stopped; Danny raised his gun then brought it back down as the bullets began to fly again.

"Grenade!" one of the Marines shouted over the din.

Danny curled as low to the ground as he could. The explosion was a low thud, a soft sound that seemed to come from very far away. It was followed by the loud buzzing of several M16s as the Marines poured bullets into the sniper's position.

Finally the gunfire stopped. Danny raised his head, then his body. Raising his left hand, he ran toward the rocks.

A slight figure lay hunched over in the bottom of the shallow depression, head and back drenched black with blood. An AK-47 and two magazine boxes lay nearby. The moon coaxed a gleam from the weapon's polished wooden furniture.

"Make sure we don't have any more of these bastards around," Danny told the Marines running up to him. "And good work."

"Corpsman!" yelled a Marine back by the missile wreckage. "We need a corpsman!"

"Oh, Jesus," muttered Danny, running for him. Somehow he knew that Jennifer had been hit, even before he saw her prone figure splayed on the ground.

**Aboard Dreamland *Bennett*,
over India
0028**

THEY MANAGED TO DUCK TWO MORE SETS OF SAM missiles, then had an uneventful thirty minutes flying an almost straight line southwest. But as they passed south of

Ahmadabad, Englehardt found himself targeted by a trio of SA-2 missile sites; he decided he had no choice but to take out their ground guidance units. No sooner had the three Anaconda missiles left the bomb bay than Rager reported a pair of Su-27s taking off from Jamnagar, to the northwest.

The Sukhois chased them for only ten minutes before giving up. By then Englehardt had altered his course to avoid yet another set of missile batteries.

They were almost to the coast when Rager sounded another warning—four Su-30s, advanced versions of the Su-27 and the most capable aircraft in the Indian air force, had just taken off from Daman.

"Target them," Englehardt told Sullivan.

"We only have three missiles."

Which is exactly why he didn't want to use them earlier, Englehardt thought.

"Use what we have."

"I'LL TAKE THE LEAD SUKHOI," STARSHIP TOLD ENGLEHARDT and Sullivan. "You guys get everything else."

A two-seater, the Su-30 bore roughly the same relationship to the Su-27 as the Super Hornet bore to the original F/A-18 Hornet. Starship knew that if he didn't fly just right, the Su-30 could easily get past him. And even if he did, it still might.

His first move was to push *Hawk One* ahead of *Hawk Two,* increasing his separation to roughly five miles. Expecting the Sukhoi radar to pick up the Flighthawk, he put *Hawk One* on an intercept that would take it directly into the Sukhoi's windscreen. The two aircraft were closing at a rate of almost 1,400 miles an hour, or roughly 23 miles a minute. That would give the Sukhoi pilot only a few seconds to react before his aircraft was in range of the Flighthawk's cannon.

A head-on attack at high speed had a limited chance of success, even with the computer aiming the gun. But Starship wasn't counting on *Hawk One* to shoot the plane down. He wanted to attract the Indian's attention and break its charge. Once it began to maneuver, it would necessarily lose speed, taking away some of its advantage over the Flighthawks.

Hawk One was still thirty miles from the Sukhoi when the Indian pilot showed he wasn't a pushover either—he fired two AMRAAMskis, not at the EB-52, but at the Flighthawks.

"Missiles in-bound for Flighthawks," Rager warned from his station upstairs. His voice was so loud in Starship's headset that he could have heard him without the interphone circuit.

"Yeah, roger that," said Starship.

He guessed that the missiles had been launched in the equivalent of a boresight mode, with the hope that their onboard radars would pick up the Flighthawks as they drew close. But it was also possible that the Su-30 was hoping to simply clear the path in front of him: Once the Flighthawks began maneuvering to avoid the missiles, his path to the *Bennett* would be clear.

Starship pulled *Hawk One* up, discharged some chaff, then rode the robot straight upward increasing the ship's radar signature to make it easier for the missiles to find him. At the same time, he continued *Hawk Two* on its course. The missiles saw *Hawk One* and began to follow—only to lose the slippery aircraft as Starship pumped more metal tinsel in the air and pushed down hard on his wing, spinning away as he reduced his radar signature to that of a pygmy grasshopper. The missiles exploded several miles behind *Hawk One*; the Flighthawk had gone a little farther south than he wanted, but it was still close enough to recover if *Hawk Two* slowed the Sukhoi down.

Hawk Two was seven miles from the Sukhoi. Starship's gun sight began blinking black, the other plane lower than he expected; as the sight blinked red, the Sukhoi veered north.

"Lock and fire," Starship told the computer, letting C^3 shoot while he flew the plane.

Always optimistic, the computer wound the Vulcan cannon

up and began spitting its bullets in the Sukhoi's direction a few seconds before it was actually in range. Starship nudged his stick to follow the Sukhoi, trying to give the computer as much time on the target as possible without trading too much altitude or speed.

The Sukhoi rolled out and disappeared below him, heading almost straight down. Starship didn't follow, knowing the Indian would only pull up abruptly and try to outmuscle him. Instead, he slid *Hawk Two* back in the direction of the *Bennett*.

Hawk One was now about eight miles to the east and two miles south of the Sukhoi, and at 30,000 feet, roughly 10,000 over the plunging Su-30. Starship pushed the aircraft toward an intercept, trading altitude for speed, but still staying east in case the Indian pilot decided to hit the gas in that direction.

"Launch warning! SA-3s," said Sullivan, the copilot, over the interphone.

The Megafortress lurched beneath Starship. He tried to shut out the cockpit conversation and focus on the Sukhoi, pushing *Hawk One* closer. The Indian had to turn to stay on course for the Megafortress. His turn inadvertently closed the distance with *Hawk One*. His tail appeared at the bottom of the screen. The targeting piper boxed it in black—out of range.

Starship told the computer to pursue the Sukhoi and took over *Hawk Two*. As he did, the Sukhoi began a hard turn west. It was far too early to get behind the Megafortress, Starship thought; he checked the sitrep and realized what was going on—the *Bennett* had altered its course to avoid the SA-3s, and was now flying almost due south toward the Indian. The Sukhoi was lined up and ready to launch its missiles at the Megafortress's nose.

"Flighthawk leader to *Bennett*—you're closing the distance with the Sukhoi."

"Take care of him."

"It would help if you kept your distance," muttered Starship.

· "Just fly your own damn plane," answered Englehardt.

Starship pushed *Hawk Two* at the Sukhoi from above, taking on the plane from the forward right quarter. He managed to get a short burst into the fuselage before passing. The Sukhoi didn't even seem to notice.

A warning sounded; the Indian pilot had managed to fire his two remaining radar missiles, both AMRAAMskis.

"Missiles," warned Sullivan.

"ECMs. Hang on." Englehardt began pushing the Megafortress into a series of evasive maneuvers. He was tired, as tired as he'd ever been, yet so keyed on adrenaline his hands were shaking.

"Still on us," said Sullivan.

"What's with the SA-2 battery near the coast?"

"Tracking. No launch."

"Sukhoi is breaking off, moving east," said Rager.

"Sure. He's out of missiles," snapped Sullivan.

Englehardt's neck was swimming in sweat. Even though the controls were electronic, pushing them felt like heavy work, and his arms and legs felt as if they were going to fall off.

"Missile two is gone. The first one is still coming," warned Sullivan.

Englehardt slammed the airplane back to the north one more time, putting enough g's on the air frame to get a warning from the computer. The AMRAAMski slipped by—but as it did, the guidance circuit in its tiny brain realized it had been fooled, and self-detonated out of spite.

Shrapnel spun through the air. A succession of light thuds peppered the right side of the plane.

The aircraft shuddered but responded to his controls, leveling herself off as Sullivan glanced at the sitrep to get his bearings. Warning lights began to blink on the dashboard, and before Englehardt could completely sort out what was going on, he heard a loud thud from somewhere behind him. The Megafortress seemed to move backward in the air. He knew he'd lost one of his engines, but his adrenaline-soaked brain couldn't figure out which one at first.

"Copilot, status. Engines," he said.

"Three is out. Problems with four. Temp high, moving to yellow. Shit. Red."

"Bring it down. Trimming to compensate," said Engle-hardt.

"SA-2 site has fired two missiles," said Rager.

"Bastards," muttered Sullivan.

THE SUKHOI BROKE EAST AFTER FIRING, EITHER UNAWARE that *Hawk One* was shadowing him or thinking he could simply slip by.

Or maybe his pass had damaged the Sukhoi, Starship thought. The Indian aircraft was trailing black smoke from one of its engines.

The aiming cue on *Hawk One* went solid red, and Starship pressed the trigger. The first two or three rounds sailed to the right, but the rest ripped a large hole in the enemy's wing.

"Get out," Starship said aloud, even as he continued to press the trigger. "Bail. Time to bail."

The wing flew entirely off, and the Sukhoi disappeared in a steaming cloud of smoke and flames. Starship throttled back and pulled his nose camera out to wide angle, looking for a parachute. But it was too late for the Indian pilots to hit the silk, too late for them to do anything. He felt a twinge of regret, sadness for the men and their fate, despite the fact that they'd been trying to kill him.

It was only as he pulled *Hawk One* back toward the *Bennett* that he realized the Megafortress had been hit. The pilots were talking about the engines—they'd lost one and were about to lose another. The Indians had also just launched a pair of SA-2s at them, though from very long range.

Somewhere above the cacophony he heard a radio call, faint, indistinct, and yet familiar; very, very familiar.

"Zen Stockard to any American aircraft. You hear me?"
Zen? For real?
"Zen Stockard to any American aircraft."
Starship punched into the emergency frequency.
"Zen! Zen! Where are you? Zen, give me a location."
He waited for the answer. After ten or fifteen seconds passed, he tried again. Still nothing.
Had he imagined it?
No way. *Hawk Two* had picked up the communication; the aircraft was flying near the coast, now about ten miles south of the *Bennett.*
"*Bennett,* I think I had Zen on the emergency band," Starship said. "I think I had Zen. Can we tack back?"
"We're down one engine and about to lose another," said Englehardt. "Try and get a location and pass it on. That's the best we can do."

THE SA-2S WERE FOLLOWING THEM, BUT ENGLEHARDT thought they could outlast them as long as he held the Megafortress's speed above 350 knots. They throttled engine four back but left it on line even though the instruments showed it running well into the yellow or caution area. Not only did he want all the thrust he could manage at the moment, but compensating for the loss of both engines on one side of the plane would cost even more speed.
He worked with Sullivan to trim the aircraft manually, hoping to squeeze a few more knots from it by pushing against the computer's red line. The nose felt as if it was plowing sideways through the air, like the prow of a small canoe being pushed by the current in a direction its owner didn't want it to go.
"Temperature on engine one is coming up," warned Sullivan. That was the engine that had given them problems earlier in the flight.
"We'll have to try backing it off a little," said Englehardt.
"SA-2 is still tracking."
Englehardt wanted to scream. Instead he took off power on

engine one, then scrambled to adjust his trim as the aircraft bucked downward. One of the motors that moved the outboard slotted flap on the right wing had apparently been damaged by the missile strike, and now the control surface began to balk at moving further. Finally it stopped responding completely.

"SA-2 is still climbing," said Sullivan. "On our left wing."

If he looked over his shoulder, Englehardt thought, he'd see the big white lance as it spun in his direction. He kept his eyes glued straight ahead, trying to keep the Megafortress as level as possible. There was no question of evasive maneuvers; they'd never survive them.

They wouldn't survive a missile strike either. Better to go out fighting, no?

"Hang on," said Englehardt, and he pushed the stick down hard, diving toward the earth.

Near the Chinese-Pakistani border
0046

THERE WAS A BUZZ AROUND HER, LIFTING HER IN THE AIR.

"What's going on?" Jennifer asked. Her words morphed as they left her mouth, changing into the chirping of birds.

What was going on?

Danny Freah's face appeared above hers.

"You're gonna be OK, Jen," he said. "All right?"

She understood the words, but they sounded odd. Then she realized he was singing.

Danny Freah, singing?

"You got shot. Your vest and helmet took most of the bullets, but one got your knee. We gave you morphine for the pain, all right? It shouldn't hurt."

"Shouldn't hurt," she said, her words once again changing, this time into the caw of a bird.

DANNY WATCHED THE MARINES SECURE JENNIFER'S SLING inside the Osprey. One bullet had gone in the side of her kneecap, exiting cleanly but doing a good deal of damage on its way. Though the other bullets hadn't penetrated her body armor, she still had two cracked ribs and a good-sized concussion. The corpsman who treated her thought she'd be OK, as long as she got treatment soon.

Three Marines had been hurt during the operation. Two had relatively minor injuries to their legs, but the third had been hit in the face and lost a great deal of blood.

But it was Jennifer he worried about. He had to tell Dog—but he certainly didn't relish the conversation.

He pressed the button on his helmet, then reconsidered. Better to wait until they were in the air.

"All right, let's go," Danny yelled. "Let's get the hell out of here. Come on! Move it!"

**Aboard Dreamland *Bennett*,
over India
0050**

THE *BENNETT* MOMENTARILY TURNED INTO A FALLING BRICK, accelerating toward the earth as Englehardt put her into a power dive. She leaned on her good wing, accelerating briefly to the speed of sound. The air frame shuddered but held, a thoroughbred celebrating its sudden release from the gate.

The SA-2 that had been tracking them began to arc in pursuit, but there was no way it could turn quickly enough. Fuel gone, it flailed helplessly for a few more seconds before self-destructing several miles beyond the Megafortress.

Englehardt had avoided the missile, but now he and Sullivan had another fight on their hands. Giddy with the burst of speed, their racehorse didn't want to come level, let alone slow down.

"Engine four is in the red," said Sullivan.

"Take it offline," said Englehardt.

"Shutting down four."

Englehardt backed off engine one himself. That left him one good power plant.

"Unidentified aircraft coming from the west," said Rager. "Two planes. Three hundred miles."

Just what I need, thought Englehardt.

"Starship, we have two aircraft coming from the west."

"On it, *Bennett*."

"Feet are wet," said Sergeant Daly at the surface radar, signaling that they were over water.

"Planes ID'd as Tomcats," said Rager.

"Sullivan, contact those guys and let them know we're on their side," said Englehardt. "Then help me set up a course to the refuel. We've got a long way home."

**Northeastern Pakistan
0100**

"MANY OF THE CIRCUITS ARE BURNED OUT, GENERAL. I cannot make it work as it was designed to. I simply don't know enough."

Abtin Fars stood up slowly. He was a tall, thin man well into his fifties; he wore glasses but clearly needed better ones, for he was constantly fiddling with them as he examined things.

"You are an expert, Abtin," General Sattari told him gently. "You can fix anything."

"Some things. This is beyond me."

Abtin seemed pensive, and Sattari feared that the true problem here was not his lack of knowledge but his conscience. The general worried that he was withholding his knowledge because he did not want to arm a nuclear weapon.

"The intention is to use it against Dreamland," said Sattari. "The American force that killed our people at Anhik."

Abtin had been friends with several of the engineers and technicians slaughtered at Anhik when the Americans raided the laser project Sattari had started there. But no emotion registered on his face.

"A difficult problem," said the engineer finally, ducking back to look at the warhead.

Sattari watched him work with his various instruments and tools. The general himself knew nothing about how to make the weapon work. It had taken considerable trouble and expense to locate Abtin; finding a replacement would be very difficult.

He could put a gun to the man's head and order him to fix the bomb, but how could he be sure it would explode?

He had to be patient, but that was nearly impossible.

"I could put in a very simple device," said Abtin finally, still bent over the warhead. "It would allow the weapon to detonate at a set time. There would be no fail-safe. Once set, it would explode. These circuits here," added Abtin pointing, "these are good. But placing the new circuit in, there is a chance that it will accidentally initiate the explosion."

"If you tell me what to do, then I will take the chance myself. You won't have to. You can be far away."

"With this device, General, it would take many hours to reach safety." Abtin rose. "I'll make a list for you. The items we need are easily obtained."

Aboard the *Abner Read*
0110

"We're on station."

Storm turned toward Eyes and nodded. The executive officer blinked and looked around the bridge apprehensively. He seemed out of place, as if he were a gopher who'd popped up from underground and arrived in the middle of a wedding.

"Say, Captain, do you have a minute?" Eyes asked.

Storm pointed in the direction of his cabin, which was reached through a door at the back of the bridge.

"You're treating me like I'm the enemy," Eyes told him after they reached Storm's quarters. "I'm not."

"No?"

"The order to stop trailing the *Khan* was Admiral Woods's order, not mine."

"You're on his side."

"I don't take sides, Storm. I follow orders."

"Damn it." Storm pounded his desk. Since his "talk" with Admiral Woods, he'd kept his emotions bottled up and stayed mostly to himself. He'd said no more than was absolutely necessary, and to some extent managed to push his disappointment and anger away. Now it raged free in his chest, surging through his whole being. "I was so damn close," he told Eyes.

"Close to what?"

"To sinking the damn *Khan*."

"Storm, we crippled it. We sank the *Shiva*. The *Shiva*, Storm. Do you realize what we've accomplished?"

"It's not enough!"

Eyes stared at him.

"It's not enough," repeated Storm, his voice closer to normal.

"Sure it is."

Both men were silent for a moment.

"No destroyer has ever engaged an aircraft carrier in a one-on-one battle before," said Eyes finally, his voice now almost a whisper. "This is what Pearl Harbor was for battleships. It's a revolution."

"It's not enough, though," said Storm.

"It should be, Captain. It should be."

Storm stared at his executive officer. Eyes was a good man, an excellent first officer. But he didn't understand—he didn't have the ambition a truly great captain needed. He just didn't understand.

But he was loyal. And Storm felt he owed him an explanation, or at least an attempt to explain.

"I can't put into words what I feel," Storm told him. "It's just—I can't."

"Your men need you," said Eyes. "They see you quiet, brooding, barely talking to them. Not leading them. They don't know what's going on. They need their captain."

Storm frowned. He wanted to sink the *Khan,* to do what no one else had ever done. Having taken down one carrier, he wanted—needed—more.

But those victories were not necessarily who he was, just expressions of what he might achieve. Who he was went deeper than that. It was more important than a medal or a line in a history book that he'd never read. He wasn't the snap in a sailor's salute when he came on board, he was the look in the scared kid's eyes when the bullets were flying and the young man needed something, someone, to believe in.

As Eyes was telling him.

"Dismissed," Storm said sharply.

The executive officer frowned, then began to leave.

"Eyes?"

He turned back around.

"Thank you very much, my friend. I appreciate it."

White House West Wing
1230, 18 January 1998
(0130, 19 January, Karachi)

"Mr. Barclay, do you ever go home? It's Sunday!"

Startled, Jed spun around to face his boss, National Security Advisor Philip Freeman.

"Um, but—"

"Just joking, Jed. How are we doing?"

Jed gave him a quick update, starting with the newly located warheads and ending with the fact that the two Dreamland pilots—his cousin and cousin-in-law, though he didn't mention this—were still missing.

"That's too bad," said Freeman. "I hope we find them."

Jed nodded.

"Now that Samson is taking direct control of Dreamland," said Freeman, "are you worried about your role with the staff?"

"No, sir."

"Good. You shouldn't be. There are going to be a lot of changes at Dreamland due to the restructuring. It's going to be a real command. The President—" Freeman caught himself. "Well, it's the President's decision. Things will work out. As for you, you're still an important part of my team. Frankly, I think we've been wasting some of your talents. Dreamland has eaten up a lot of your time."

"Um, yes, sir. Uh, th-th-thank you."

Freeman reached into his jacket pocket and took out a business card. "I don't want you to take this the wrong way," he said, handing it to Jed.

"Um, OK."

"This is a speech therapist. She's the best. She helped my daughter. I want you to see her."

Jed took the card. He tried to smile. He'd been to several professionals over the years. Some had helped for a brief time, most hadn't.

"Um, thanks."

"I'm going to make sure you keep your appointments," added Freeman. "And don't worry about paying."

"Uh—"

"A friend of yours who wishes to remain anonymous is footing the bill, not me. And I'm going to make sure you have time. The stutter is going to hold you back, Jed," added Freeman. "It gives people the wrong impression. All right?"

"Um, y-y-yeah. OK. Thanks."

Diego Garcia
0130

"THIS IS BASTIAN," DOG SAID WHEN HE REACHED THE COM-munications station in the Dreamland trailer. "What's up, Danny?"

"Bad news, Colonel. The last warhead is missing. And Jennifer's been hit, along with three of our Marines."

Dog felt as if he'd been punched in the stomach.

"Tell me about the warhead," he said. He struggled to keep his voice even.

"There were guerrillas nearby when we arrived," Danny began. He explained what they'd found—that the tapes made it seem as if the guerrillas hadn't been there long enough to get the weapon, and that they'd also taken a prisoner, though so far he hadn't said much.

Dog questioned Danny about the warhead and what might have happened to it, even though it was obvious Danny didn't know. Finally, he couldn't think of any other questions, except the one he wished he didn't have to ask.

"And Jennifer?" he said, biting his lip. "How bad—"

"She's going to be OK, they think," said Danny. "She got hit in the knee, but she'll be OK."

The rest of what Danny said didn't register—she was going to be OK. That was the only information he wanted. Danny mentioned the others who'd been wounded, the plan to get back to the base camp—none of it registered.

She'll be OK.

Jennifer shouldn't have been there in the first place, he thought. It was his fault. He should have ordered her home.

"You OK, Colonel?"

"I'm all right," Dog told him. "Take care of your wounded. And get back in one piece."

"Absolutely."

Dog closed the transmission. There was another one wait-ing to connect—Starship, aboard the *Bennett*.

"Bastian."

"Colonel, I think I heard a broadcast from Zen. I haven't been able to get him back. We're under fire," added the pilot, almost as an afterthought.

"Give me the position."

The Flighthawk and *Bennett* were considerably farther south than the crew members who had already been rescued. Was that an odd quirk in the radio waves? Or had Zen and Breanna parachuted out much farther south than anyone thought?

"Were you over the water?"

"The Flighthawk was. It was a faint signal, Colonel. I'm sorry I can't be more definitive."

"That's OK. Are you guys all right?"

"Oh, yeah, Colonel. We're great."

"Take care of yourself. Dreamland trailer out."

Dog switched over to the fleet liaison and told them he had important information about the search for his people. He was quickly relayed to one of the wing commanders aboard the *Lincoln*. The commander thanked him for the information—then told him it would be hours before they could respond.

"I know how important it is, Colonel," the man said before Dog could protest. "Right now, though, we're covering the evacuation of the warheads from the desert. The Indians are throwing everything they have in the air, and the Pakistanis and Chinese look like they're going to respond. The warheads are our priority."

"Switch me to Admiral Woods's staff," said Dog.

"If it were my people, I'd do the same thing," the commander replied before making the connection.

The lieutenant who came on the line was considerably less sympathetic.

"The carrier cannot be in two places at one time. That position is nearly twelve hours from where we are. And the entire task force is needed to shelter the warheads and get them away safely. You have your own people involved," said the lieutenant. "You don't want us to abandon them."

"I'm not talking about abandoning them," said Dog. "I'm talking about recovering two of my people."

"I'm sympathetic," said the lieutenant, sounding anything but. "For now, this is what we can do."

Dog smacked the connection button, killing the line. He was about to call General Samson, then thought better of it. From the remarks he'd heard Woods's staff make earlier, Samson had even less influence with Tex Woods, who saw him as a rival for a future command appointment.

And the truth was, all Dog had was a single radio transmission, without a real location.

He laid out the paper map on the large table in the trailer's common area. He plotted the point where the others had been picked up and where the Flighthawk heard the call. The area to the north had been searched. So it could be that Zen was even farther south, near the small islands off the Indian coast.

Maybe he could have the *Cheli* come south along the coast on its way back to Diego Garcia.

He got up and went to the communications area, located just behind the large open room.

"Things are hot down there," Brad Sparks told him. "A couple of guys took hits. They're going to evac any second. We'll shadow them to Base Camp One. A lot of action up here, Colonel."

"Right. Stay with it."

"Colonel, did you want something specific?"

"Just making sure everything is OK."

"Hey, not a problem, Colonel. We were born ready."

Dog checked back with the *Bennett*. "Englehardt, what's your situation?"

"I'm down to one and a half engines, but clear of the Indian defenses."

Dog listened soberly when Englehardt explained the extent of the *Bennett*'s damage. He figured they could make it back to Diego Garcia, but it would take an extremely long time.

And maybe a little luck.

He wished he'd taken the plane himself.

"All right, Mike. I know you can do it."

"Thanks, Colonel."

Dog rose. If Zen's transmission was going to be checked out, he'd have to do it himself.

VIII

Homecoming

———

DOG HAD ONLY ONE AIRPLANE AT DIEGO GARCIA THAT WAS
both available and had sufficient range to get up to the area
where the communication had been received—*Quickmover*,
Dreamland's MC-17.

Based on the McDonnell-Douglas Globemaster III C-17,
Quickmover had been specially upgraded by the Dreamland
design team to act as a front-line, combat cargo ship.
Equipped with state of the art avionics and locating gear that
would allow the aircraft to drop supplies and paratroopers
deep inside hostile territory, *Quickmover* had proven herself
in combat several times. But she was still a cargo aircraft
with no offensive capability; if things got nasty, her only option would be to run away. The ship would have virtually no
chance of surviving a gauntlet like the one the *Bennett* had
just gone through.

But that didn't prevent the crew from volunteering for the
mission as soon as Dog told them what was going on.

"Let's get the hell in the air," said Captain Harry "Whitey"
Golden, the pilot, when Dog told him about the transmission.

Whitey—his premature gray dome made the nickname a
natural—spoke for the entire crew. The aircraft was airborne
and winging north inside of twenty minutes.

As in a standard C-17, the flight crew worked on a deck at
the front of the aircraft, sitting above the auditorium-size
cargo area. Automation allowed the aircraft to operate with

only three crewmen: a pilot, copilot, and combination load-master/crew chief.

Dog sat in one of the auxiliary crew seats, studying a set of paper maps of the western shore of India and trying to puzzle out what might have happened to the *Levitow* after its crew had bailed out. The first six members of the crew had been rescued about 160 miles west and twenty south of Veraval; according to the copilot, the plane was flying due west at the time and the search had concentrated in that general area.

They'd widened the search, of course, but among the assumptions they'd made were that the plane had continued roughly on the course and that Zen and Breanna had gone out within two or three minutes of the others—reasonable guesses, especially as the plane had been descending rapidly before the others bailed.

But what if, right after the bulk of the crew bailed, the plane had turned back toward India or gone south, staying in the air for ten or even fifteen minutes longer before Zen and Breanna jumped?

The Megafortress's computer was supposed to hold it on course, but Dog had seen firsthand how difficult the plane could be to steer with the holes torn in the skin when the ejection seats blew.

He drew a long box along the coast of India, extending nearly three hundred miles south from where the others had been found. Below the box, another hundred miles or so, were the Aminidivis islands.

Could they have made it that far south?

Probably not, he thought. But they would go over them anyway. He extended his box.

"Fly us up through here," he told Whitey. "We'll broadcast on the Guard band and listen on all of them."

"Got it, Colonel."

"If you get a radar warning from one of those SA-3 batteries along the coast, you get the hell west. Don't stop, just go."

"We're well above them."

"You go west, you got me?"

"Yes, sir."

"Colonel, how long should we search?" asked the copilot, Sandra McGill.

"Until we find them or have to refuel," said Dog. "Or until General Samson finds out where I am and has my head."

Aboard Marine Osprey *Angry Bear One,* over northern India 0403

AS DANNY FREAH SAT BACK IN THE RACKLIKE BENCH OF THE Marine Osprey, two thoughts filled his head:

Man, am I tired.

Man, do we have a long way to go before I can get some rest.

His eyes started to droop. As he drifted toward sleep, he saw Dancer in front of him.

Out of uniform.

Way out of uniform.

Nice, he thought. Very nice.

Someone shook his leg.

"Yeah, what?" said Danny, sitting upright.

"Pilots want to talk to you, Captain," said Gunny.

Danny got up and leaned into the cockpit.

"Troops are moving on both sides of the border near Base Camp One," said the pilot. "They want us to go straight on to the *Poughkeepsie.* We'll have to set up a refuel. Can you tell the Megafortress what's going on while I work out the refueling details? We need to meet an Osprey from the *Lincoln.*"

"Not a problem."

Brad Sparks was his usual overcaffeinated self, telling him the escort would be no problem. Danny next checked in with Sergeant Liu and the Whiplash detail back at the Base Camp; Liu told him tersely that things were under control "but we're moving triple time."

Clearly, the sergeant was still shaken by what had happened at the house, thought Danny. But he sounded a little better, or maybe just busier—the two sometimes went together.

The corpsman was checking on Jennifer when he snapped off the line.

"How's she doin'?" Danny asked.

"She's lost a good bunch of blood from that knee," said the corpsman. "Like to get her treatment as soon as we can. Real soon."

"We're working on it."

**Aboard Dreamland *Cheli*,
over India
0440**

CHEECH LONG'S NASAL DRAWL BROKE THE SILENCE.

"MiGs look like they're taking an interest," the radar officer told Sparks. "Changing course."

"We're ready," said Sparks. "Keep watchin' 'em."

The MiGs were Indian MiG-21s, flying a little more than two hundred miles to the west—behind them now as they swung with the Osprey. Sparks decided the MiGs weren't going to catch up; he'd save his missiles for planes that would.

"Spoon Rest radar," said his copilot, Lieutenant Steve Micelli. "A hundred miles south."

The radar indicated an SA-2 ground-to-air battery. Their present flight plan would keep them out of the missiles' range.

"All sorts of goodies under the Christmas tree today, huh?" said Sparks.

"Looks like somebody told them we were coming," said Micelli.

"I think it was Cheech," said Sparks. "He's always looking for a fight."

"Had to be Cowboy," Cheech retorted. "Those Flighthawk guys live for trouble."

"You got a problem with that?" said Lieutenant Josh "Cowboy" Plank.

"Negative, Cowboy," said Sparks. "Just keep your Flighthawk juiced and loose."

"Just remember I'm on your tail," replied the Flighthawk pilot.

"Hard to forget."

"Chinese J-8s, coming at us hard," warned Cheech, his voice now serious. "Four planes. Two hundred miles. They're doing Mach 2."

"Micelli, target them with the Anacondas," Sparks said.

"Not supposed to shoot until they threaten us," answered the copilot.

"I interpret afterburners as a threat. Take the mothers out," said Sparks.

Aboard Dreamland MC-17 *Quickmover*
0453

COLONEL BASTIAN KEYED THE MICROPHONE AGAIN.

"Dreamland MC-17 *Quickmover* to *Levitow* crew. Come in, Major Stockard."

He paused to listen. Something was scratching at the back of his throat, and he took another sip of the herbal tea the crew chief had brewed. Then he tried the broadcast again.

"Colonel, we have a surface ship in our search box," said Whitey when Dog paused to listen for a response. "The *Abner Read*. Very northern end."

"Ask them if they'll help."

"Already have."

"And?"

"Captain Gale wants to talk to you."

Dog punched into the circuit. "Bastian."

"Colonel, I understand you require assistance. What's the status of your search?"

"Two crewmen are still missing," said Dog. He told Storm about the radio transmission and briefly explained his theories about where the crew might have bailed.

"We're inside your box. We'll do what we can," said Storm.

"Thanks. Bastian out."

Aboard the *Abner Read*,
Indian Ocean
0500

STORM FROWNED AS THE LINE SNAPPED CLEAR. BASTIAN had been abrupt as always, barely acknowledging his offer of help.

Some people were just social jerks, he thought.

It didn't matter, though. This was their chance to get back in the game, if only a little. Anything was better than sitting at sea and twiddling their thumbs like a garbage scow waiting to sweep up the slops. The crew was starting to get *bored*: a disease worse than death, in Storm's opinion.

"Eyes, I want to set up a thorough search for two downed Dreamlanders," Storm said, switching over to his internal line. "The Werewolf, everything we've got."

"Already working on it, Captain."

Aboard Dreamland *Cheli*,
over India
0512

SPARKS THOUGHT THEY HAD THINGS PRETTY WELL COVERED. The Anacondas were about sixty seconds from hitting the Chinese J-8s, and the SA-2 radar had turned itself off.

Then a mobile SA-3 battery turned on its radar and began directing it at the Marine Osprey.

"Get *Angry Bear* out of there," Sparks told his copilot, Micelli. "Flighthawk leader—yo, Cowboy, toast the SAMs."

"SA-3 toast coming up."

"More aircraft. No IDs," said Cheech at the airborne radar. "Three, maybe four planes. Two hundred fifty miles, bearing—"

"What do you mean, 'maybe four'?" snapped Sparks.

"Make it three. Things are getting a little hot here, Sparks," added the sergeant. For the first time since Sparks had worked with him, Cheech's voice contained a note of stress.

"What are they?"

"Working on it. Tentatively, Sukhois. Su-27s."

"Find out for sure and keep an eye on them."

"Missile one has hit lead J-8," said the copilot. *"Bam!"*

"I can do without the sound effects, Micelli."

"Bam!" repeated the copilot, even louder. "Splash the second J-8. Kick ass."

The crew's banter level continued to edge up over the next few minutes, even as the threat board reddened with fighters and ground radars. No sooner had the Flighthawk taken out the radar for the SA-3s than a small dish radar for an ancient ZSU-23 lit up a few miles down the road. The ZSU-23 was a four-barreled cannon. Though old, it was hell on low-flying aircraft like the Osprey. While Cowboy got after it, Spark urged the pilot in the Osprey to get the hell out to sea.

"I'm moving," said the Marine.

"Move faster," said Sparks.

"You want to go like a bronco with a firecracker in its papoose," cut in Cowboy.

Micelli and Cheech heard the communication and started roaring.

"I'm glad you guys are having fun," said Sparks. "Keep at it."

"Tracking Indian Sukhois," responded Cheech, his voice somewhat more serious. "Two hundred miles. Losing them."

The Sukhois turned off, but two Chinese planes joined the fray, flying over Pakistan. These were MiG-31s, similar to the aircraft Colonel Bastian had encountered some days before. Sparks decided he would target them with Anacondas right away—and wasn't surprised when they fired their own missiles, apparently radar homers, just as the first Anaconda left the bay.

"Launch the Quail," he told Sparks, referring to the radar decoy.

"Still trying to get a lock on the second MiG," replied the copilot.

"Well, lock the motherfucker and let's go."

"I'm working on it, Sparks. Relax."

The pilot brought up the decoy screen and handled the Quail II himself. Similar in many respects to its Cold War era forebear, the Quail II had an artificial radar profile and could broadcast radio and radar signals similar to the Megafortress's own. With the decoy launched, Sparks took a sharp turn away, making sure the bait was between him and the missiles.

"Foxfire One," said Micelli finally. "Anaconda away."

The missile ripped out from under the *Cheli* as if angry that it had been delayed.

"Why are you having so much trouble?" Sparks asked. "You were one-two-three on the test range."

"We ain't on the freakin' test range," said Micelli. "The radar isn't interfacing right. It's getting hung up in the ident routine. I don't know. Where's Jen Gleason when you need her?"

"She's in that Osprey we're trying to protect," said Sparks. "So we better do a good job."

**An atoll off the Indian coast
Time and date unknown**

WHAT WAS THAT SOUND? ZEN WONDERED. AN AIRPLANE?

If so, it was very far away—beyond his imagination. Beyond everything. He only existed on this tiny collection of rocks; he could not think beyond it.

An airplane.

He picked the radio up mechanically, made sure it was set to broadcast, made sure the voice option was selected.

He should broadcast, shouldn't he? That was his job, even though his life was here.

"Zen Stockard—" His voice broke. He stopped speaking for a few seconds. Could he imagine himself beyond these rocks? Was there another place to go?

"Zen Stockard to any aircraft. Any aircraft," he repeated. "Mayday. Mayday. Airman down . . . Pilot down . . . Mayday. Zen Stockard."

He listened for the inevitable silence. But instead words came.

"Give me your location, Zen."

Had he heard the voice yesterday, the day before, he would have laughed and answered with glee. He would have made a joke or said something grateful, or done one of a dozen other things.

Now he simply replied, "Colonel Bastian, I'm on a treeless atoll somewhere off the coast of India. I don't have a GPS."

"Roger that Zen. Jeff—Breanna? Is she with you?"

Zen glanced toward her, unsure what to say.

"Yes," he managed finally.

"Thank God. Keep talking to me. Just keep talking. We're going to find you. Keep talking so we can home in your signal."

Was there anything to say?

Anything?

"Zen?"

"I guess I'm a little thirsty," he said finally. "And hungry. But mostly thirsty."

**Aboard Dreamland *Cheli*,
over India
0515**

"ANGRY BEAR, CUT NINETY DEGREES," SAID MICELLI, warning the Osprey of yet another ground battery. "Cut and stop. Shit. You got a zsu-zsu dead ahead."

"Get 'em, Cowboy," said Sparks.

"Yeah, I'm on it," said the Flighthawk pilot. "Take me two minutes."

"Splash Chinese *MiG One. Bam!*" said Micelli.

Sparks didn't have time to celebrate with his copilot. He checked the radar warning indicator at the bottom of his dashboard. Another Spoon Rest radar—SA-2—was operating to the south, but they were well out of range.

"What's the status of those Chinese missiles?" Sparks asked Micelli. "They still following us?"

"Sucking on the Hound Dog's signal. Going east. Both of them," said the copilot. "No threat. Anaconda missile has missed *Bandit two,* the Chinese MiG."

"We missed?"

"Must've been the trouble locking. Both MiGs turned as soon as they launched. They're not a threat."

"No SA-3 battery here," said Cowboy, guiding the Flighthawks. "What's the story, dude?"

"You need to go two miles south," said the ground radar operator.

"Oh yeah, yeah, yeah, my bad."

"I need that refuel," said the Marine pilot in *Angry Bear.*

"We're going to get you there," said Sparks. "You're ten minutes away. Relax."

"I have fifteen minutes of fuel, no reserves."

"And you're complaining?"

As soon as Cowboy started his run on the antiaircraft gun, Sparks told the Osprey to proceed. The area for the refueling rendezvous had been carefully plotted so it was far from any Indian or Pakistani radars. The tanker aircraft—another Osprey rigged for refueling—approached over southern Pakistan, sneaking away as its F/A-18 escorts tangled with a pair of Pakistani F-16s.

As the Flighthawk tracked back to cover *Angry Bear,* Sparks took the Megafortress west, checking the path to the ocean. With roughly two hundred miles to go, their best course was a beeline over the Rann of Kutch. There were several radar installations there, but only one missile site; Sparks had Micelli target it and was just about to give the order to fire when a fresh flight of Indian Mirage 2000s showed up on the radar to the south.

"Four of them," announced Cheech. "Just coming in range—they're at 35,000 feet."

"I don't think they're going to be a problem if I hurry these Osprey guys up," said Sparks.

"Where are those Navy jets?" said Micelli. "We're supposed to have help."

"They have their hands full," said Sparks.

"We don't need no effin' Navy," said Cheech.

"Keep your mind on your scope," said Sparks.

"My eyes are there. That's what's important," said Cheech. Then his voice settled into a more serious, clipped tone. "Another aircraft coming off the field at Jamnagar."

Jamnagar was a major military base on the Gulf of Kutch, less than a hundred miles south of their planned exit route.

"You have an ID?"

"Negative. Two engines—patrol type."

"All right. Track him. Micelli, let's get that missile site."

They fired the Anaconda, then swung back toward the Ospreys. A fresh pair of Hornets from the *Lincoln* checked in, saying they were about ten minutes off. Sparks told them to concentrate on Jamnagar; he'd watch the Mirages.

"Another pack of MiGs," added Cheech. "The Mirages are on afterburners. I have some other contacts. A hundred and fifty miles."

"What the hell did they do, save up all their fuel just for us?" said Micelli.

"They're bored from being grounded the last few days," said Cheech.

"All right, we're going to have to deal with these guys," Sparks told them. "Who's the biggest threat?"

"We have only three Anacondas left," said Micelli.

"Well, you'll just have to get a two-for-one shot," Sparks replied. He pulled up the stick, taking the Megafortress up another 5,000 feet and aiming southward. He'd keep as much distance as possible between the *Cheli* and the Ospreys. Most likely the Mirage radars wouldn't be able to see the rotor tilts after they tanked and would concentrate on him.

The Mirages were in two groups, two planes apiece. Sparks had Micelli target the lead plane in the first group, hoping that with their leader gone, the others would lose heart, or at least hesitate enough for them to get away.

"Trouble locking—IFF says it's a civilian."

"Override the bitch."

"It's not that simple."

"Override and lock."

"I'm working on it, Sparks," said Micelli. He finally got the lock and fired.

The ground radar operator reported a contact moving on a highway twenty-five miles ahead of the Ospreys. Sparks had Cowboy check on it.

The cacophony continued. They'd trained for encounters like this, but the real thing was twenty times as draining and as confusing as the simulations. Even his crew of wiseasses was showing the strain.

"New bogey—unidentified plane thirty miles from *Angry Bear*," said Cheech. "Designated *Bogey Seven*."

"Where'd that come from?" said Sparks.

"Thirty-five thousand feet—looks like it's one of the ones that came off from Jamnagar."

"Tell the Navy flight."

"They're too far away to intercept," said the radar officer. "They're on a pair of MiGs."

"ID the plane."

"Working on it. *Bogey Seven* is in range to fire radar missiles."

"Missile one is terminal," said Micelli. "Locked on the lead Mirage."

"No ident from *Bogey Seven*," reported Cheech.

"Query the mother again. Micelli—get him on the radio."

"Roger that," said Cheech. "*Bogey Seven* is twenty miles

from *Angry Bear*. Direct intercept. Turning—looks like they're moving to get behind them. Shit. Fifteen miles."

"No reply," said Micelli after trying to hail *Bogey Seven*.

"Micelli—lock on *Bogey Seven* and fire."

"Do we have an ID?"

"*Bogey Seven* closing!" said Cheech.

"Flighthawk leader, leave the ground gun and get between the Ospreys and bogey."

"He's too far. I won't make it."

"Micelli—lock on the mother and fire!" Sparks hit the radio. "*Angry Bear,* you have a bogey coming at your tail. Get as low as you can go."

"Can't lock. The IFF module—"

"Shoot the damn thing in bore sight if you have to," said Sparks. "Nail that mother *now*."

"Override. Locked. Foxfire One."

The missile shot away from the Megafortress. As it did, the missile fired at the lead Mirage hit home.

"Splash Mirage," said Micelli, his voice drained.

"Mirages are turning away," said Cheech.

"Anaconda is terminal."

"Lightning Flight to Dreamland *Cheli*. You read us?" asked a Navy unit.

"Roger, Lightning Flight," said Sparks.

"We're coming for you," said the leader of Lightning Flight, a group of four F-14s dispatched from the *Lincoln*. "Rest easy."

"Screw him," said Micelli.

"Not today," muttered Sparks. He clicked the radio transmit button. "Stand by, Lightning Flight."

"Splash bogey," said Micelli. "Bogey is down. The way is clear."

"*Angry Bear,* your nose is clean," said Sparks. He told the Marine pilot about the F-14s and had him contact them. "Did we get an ID on that plane?" he asked Micelli when he was done.

"Negative."

"Cheech?"

"It was one of the MiGs, I think."

"All right. We'll sort it out later. Let's make sure these guys hook up with the Tomcats so we can home."

**Aboard Marine Osprey *Angry Bear One*,
over northern India
0518**

DANNY FREAH LEANED OVER THE BACK OF THE COPILOT'S seat, trying to get a better view of the source of the smoke as they approached.

"Got to be the gun the Flighthawk smoked," said the copilot.

There was way too much smoke, thought Danny. He pulled down his visor and put it on maximum magnification, zooming in on the black cloud. The first thing he saw was a large flat piece of metal. Beyond it, red flames and a roiling cloud of smoke furled from a long tube.

A fuselage. He was looking at the wreckage of an aircraft.

"One of the MiGs," said Danny, but almost immediately he realized he was wrong. The fuselage was too long, out of proportion to the tailfin for a fighter. Then he saw a large aircraft engine sitting off to the side.

He hesitated, then reached for the control on the smart helmet to record the image.

"Path is clear to the *Lincoln*," said the pilot. "We'll drop our injured and get over to the *Poughkeepsie* with the warhead."

"Good," said Danny. "Good."

**Northeastern Pakistan
0521**

GENERAL SATTARI WATCHED AS ABTIN FARS TOOK A LONG, deep breath, then bowed his head and said a silent prayer before reaching to connect the wire with the trigger device he had devised. To a layman, at least, the device seemed almost overly simplistic. There was a small digital clock, two different types of very small watch batteries, and a three-inch board containing a few diodes and two small capacitors.

Sattari took his own deep breath as Abtin reached into the bomb assembly.

The engineer jerked backward. Sattari reflexively shut his eyes, expecting the inevitable.

"OK," said Abtin after a few moments passed. "OK."

The general found he had trouble catching his breath. "It will work?" he asked when he did.

"It should. I cannot make any guarantees. Let me solder the connections."

Sattari bent over the device.

"Please, General," said Abtin. "If you don't mind, having someone looking over my shoulder makes me nervous. Inspect the work when I am done."

"Of course," said Sattari, backing away. "Of course."

An atoll off the Indian Coast
Time and date unknown

EVERYTHING HURT. EVERYTHING.

Breanna's heart thumped against the ground.

"Oh," she said.

Pushing the word from her mouth took supreme effort. She tried to say something else but was too exhausted.

"Oh," she managed finally. "Oh. Oh."

Aboard Dreamland *Quickmover*,
over the Indian Ocean
0530

"WE GOT IT, COLONEL. A DEFINITE LOCATION."

Dog flattened the folds out of the paper map, translating the GPS coordinates to the grid. Zen and Breanna were on an unmarked island northeast of the Chebaniani Reefs, about seventy-five miles from the mainland and roughly parallel to Magalore—farther south than even he had thought. According to the map, there was no land there, just sea; the nearest marked island was about three miles away.

But they were definitely there. Disoriented, barely able to talk, and clearly thirsty and hungry, but there.

"Dreamland *Quickmover* to the *Abner Read*," said Dog, contacting Storm with the information. He spoke to Eyes first, then Storm.

"There's nothing there on the chart, Bastian," said the ship captain. "Are you sure about this?"

"I'm sure."

"It'll take us three hours to get there. We'll have the Werewolf over as quickly as possible."

"Thanks. I appreciate it."

"Is your daughter all right?"

"She's there. They're both there. What kind of shape they're in, I'm not sure."

After a moment Storm replied, "I hope she's OK."

"Me too."

An atoll off the Indian Coast
Time and date unknown

THE SOUND WAS SO FOREIGN HE COULDN'T PROCESS IT, almost couldn't hear it.

A moan, soft, long, plaintive . . .

Breanna, talking to him from the grave.

Calling for him.

"Jeff. Jeffrey. Zen. Where are you, Jeff?"

It was so far away, so injured, so lonely, he couldn't stand it. A buzz descended from above, a cloud of hums as if angels were surrounding him. The air vibrated with a cold, parching dryness.

Is this what death was like? Or was it just loss, empty of all hope?

"Jeff. Jeff. Where are you?"

"I'm here," he said. And the spell broke, and he turned and pushed himself back to the tent, where for the first time in days—for the first time ever it seemed like—Breanna's eyes were wide open.

"Hey."

He twisted his head down and kissed her, pressing his lips to her face, then pausing as the flesh touched, afraid that the pressure would hurt her—or worse, that the kiss would shatter an illusion and he would find she wasn't here, wasn't looking at him, wasn't softly moaning for help.

He pulled back, eyes closed as they always were when they kissed. Fear overwhelmed him, choked out his breath. Zen shook his head and forced his eyes open, forced himself to face the inevitable mirage.

"Jeff. Everything hurts," she said.

It was real, not a mirage, not a dream, not death or hopelessness, but life—she was alive.

He pushed in and kissed her again, happy beyond belief.

IX

Payments Due

EVEN THE MOST AVARICIOUS OF MEN HAD LIMITS, MORAL lines they would not cross for any amount of gold. So General Sattari was not terribly shocked when he found that Abul Amin, the Egyptian whom he had contracted with in Rawalpindi, balked when he saw the shape of the cargo that was to be loaded into the Airbus 310. Sattari countered the man's frown with one of his own, then suggested they discuss the matter in a corner of the nearby hangar while his men proceeded.

"No, you must stop," said the Egyptian in his heavily accented English. "I cannot allow my plane to make such a transport. If the Americans found out—"

"Why do you think that the Americans don't know?" asked Sattari. "Come, let us discuss the matter and make sure our payments are arranged. Then a pot of tea."

More confused than mollified, the Egyptian began walking with Sattari toward his small office inside the hangar. The Egyptian employed a single bodyguard, who stepped out from near the door and glanced nervously at his boss. Abul Amin shook his head slightly, and the man stepped back into the shadows.

That was the problem with people like him, who made their living in the shadow of the law. They were too trusting of others they thought were corrupt.

Most of the Egyptian's money came from transporting embargoed spare parts for oil equipment, with the occasional military item thrown in as an extra bonus. He would be hired to pick them up from a country on decent terms with the West, like Pakistan, and fly them to a place such as Iran, where the international community had prohibited their direct sale. Amin had been doing this for so long that he'd come to believe not so much that it was legal, but that there was only minimal danger involved, that he did not have to be on his guard when with someone like Sattari—for whom he had transported everything from circuit boards for F-4 Phantom jets to Western-style blue jeans over the years.

Sattari's greatest difficulty was waiting for the right moment to pull his pistol from his pocket. He waited until Amin had sat down at his desk, then took out the pistol and shot him twice in the head.

Amin fell backward, his skull smacking against the Sheetrock wall and leaving a thick splatter of very red blood as he slumped to the floor.

Sattari aimed his gun at the door, expecting the bodyguard to respond. After waiting a full minute, he went calmly to the door, pushed it open and waited again.

His own bodyguards would be in the hangar by now, but he hadn't heard more gunfire and didn't want to take a chance.

A few seconds passed, then a few more; finally there was a shout from outside.

"General?"

"It's OK, Habib," he said. "Where is the bodyguard?"

"He ran as soon as the door was closed," said Habib Kerman, appearing at the door. "We let him go. It seemed wiser."

"Very good, nephew. We need to be ready to take off very quickly. There is a long night ahead, and I have not yet arranged the refueling."

"Yes, General."

Sattari smiled, then reached over to turn off the office light.

Aboard the *Abner Read*,
Indian Ocean
0610

THE ATOLL WAS ONLY VISIBLE ON THE HIGHEST DETAIL SATEL-lite images in the *Abner Read*'s library, and then it appeared as little more than a squiggle on the ocean. The small rock was completely barren; its vegetation appeared to consist largely of moss.

"I want the Werewolf there. Now," Storm told Eyes. "I want these Dreamlanders rescued."

"Aye aye, Captain. We're moving as expeditiously as possible."

"Don't move expeditiously—move *quickly*!"

Storm grinned to himself. He was better, back in control. Woods and the others weren't going to win.

Turning from his holographic chart table, he looked out the "windshield" at the front of the *Abner Read*'s bridge. Specially tinted and coated with radar-absorbent material, the view through the glass was one of the few things about the *Abner Read* that Storm did not like; the material made it difficult to use his binoculars. And unlike the younger members of the crew—though he would never admit that age had anything to do with it—he did not entirely trust the long-range images provided by the video cameras. So after checking with the helmsman to make sure they were on course and making the best speed possible—"Faster would be better," he commented—Storm stepped out onto the flying bridge and brought his binoculars to his eyes.

Nothing but sea before him, and a high sky as well. The sun bloomed to the east, announcing a glorious day.

"Storm, looks like there's an Indian destroyer on the move from the north, running in the general direction of the atoll," said Eyes, breaking into the captain's brief reverie. "Ex-Soviet Kashin-class ship. Looks like it may be the *Rana*. The Were-wolf's radar picked it up. You want to go to active radar?"

"Negative," said Storm. "The fox doesn't let the hen know it's in the barnyard. Plot its position. I'll be back with you in a moment."

An atoll off the Indian Coast
Time and date unknown

ZEN CUPPED HIS HANDS BELOW BREANNA'S LIPS, THEN tilted the small canteen so the water would flow. He had to tilt it more than he'd expected—the water was nearly gone.

"Oh," said Breanna as it touched her lips. "Oh."

She sucked at it, then started to cough. Zen stopped pouring, waiting patiently for her to regain her breath. She shook her head, and he took the water away.

"How long?" she asked.

"Days."

"How did we get here?"

"We drifted. I don't know how I found you. God, I guess."

"Yeah." She started to move, as if she wanted to stand up.

"No, no, stay down."

"No, I gotta move." She stirred, pushed herself, then stopped with a groan. "Oh, my legs are killing me."

"Mine too," said Zen.

"Yours?"

"Phantom pain. We're going to be OK," he told her. "I just talked to Dog—they're circling above us."

"Oh," said Breanna.

She struggled to get up again. This time Zen helped and she managed to sit.

"I think this leg is broken," she said, pushing her right leg. "It really hurts. And the knee is twisted."

Something caught her eye.

"What's that?" she said, looking toward the beach.

Zen turned. It was the Bart Simpson kid. He had a bottle of water in his hands and he was walking slowly up the rocks.

"Bart Simpson," said Zen. He waved at the boy. The boy, staring curiously at Breanna, waved back.

"He loves Bart Simpson," he explained to Breanna. "He must see it on TV. He thinks we know him."

"Does the kid live here?"

Zen explained that they were on a barren island but that the boy and his friends seemed to live on another island a few miles away. The kid, meanwhile, stopped a few feet from Zen and held out the water bottle.

Zen took it.

"We probably should boil it or something," said Breanna.

"I'm really thirsty," he said. But he didn't open the bottle.

"I think I hear something," said Breanna.

Zen held his breath, trying to listen.

"A helicopter, I think," said Breanna.

"I gotta get the radio," he said, crawling back for it.

Aboard Dreamland *Quickmover*
0630

"YOU CAN HEAR IT?" DOG ASKED ZEN.

"Yeah," Zen answered, his voice hoarse.

"Good. I'm telling the *Abner Read* right now . . . Zen?"

"Yeah, Colonel?"

"Breanna? Is she all right? Really all right?"

"She's OK." Zen's voice trailed off. "You want to talk to her?"

Tears flooded from Dog's eyes. He was so overcome he couldn't answer, and when he did, it was between sobs. "Please."

The silence seemed unending.

"Daddy?"

"I thought we agreed . . . you'd never . . . call me that . . . at work."

Dog held his arm up, burying his face in it as the tears flowed uncontrollably.

"That's right, Colonel," said Breanna. "Sorry. I thought this was R and R."

"All right. We'll pick you up soon. Hang in there."

"I love you too, Dad."

Aboard the *Abner Read*,
Indian Ocean
0630

STORM STUDIED THE HOLOGRAPHIC PROJECTION OF THE ocean around them. They were about two and a half to three hours from the atoll. The Indian destroyer was closer; it could reach it in an hour and a half at flank speed.

It seemed too much of a coincidence that the other ship would be steaming in that direction; clearly, it was homing in on the radio transmissions from the survival radio. Perhaps it had picked up the MC-17 first, then gone to investigate.

With hopes of capturing the American fliers, he had no doubt.

He could sink the bastards with the Harpoons if it came to that. But by the time he got into range, the Indian would be at the atoll.

"Dreamland *Quickmover* looking for you, Captain," said the communications specialist over the ship's intercom circuit. "It's Colonel Bastian."

"Yes, Dog, what's going on?"

"We spotted an Indian destroyer that seems interested in the atoll."

"Yes, we copy," Storm told him. "I'm not in range to deal with him."

"Given what the Indians have been doing to our aircraft up north," said Dog, "we should consider him hostile."

"Agreed." Storm felt his irritation growing.

"I can broadcast a warning," offered Dog.

"You're in a cargo plane, aren't you?"

"I'll fight the bastard with my bare hands if I have to," said Dog.

"That won't be necessary," replied Storm.

Aboard Dreamland *Quickmover*
0704

"MAIN ANTIAIR WEAPONS ARE SHTIL MISSILES," SAID THE copilot, consulting the onboard reference to ID the Indian destroyer's capabilities. "They're Indian versions of the Russian SA-N-7s. They have about a three kilometer range. Maybe 15,000 meters—roughly 50,000 feet. We're OK as long as we keep our distance."

Dog looked at his paper map, mentally calculating the *Abner Read*'s position against the Indian destroyer's. The Indian was north; Storm was south and to the west. The *Cheli* was more than an hour and a half north, still covering the warhead recovery operations. By the time they got down here it would all be over.

"Dreamland MC-17 *Quickmover* to Indian destroyer," said Dog, switching his radio into the international communications frequencies. "We are conducting a recovery mission in the area and request you hold your position."

When the destroyer did not reply, Dog repeated the message, this time giving the destroyer's position and heading.

"Dreamland *Quickmover*, you are over Indian territory and will be shot down if you remain," replied the destroyer.

"This is Colonel Tecumseh Bastian. I'd like to speak to the captain of the ship."

"This is the Republic of India naval vessel *Rana*. You are in Indian territory."

"I'm in international airspace, conducting a Search and Rescue mission for downed airmen."

"Give us their location and we will pick them up."

"Thanks, but we've got it covered," replied Dog. "Please just stand by."

The Indian destroyer continued on its course.

Its offer, though, gave Dog an idea.

"*Rana,* if you desire to assist, I can give you a search grid. Your assistance would be appreciated."

Dog gave the destroyer a GPS reading that would take it to the east of the atoll. The destroyer didn't acknowledge—but it did change course.

"Good one, Colonel," said the crew chief, who'd been standing next to him, nervously shifting his weight back and forth the whole time.

"It won't work for too long," said Dog. "As soon as Zen broadcasts again, they'll figure it out."

"Maybe you should tell him to keep quiet."

"I will, as soon as I think of a way to do that without tipping off the Indians that it's a ruse."

An atoll off the Indian coast
0715

THE KID WHO HAD BROUGHT THEM WATER WAS FASCINATED by the Werewolf, staring at it as it circled around the small island.

"You like helicopters?" Zen asked.

The boy was so engrossed in watching the helo that he didn't seem to hear.

"That's a robot," said Zen. "It's being flown from a ship."

"Robot?" said the boy.

"Yeah." Zen pushed himself a little farther down the rock-strewn beach. There was something on the horizon to the north, a long sliver of white.

A ship.

The *Abner Read*?

Zen stared. The bits of white separated into distinct pieces. There was a mast at the center of the figure, a sleek smoke-stack.

The *Abner Read* didn't have a mast. She was a special ship, very low to the water.

And black, not gray. She wouldn't reflect the sun like this.

"Zen, what's up?" asked Breanna.

"I see a ship," he told her. "It's going in the wrong direction. Give me the radio."

**Aboard the *Abner Read*,
Indian Ocean
0725**

STORM WATCHED THE PLOT OF THE INDIAN DESTROYER, now positively identified as the *Rana*, veer toward the mainland. He had to hand it to Bastian, the old Dog had a plentiful bag of tricks.

They could be friends if he weren't such a jerk.

The holographic unit included a navigational module that could calculate and project courses. Storm simply pointed at the atoll and asked, in his clearest voice, "ETA?" The computer flashed a set of numbers above the small rock: 1:42:06.

"I want more power, engineering," he said. "Helm, find some way to get us to that rock faster. I don't care if you have to put up a sail. Get us there!"

**Aboard Dreamland *Quickmover*
0730**

"ZEN STOCKARD TO RESCUE OPERATION. COME IN," SAID ZEN.

Dog immediately hit his transmit button.

"Zen, we need radio silence. Complete radio silence. We will get you. *We will get you.* We don't need a broadcast."

Dog leaned over the radio console, hoping that Zen's brief transmission—and his own—would go unnoticed by the Indian destroyer.

But it was a vain hope.

"Destroyer is changing course, Colonel," said the copilot, who'd been monitoring it. "Going back in the original direction."

"I'll notify the *Abner Read*," said Dog grimly.

An atoll off the Indian coast
0731

"WHAT'S WRONG, ZEN?"

Zen put down the radio without answering. He shaded his eyes and stared at the ship on the horizon.

"Jeff?"

"I think the Indians are looking for us too," he told Breanna. "And I gather that we don't want them to find us."

Breanna struggled to get up, pushing as much of her weight as she could onto her left leg. But her head swam and the pain in her side seemed to explode. She collapsed to the ground.

Zen was over her when she opened her eyes.

"Hey, are you OK?" he asked.

"Yeah. I was just getting up."

"Who asked you?"

"Well, I'm not going to stay on the ground the rest of my life. And I'm not going to stay on this island either."

He smiled.

"What?" she asked.

"You're beautiful."

"If I look half as bad as you, I look like a zombie."

"Oh, you look worse than that."

Zen looked up at the Werewolf, which was doing a slow turn about a half mile off shore.

"You really think you could move?" he asked her.

"I *can* move, Jeff. It hurts, but I can move. I don't know if I can stand, though."

"You're a gimp like me, huh?"

"You're not a gimp."

"I have an idea. Maybe we can meet the *Abner Read*."

"I don't think I can swim."

"That wasn't what I had in mind."

Aboard the *Abner Read*,
Indian Ocean
0735

"THE *RANA* FIGURED IT OUT," SAID EYES. "THEY'RE BACK ON their original course."

"How long before they're in range of the Harpoon?"

"Ten minutes, tops."

"All right. Stand by."

"Storm—there is the possibility that they'll shell the atoll if we open fire," said Eyes. "There's not much shelter there."

"Noted."

Eyes was right, of course, but what other options did he have? He certainly wasn't going to let the Indian pick up his people right under his nose.

A full volley of Harpoons would sink the bastard before he had a chance to react.

No, they'd have a launch warning. It would take the Harpoons roughly three minutes to get there; by then the atoll would be obliterated.

"Storm, listen in to the emergency channel," said Eyes over the intercom radio. "Major Stockard is up to something."

Storm looked down at his belt to get the proper combination of buttons that would allow his com unit to listen in. The broadcast came in, weak and breaking up.

"Hey, Werewolf. We're looking for some navigational guidance," said a tired voice. "Wag your tail if you understand what I'm talking about."

"Eyes, have the Werewolf pilot zoom his video on the beach," said Storm.

"I think he's getting into a canoe," said Eyes.

"I'm going to automated beacon," said Zen. "So you can home in on me."

Clever, thought Storm.

"Have the Werewolf lead them south," he told Eyes. "Get the Harpoons ready—he's leaving the radio on so the destroyer thinks he's still on the island. Move, let's go people!" shouted Storm. "Let's show these Air Force people what we're made of."

**An atoll off the Indian coast
0745**

"NOW THEY'RE GETTING IT," SAID ZEN AS THE WEREWOLF ducked to the left. "Come on, Bart Simpson. Help me paddle."

Zen pushed the boy's small canoe through the shallow water, avoiding the rocks. Breanna was inside the boat, leaning over the side and paddling with her hands.

"Yeah, come on, guys," said Zen as the current pushed up against the boat. "We have to go south. Stroke! Come on, Bart Simpson, follow that helicopter."

BREANNA COULDN'T SEE MUCH FROM WHERE SHE WAS, BUT she could hear the helicopter. She had no more strength to paddle, and let her arm drag in the water.

Everything hurt so badly. She closed her eyes and remembered the night she'd seen Zen after the accident, the longest night of her life. She'd become a different person that night, though of course at the moment she hadn't understood.

Who had she become? Someone wiser, more patient.

Not wiser, but definitely more patient.

She'd laughed a lot less since then. Much, much less.

That was a mistake. That was something she had to correct. She should be happy. They had so much.

"OK, baby, time to go."

Disoriented, Breanna expected to see Zen in his wheelchair hovering over her when she opened her eyes. But she wasn't at home, she wasn't in bed—two men in wet suits were picking her up, helping her into a rigid inflatable. The

Werewolf was hovering somewhere behind her, and the black shadow of the *Abner Read* loomed about a half mile off.

"What?" Breanna muttered. "Where are we?"

"We're with the USS *Abner Read*, ma'am," said one of the sailors. "You just relax now and enjoy the ride. We all are goin' to take you home."

**Aboard the USS *Poughkeepsie*,
Arabian Ocean
0800**

WITH THE LAST OF THE NUCLEAR WARHEADS STOWED aboard the ship, Danny Freah asked the *Poughkeepsie*'s captain if he could find him a relatively quiet place for a private communication. Quiet turned out to be a precious commodity aboard the ship, harder to find than water in the desert. The communications shack sounded like a tollbooth at rush hour, and Danny couldn't find a spot below that wasn't overflowing with sailors and Marines, or sounded as if it were. He finally went onto the deck, and standing near the railing just below the bridge, put his visor down and contacted Dog.

"Bastian."

"Colonel, it's Danny Freah."

"Yes, Danny. Go ahead."

A small legend in the view screen indicated that no video was available. Danny knew that Dog was aboard *Quickmover* and guessed that the colonel had chosen to communicate with voice only—probably because he knew he looked tired.

Somehow that made it harder. Danny wasn't sure why.

"Jennifer's aboard the *Lincoln*," Danny said. "They're thinking they're going to have to operate on her knee. It's pretty bad."

"But she's OK," said Dog.

"Yeah. She might have a concussion. Bullet splinter hit her helmet, knocked her out. That and the shock scrambled her head a bit. But she's OK."

"What about the mission?"

That was Dog, thought Danny—stone-faced and proper, insisting the focus be on duty and the job that had to be done, not personal emotion.

Even if he had to be breaking inside. First Bree, now Jennifer. But at least Jen was alive.

"We've brought the warheads back to the *Poughkeepsie*," Danny told him. "Base Camp One has been evacuated. We have no further information on the last warhead; it just wasn't there."

"I understand."

"The prisoner we took insists they didn't recover the warhead before we got there. Maybe the Pakistanis were there yesterday or the day before."

"It's possible. Dreamland Command is already working on some theories with the CIA," said Dog. "It's all right. You did a hell of a job. A hell of a job. Where's Sergeant Liu and the others?"

"They're getting some rest."

"We have to arrange for them to go back to Dreamland," Dog told him. "General Samson wants to talk to them personally, before anyone else."

"Samson?"

Dog explained that Samson had taken over as the new commander of Dreamland.

"Admiral Woods directed that they be taken over to the *Lincoln*."

"Samson wants them himself."

"It was an accident, Colonel."

"I know that. Samson does too."

"OK."

Neither man spoke for a moment.

"We've found Zen and Breanna," said Dog finally.

"You found them!" Danny practically yelled.

Colonel Bastian's voice remained drained as he told Danny what had happened—once more the calm, understated commander.

"Jesus, that's great, Colonel. That is damn great. Damn great."

"It is," said Dog.

For a moment Danny thought his commander's voice was going to break. But it didn't.

"All right," said Dog, preparing to sign off.

"Colonel, there's something else," said Danny.

He told the colonel about seeing the airplane wreckage as the Osprey headed out to sea. The plane, he said, had almost certainly been a civilian aircraft.

"The Osprey pilot had the *Lincoln* call in a location with the Indian authorities. It was a pretty severe crash; I doubt there were any survivors."

"I see."

"The Navy people are investigating. It's possible one of the Tomcats fired at it, but they think the Indians accidentally shot it down."

He gave Dog the approximate location.

"Things were pretty heavy up there," Danny added. "All sorts of stuff was in the air."

"Thanks for the information," said Dog. "We'll make arrangements to get you to Diego Garcia as soon as possible. Bastian out."

Diego Garcia
1502

DOG ROCKED HIS SHOULDERS BACK AND FORTH AS HE walked down the ladder from the MC-17, fatigue riding heavy on each one. He'd managed to talk to one of the doctors on the *Lincoln* and found out that Jennifer was all right; the doctors believed she'd keep her lower leg, though her knee would have to be reconstructed.

Maybe now he'd be able to keep up with her when they went jogging, he thought.

Breanna and Zen were aboard the *Abner Read*, very dehydrated. Breanna had a broken leg, badly bruised ribs, and a concussion—but she was alive, damn it, alive, and that was more than he'd hoped for, much more.

"There you are, Bastian! It's about time."

A large black man stepped from the passenger side of a black Jimmy SUV. It was General Samson.

"General, what brings you out to Diego Garcia?"

"I'm taking charge of this operation personally, Bastian. You're headed home."

"Well, that's good," said Dog, struggling to keep his anger in check. "Because we're done. All of the warheads, save one, were recovered. My people have been picked up."

Clearly flustered, Samson shook his head.

"I'm going to turn in," said Dog. "I don't need a lift. Thanks."

"Listen to me, Bastian. I know you think you're untouchable, but that's about to change. Your men created an international incident—"

"Which men?" demanded Dog, facing the general. "What incident?"

The general and the colonel stood facing each other on the concrete, both with their hands on their hips. Samson was several inches taller than Dog, and wider. More important, he outranked the lieutenant colonel by a country mile. But they were evenly matched where it counted—in their anger and distaste for each other.

"Your Whiplash people, on the ground, shooting up that house. The UN got ahold of that. I've just been on the phone with our ambassador."

"Those people were trying to deliver a baby and save the mother's life," Dog said. "You know that."

"Whether I know it or not isn't the point."

"Then what is the point?" Dog turned and started away, but his anger got the better of him. He pitched around. "You have a lot to learn if you think any man or woman who works for me, who works for Dreamland, anybody in this command, would kill innocent people deliberately. That's just total bullshit. And if you're going to lead these people, you better stand up for them, loud and clear, right now. Loud and clear."

"Go to bed, Bastian." Samson jabbed his finger in Dog's direction. "Get the hell out of my sight."

"Gladly."

STARSHIP RAN HIS FINGERS ACROSS THE TOP OF HIS SKULL. His hair, normally cut tight to his scalp, was nearly two inches high. It felt like a thick brush.

"So what do you think, Starship," asked Sullivan, the co-pilot of the *Bennett*, "are you with us or against us?"

"I don't know how far you can really push this," said Starship.

"Man, Englehardt almost got us killed. All of us. Including you. You were in the belly of the plane, you know. Not out there with the Flighthawks."

Starship looked across the cafeteria table at Rager and Daly, the other members of the *Bennett* crew. He didn't know them very well, nor did he really know Sullivan, except to occasionally shoot pool with on a night off.

"I mean, basically, you guys want to call the guy a coward," Starship told them finally. "I don't know. I'm not saying he made all the right decisions, but who does? And we had orders—"

"First order is not to get shot down," said Sullivan. "He ran away from every battle, he didn't want to use his weapons—"

"He used them," said Starship. "Listen, you guys haven't been in combat before. I'll tell you, you just don't know how some people are going to react. Bottom line is, he got us home. Flying that plane on two engines—"

"I had something to do with that," said Sullivan.

"So you do agree, he wasn't aggressive enough," said Rager.

Starship shrugged. It was a tough call. There was no doubt Englehardt's decisions could be questioned, but he'd been in a no-win situation. Starship knew from his own experience how hard it was to make the right call all the time, and how easy it was to be second- or even third-guessed.

"Look, we were hundreds of miles inside hostile territory, or what turned out to be hostile territory," he said. "Give the guy a break, huh?"

"He's against us," said Sullivan, standing. "Thanks, Starship."

The others rose.

"This isn't an us versus them," said Starship.

"We can't do anything if you're not with us," said Rager. "It doesn't make any sense."

"Listen—"

Sullivan frowned at him, then stalked out. Rager and Daly quickly followed.

THOUGH SORELY TEMPTED TO JUST GO TO BED, DOG INstead walked back to the Dreamland Command trailer to check on the *Cheli*. He'd just gotten to the door when he heard the Megafortress's engines in the distance. He watched the aircraft touch down, then went inside.

A young sergeant named Sam Bautista, a Whiplash team member who'd flown in with Samson, was on duty inside. Bautista jumped to his feet as Dog came in.

"Relax, Sergeant," said Dog.

"Sorry, Colonel. I thought you were General Samson. He said he was going over to see the base commander, but I thought he came back for something."

"No, it's only me," said Dog, passing through to the secure communications area. He slid into the seat in front of the console and authorized the connection to Dreamland Command.

Major Catsman's worried face appeared on the screen.

"Good even, Natalie. Or should I say good morning? Can you give me an update?"

Catsman started with things Dog already knew. The warheads were aboard the *Poughkeepsie*, Zen and Breanna were aboard the *Abner Read*. Further analysis of the last warhead site seemed to show that the warhead was gone when the guerrillas arrived, though the imagery was still being examined. The image experts asked to see everything recorded in the area since the EEMWBs had exploded.

"A passenger plane is down in the area the Marine Osprey flew through," said Catsman finally.

"Yes, Danny mentioned it to me," said Dog. "Do we know what happened yet?"

The major hesitated.

"Better tell me what you know," said Dog.

"A Global Hawk went over the area about a half hour ago. This is a photo from the area of the wreckage."

An image appeared in the corner of the monitor. Dog pressed the control to zoom in.

A triangular piece of white metal with black letters and numbers filled the screen. It was part of a fin from a missile.

"It's one of ours," said Catsman.

"From the Navy fighters?"

"No *ours* ours. It's one of the control fins from a Anaconda."

"From the *Cheli*?"

"Has to be. I haven't talked to Captain Sparks. I figured you'd want to do that."

Dog pushed his chin onto his hand. "Yeah."

"I haven't talked to General Samson either."

"I'll take care of it," said Dog.

"I— He ordered me not to tell you he was on his way," Catsman blurted.

"It's all right, Major. It wouldn't have made any difference at all."

WHEN YOU'RE BASED NEAR A PLACE LIKE LAS VEGAS, JUST about anywhere else in the world can seem spartan. But Diego Garcia was spartan in the extreme, which limited the crew's options for celebrating their mission.

"First we debrief, then we go over to the Navy canteen," said Brad Sparks as the crew shut down the *Cheli*. "Or whatever they call their bar."

"Hell, Brad, just listing the planes we engaged will take an entire day," said Cheech. "Let's debrief tomorrow."

"Oh sure," said Cowboy. "Like we're gonna want to do that with hangovers."

"Colonel Dog will have my butt if we wait," said Sparks. "Let's just get it over with."

"Where are the unintelligence officers?" said copilot Steve Micelli, getting up from his seat.

"Micelli, that joke is older than our airplane."

A combat-suited Whiplash security sergeant stuck his head up from the Flighthawk bay at the rear of the cockpit.

"Excuse me, Captain Sparks, Colonel Bastian wants to talk to you right away. He wants the entire crew over at the Command trailer."

"All right, Sergeant. We'll be right down as soon as we grab all our gear."

"Begging your pardon, sir, but you're to leave everything here. The memory cards and tapes from the mission especially."

"What the fuck?" said Micelli.

"If anything's missing or erased, we're going to be court-martialed," added the Whiplasher. "I'm really sorry, sirs."

DOG DECIDED HE WOULD TALK TO THE *CHELI*'S CREW ONE at a time. Sparks, since he was the captain, went first.

"Describe to me what happened on your sortie," Dog said, sitting across from him at the table in the Dreamland trailer. The others were outside, sitting in the shade of the nearby hangar.

"It was a long mission, Colonel. I don't know if I can remember every last detail."

"Do your best."

"OK. Can I have a drink?"

"I just made some coffee. And there's water in the fridge."

"I was thinking about a beer."

"Better not just now."

Sparks nodded. Dog recognized something he rarely saw in a pilot's face, certainly not at Dreamland: fear. Sparks must have sensed what had happened.

Dog had heard enough before Sparks was halfway through. The Anaconda aiming system had been giving them problems; they encountered a plane in the area near fighters that seemed to be a threat; the plane had not had a working friend or foe identifier.

Those were the mitigating circumstances. On the other side of the ledger, the plane should have been better identified by the radar operator, or, lacking that, visually identified by the Flighthawk before being fired on.

Should have been.

That was a judgment call, Dog thought, an extremely difficult decision to make in the heat of a battle, especially under the circumstances.

He truly understood how difficult that call was to make. Others might not.

"Did we screw up, Colonel?" asked Sparks when he was done. "What happened?"

"An airliner went down in the area the Osprey went through. There's a good possibility it was shot down by a Anaconda missile that came from your plane."

"Jesus."

Both men sat in silence for a few moments.

"What's going to happen?" asked Sparks.

"I don't know," said Dog. "It's up to General Samson. He's in charge of Dreamland now. And Whiplash."

"Am I going to be court-martialed?"

Dog wanted to shake his head, to stand up and pat Sparks on the shoulder and tell him it was all going to be all right. But that would be lying. There would be an inquiry—a long one, no doubt—before any decision was made on whether charges would be brought.

"I don't know what will happen," said Dog honestly. "At

this point anything is a possibility. I want you to go to your room and just stay there until you hear from me."

"Or the general?"

"Yes. Or the general. He's the one that has the final say now."

Malaysia
1730 (1530, Karachi)

GENERAL SATTARI FOLLOWED THE CONTROL TOWER'S IN-structions, taxiing the airplane away from the main runway. He felt physically drained. It had been years since he flew a large jet, and even with his nephew, an experienced multiengine copilot, managing the Airbus's takeoffs and landings had not been easy.

"Turn coming up ahead, Uncle," said Habib Kerman.

"Very good."

Sattari's eyes shuffled back and forth from the windscreen to the speed indicator. He could give the airplane over to Kerman if he wished, but his pride nagged him.

"You haven't lost your skills," said Kerman as they pulled into the parking area. "Outstanding."

Sattari smiled but said nothing. Kerman was his sister's youngest son. He had been a close friend of his own son, Val, though a few years younger; at times he reminded him very much of Val.

Four or five men trotted from a nearby hangar, followed by a pickup truck.

This was the most dangerous moment, Sattari knew—when his plot was nearly but not quite ready to proceed. He needed to refuel the jet in order to reach his destination. The airport had been chosen not for its geographic location but the fact that he had agents he believed he could count on to assist. He himself had not been here in many years, so he could not be positive they would help—and indeed might not know for sure until he took off.

The men ran to chock the wheels. A good sign, he thought. They were unarmed.

Sattari glanced at his nephew. "You have your gun?"

"Yes, Uncle."

Sattari nodded, then rose. He went to the door behind the flight cabin and opened it, pushing it with a sudden burst of energy. A fatal dread settled over him as the muggy outdoor air entered the cabin. He was ready; ready to die here if that's what was ordained.

But it wasn't, at least not at that moment. A metal stairway was being pushed close to the cabin.

"God is great, God is merciful, God is all knowing," shouted a man from the ground, speaking in Persian.

"Blessed be those who follow his way," said Sattari, completing the identifier he had settled on in their e-mail conversation.

"General, it is my pleasure to serve you," said Hami Hassam, climbing eagerly up the steps as soon as they were placed. "What cargo do you have?"

"That should not be relevant to you."

Hassam smiled, then reached inside his light jacket. "You have perishable dates," said Hassam confidently. "With all necessary papers and taxes paid."

"Good work."

"For our air force, nothing is too good. I have taken the precaution of purchasing several crates of fruit, in case there are any complications. I can have them loaded aboard the aircraft in a few—"

"That won't be necessary," said Sattari.

"Sometimes, the inspectors do come aboard."

"It won't be necessary," repeated Sattari.

The man's crestfallen face made it clear he was being too strident. He'd given Hassam to believe he was transporting banned missiles and other aircraft parts, a matter sufficiently important and clandestine that Hassam would probably not probe too deeply.

"The items we have are packed very delicately," said Sattari, explaining while not explaining. "And the fewer in contact with them, the better. We can put a few crates here if necessary," he added, pointing to the rear of the flight cabin. "But—should I expect trouble?"

"No," said Hassam, a bit uncertainly. "Usually there are no inspections at all. Not once fees are paid. Which has been done."

"The money transferred properly?"

"Yes, General. Of course."

"Can we get some food?" asked Sattari.

"There is a place in the terminal."

"Come, then," said Sattari.

"Your copilot?"

"He and the others will stay with the plane."

"You have others in the plane?"

"Not important," said Sattari, unsure whether his bluff had been detected or not. "I'll bring back a few things."

Diego Garcia
1900

REVIEWING ALL OF THE RECORDED SENSOR AND OTHER data from the flight would take several days, but the tapes made it clear that the *Cheli* crew believed they were looking at an enemy aircraft about to shoot down the plane they were protecting. The plane's transponder had not been working, or had been turned off for some reason.

Dog got up from the copilot's station and walked slowly through the *Cheli*'s flight deck.

"No one comes aboard this aircraft without my explicit permission," he told the sergeant standing near the ladder to the lower deck. "You understand?"

"Yes, sir."

"You noted that all the systems were intact when I left?"

"Uh, yes, sir. OK."

"It's OK, Sergeant, they were. You saw them playing, right?"

"Yes, sir."

It was a long, long walk to the borrowed Navy Hummer, and a short, short ride to the base commander's office. General Samson had concluded whatever meet and greet operation he'd been conducting and was striding out to his SUV when Dog arrived.

"General, I need to talk to you," said Dog, leaning out his window.

"Not now, Bastian. I'm meeting the commander for dinner."

"You're going to want to talk to me first, General."

"What about?"

"We'd best go someplace a little more private."

THE FIRST THING SAMSON THOUGHT WAS, *NOW I'VE GOT* him. Bastian wouldn't be able to wiggle out of this.

The next thing he thought was, *What if they blame me somehow?*

The incident with the family in the desert was bad, very bad, but the video vindicated the men, and it could be argued that the Dreamland people were on a mission of mercy. Whether they should have undertaken it or not was beside the point.

But this was very different.

"You're sure it was a civilian plane?" Samson asked Bastian.

"Dreamland Command says there's no doubt. It's a small airline that flies in northern India. This wasn't a scheduled flight," added Dog. "It apparently was some sort of relief plane or charter flying workers north to do electrical repairs."

"Why the hell wouldn't they have had a working transponder?"

"I don't know. We've encountered plenty of planes that haven't. Usually, though, it's because they're up to something they shouldn't be. This might just have been a malfunction."

"Why the hell wasn't it visually identified before they fired?" Samson asked. "That's standard procedure."

"There wouldn't have been time to visually check before the Osprey was in danger."

"That's their excuse?"

"That's my assessment. They haven't offered an excuse."

"That's not going to be good enough, Bastian."

Dog didn't reply. Samson rubbed his forehead.

There must be some way out of this, he thought. Forget the damage to his career—this was going to make the Air Force look bad. Very, very bad.

"What's the status of the plane?" snapped Samson.

"I have it under guard."

"All right. Dismissed."

"That's it?"

"Of course that's not it. But at the moment, Bastian, I don't want to see your face. And let me make one thing perfectly clear: You have no command. Do you understand? You are not in charge here. You cannot give an order relating to Dreamland, not even for coffee," he said. "Got me?"

"Loud and clear."

"Catch the first flight you can back to Dreamland. I'll deal with you there."

"Remember what I said about standing up for your people," said Dog.

"When I want advice from you, I'll ask for it."

**Aboard the *Abner Read*
1900**

THE *ABNER READ*'S SICKBAY HAD SOME OF THE MOST MOD-
ern medical equipment in the world, crammed into a space that would have made a broom feel crowded. Zen and Breanna occupied exactly fifty percent of the beds.

Zen had cuts all over his body. Acting on the advice of a doctor aboard the *Lincoln*, the *Abner Read*'s medical officer had started him on a course of intravenous antibiotics to combat any infection. Otherwise, his main problem was dehydration.

Breanna's case was more difficult to diagnose. Besides her broken bones, there appeared to be some light internal bleeding in her chest cavity. After consulting with a doctor on the

Lincoln, the *Abner Read*'s medical officer decided to have her moved to the aircraft carrier, where the larger facilities would make it easier to monitor her condition and operate if necessary.

Breanna was awake when the helicopter arrived. Zen, exhausted, was snoring loudly.

"Don't wake him," Breanna whispered to the doctors when they came in to examine her. "He needs to sleep."

"A good prescription," said the doctor.

"I'll see you later, babe," Breanna told her sleeping husband as her cot was gently lifted. "Pleasant dreams."

"I HEAR SAMSON'S A REAL PRICK," SAID JONES AS THEY waited in the dark.

"I don't think it matters whether he's nice to us or not," said Liu. "The facts are the facts."

"I wish I could be as calm as you," said Blow. He rubbed his hands together; the night had turned chilly. "Look at these arrangements—we gotta fly halfway around the world, land in Germany, catch a plane to D.C., then over to who knows where before we go home."

"'Cause he's keeping us away from the Navy," said Jones. "That might be a good sign."

"It's not going to be bad," said Liu calmly.

"Man, I can still see that baby." Jones pounded his eyes with his fist. "I can't stand it."

"It'll be OK," said Liu. He touched the other man's back. "The baby's in heaven."

No one said anything else until Blow pointed out the Osprey in the sky, its searchlight shining through the darkness.

"That's ours," said the sergeant. "Coming for us."

HE WAS IN THE AIR, TUMBLING AND FALLING. BREANNA WAS there too, but just out of reach. He kept trying to get her, though, throwing his hands out, grabbing for her.

Then suddenly she stopped. He continued to fall, plummeting toward the sea.

"Breanna," he called. "Bree. Bree."

The water felt like cement as he hit. His legs were crushed beneath him.

"Breanna!" Zen cried, and he woke in the sickbay.

He knew where he was, knew they were OK, but whatever part of his consciousness controlled his emotions was stuck back in the frightful dream. When he finally caught his breath, he turned and looked for Breanna.

The cot was empty.

"Bree!" he shouted. *"Breanna!"*

He pushed to get up, but couldn't. There were straps across his chest.

"Breanna!" Zen bellowed.

"Major Stockard, what's wrong, what's wrong?" said a corpsman, running in.

"My wife. Where is she?"

"She's OK, sir. They've taken her to the *Lincoln*."

"Why?"

"The aircraft carrier, Major. It has better facilities. She's fine, believe me. They've got great doctors. We just want to make sure there's no bleeding. If there is any, if by any chance they needed to operate, they have the facilities."

"Why the hell didn't you wake me up?"

"She said not to."

Zen dropped his head back on the bed. His whole body felt cold, and bruised.

"Can you undo me?" he asked the man.

"Don't want you falling out of bed, sir."

"Just undo me. I'm not going for a walk."

"Yes, sir."

Zen pulled his hands free but couldn't reach the strap over his chest. As soon as he was able, he pushed himself into a sitting position.

"You know what the weird thing is, sailor," he said as he sat up.

"You can call me Terry, sir."

"I'm Zen."

The sailor smiled, and pushed a pillow behind his patient's back.

"The weird thing is that I could swear I actually feel pain in my legs."

"Yes, sir."

"I haven't walked in a couple of years. I don't feel anything."

"Doctor said it's like a normal thing. Phantom pain."

"Yeah. But I haven't felt it in years. Sure feels real."

Zen stared at his legs, then did something he hadn't done in a long, long time—he tried to make them move.

They wouldn't. But they did hurt. They definitely did hurt.

"Yeah. Weird thing, the body," said Zen. "Real weird."

Diego Garcia
2350

"Ms. GLEASON IS SLEEPING," SAID THE NURSE ON DUTY in the *Lincoln*'s sickbay when Dog finally managed to connect with the carrier. "Even if I was allowed to wake her, she'd been pretty incoherent with the painkillers. She'll be OK," added the nurse, her voice less official and more emphatic. "All her vital signs are stable and she's headed toward a full recovery."

"How is her knee?"

"The primary problem is her kneecap, or the patella. They'll have to replace it. But there's a lot of work with prostheses over the last ten or twenty years. She'll definitely walk again, after rehab."

"Will she run?"

"Did she run before?"

"Yeah," said Dog. "She's pretty fast."

"Then, maybe. The doctors will have a lot more information. You're her commanding officer?"

"I'd like to think I'm more than that," said Dog.

"Encourage her. The rehab can be very difficult."

"She's up to it," said Dog. "If there's one thing I know about Jennifer Gleason, she's up to it."

RELIEVED OF COMMAND AND CLEARLY UNWANTED, DOG saw no point in hanging around Diego Garcia. Responsibility for locating the last warhead had now been shifted to the CIA; with more Navy assets on the way, Dreamland's help was no longer needed. The entire Dreamland team would be shipping back to base within the next few days; better to leave sooner rather than later, he decided.

The *Bennett* was the first aircraft scheduled to go home, once her damaged engines were replaced and the others repaired. Pending completion of the work, the plane was tentatively scheduled to take off at 0400, and Dog decided he'd hitch a ride.

He stayed up the rest of the night, slowly sipping a beer as he stared at the stars. Once or twice he tried thinking about his future in the Air Force, or rather, if there was a future for him in the Air Force, but he quickly gave up. That was the sort of thinking that required a quiet mind, and his was anything but. A million details, a thousand emotions, battled together below the surface of his consciousness, ready to interfere with any serious thought. The only way to hold them at bay was to stare blankly at the sky, just watching.

Just before 0200 he found Englehardt and his crew briefing their flight. He interrupted them and, calling Englehardt out into the hall, asked permission to grab a flight home.

"Um, you don't need my permission, Colonel."

"Well, as it happens, I do," said Dog.

He told Englehardt that Samson was reorganizing things and at the moment he didn't have any authority concerning Dreamland.

Pride kept him from saying he'd been shafted, though that's what it was.

"It's OK with me, Colonel. It'd be fine with me."

"Great. I'll meet you and the crew at the plane with my gear."

Malaysia
0600, 20 January 1998 (0400, Karachi)

GENERAL SATTARI TWISTED ANOTHER PIECE OF BREAD FROM the loaf and pushed it into his mouth. He hadn't realized how hungry he still was until he began nibbling on one of the loaves he'd bought for his nephew at the airport workers' cafeteria.

The refueling was nearly complete. Sattari paced on the tarmac as the men finished, waiting, impatient to be gone.

There were voices in the darkness beyond the plane. Some trick of the wind or his brain transformed them, made them seem familiar: his son, Val Muhammad Ben Sattari, speaking with his wife in the family garden many years before, when Val was just a boy.

Oh, Val, the loss, the loss of your precious life. What would I tell your mother, after my promises to see you happy, and with many children on your knee?

Sattari took a step in the direction of the voices, but they had faded. The fuel truck was finished; a worker recoiled the hose on the spool.

General Sattari thought back to the time when his son told him he wanted to be just like him. He'd been very proud— too proud.

How much would he trade to have that moment back?

He climbed up the steps to the cockpit. His nephew was just finishing the dinner he had brought.

"Are you ready?" Sattari asked.

"Yes, General."

Though they were cousins, Habib Kerman bore little resemblance to Val; he was flabbier, shorter. But for some reason he now reminded Sattari of Val, and the general felt a twinge of guilt.

"Habib, I have been thinking," he said, and put his hands on the back of the first officer's seat. "I think I will take the plane myself."

"You can't fly it by yourself, Uncle."

"I can. You saw yourself."

Kerman stared at him, his front teeth biting into his lip. Then he shook his head.

"I want to do this," he told Sattari. "Since my wife died, I have looked for a way to make my life meaningful. Allah has given me this chance, praised be his name."

"Once we take off, Habib, there can be no turning back."

"I wish to do it."

If it were Val, Sattari thought, would he let him go? It was one thing to undertake a hazardous mission, and quite another to face certain, absolute death.

"Are you sure?"

Kerman nodded.

"I am very proud of you," Sattari said. He tapped Kerman on the shoulder, then quickly turned and walked out of the cockpit, not wanting the younger man to see the tears welling in his eyes.

He found someone waiting at the base of the boarding ladder. It was Hassam, the spy who had helped arrange the refueling.

"What is it?" said Sattari.

"General, I trust all is well," said Hassam, coming up a few steps.

"Yes." They met halfway.

"I didn't mean to startle you."

"What is it you need?" said the general harshly. He had an impulse to reach for the gun in his belt and shoot the man, but that might ruin everything.

"The flight plan that was filed. It indicates you are going to America." Hassam was grinning.

"Flight plans do not necessarily tell the entire truth," said Sattari.

"Still, that is curious."

"What is your point, Hassam?"

The general placed his hand closer to his gun.

"I took the liberty of finding alternate identifiers and

flights for you, in case you are tracked once you take off," said Hassam.

Sattari's hand flew to his gun as Hassam reached to his jacket. Hassam smiled, opened the coat to show that he had no weapon, then took out a wedge of papers.

"I assume you want no questions asked when you appear at the airport to refuel," said Hassam. "But in the meantime, these may help you."

Sattari stood speechless on the tarmac, eyeing the folded documents. The smuggler's plane could send false ident signals, but he had not had time to research other IDs or flight numbers. These would very useful.

And yet, he didn't trust Hassam. There was something in the man's manner that kept Sattari from reholstering the gun as he took the papers.

"You'll find they're in order, I'm sure," said Hassam.

"How?" Sattari asked.

"Do you think the leaders of our country are blind and ignorant?"

Sattari felt his face flush.

"General, there is another question I must ask, though. Going to America—do you really feel that is wise?"

Sattari was once more on his guard. "If you know everything, then you know why I am going."

"Such an important man as yourself. It would be a shame to lose you. Especially when there is someone much younger ready to take your place."

Sattari heard something behind him. As he turned to glance up at the ladder, he realized his mistake. Before he could react, Hassam had leapt at him.

The general was still strong, but he was tired from his exertions over the past few days. He tried to bring his pistol around to shoot Hassam but couldn't manage it. Then there were others—someone stomping on his arm, kicking. Sattari's finger squeezed on the trigger. The loud pop of the pistol so close to his ear took his hearing away for a moment, and with his hearing went the last of his strength. The others continued to wrestle with him, but he was done, drained—angry and humiliated, a failure, a man who could not even get justice for his son.

"Wait! He has been injured!" yelled Hassam. "Careful! Take the gun."

Sattari's body had become a sack of bones. The gun was taken from him. Hassam got up; one of the men who'd come to his aid pushed the general onto his back.

"Gently," said Hassam. "He is a general."

Sattari could not see who he was speaking to. His eyes were focused on the face that appeared above him: Kerman.

In the darkness, he looked like his son, gazing down on him from Paradise.

"I will not fail you, Uncle."

"You SAID HE WOULD NOT BE HURT," KERMAN TOLD HASsam after Sattari had been carried to one of the cars. "Your thugs knocked him unconscious."

"He's not unconscious," said Hassam. "A few bruises."

"He wasn't talking."

"Don't worry so much about your uncle. Worry about yourself."

Kerman felt a surge of anger. But who was he really mad at—the spy or himself? He had told the ayatollah what Sattari was up to, knowing what the result would be.

"Nothing more to say, young man?" Hassam sounded almost as if he was jeering.

"Give me the papers."

"Can you be trusted? Ayatollah Mohtaj says yes, but I am not sure."

Kerman took the documents with the false IDs.

"You'll find out in less than twenty-four hours," he said, jogging toward the airplane's ladder.

X

The Long Ride Home

———

DANNY FREAH STRUGGLED TO SHUT OUT THE NOISE FROM the ship as he continued reviewing the mission with Major Catsman back at Dreamland. The Dreamland people had reviewed the available satellite and aerial reconnaissance data, looking for whoever might have been to the final warhead site before the Whiplash team. There were gaps of several hours in the records, but Catsman seemed fairly confident that the photo analysts would have been able to spot a Pakistani task force somewhere in the mountains. Trucks just couldn't move that quickly on the roads.

"There were tribespeople through the area on horseback two days before," said Catsman. "Then we think there was a Chinese reconnaissance flight, though we can't be sure it went over that area."

It still wasn't clear that the Chinese were actually working with the guerrillas Danny had encountered, or were competing with them to recover the weapon—a claim the Chinese ambassador to the UN had made when pressed about encounters in the area.

The politics didn't concern Danny much; he wanted results.

"The specialists have gone back and analyzed the satellite imagery," said Catsman. "They think the warhead was removed sometime after 1600 yesterday. They're going by some changes in the shadows on the ground. There is some debate on it—a lot of debate. They're comparing the satellite image to the Global Hawk image, and there's a large margin of error. The warhead itself was obscured; it was the missile's engines it focused on."

"Maybe some of the guerrillas got away while we were fighting," said Danny. "Maybe I missed them."

"We've gone over all the data, the Global Hawk feed, the video from the Flighthawk—none of them got away."

"I want to check it out anyway," said Danny.

"Fine. We'll stream it all back to you."

Danny moved the rolling chair he'd borrowed back against the wall of the communications compartment, watching the footage after it finished loading. In the earliest images it looked as if the guerrillas were just arriving, securing lookout positions and then moving down toward the warhead.

The rest of the video showed the battle. He saw his people come under fire, and could even make out himself in a few frames. It was odd to watch a replay of something that had been so intense—the tape seemed several times faster than real life, cold and quick, without any of the real emotion. Or fear.

"You have anything earlier than this?" he asked.

"We have the satellite shots. I'll download them."

"Instead of looking at the site, what if we looked at the major roads through the area?"

"The major road is a cow path," said Catsman.

"Well, any truck on it would be significant."

"Sure. We've checked the area," added Catsman. "And the photo interpreters at the CIA and Air-Space Command have been all over it."

"What if you look at the grids around it?"

"Just because we see a truck on the road doesn't mean it was at the site. The CIA has taken over the search—"

"Look, I'll do it. I don't have anything better to do anyway."

"We'll look at it and get back to you."

Dreamland
1100, 20 January 1998

MACK SMITH HAD BEEN TO GERMANY EXACTLY THREE times, and each time it had been far less than exciting. It was the *fräuleins*; they just didn't appreciate American men. And the police lacked a sense of humor.

Evacked to Germany for medical observation, Mack had no trouble convincing the doctors that he was fine. Or rather, he would have convinced them if he'd stayed around long enough to listen to their excuses about why someone in perfect health needed to take umpteen tests. He checked himself out—more precisely, he waved at the people at the desk as he strode into the lobby—and found himself the first flight back to the States, and from there, to Dreamland.

His bad experiences in Germany were only part of his motivation. He had surmised from the paperwork that changes in the Dreamland Command structure were afoot. A call back to the base informed him that the changes were even broader than he had thought, and he decided that the sooner he shook the new commander's hand, the higher up on the food chain he'd find himself when the dust settled.

Mack was so anxious to get back that he even accepted a C-130 flight into Nellis, sitting in steerage—that is, on the floor in the cargo hold of the notoriously loud aircraft. By contrast, the Dauphin helicopter that took him from Nellis to Dreamland was a sleek limo, and he found himself bantering with the pilots, telling them how great a place Diego Garcia was, with the sun always shining and girls fawning over him 24/7.

Half of the story was true, after all; how much more could they expect?

As he made his way over from the landing "dock" to the Taj, he developed a cocky spring in his step. Dreamland's new commander wasn't a fighter jock; he flew Boners, as the go-fast community disparagingly called the B-1B Lancer. But he was a general, and as such, Terrill Samson would have a lot more muscle than Lieutenant Colonel Bastian—a decent guy and a fellow fighter pilot, but when all was said and done, a lightweight in the political department. And politics was the name of the game these days.

Mack sailed into the base commander's outer office, gave a quick wave to the cute secretary at the far desk, ignored the bruiser at the close one, and stuck his head into the open door, where Samson's name had replaced Colonel Bastian's.

"Hey, General," he said. "Got a minute?"

"Thanks for the promotion," said Chief Master Sergeant Terence "Ax" Gibbs, who was arranging folders on the general's desk.

"Hey, Axy," said Mack, sauntering inside. "Where's the majordomo?"

Ax cleared his throat. "Major General Samson is on Diego Garcia."

"No shit. I just left there. Well, not just." Mack went around to the desk and plopped into the general's chair. "So he already kicked Dog out of his office, huh? I figured he would. Too nice for a colonel."

"Colonel Bastian has an office down the hall."

"What's that for, transition? Where's the old Dog headed next anyway?"

"I don't know," said Ax.

"Jeez, Axy, I thought you knew everything."

"From what I understand, it hasn't been decided. Is there something I can do for you, Major?"

"Just enjoying the view," said Mack, spinning from side to side in the seat. "Not bad."

Ax frowned.

"You know what your problem is, Chief?" Mack asked, getting up.

"I couldn't guess."

"All you chiefs—you think you outrank everybody, even a general. But don't worry." Mack slapped Ax on the back. "Your secret's safe with me."

"I'm most obliged," said Ax.

Tehran
0110, 21 January 1998
(1410, 20 January, Dreamland)

"YOU SEEM TO HAVE LOST YOUR SPIRIT, GENERAL."

Sattari blinked at the dark shadow in front of him. He wasn't quite sure where he was.

In Tehran somewhere, of course, but where?

The seat he was sitting on was hard. There were several people in the room besides the man talking.

"You should be quite proud of what you accomplished," continued the man. "Soon, you will have struck a blow against the Americans that will be remembered for all time."

"Why did you not let me fly the plane?" said Sattari.

"General, a man such as yourself is very valuable. Our country needs you. And what do you think would happen when the Americans found out that a general of the Iranian air force—an important man in our country—was at the controls? We could say you were a rebel, but the Americans would not believe it. This will be much easier for them to accept. There will be trouble, of course, but we will overcome it."

Sattari finally recognized the voice. It belonged to Ayatollah Hassan Mohtaj, an important member of the National Security Deputate, Iran's national security council.

"My nephew," said the general.

"Your nephew was proud to be chosen. He will be a great martyr. Of course, we will say he was crazy, but we will all know the truth in our hearts."

"He's too young."

"You did not seem to feel that was a concern when you asked him to be your copilot."

Sattari felt a stab of guilt. He should not have enlisted the young man. He shouldn't have let Val lead the mission to provoke the Indians either.

So many things he shouldn't have done. He should not have trusted Hassam, above all.

Sattari's eyes finally came into focus. He was in a small basement room. He didn't recognize it, but guessed it was in the government complex.

"Was I drugged?" he demanded.

Mohtaj waved his hand. "Do not concern yourself with the past. You must work for the future. You have many important tasks ahead. Many. You're not an old man."

"I want revenge against the bastards who killed my son," said the general. With every breath, his mind became sharper.

"You will have it. And the longer you live, the more revenge you will have."

It wasn't going to be enough—this wasn't going to be enough.

Sattari rose from the chair. The men behind the Ayatollah jerked forward, submachine guns suddenly pointed in his direction.

"He means no harm," said Mohtaj calmly. "He is back among friends."

"I need time to think," said Sattari.

"By all means. As long as you need."

Mohtaj smiled, then turned and left the room.

Sattari thought of Kerman, then of Val.

It wasn't going to be enough, destroying Las Vegas and Dreamland. Someday, he would drink his enemy's blood.

Aboard Dreamland *Bennett*,
over the Pacific Ocean
1410, Dreamland

DOG FOLDED HIS ARMS AND LEANED AGAINST THE BACK OF the ejection seat in the lower bay of the *Bennett,* trying to stretch a few kinks from his legs and neck. He'd thought vaguely about sleeping on the flight back, but the cots upstairs seemed almost claustrophobic, and his nervous adrenaline just wouldn't let him rest.

That was the way his life ran: Every time he was really tired, he was too busy to sleep, and when he wasn't busy, he wasn't tired.

Starship seemed equally antsy, sitting in the seat next to him, monitoring the flight. Since it was highly unlikely they'd be needed, the Flighthawks were stowed on the wings to conserve fuel.

"Shoulda brought a deck of cards, huh?" said Starship as Dog settled back.

"That or a nice stewardess, huh?"

Starship laughed.

"You have a girlfriend, Starship?" asked Dog. He knew almost nothing about his junior officer's personal life.

"Uh, no, sir. Not at the present time."

"You can relax, Starship. I'm not going to bite you."

"Yeah, Colonel. Um, no. I did. I mean I've had a couple, but things didn't work out that well. You know, like, I was traveling and stuff."

"I know what you mean."

"I'll probably get married someday," added Starship. "But pretty far in the future, you know what I mean? I wouldn't mind kids. But, in the future."

"I know what you mean," said Dog again. But what he was thinking was how small a place the future sometimes could be.

ENGLEHARDT HAD FELT THE CREW'S RESENTMENT TOWARD him from the moment he walked into the little room they used to brief the mission. None of them had the guts to say anything, but he knew what they were thinking. They thought he hadn't made the best decisions under fire, hadn't moved quickly enough, had hesitated a few times when he should have been aggressive.

But what the hell did they want? Look at Sparks and the *Cheli*. They were in deep, deep shit. Did his guys want security standing over them in the restroom everytime they had to take a leak?

Not likely.

Colonel Bastian's presence downstairs made things ten times worse. In a way, he felt sorry for the colonel—everybody knew Samson was screwing him because he was jealous. Still, it was Bastian who had caused him so much trouble. The crew compared them unfairly. Of course, Dog had done a great job when he piloted the plane; the man had been in combat countless times, and he was a colonel, for cryin' out loud. He was supposed to be good.

Not that he wasn't good, Englehardt thought. He was. And even if the nitpickers had problems with his mission, he knew he'd done a hell of a job—a hell of a job—getting the plane back on two engines.

One and a half, really.

More like one and a quarter.

"Waypoint coming up," said Sullivan, his copilot.

"Noted," said Englehardt quickly. He tried to get a little snap into his voice, a bit of professionalism, though it sounded a little hollow.

From now on he was going to do everything by the book. If his crew didn't like him, at least they wouldn't have anything to complain about.

Dreamland Command Center
1500

UNDER ORDINARY CIRCUMSTANCES, TRACKING TRUCK traffic through the Pakistani northeastern territories would have been close to impossible.

Fortunately, these weren't ordinary circumstances.

Which wasn't to say that the task was a piece of cake. Or a Yankee Doodle, which the head of the Dreamland photo analysis team was eating as he discussed the possibilities with his counterpart at the CIA.

"One of these six," the techie agreed, stuffing the last of the snack in his mouth. "Gotta be."

Ray Rubeo, standing behind his console, frowned. The scientist hated sweets of any kind, but most especially ones that threatened the equipment he had personally helped design. The Command Center's no food rule had been eased by Catsman as a morale booster as the mission stretched on. Without any authority over operations or military personnel now, Rubeo couldn't order it reinstated; the best he could do was frown.

"Problem is, so we see those two trucks together, so what?" said the analyst. "We can't search every inch of Pakistan."

"What you should do," said Rubeo dryly, "is search the places where it's possible to leave Pakistan."

The techie looked up at him. "Excuse me, Doc, but, uh, I wasn't talking to you."

The expert was an Air Force captain, one of many Rubeo had never particularly cared for. The feeling was undoubtedly mutual.

"Whether you are talking to me or not, you have photos of every airport and dock in the country. You can judge how long all of these vehicles would have taken to get to those positions, and see if they are there."

"Lot of work. And, you know, a pickup's a pickup."

"What else do you have to do?" snapped Rubeo. "And each pickup is different. Look at the bumper and the right side fender—you can use those to identify it."

"Smudges."

"Hardly."

"I didn't say I wasn't going to do it." The captain pushed the rest of the Yankee Doodle into his mouth and went back to work.

Diego Garcia
0600, 21 January 1998

THE SUN BLOSSOMED ON THE HORIZON, THROWING A REDdish yellow stream of light on the long concrete runway and its nearby aprons. Major General Terrill "Earthmover" Samson,

standing at the edge of one of the aprons in front of the Dreamland Command trailer, took a deep breath, as if he might suck
in the sunshine and all of its energy.

He might need it. He'd spent half the night talking to the
Pentagon, and nearly every friend he had in the upper echelons
of the service. He told them about the incident, of course—the
metal from the missile made stonewalling moot, even if he'd
been inclined to try it. He'd put his best spin on the situation
from a personal point of view, saying that he'd come to personally take charge and to get things in order.

The results had been mixed. The head of the Air Force
was openly hostile, but the chairman of the Joint Chiefs of
Staff, Admiral Balboa, was almost sympathetic. Most of the
rest were somewhere in the middle.

The administration, meanwhile, was obsessed with finding the last remaining warhead. That, at least, was out of his
hands: Though ordered to continue providing "all due assistance," the search had been turned over to the CIA.

Samson vowed that if he got through this—*when* he got
through this—he would remake Dreamland in his image. No
more EB-52s, and in fact, no more manned planes. They
were going to concentrate on their robot and unmanned aerial vehicle technology. Improvements could be made to the
Flighthawks so they could be flown remotely from Dreamland Command, just like the so-called UMB, or Unmanned
Bomber, project. He'd push the remotely controlled B-1
bomber idea further along; Bastian seemed to have side-
tracked it, probably because he had no feel for the aircraft.

As for some of the *truly* weird stuff going on at
Dreamland—the Minerva mind thing, the plasma ray, the
airborne laser project—they were on his short list to be
axed.

As were the egghead scientists who went with them. Ray
Rubeo would lead the parade out.

"Dreamland will be run like a military unit, not the personal toy box of its commanding officer," said Samson to
himself, the line suddenly occurring to him.

It would be the perfect opening sentence for the orientation speech he planned on giving when he got back to the States. He scrambled inside for a pen and paper to write it down.

Aboard Dreamland *Bennett*,
over the Pacific Ocean
2000, 20 January 1998
(0900, 21 January)

DOG FINALLY MANAGED TO DRIFT OFF TO SLEEP DURING THE flight. The ejection seat at the Flighthawk station was about as comfortable as most ejection seats, which meant not at all. His head drooped to his chest and his shoulders tightened; when he woke he felt as if someone had him in a headlock.

Stretching helped a little, but not much.

"Couple of beef Stroganoffs in the galley," said Starship, who was watching a video on his auxiliary screen. "Not too bad if you put Tabasco sauce in it."

"Tabasco?"

"Just a little punch, you know?"

"Is that *Batman* you're watching?" asked Dog.

"I've only seen it ten times," confessed Starship. "Practically new."

Dog laughed, then went upstairs. While his food was cooking in the microwave, he walked over to the pilots and asked them how they were doing.

"Just routine, Colonel," said Englehardt. "Haven't even hit turbulence."

"Great," said Dog. "How are you, Sully?"

"OK, Colonel," said Sullivan.

The copilot's tone seemed a little cold. Maybe that was the reaction he was going to get around the base from now on, Dog thought; no one would want to associate themselves with him. Senior officers would view him as a political pariah, and junior officers would figure he was washed up.

No one wanted to be associated with a commander who'd been relieved.

Technically, he hadn't been relieved for cause—not yet, at any rate. But Samson would undoubtedly go in that direction. While explainable and to some extent excusable on their own, taken together the baby incident and the airliner could easily be whipped into a case against him.

He'd have to get a lawyer if something like that happened.

The microwave began beeping, but Dog left his dinner inside and sat down next to Rager at the airborne radar station. The sergeant was considerably more relaxed now that they weren't in combat; he had a dozen contacts on his scope, all civilian flights.

"Now that you've seen the system in combat, you have any ideas for improvement?" Dog asked.

"A couple, Colonel." The sergeant ran Dog through some of the identification routines and the automated processes, which were supposed to reduce the operator's workload by letting the computer take over. In theory, the system let one man do the work of six or eight in the "old" style AWACS. In practice, said Rager, the workload became overwhelming after a half hour in combat.

"Thing is, you just get tired after a couple of hours," said the sergeant, who'd had extensive experience in AWACS and other systems before coming over to Dreamland. "It works fine in the simulations, but when we were getting shot at for over an hour, at the tail end of a long mission—I have to be honest with you, Colonel, I'm sure I made some mistakes. I haven't had a chance to review the whole mission tapes, but I'm sure I could have done better. Adding two guys on the board during a combat mission makes sense, but it's not just that. There are some software improvements you could make."

Rager listed them. Surprisingly, at least as far as Dog was concerned, the improvements included several that would provide the operator with less information up front; details, he explained, could clutter the board and your head when things got heavy.

"Give it more thought, then write it down for me," said Dog. "I mean—write it down for General Samson. And the techies."

There was a flash of pity in the sergeant's eyes before he spoke. "Yes, sir, I will."

Dog got up and went to get his food. Best thing for everyone, he thought, would be to move on as quickly as possible.

Over the Pacific Ocean
2015, Dreamland

KERMAN MARKED THE DISTANCE IN HOURS. HE WAS NOW two hours away.

He put the aircraft on autopilot and got up from the plane to use the restroom.

The small closet smelled like a chemical waste dump. Kerman did his best to hold his nose. He washed his hands fastidiously, then returned to the flight deck, ready. Before taking his seat, he decided he should pray. He fell to his knees, but before he could say the simple prayer he had learned as a child, he was seized by an overwhelming sense of dread. It was not about his mission. He had always known that it was his destiny to strike a blow against Satan, and had known since before he learned to read that America was evil, an enemy not just to Iran but to Islam. It was an abomination, and any blow struck against it would be rewarded in the everlasting days that followed life on earth.

His dread came from the way his uncle had been treated, used and then tossed aside. Hassam had said he was too important for the country to lose, something that Kerman completely agreed with. But the image of his uncle on the pavement haunted Kerman now. If he was so valuable, why was he treated like a piece of dirt?

The general had always had his trouble with the religious leaders. Kerman had always regretted that—secretly, of course; he would not criticize his uncle to his face or even behind his back, not seriously at least, for whatever else, the general was a great man.

Perhaps, thought Kerman, his uncle had reason to denounce the clerics.

He struggled to put the idea out of his mind. It was a distraction: He had to focus on his mission.

"I will pray," he told himself, as if chiding a small boy. "I will pray for success."

**Dreamland Command
2038**

"IT WAS THE DOC'S IDEA. HE WAS RIGHT," SAID THE PHOTO interpreter. "Look—same pickup trucks at the airport."

Rubeo scowled. The analysts had found a pair of pickup trucks in the region where the warhead was found—albeit miles away, and at roughly the same time that the attack was going on—in some of the shots taken by the Global Hawk as it circled away. The same truck showed up on an access to the airport at Rawalpindi.

"So it must've left from this airport," said Catsman. "Have you checked the flight plans?"

"I turned that part over to the CIA. They said it could take anywhere from hours to a couple of days to get the information."

Catsman looked up at Rubeo. He frowned again. "Days?" she asked.

"If they keep the information on a computer," said Rubeo, "I believe we should be able to shorten the time considerably. Unless you insist on working through channels."

"Do it," answered the major.

Aboard Dreamland *Bennett*,
over the Pacific Ocean
2047

"URGENT INCOMING MESSAGE FOR YOU, COLONEL, ON THE Dreamland channel," said Sergeant Daly, descending from the flight deck. "They need to talk to you right away."

Dog authorized the communication at the Flighthawk station.

"Colonel, we think we may have traced the missing warhead," said Ray Rubeo from the Dreamland Command Center.

"I'm afraid you have to give that information to General Samson," Dog said.

"Yes, well, Major Catsman is attempting to contact him through channels. In the meantime, I thought I would tell someone who could do something about it."

That was, by far, the highest compliment Ray Rubeo had ever paid him.

"What's the story, Doc?"

Rubeo explained about the pickup trucks and how they were tracked to an airport near Pakistan's capital. A number of aircraft had taken off since, including several that were somewhat suspicious because of their registry or stated cargo.

"Apparently a popular stop for the nefarious of the world," said Rubeo. "But there is one in particular that is interesting."

"Why?"

"Because after flying to Malaysia, its pilot filed a new flight plan that said it was heading to McCarran International Airport. Since then, it has disappeared."

Over the Pacific Ocean
2115

KERMAN CHECKED HIS WATCH, THEN UNDID HIS SEAT BELT and walked to the back of the flight deck. The cargo area was not pressurized, but at the moment they were low enough that he did not need an oxygen mask.

The pilot could see his breath as he opened the door. A bank of overhead lights illuminated the warhead's crate, strapped to the floor about a third of the way back.

The timer was wrapped in a towel and tucked beneath the strap. As he got down on his hands and knees to remove it, he began to shiver. He put his hands together for warmth and blew into them.

Was he shaking from cold or fear? Did he have the courage to do this?

For Allah, blessed be his name, he could do anything.

He pulled the towel out and unwrapped it carefully. His uncle's expert, Abtin Fars, had preset the timer for exactly one hour; all he had to do was push two small toggle switches.

He pushed the first. A small LED light lit on the device, showing it was working.

As his hand touched the second switch, it began to tremble so badly that Kerman dropped the timer onto the blanket. He thought he had broken it and for a moment was overcome with grief. All his plans, his entire life, completely in vain. To fail now, so close—it was the most unimaginable disaster. He closed his eyes, cursing himself. He could have remained silent, not called the Ayatollah; his uncle would then still be here, helping him, guiding him. Together they would have carried out the mission—the general to revenge Val's death, Kerman to fulfill God's plan.

The pilot felt a burst of warm air flow around him. It was a draft, he knew—and yet part of him thought it was another presence, his cousin perhaps, coming to reassure him.

Or his uncle.

Kerman opened his eyes.

The light was still lit.

He turned the trigger over gently and pushed the second switch. The numbers on the display began to drain away slowly: 59:59, 59:58, 59:57 . . .

"Thank you, Lord, thank you," whispered Kerman, nestling the timer on the towel and tucking it beneath the strap before retreating to the cockpit.

Aboard Dreamland *Bennett*,
over the Pacific Ocean
2115

DOG CALLED THE NORTH AMERICAN AEROSPACE DEFENSE Command himself so they understood the situation. An air defense order had already been issued, thanks to Major Catsman, but he wanted to make sure the pilots knew that shooting down the aircraft over a populated area would be problematic—the bomb could easily be set to detonate via a barometric fuse.

His preferred solution would have been to explode an EEMWB in the plane's vicinity. But Dreamland had used all of the weapons over India.

After talking to NORAD, Dog decided to call Samson himself over the Dreamland channel. He got one of the boneheaded lieutenants who had traveled to Diego Garcia with the general. The idiot told him that Samson was "on the line with the White House" and would probably not get back to him for a while.

"He knows about this?"

"Major Catsman already told him," said the lieutenant. "That's what he's talking to the White House about."

"You have to scramble what we have at Dreamland," said Dog. "Get the Megafortresses and their Flighthawks up, the airborne laser—"

"I am sure that the general has it under control, Colonel."

"Right." Dog snapped off the line.

He'd accomplished what needed to be accomplished— Nellis was scrambling fighters. A full air alert had been issued. But it felt wrong that he wasn't leading the charge.

Not that his personal feelings should matter.

"Colonel, Nellis Group One is on the air with us," said Sullivan up in the copilot's seat. "Requesting further details."

"Well, give it to them."

"I thought you would want to talk to them, sir."

Dog hesitated a moment, then pushed the button to connect to the frequency the fighters were using. Nellis Group One was a two-ship of F-15 fighters sent to investigate.

"What do you have for us, Dreamland?" asked the lead pilot. "Where are these bastards?"

Dog told him what he knew.

"So where is this Airbus?" asked the F-15 jock.

"Unknown," said Dog. "The plane filed a flight plan but since then hasn't shown up in the international air traffic control system. We believe they were able to turn off their identifier and simply used different call signs, but we're not clear yet. We're working on locating it."

"Roger that."

Rubeo had supplied a theory about the flight plan: It had been filed so that the plane's appearance over Las Vegas would not arouse too much suspicion. After taking off, though, the pilot had taken steps to make it difficult to be followed, deviating from his course and probably flying through countries or ocean areas where air traffic control was not as thorough as in the U.S. and developed parts of Asia and Europe.

Dog went on the interphone to speak to Englehardt.

"Mike, we should join the search immediately," he told him. "Launch the Flighthawks."

"Yeah, that's what we're going to do, Colonel," said Englehardt. His voice sounded a little shaky. "I was just going to suggest that."

"You don't have to wait for me," Dog told him. "Do it on your own."

"Yes, sir. Thank you. You heard him guys—let's go."

Dreamland Command Center
2120

"HOW DO WE EVEN KNOW LAS VEGAS IS REALLY THE TAR-get?" asked Secretary of State Jeffrey Hartman as the video conference continued. "If I had a nuclear weapon, I would target New York City or Washington, D.C."

"I agree," said General Samson. "And why telegraph it?"

Rubeo scowled.

"You don't think that's correct, Dr. Rubeo?" said National Security Advisor Philip Freeman.

Rubeo bent to the keyboard on the computer near where he was standing.

"Admittedly a possibility. However, this is the flight data," he said, flashing a copy of the information one of his computer geeks had hacked. "You notice the name of the pilot?"

"H-H-Habib Kerman," said Jed Barclay.

"Kerman is related to General Mansour Sattari," said Rubeo. "You remember General Sattari, don't you, Jed?"

"Iranian Air Force. He led the Iranian d-d-development team, the bomb and laser, the R-R-Razor knockoff."

"That was two years ago. What does that have to do with this?" said Hartman.

"The CIA thinks Sattari's son was involved in th-th-the plot to provoke war between India and Pakistan," said Jed.

Well, at least someone can connect the dots, thought Rubeo. Probably they'll demote him out of Washington next.

"Sattari knows that Dreamland took down his facilities in Iran," Rubeo told them. "He's promised revenge."

"You think too much of yourself," snapped Samson. "He doesn't even know where Dreamland is."

"P-P-Plenty of reports have said it's near Las Vegas," said Jed. "The book the journalists did of the campaign—*Razor's Edge*, h-h-hinted."

"Combined with the flight plan, I believe it's highly likely that it's a target," said Rubeo. "We're rechecking the flight control network," he added, choosing the much more neutral "checking" over the more descriptive, and accurate, "illegally hacking into." "In the meantime, I suggest all flights be inspected. Sattari may have changed the ident device, or may simply fly without it."

"Do what you need to do. Find the plane," said President Martindale. It was the first time since the conference began that he had spoken. "Restrain it. Shoot it down over the ocean. Whatever has to be done. Do it."

Rubeo had never met the President in person, but he'd seen him on Dreamland Command's large screen many times. He seemed old and tired, drained by the continuing crisis. His voice was weak, almost frail, and his face pale white.

"We're going to find it, Mr. President," said Samson, but the others were already signing off.

Rubeo nodded to the communications specialist, signaling that he could kill the connection. Samson cut in before he did.

"Listen, Rubeo, I know we've had problems, but—"

"Problems doesn't begin to express it, General." Rubeo turned from the console. "I'll be with the programmers hacking into the flight control networks if you need me," he told Major Catsman as he walked toward the door.

Aboard Dreamland *Bennett*,
over the Pacific Ocean
2122

ENGLEHARDT TURNED THE AIRCRAFT OVER TO THE COMputer for the Flighthawk launch. The Megafortress tugged downward for a moment, then lifted, increasing the separation forces as the Flighthawk released and sailed off. He moved through the procedure quickly, getting the second robot off its wings, then climbed toward 50,000 feet, still moving toward Dreamland, a few hundred miles away.

It seemed to Englehardt that the alert had brought the crew back together, though he wasn't sure how long that would last.

"Airliner contact, two hundred miles, zero-five-zero, altitude 35,000 feet," said Rager at the airborne radar station. "Tracking. Computer IDs aircraft as a Boeing 777."

Rager queried the plane's friend-or-foe identifier. The aircraft came back as a United Airlines flight. Englehardt told Starship to get a visual verification anyway, and the Flighthawk pilot hopped to it.

Maybe it was some trick with his voice, Englehardt thought. Maybe he just had to speak sternly, or quickly, or maybe just not think about what he was saying. Maybe it had nothing to do with him—maybe adrenaline pushed them to do their jobs.

Whatever, the crew was definitely responding.

DOG WATCHED RAGER SORT THROUGH THE AIR TRAFFIC. There were plenty of airplanes in the vicinity, but less than a third fit the general profile of the Airbus. Each would have to be visually inspected.

"Colonel, Ray Rubeo for you," said Sullivan.

Dog clicked into the Dreamland Command channel.

"Doc, what's up?"

"We tracked the discrepancy in the flight plans and control system to Thailand. That seems to be where he took on a new identity. There were a number of flight plans filed that we're not finished tracking, but there's an aircraft passing through Mexican control over the Pacific that seems to have the wrong ID. It's definitely an Airbus, and it's on a course that will get it to Las Vegas."

Rubeo began running down some of the information they had obtained. As he did, Dog saw Rager wave at him out of the corner of his eye.

"Stand by, Ray."

"I have an Airbus 310, just now coming up to the California coast," said Rager.

"That's our priority. Tell Starship," said Dog. "Get *Nellis Flight One* there. Now."

Over the Pacific Ocean
2123

KERMAN TIGHTENED HIS GRIP ON THE AIRLINER'S CONTROL wheel. He was thirty minutes away from Las Vegas. The bomb would explode in a little more than fifty.

So close, and yet an eternity away. He throttled back, starting to slow.

Something was going on with the air controllers. They were asking aircraft to identify themselves and sending them into holding patterns back over the sea. *Every* plane was being queried.

Kerman ignored the request when it was his turn.

A minute passed. Another. And then another. The controller asked him to acknowledge. The man's nervousness made his voice harsh and his words difficult to understand, though Kerman knew what he was saying.

He listened as flight control became increasingly exasperated with their failure to respond. There was a short respite, followed by a new controller calling, asking for the flight to contact him and take an immediate new course.

A few seconds later an American with a slow drawl identified himself as an interceptor pilot and told him that he was to check in with flight control and follow their guidance immediately.

Kerman realized that if the Americans were on alert, he'd never make it.

He glanced at the radar, but couldn't see them. They must still be relatively far away.

He blew a slow breath from his lungs, trying to relax and think of what to do.

Aboard Dreamland *Bennett*,
over the Pacific Ocean
2124

"THIS LOOKS LIKE THE REAL THING," SAID RAGER. "THE plane isn't answering the ground controllers or the F-15s."

Dog studied the display, getting his bearings. The Airbus—officially identified as Pakistan Air Crating Flight 201—had just crossed the California coast. The two Air Force F-15s were only a few minutes away; *Hawk One*, one of the robot Flighthawk aircraft controlled by Starship, was maybe two minutes behind them.

Dog switched into the Dreamland channel. "Colonel Bastian to Dreamland Command. I need to speak to Ray Rubeo."

"Ray's down in the computer center, Colonel," said Major Catsman. "I'll switch you."

"Wait. What I want are the warhead experts," Dog told her. "What happens if we shoot this thing down? Is it going to explode?"

"They're already trying to work up a simulation based on the other warhead," said Catsman.

"We don't need a simulation, we need an answer right now. Get everyone on the line, wherever they are. We need to know."

"Yes, Colonel."

Dog switched over to the regular frequencies and contacted *Nellis Flight One*. The F-15 pilot said he was about a minute from visual range.

"What exactly are your orders?" Dog asked.

"At the moment, find and identify the plane."

"I don't know how much of this they've told you, Captain, but here's the deal: That plane is carrying a nuclear warhead, and it may be rigged to explode in any number of ways."

Nellis Flight One didn't respond.

"Do you copy, *Nellis Flight One*?"

"Copy. We copy you, Colonel. What the hell are we going to do?"

Over California
2132

KERMAN WAITED UNTIL THE F-15S WERE VISIBLE OVER HIS
left wing before responding.

"This is Pakistan Air Crating Flight 201, to any control
unit. Pakistan Air Crating Flight 201, to any control unit.
There has been a hijacking situation. We are now back in full
control of the flight."

"Pakistan Air Crating Flight 201, this is *Nellis Flight One*.
Repeat your status."

"We have overcome the hijackers," said Kerman. He was
so nervous he was almost out of breath as he spoke. But that
would play in his favor. "Some injuries to crew. We have
control. Two men are dead. Both are the hijackers. My navigator is critical. He may already be dead."

"Pakistan Air Crating Flight 201, I want you to execute an
immediate turn."

The pilot repeated the instructions the controllers had
given him earlier, telling him to go out to sea.

"I have damage to my instrument panel. I have two holes
in the fuselage and am losing pressurization," said Kerman.
"I need immediate clearance for an emergency landing. Repeat, I have a flight emergency landing. Repeat, I have a
flight emergency and require assistance."

He throttled back and dipped his wing slightly. There was
a fine balance—he couldn't overact, but he had to seem as if
he was truly in distress.

"Pakistan Air Crating Flight 201. I need you to execute
that turn."

"Repeat directions."

The American pilot once again gave him a heading that
would have him turn south and then head out to sea.

"I am going to try," said Kerman. "Stand by. My navigator
is critical. We require ambulances on the runway. My own
wounds are not serious."

He glanced at his watch. He still had nearly forty-five minutes before the weapon would explode.

But there was a bright glow in the distance, an arc of light brighter than anything he'd seen for hours and hours.

Las Vegas.

**Aboard Dreamland *Bennett*,
over the Pacific Ocean
2135**

STARSHIP SLID HAWK ONE IN BEHIND THE F-15 EAGLES, lining the small robot up to get a good visual of the aircraft.

"They're claiming they have wounded crewmen and damage to the plane," radioed one of the F-15 pilots. "Asking for an immediate clearance to land."

"Negative," said Colonel Bastian over the circuit. "That plane does not land. Stand by while the Flighthawk gets a good look at the plane. Flighthawk leader?"

"Yeah, roger that, Colonel," said Starship. "I'm on it now."

"COULD BE AS SIMPLE AS TOUCHING TWO WIRES TOGETHER, Colonel," said Rubeo, whose voice sounded distant. "But as I told you earlier, we're not convinced the warhead will explode. The odds are at least fifty-fifty that the pertinent circuitry was fried by the T-Rays."

"Ray, I doubt they would have come all this way if they didn't think it would explode," said Dog.

"Just because *they* think it will explode doesn't mean it will," said the scientist.

"How can we take him down safely?"

"Get him out to sea and shoot him down. There is no other guarantee. It's possible that the warhead is set to explode if the airplane is destroyed, or if it drops below a certain altitude. There is just no way of knowing."

Over Nevada, approaching Las Vegas
2138

THE FIGHTER JET PASSED SO CLOSE TO THE AIRBUS'S WIND-screen that Kerman thought the glass would implode from the jet's thrust. But he held his control steady. He was going to win. All he had to do was stay in the air a few more minutes and he would be over Las Vegas.

This one's going to hit us, he thought as another fighter pushed in.

The Airbus shuddered as the F-15 swept over the fuselage. Kerman felt the plane slipping from his grip, responding to the violent air currents rather than his controls. He jabbed the pedals, desperate to keep it on its course. The Airbus dropped straight down about 2,000 feet, then abruptly jerked back, level, to just below its original altitude.

The two fighters had moved off. Before Kerman could exhale, a small missile whipped in front of the windscreen. The missile twirled and danced before his eyes, rising upward and then curling back, as lithe as an ocean, before plunging a few feet from the Airbus's nose.

As it turned, he realized it wasn't a missile, but an aircraft.

A small one, far too small and sleek for a man.

It must be a Flighthawk. The Dreamland people. They knew he was coming for them.

"I will not fail," Kerman said aloud, hunkering closer to the wheel.

Aboard Dreamland *Bennett*
2139

ENGLEHARDT HAD CLOSED THE GAP BETWEEN HIMSELF AND the Airbus; as he descended through 30,000 feet, he saw the airliner a few miles ahead. The F-15s had backed away and the Flighthawk—a small black dart—wheeled over the plane. The Airbus continued on its path.

Englehardt sized up the distance between the *Bennett* and the Airbus. He could ride right over it—that would get their attention.

"Dreamland *Bennett* to Flighthawk leader and *Nellis Flight One*. Stand back—I'm going to take a pass."

"Negative, Dreamland," said the Nellis F-15. "Stand by. We are under orders to take this airplane down."

"Negative, negative," said Dog, practically shouting over the radio. "You can't shoot it down."

"Those are my orders, Colonel."

"Sullivan, open the bomb bay doors," said Englehardt over the interphone circuit.

"What?"

"Just open the damn the bomb bay doors." Englehardt switched back to the radio. "*Nellis One*, stand off—this is our shot. We have the Airbus targeted."

The Eagle pilot didn't acknowledge.

"I'll take you next if I have to," snapped Englehardt. "Get the fuck out of my way."

"Hey, slow down, cowboy," said *Nellis One*.

"All right. Everyone, take a deep breath," said Colonel Bastian. "We're on the same side here. Remember who the enemy is. They may have the bomb rigged to go off when the aircraft descends. We're working on a solution. So everyone calm down and let the scientists think."

"*Nellis,*" said the F-15 flight leader, acknowledging though clearly unhappy.

"Good outburst, Mike," Dog told Englehardt over the interphone.

"Colonel, I think I can fly right over him and push him away from the city," said Englehardt. "If the F-15s stay out of the way, I can herd him out over the desert and have them shoot him down there. We're never going to get him back out to sea."

"I have a better idea," said Starship.

Over Nevada, approaching Las Vegas
2141

KERMAN'S HEART FELT AS IF IT WERE BEING JOLTED BY ELEC-
tric shocks. It was racing, and every so often skipped a beat.

He was here. He was here. The Las Vegas airport directly
below him. In little more than half an hour the city would be
gone. All that waited was for the timer to run its course.

He checked his altitude. He'd come down to 15,000
feet.

Every nuclear weapon had an optimum detonation altitude, where the effects of the blast were at their highest. Not
being privy to the design of the Indian warhead, Kerman
simply planned on flying the aircraft at 2,000 feet when the
bomb exploded.

Fifteen thousand feet would be fine, though. So would the
ground. There'd be plenty of destruction no matter where it
exploded.

But he needed more time. His bluff about being hijacked
had to work. He had to make it work.

"Pakistan Air Crating Flight 201 to tower," said Kerman.
"Requesting emergency clearance to land."

"Pakistan Air Crating Flight 201, you are *not* cleared to
land. Follow Air Force instructions."

"We are having trouble with our radio," said Kerman. "Is
our landing gear down? Can someone confirm that our gear
is down?"

There was a clunk from the back of the plane. The Airbus
rocked, buffeted by something. Kerman glanced at the panel
for the landing gear—he hadn't put the wheels down, had he?

Of course not.

Then he realized what was going on, and jammed his hand
on the thrusters.

Aboard Dreamland *Bennett*
2143

STARSHIP CURSED AS THE AIRBUS LIFTED AWAY FROM THE Flighthawk.

"Didn't work," said the pilot over the interphone.

"Try again," said Dog. "Get *Hawk Two* in. Try them together."

Hawk Two, which Starship had used to continue checking airliners, was just catching up. The pilot told the computer that he wanted to control them in parallel, and had it help him line them up precisely together.

By the time Starship was ready, the Airbus had begun to circle to the south.

Maybe they'd made a mistake—maybe it actually had been damaged by hijackers, perhaps the men with the bomb. The real crew would take it out to sea, now that they were convinced the Americans were serious.

No such luck—it was turning back now, headed toward Vegas.

"Flighthawk leader, this is *Nellis One*. Take one more shot at it. Then we're going in."

"Keep your shirt on."

ENGLEHARDT FOUND HIMSELF ABOUT TWO MILES BEHIND the Airbus as the aircraft began banking back to the north, once again moving in the direction of Las Vegas. He had a good view of the Flighthawks as Starship eased them in, one under each wing. The operation was a delicate one; Starship didn't want to damage the Airbus and make it crash.

The small jets slid in close to the wing roots.

"You're there," said Englehardt.

"All right, all right," said Starship. "We're going north."

The Airbus lifted slightly—then dropped abruptly. One of the Flighthawks twisted off to the left, slowly at first, as if it were a leaf being pealed from a tree. A few seconds later smoke began pouring from the robot aircraft.

Pakistan Air Crating Flight 201, meanwhile, banked back toward Las Vegas.

"Dreamland aircraft, back off," said *Nellis One*. "We're going to fire."

"I'm taking a shot," said Englehardt. He reached for the throttle. "Come on, Sullivan. Help me."

Sullivan was silent for a moment, then sprang to help. "Yeah. Yeah, it's what we got to do."

Englehardt had worked with the 757 tanker project, and had a great deal of experience pulling up under two-engined aircraft similar to the Airbus. But he'd never tried to pick one up before.

Screw that. This was happening. He could see it in his head.

The airliner's shadow grew steadily. The computer's automatic warning system was screaming alerts.

"Kill the auto system," said Englehardt, narrowing his focus to the small area in front of him.

"Killed," said Sullivan.

Slowly, the Megafortress eased forward. Then, just as he was going to nose up, the Airbus lurched to the left.

Englehardt felt a hole open in his stomach. His hands trembled and all of sudden he was sweating again. His entire body turned to water. There was no way he could do this. No damn way.

Tears welled in his eyes. He was scared, too scared—not good enough.

A coward. A failure.

"Hang in there, Mike," said Colonel Bastian, putting a hand on his shoulder. "You almost had him. Just hang with him and push it in. I know you can do it."

"Yeah, I'm gonna do it," said Englehardt. His voice cracked and trembled, but he tightened his grip on the stick. He pushed the Megafortress back toward the Airbus. "I am going to do it."

Over Las Vegas
2144

SOMETHING CRACKED BELOW HIM. THE AIRBUS FELT AS IF it were being pushed upward, shaking violently with a loud scraping and crackling.

Kerman cursed. He was so close—he needed only a few more minutes. Only a few more. He pounded his hand on the throttle and pulled back on the yoke.

Aboard Dreamland *Bennett*
2145

ENGLEHARDT FELT LIKE A BULL HAD CLIMBED ON HIS BACK and he was struggling to hold it there.

"Power!" he yelled at Sullivan.

"It's working!" Sullivan shouted back.

The *Bennett* shook violently as the Airbus ramped up its engines. The Megafortress shot upward, slapping against the belly of the smaller plane.

"Starship—take out the bastard's engines!" yelled Englehardt, pushing his nose up to stay on the Airbus.

The two planes were now rocking violently. Englehardt struggled to keep his nose angled up while Sullivan concentrated on the power. The Megafortress drove against the Airbus, pushing and pulling the lighter commercial plane through the air. Three or four people, including Nellis ground control, were trying to talk over the radio, but Englehardt kept them blocked out. He was sweating and his head pounded and his stomach was a knot, but he was doing this, he was definitely doing this, and no one was going to stop him.

HAWK ONE'S CONTROL SURFACES HAD BEEN BADLY DAMaged by the pressure from the Airbus; worse, her engine had sucked in bits of metal, shredding most of her turbine. Starship tried to get the aircraft to the west of the city, into the open terrain, but he didn't have enough momentum. The Flighthawk spun toward a tight cluster of homes, their light brown roofs looking like the sides of a zipper. White sand appeared—Starship pulled back on the stick, trying to push the plummeting aircraft into a golf course built in the middle of a condo development. Green grass flashed in the screen, and then everything went blank.

"Connection lost," said the computer.

There was no time to see whether he had missed the houses. He took over *Hawk Two,* selecting the cannon.

The computer refused to let him fire. He was too close to the mother ship.

"Override," he said.

"Forbidden."

"Override Authorization StarStarTwoTwoTwo."

"Forbidden," insisted the computer.

"I can't get the Flighthawk to fire!" he told Englehardt. "It thinks it's shooting on us."

THE MEGAFORTRESS WAS FLYING WITH HER NOSE PRACTI-cally thirty degrees downward, but she was still pushing the Airbus forward. They were past Nellis, into the Dreamland test ranges.

How far did he need to go? Twenty miles, fifty?

He might be able to hold it for another sixty seconds.

"All right—everybody get the hell out!" he said. "Get down to the Flighthawk deck and bail."

"We're staying with you, Mike," said Sullivan.

"Yeah, we're with you, Englehardt. Right down to the line," said Daly.

"I ain't leaving," said Rager.

"No way," said Starship.

The long expanse of Dreamland's main runway passed the left side of the airplane. The Airbus bucked upward, escaped—Englehardt pushed the ganged throttle, his hand on Sullivan's, ramming into the cargo plane.

No way it was getting away.

Tears streamed from Englehardt's eyes.

"We're doing this!" he screamed.

Over Nevada
2147

KERMAN STRUGGLED TO FIND A WAY TO RELEASE THE AIR-
bus, but everything he tried seemed to fail. He was being
pushed sideways and forward at the same time. The bigger,
more powerful aircraft below him had him in its claws, pushing him away from the city, toward the open desert.

He wasn't going to make it. By the time the bomb exploded
he'd be much too far from Las Vegas to do any damage.

He pulled his seat belt off. He'd have to find a way to detonate the bomb immediately.

Aboard Dreamland *Bennett*
2148

"THIS IS FAR ENOUGH, MIKE!" DOG YELLED AT THE PILOT.
"Let it go!"

The Megafortress lurched to the left. Suddenly free of
the weight she had been carrying, she shot upward, out of
control.

Dog flew backward as the plane lurched. He tumbled
against the airborne radar operator's station, then pulled
himself up.

The pilots were wrestling with the controls, trying to keep
the plane in the air. Dog fumbled for his headset, resettling it
on his head.

"Station Five, operational, authorization Bastian Nine-
nine-one," he told the computer, double tapping the power
button to bring the station on line.

"On line."

"Anaconda weapons section on line. Authorization Bastian Nine-nine-one."

"Bastian authorized."

The targeting screen came up.

"Target aircraft identified as PC-1."

A message flashed on the screen—the aircraft was identified as a civilian by its identifier.

"Override."

A targeting reticule appeared. The plane had begun to turn back to the south, toward Las Vegas.

Dog was about to tell the computer to fire when the symbol went from red—locked—to yellow. The radar had lost the lock.

"Lock, damn it," said Dog.

If the computer heard him, it didn't let on. Dog switched to the manual control, using a small joystick that would let him designate the target the old-fashioned way. He hit the reset, moved to the cursor, and this time got a lock.

"Fire," he said. "Fire Fox One!"

The missile ripped from the belly of the aircraft.

Over Nevada
2150

KERMAN FINGERED THE WIRES ON THE BOMB'S TIMER AS the aircraft jerked up and down. He hadn't been with his uncle when the timer was explained, and Sattari hadn't bothered to show him how it worked. Still, it seemed like a simple device; there had to be a way to set it off immediately.

A set of wires had been soldered to contacts at the top of the switch. Kerman decided he had only to cross the contacts for the weapon to be triggered.

He had nothing to cross them with.

He could do it with a pen.

The plane jerked as he reached to his pocket. He fell backward to the deck.

There was no time. *Just strip the wires and touch them together*, he told himself. *Be done with it. Be done with it.*

He clawed his way upright, then hunched over the timer.

As his fingers touched the wires, the plane lurched again. Kerman pushed down on the device with one hand and managed to pull the wires off the contact with his other.

The plane suddenly jerked upward and stopped shaking.

He was free! The American had given up!

He started to rise to run back to the cockpit. Then he stopped, realizing there was no sense doing that now. He reached back to the wires to push them together.

As he did, the front of the aircraft turned silver. It looked like a flash of light, but it was pure silver, a brilliant shade that he had never seen before.

Paradise, he thought.

Then silver turned to red, then black, then nothing.

Aboard Dreamland *Bennett*
2151

STARSHIP SAW THE ANACONDA MISSILE CLOSE IN ON THE Airbus's cabin just as he was pressing the trigger on the Flighthawk's gun. He rolled away, escaping most of the explosion. The Anaconda struck at the front cabin, decapitating the aircraft. The cockpit disintegrated, but the rest of the fuselage continued on, flying toward the highest of the Glass Mountains about sixty miles northwest of Dreamland.

By the time he got the Flighthawk turned back around, the headless Airbus was down to 2,000 feet. Its left wingtip hit the ground first, skittering along for a hundred feet or so before collapsing. The rest of the plane spun in toward the missing wing, tumbling into a rising cloud of smoke and dust.

"It's down! It's down!" said Starship.

Then he braced himself.

ENGLEHARDT CLOSED HIS EYES, WAITING FOR THE INEVITAble flash of light. He pushed himself against the back of his seat, expecting the air burst that would follow a nuclear explosion.

It didn't come. After a minute he swung the aircraft back toward the site. Nothing.

They were a little more than twenty miles away, climbing back through 25,000 feet. He moved into a figure eight, intending to climb as high as possible.

"Sully, you with me?"

"With you, Mike."

"No explosion."

"Yeah, nothing."

"Maybe coming. We high enough?"

"Yeah, just about."

"You got the engines."

"Yeah, I'm on it, bro," answered Sullivan.

DOG STARED AT THE IMAGE ON THE SCREEN, WAITING FOR the massive white cloud—the famous mushroom cloud—to rise above the desert mountainside.

But it didn't. Their missile had prevented it.

"Dreamland is sending a response team," reported Sullivan.

"I have a helicopter en route," reported Rager at the airborne radar, "and two Ospreys."

Dog waited, listening. He knew every man aboard those aircraft, had brought most of them to Dreamland, or had at least approved their assignments.

Somehow, the fact that he was no longer their commander didn't enter into his thoughts.

Minutes passed that seemed like days. He began to feel numb.

"Neutralized," said Sullivan finally. "The bomb's trigger section is off. It's inert."

"Take us to Dreamland," Dog told Englehardt. "Take us home."